STORM FRONT

STORM FRONT

Twilight Of The Gods 1

CHRISTOPHER G. NUTTALL

Text copyright © Christopher G. Nuttall

ISBN: 1523472464
ISBN-13: 9781523472468

http://www.chrishanger.net
http://chrishanger.wordpress.com/
http://www.facebook.com/ChristopherGNuttall
Cover by Brad Fraunfelter
www.BFillustration.com

All Comments Welcome!

AUTHOR'S NOTE

I'm not particularly fond of books, even alternate history books, that attempt to reproduce foreign accents or make excessive use of foreign terms. Unfortunately, writing a book set in Nazi Germany makes it impossible to avoid the use of *some* German words, including a number specific to Nazi Germany and the SS. I've done my best to keep this to a bare minimum and, just in case the meaning of the word cannot be deduced from context, I've placed a glossary at the rear of the book.

Please don't hesitate to let me know if there's a word I've missed during the editing.

CGN

PROLOGUE

India, 1949

"It's time, Your Excellency."

Winston Churchill, 44th and last Viceroy and Governor-General of India, sighed as the functionary entered the office. It was a magnificent office and Winston knew he would be sorry to leave it, but it wasn't important. The important matter had been decided long ago, in London and Delhi, and Winston's opinions had been dismissed as unimportant. India would be granted her independence, the government in London having decided that a peaceful separation was better than a brutal civil war that would destroy everything Britain had worked so hard to build. The Raj was dead. It had died when Hong Kong and Singapore fell to the Japanese, when Japanese troops had reached the borders of India itself. And Winston Churchill, who had fought so hard to save it, was charged with its funeral.

He rose slowly, feeling his old bones creaking under the weight. It had been years since he'd been a reporter, years since he'd served as a soldier, years since he'd been able to keep up with the younger men. The boundless determination that had driven him onwards, through years in the political wilderness and three years as Prime Minister, as Hitler's armies scored victory after victory, was fading. He had hoped - prayed - to go to his rest after the Nazi beast was slain in its lair, but he knew he wouldn't live to see it. Hitler's enemies had fallen before him, one by one; Stalin assassinated during the retreat from Moscow, De Gaulle killed by a sniper's bullet in Indochina, Roosevelt felled by his own heart. Winston was the last to survive and he knew it wouldn't be long before he too was lowered into the grave. And the hopes and fears of the free peoples of the world would die with him.

Perhaps not, he thought, as he looked up at the map. *Hitler may yet over-reach himself.*

He had never admitted, not even to his wife, just how much he'd hoped Hitler would declare war on the United States. Roosevelt had done all he could, but America couldn't - wouldn't - enter the war against Germany without good cause. Winston had no illusions about what would have happened to the British Empire, overshadowed by its mightier cousin across the ocean, yet Nazi Germany would have been crushed. Instead, Hitler had declared war on Japan, a stunt that had fooled no one but had been treacherously difficult to overcome. He'd even withdrawn the u-boats from the Atlantic, gambling that it would avoid an incident that would bring America into the war. And he'd been right.

Winston shook his head, silently tracing the lines on the map. Hitler's armies had fallen back from Moscow, true, only to resume the offensive in the following spring. The Russians, their armies faltering as their industry staggered under the weight of the war, couldn't keep Hitler from seizing Stalingrad, then resuming the drive on Moscow. And, if that hadn't been bad enough, Hitler's forces had thrust into Egypt and then Palestine. If the Americans hadn't moved troops into Iran, as part of an agreement to withdraw the Anglo-French occupation force, Winston knew that they might have stabbed into India itself. The weakness of the British Empire had been exposed for all to see.

And now he sits, consolidating his gains, while we have to struggle to survive, he thought, as he followed the functionary down the stairs. He doubted Hitler could hold Russia indefinitely - although the horror stories from refugees had made it clear that the Nazis were far more brutal than the communists - but there was no one left on the continent who could challenge him. *He may even start preparing to launch an invasion of Britain.*

Outside, the hot air slapped him in the face as he made his way towards the podium. Hundreds of thousands of people were gathered, watching and waiting for the moment when Britain finally granted India her independence, when they could set foot on the world stage as an independent country. Winston couldn't really blame the Indians for wanting independence - thankfully, the looming threat of the Germans had forced the INC to come up with a reasonable plan for governing the country - but, at the same time, he couldn't help feeling a pang for everything that would be lost. The Raj had been a proud achievement, bringing government and civilisation to India.

Winston stopped in front of the podium and looked down. The Indians were waiting, dark men in sober white suits; beside them, diplomats from the rest of the world watched with great interest, flanked by reporters ready to jot down whatever he said and misquote it to the world. Winston had been a reporter himself, once upon a time, but his time in the political wilderness had left him with little love for the breed. The age of the daring reporter, along with the brave explorer who brought civilisation to the natives, was over. Instead, there were hacks, liars and bureaucratic beancounters. The glories of the past were long gone.

He cleared his throat and stumbled through the speech Prime Minister Atlee had had written for him. It was a cumbersome thing, clearly written and approved by committee; it was hard, so hard, to put any of his passion into his words. But it was what the Indians wanted to hear and they cheered loudly as he told them that India was, from this moment forward, an independent dominion of the British Commonwealth. Thankfully, they'd agreed to stay in the Commonwealth for at least five years. The British Government had that long to convince them to stay permanently.

"But there is another matter I must discuss," he said, putting the paper notes aside. He hadn't told Atlee that he intended to add his own words to the speech before the world's reporters - and the assembled world leaders and diplomats. It would only have upset him. "The world is not what it used to be."

He took a breath. "When I was a young man, a quarter of the world was red and the sun never set on the British Empire. I remember campaigning along the North-West Frontier and fighting a war in South Africa, never dreaming that the glories before me would come to an end. It never crossed my mind that Europe would destroy itself in war. Nor did it occur to me that a great beast would rise from the ashes to enslave the entire continent. I would have thought it impossible, if someone had told me, and laughed in his face.

"But I would have been wrong.

"An iron curtain has descended across Europe, yet we may still see glimmers of the horrors unleashed by Adolf Hitler. A dozen nations have simply ceased to exist. Countless populations have been enslaved or exterminated by the black-clad SS. Those who dare resist are subjected to torture before they are killed. A horror has descended that holds all of Europe, even Germany itself, in the grip of fear.

"I remember when the cabinet debated what to do, the day that Hitler's troops marched into the Rhineland and dared us to evict them. If we had known then what we know now, we would have gone to war and forced the Germans to retreat. But we did nothing. I remember when Hitler demanded the most valuable regions of Czechoslovakia and Chamberlain, a weak man, chose to appease the fascist beast rather than make a stand. We allowed Czechoslovakia to be dismembered and, in doing so, sacrificed our best chance to stop Hitler without major bloodshed. But we lacked the nerve to make a stand.

"We had our excuses, of course. Britain lost nearly a million lives in the first Great War against Germany. The French lost nearly twice that and had their country devastated by the war. Our economies were weak, our forces ill-prepared and Hitler seemed to hold the moral high ground. *Anything* seemed better than war.

"But all that matters, in the end, was that when we determined to take a stand, we had already surrendered far too much to the Germans. When the Phony War ended, Hitler's forces smashed France and pushed Britain to the wall. Had Hitler focused more on naval matters, Britain too might have been invaded and occupied. Instead, we were forced to watch as Hitler overwhelmed Russia and the Middle East.

"There is a temptation, on this day of all days, for us to forget the threat posed by the Germans. There is a temptation to believe that Hitler is satisfied, that he will be happy with what he has taken by force. There is even a temptation to be *pleased* that the communist regime that dominated Russia has been destroyed..."

He paused, silently cursing the American industrialists under his breath. They'd *hated* communism - and, after Finland, they hadn't been alone. Sending supplies to Britain was one thing, yet sending supplies to Russia was quite another. They had hoped the communists would be destroyed, but what they'd got in exchange might destroy them.

"We can never relax," Winston said. "Right now, *Herr* Hitler is experimenting with jet aircraft, with atomic weapons, with rockets that will allow him to target New York or land a man on the moon. It would be dangerously reckless of us to assume that the threat will go away, even if we do nothing to provoke it. We must stake out our perimeter, establish our defences and never, ever, drop our guard until the day the fascist beast is slain in its lair.

"There can be no compromise with evil," he concluded. "The Nazis will never be satisfied until they have overrun the entire world. And so we must remember, at all costs, that freedom is something that must be defended. Europe forgot that and now Europe is lost. I charge you all to remember that, when they start trying to soothe us. We must hold the line or we will all be lost."

He stepped back from the podium as the crowd burst into cheers, wondering just how many of them would understand what he'd said. Far too many Indians considered democracy a joke - and who was to say they weren't wrong? India had seen very little democracy under the Raj. But they'd see less of it under Hitler. The Nazis wouldn't hesitate to do whatever it took to crush resistance.

Atlee wouldn't be happy, Winston knew. It was unlikely he'd be offered another government post in the future, but he'd assumed the Labour Government wouldn't have a use for him in any case. He was, after all, an embarrassing old lion, a relic of the past...

... But as long as he lived, he would do what he could to alert the world to the dangers of Nazism. He could do naught else.

CHAPTER ONE

Berlin
17 July 1985 (Victory Day)

It was, Finance Minister Hans Krueger concluded darkly, a very impressive parade.

He stood with the other ministers, one arm raised in salute, as endless rows of tanks, armoured personnel carriers and mobile missile launchers drove down the parade route and past the stand, before being carefully directed to staging areas on the outskirts of Berlin. The crowd roared its approval as the vehicles passed, followed by thousands upon thousands of soldiers wearing their fanciest uniforms. They'd have no trouble finding companionship tonight, Hans thought wryly, as the soldiers vanished into the distance. All the nice German girls loved a man in uniform, particularly if he were unmarried...

Not now, he told himself firmly, as the crowd roared again. *Not on Victory Day.*

He twisted his head, slightly, as a dull roar echoed over the city. A trio of heavy bombers, capable of flying from Berlin to Washington without refuelling, flew overhead, so low he almost felt as if he could reach up and touch them. They were followed by a force of fighter jets, antiaircraft missiles slung under their wings; they in turn were followed by a small flock of assault helicopters, freshly painted after their return from the front. The crowd went wild with delight; he smiled to himself as he saw a line of uniformed schoolboys breaking ranks to wave at the aircraft as they passed overhead. Their teachers wouldn't be happy - discipline was everything in a parade - but hopefully they'd let it pass.

"Little brats," Foreign Minister Engelhard Rubarth muttered. "Can't they stand in line like everyone else?"

"They're eight," Hans told him, dryly. The boys would have been gotten out of bed at six in the morning, forced to don their dress uniforms and marched to their spot in the square, where they'd then had to wait while standing in line for hours. He still had nightmares about *his* time at school, even though he'd been lucky enough to avoid a Victory Day parade. "Let them be children, just for a while."

"They're disrupting the parade," Rubarth said. "The teachers will be furious."

"I don't envy them tomorrow," Hans agreed. "They'll be spending half the day running laps around the school."

He made a mental note to have a word with the parade organiser about the children, although he knew it might be nothing more than tilting at windmills. Everything must be in order, they'd say; it had been a principle of the state since Adolf Hitler had become Chancellor of Germany and set out to reshape the world in his image. Clearly, they'd never seen the confused mishmash of ministries that made up the government. When he'd been younger and more idealistic, Hans had planned a cull of government officers; older and wiser, he knew there was no way to streamline the system. Too many people had a vested interest in keeping the system as it was.

Another pair of aircraft flew overhead, disgorging a line of black-suited figures that fell towards the ground. Hans knew the whole routine had been carefully rehearsed, but he couldn't help feeling a flicker of doubt as the figures kept falling, without even *trying* to open the chutes. And then, in perfect unison, the chutes popped; the parachutists slowed their fall and landed neatly in front of the *Fuhrer's* box.

"*Heil Bormann,*" they snapped. The crowd picked up the salute and repeated it. "*Heil Bormann!*"

"The *Fuhrer* seems pleased," Rubarth said.

"Good," Hans muttered. Adolf Bormann might be the son of Martin Bormann, but he lacked his father's political skills. *Fuhrer* wasn't *precisely* a meaningless title these days, not when an entire continent saluted him every day, yet Adolf Bormann had little real power of his own. And he didn't even have the sense to know it. "That will keep him pleased."

He turned his attention back to the parachutists, just in time to see them turn, fold up their chutes and march off, still in perfect unison. Moments later, a long line of soldiers marched into the square, turning to salute the *Fuhrer* as they passed. The schoolboys seemed to have lost all sense of discipline; they were waving and shouting at the soldiers, some even dropping into line beside them. Hans winced inwardly as a stern-faced teacher came forward, his face darkening with fury. He'd be blamed for their poor conduct by his own superiors and probably wind up being dispatched to Germany East. It was rare for a teacher to volunteer to serve in Germany East.

Hans sighed, then waved to one of his aides. "Yes, *Mein Herr?*"

"Go tell that teacher he is not to punish the children too severely," Hans said. He *was* one of the three most powerful men in the *Reich*. What was the point of having power if it couldn't be used? "And then see to it that he doesn't suffer too badly himself."

"Yes, *Mein Herr*," the aide said.

"You always were sentimental," Rubarth commented, as the aide scurried away. "That's how it begins, you know. The problems the Americans had in the sixties started with a lack of discipline."

"And yet the Americans are richer than us," Hans pointed out. It was an old argument, one he'd found himself repeating to both the military and the SS. If the Americans were so weak and feeble why were *they* the ones who had established the first true settlement on the moon or developed the first anti-ballistic missile shield? "How does that square with a lack of discipline?"

"The Americans are protected by their ocean," Rubarth countered. That too was part of the argument. "They wouldn't stand a chance if we could cross the waters."

Hans shrugged. Very few in the *Reich* would admit it, but the Americans were more advanced than the *Reich*. Maybe they did pour fewer resources into their militaries than the *Reich*, yet their advanced weapons more than evened the balance. What was the point of investing in thousands of ICBMs if the Americans could stop more than half of the missiles before they reached their targets? The cost of trying to keep up with the United States was draining the *Reich* dry.

And their educational system is better than ours too, he thought, as he watched his aide quietly explaining the facts of life to the teacher. *They actually teach their children to think.*

He pushed the thought aside as another flight of aircraft roared over the city. There would be time enough for the endless argument tomorrow. Today... was a special day.

———

Weakling, Reichsführer-SS Karl Holliston thought, as he watched the interplay between Hans Krueger's aide and the teacher. *In Germany East, such behaviour would never be tolerated for a moment.*

He sighed, briefly considering sending an aide of his own to the school. A formal complaint from the SS would be enough to get the teacher sacked and the children severely punished, but it would be nothing more than spite. The Berliners hadn't faced war for forty years, since the last time the British had bombed the city before coming to an uneasy peace with the *Reich*. Even a handful of bombs planted by particularly foolish *Gastarbeiters* hadn't disturbed the peace of the city. The Berliners simply didn't know the true danger of living on a frontier.

The little brats should all be sent to spend a year in Germany East, he thought, darkly. It would seem an adventure, at first, until they realised that a terrorist sniper could strike at any moment. *They don't have the mindset to survive.*

He gritted his teeth in outrage. *He'd* grown up in Germany East; his father an SS trooper who'd been granted a farm in the settlements at the conclusion of his service, his mother a stout German woman who'd already buried a husband who'd been killed by the insurgents and brought two children to her second marriage. Not that Karl's father had cared; he'd been happy to bring up an additional son and daughter. Repopulating the steppes with good Germans was more important than his personal feelings, after all. Karl had grown up *knowing* he might have to fight for his life at any moment, learning to shoot almost as soon as he could walk. And, by the time he'd left school and volunteered for the SS, he'd been shot at several times by the insurgents. How many of the bratty schoolchildren below could say the same?

None of them, Karl told himself. *They grew up in safety.*

4

He pushed the thought aside as the first row of SS troopers marched into the square. They were a magnificent sight; hundreds of black-clad men, their insignia glittering under the light, marching in perfect unison. It was men like them, Karl told himself, who were the true defenders of the *Reich*. The army, as powerful as it was, didn't have the same determination to do whatever it took to protect the country. Hadn't Rommel proved that when he'd captured Jerusalem? The treacherous Field Marshal had even allowed the Jewish defenders to withdraw, with their weapons, and escape to Iraq! Rommel simply hadn't the stomach to do what needed to be done.

"*Heil Bormann*," the troopers bellowed, saluting. "*Heil Bormann!*"

Karl kept his face expressionless with an effort. Adolf Bormann was an idiot, plain and simple, and the Deputy *Fuhrer* was even worse; they should both have been put out to pasture long ago. Giving the title of *Fuhrer*, the title that had been practically *defined* by Adolf Hitler himself, to an idiot was an insult. But it couldn't be helped. No one really wanted a true *Fuhrer*, one with the power of life and death over the entire *Reich*, save perhaps for Karl. And *he* only wanted to be the *Fuhrer* himself.

If they let me claim that power, he thought, his eyes seeking Krueger. The fat man was watching the SS troopers with wary eyes. *I will be opposed by the rest of the trio.*

Karl ground his teeth in silent frustration. The Finance Minister fought tooth and nail over every funding request, doling out money as carefully as a farmwife who distrusted the local tradesmen. Krueger wouldn't let Karl become a *real Fuhrer* without a fight - and he'd be supported by the military, who wouldn't be pleased at the thought of an SS *Fuhrer*. The *Heer*, *Kriegsmarine* and the *Luftwaffe* only agreed on a handful of things, but disapproval of the SS was one of them. Karl knew, without false modesty, that he could split the different military commanders on smaller issues - the *Heer*, *Kriegsmarine* and the *Luftwaffe* heads fought each other with more determination than they fought the rebels in South Africa - yet they'd unite against the SS. Krueger, damn him, wouldn't need to call in any favours or strike bargains to block Karl from claiming the topmost position in the *Reich*.

He leaned forward as row upon row of SS stormtroopers passed through the square, silently gauging the crowd's reactions. The younger children were still cheering loudly, but there was something forced about the cheers from the older civilians. Karl had no illusions about the popularity of the SS, yet it still bothered him. The vast majority of recruits came from Germany East, where the SS was genuinely popular, but it wasn't enough. He simply didn't have enough recruits to meet the state's manpower needs in peacetime, let alone with a war on in South Africa.

And the war has to be won, he told himself, grimly. The Dark Continent was an untapped treasure trove of raw materials and he had no intention of leaving it to black communists and American capitalists. *No matter the cost, the war has to be won.*

But it was a problem. There had always been questions raised about the racial purity of Germany South. The settlers there didn't give a damn about someone's ancestry, as long as he looked white, and they resisted any attempt by the SS to hunt down rogue Jews, let alone someone who might be French or Italian pretending to be of good German stock. And South Africa wasn't much better. They'd been happy to accept the *Reich's* offer of military assistance, but they'd flatly refused to hand over their Jews to the SS. Indeed, Karl was *sure* that senior figures in the South African government had been encouraging the Jews to flee before it was too late.

Maybe we should just decapitate the local government and take over, he thought. There was a contingency plan to do just that, one he'd been putting together as a last resort. *That, at least, would make it easier for us to fight the war.*

———

"The Nasties do put on a good show, don't they?"

Andrew Barton, Office of Strategic Services, nodded in agreement. It *was* an impressive parade, all the more so for being something he would never have seen in America. The Nazis wanted to show their might off to the world, displaying their power for all to see. It just didn't happen in Washington.

"Take careful note of the number of aircraft you see at any one time," he said, dryly. A decade ago, a team of American observers had been fooled into believing that the *Reich* had over a hundred intercontinental bombers when the Germans had flown the aircraft over Berlin and then circled around, out of sight, to fly over the city for a second time. "We don't want to be fooled again."

He looked down at the crowds from the balcony, wondering absently just how many of them truly *wanted* to be there. The kids in the front rows might have thought it was going to be fun, but he doubted they were enjoying themselves after waiting in line for hours; behind them, the lines of watching civilians seemed slightly disorderly, as if the crowd was already bored and resentful. That too wasn't something he'd have seen in Washington. If there had been a parade, attendance sure as hell wouldn't be compulsory. The crowd would have been composed of men and women who wanted to be there, waving flags and cheering loudly.

"Ah," Robert Hamilton said. The CIA operative leaned forward. "The meat of the matter."

Andrew leaned forward too as the first of the heavy mobile missile launchers made its way onto the square. It was a truly impressive sight, he had to admit; the giant vehicle, the missile mounted on its back, inching forward as the crowd went wild. The Nazis had claimed, in their boastful speeches, that the mobile missile could be fired from anywhere within the *Reich* and hit the United States, although Andrew was fairly sure that was nothing more than empty bragging. Unless the Germans had made a radical breakthrough, the rocket simply didn't have the fuel to fly further than 1500km. Not that that kept it from being a major headache, he had to admit. *England* was easily within range and the Germans had enough nukes to turn the United Kingdom into a radioactive slagheap. The ABM shield simply couldn't guarantee it would stop even half of the salvo from reaching its target.

"I was thinking," Hamilton said. "Do you think they've left the nuke in the rocket?"

Andrew shrugged. The Germans would have to be insane to take the risk, no matter how many safeguards they'd worked into the warhead, but the Germans *were* the only people to ever use a nuke in combat. On the other hand, nukes didn't go off if you hit them with a hammer. It was quite possible that the warhead was completely safe, no matter what happened. But they'd still have to be insane to mess around with a nuke.

He turned his attention towards the podium at the other side of the square. The *Fuhrer* was there, exchanging salutes with the missile crew; the *Reichsführer-SS*, one of the most evil men Andrew had ever met, was sitting just two seats down from him. If something happened in the parade, the *Reich* would be deprived of both its titular head and one of its most powerful men. It was hard to be sure just how powerful the other casualties were - in the *Reich*, power and title didn't always go together - but a disaster would throw the entire state into confusion.

If nothing else, the SS will be holding competitions to see who is evil enough to become the next Reichsführer-SS, Andrew thought, darkly. *The winner must be a treacherous unprincipled bastard, with a goatee he can stroke at particularly evil moments...*

He shook his head, annoyed at himself. He could make fun of the Reichsführer-SS - God knew there were hundreds of old WW2 cartoons still running around the internet that made fun of Hitler, Himmler and Fatso Goring - but none of the people below dared say a word against the *Fuhrer* and his cronies. The military might marching through the square was one thing, yet the true horror lay in the hundreds of thousands of listening ears, ready to report a single word against the state. Wives could turn on husbands, children on parents... Nazi Germany was a nightmare few ever escaped.

And I will go back to America, when my stint is up, and wash the stench of Nazi Germany from my clothes, he added, silently. *The people below me are trapped.*

"They'll be running more soldiers and machines through the square tomorrow," Hamilton observed, as the final set of tanks rumbled past. "Hopefully, they'll get themselves some more watchers too."

"We have to be back," Andrew said, feeling another stab of pity for the children. He checked his notebook, where he'd scribbled down a brief report of what he'd seen. He'd write out a full report once they returned to the embassy. "You want to go get a beer?"

"I'd sooner go find out what's under those uniforms," Hamilton said. Andrew followed his gaze and saw a handful of blonde-haired women wearing strikingly ugly and shapeless clothes. They were army nurses, he thought. "German girls are hotter than hell."

"And you'll be in hell if the ambassador catches you in one of them," Andrew pointed out. It wouldn't be the first honey trap the Nazis had tried, either. "Let's go get a beer instead."

CHAPTER TWO

Josef Mengele Hospital, Berlin
17 July 1985 (Victory Day)

"Are you sure you want to do this?"

Gudrun Wieland took a long breath. Her heart was pounding so loudly she was sure her older brother could hear the sound. She wanted to do it, needed to do it, but she knew they could easily get in deep trouble. Their father's belt would be the least of their concerns.

"I'm sure," she said.

She braced herself. It would be easy to back out, to walk away; they could be back home within twenty minutes if they walked fast. But she'd gone to a great deal of trouble to borrow a nurse's uniform from a friend, just so she could wear it while walking into the hospital. No one would question her if she wore a uniform, she'd been told; no one, not even the senior doctors, would know *every* nurse in the building. There were over a thousand young women and, with the current fashion for blonde hair, it was a reasonable bet that three-quarters of them would be blonde too. She'd scrubbed her face clean of make-up, tied up her hair and removed anything that might identify her. As long as they weren't caught in the building, it was unlikely that anyone would be able to track them down afterwards. But Kurt...

"Are *you* sure?" She asked. "I can go alone, if necessary..."

"I can't let you go alone," Kurt Wieland said. Her brother ran a hand through his short blonde hair, cut very close to the scalp. "I'm not expected back at the barracks until tomorrow morning."

Gudrun gave him a grateful smile. She'd known, when she'd asked him, that he could have simply refused, or reported her to their father. Herman

Wieland wasn't a bad man - she knew friends who had worse fathers, mainly drunkards like Grandpa Frank - but he would have exploded with rage if Kurt had told him what his eldest daughter had in mind. Instead, Kurt had insisted on coming with her and providing support. He'd even helped her sort out what to do when she walked into the building.

"Thank you," she said, quietly.

"Then let's go," Kurt said. He caught her arm as they started to walk towards the hospital. "Remember, you're meant to be escorting me, not the other way around."

Gudrun allowed herself a nervous smile. Kurt was wearing his uniform, marking him out as a soldier in the Berlin Guard. It was unlikely that *anyone* would question his presence, not when the uniform practically screamed his legitimacy to the skies. The cover story they'd devised had her escorting him to see a friend in the hospital, which wasn't *too* far from the truth. And if someone thought they were lovers... well, as embarrassing as it was, it would be better than the alternative. Being caught would get them both in *very* hot water.

She gritted her teeth as they walked down towards the hospital and through the gates. It was a colossal building, constructed during the 1950s and staffed with the finest doctors and nurses in Germany. Her friend had told her that there were hundreds of departments; the original building was practically buried in outbuildings that were half-hidden behind other outbuildings themselves. The country had a fetish for efficiency - or so she'd been taught at school - but there was nothing efficient about Josef Mengele Hospital. It was far too obvious that the designers hadn't anticipated just how many doctors and patients would need to use the facilities.

The guards paid no attention to them as they walked through the door and into the lobby, heading straight towards the locked doors. Gudrun allowed herself a sigh of relief as they joined a dozen nurses heading though the doors, the leaders holding the doors open for the others. If they had had to wait for someone to open the doors it would have been far too revealing, she knew. Her friend had flatly refused to hand over an ID card that would open the doors.

Inside, it was surprisingly cool. Gudrun sniffed the air, the scent of antiseptic bringing back memories of the last time she'd visited a hospital, then looked around for the wall-mounted map of the giant complex. There were hundreds of wards; some identified in medical terminology she couldn't even begin to interpret, others merely identified by a number. She scanned the display quickly, hunting for the number she'd been given. Somehow, she wasn't entirely surprised to discover it was on the far side of the building, well away from the entrance. Cold ice ran down her spine as she looked up at her brother. He was frowning.

"They've got something to hide," he murmured. "That ward is pretty well concealed."

Gudrun nodded in agreement, then checked the map, memorising the route. Map-reading wasn't one of the skills she'd learned in the Hitler Youth - young women were expected to learn how to cook, clean and have babies - but she didn't dare risk asking for directions as they walked deeper into the facility. Anyone with a legitimate reason to be there would know their way around the building - or, if they were just visiting for a day, would be assigned an escort. She glanced back at her brother, then led the way down the corridor. The hundreds of doctors and nurses, some of the latter somehow managing to make their ugly blue uniforms look fashionable, ignored them.

Kurt was right, she thought, ruefully. Just how long had she spent scrabbling with her older brother as a young girl? It had taken her far too long to realise that Kurt had grown into an adult. *As long as we look as though we fit in, no one will pay any attention to us.*

She concentrated on finding her way through the corridors as Kurt followed her, no doubt keeping track of their route himself. He'd have learned to read a map in the Hitler Youth; he wouldn't have been promoted so quickly, she was sure, if he hadn't mastered the basics at a very early age. But then, young men were taught military skills in the Hitler Youth. She'd always envied the boys when they'd gone camping, leaving school for a week of mountain-climbing, mock exercises and other exciting sports. They'd even been allowed to play with real weapons. *Gudrun* and the other girls had never even been allowed to *see* a gun in school.

They turned the corner and walked towards the ward. A pair of SS troopers were on guard, but neither of them looked particularly alert. Gudrun walked forward, keeping her face utterly expressionless as she led Kurt past the guards and into the wards. The troopers gave her an appreciative look, but made no move to stop her. This far inside the building, they probably assumed that anyone they saw had the right to be there. She fought down a smile, knowing that they'd just crossed the Rubicon, and started to look for a specific bed. They didn't dare loiter where the troopers could see them.

Kurt poked her arm. "There," he said, pointing to the wall. A chart was mounted on it, showing a list of names and beds. "See if you can find him there."

Gudrun nodded and peered up at the chart. There were over two dozen names on the list, all completely unfamiliar, bar one. *Unterscharfuehrer* Konrad Schulze, her boyfriend; *Unterscharfuehrer* Konrad Schulze, who had asked her to marry him when he returned from South Africa; *Unterscharfuehrer* Konrad Schulze, who had returned from South Africa and vanished into Josef Mengele Hospital. She felt an odd twist in her heart as she stared at the name, realising that Konrad hadn't left her; his family, she'd discovered, were as much in the dark as herself. Their son had gone to war and then...

She gritted her teeth as she looked for the right bed. It had been sheer dumb luck she'd heard anything. A friend of hers, the same girl who'd loaned her the nurse's uniform, had seen Konrad's name and SS number on a list of patients in the hospital. Gudrun hadn't believed her at first - his family hadn't been told he'd been wounded and sent home, let alone allowed to see him - but as weeks went by without a single letter from a normally attentive boyfriend, she'd started to have suspicions. And then it had taken two weeks of scheming to plan an unauthorised visit to the hospital. If Kurt hadn't agreed to accompany her, it would have been impossible.

And no one had heard anything from the bureaucracy.

Gudrun scowled in bitter memory. She'd thought Konrad's family liked her, for all that she was a university-educated student rather than a proper little housewife; they'd certainly never sought to discourage their son from courting her. Hell, it had been *her* friends who'd raised eyebrows at the thought of dating an SS trooper. The university students had *never* got along with the SS, who would happily close the university down in an instant if they thought they could get away with it. But Konrad had been different. He'd been sweet and funny and never tried to press himself on her. The thought of his kisses made her lips tingle...

... And, if they knew something had happened to him, they would have told her.

She paused, just outside the curtains enshrouding his bed. All of a sudden, she wasn't sure she wanted to take the final step, to brush aside the curtains and see her lover. What if she was wrong? What if it wasn't him? Or... what if something had happened...?

"Go," Kurt urged, quietly. "We may not have long."

Gudrun reminded herself, firmly, that she came from a brave family and pushed the curtain aside, then froze in horror at the sight that greeted her eyes. Her boyfriend was lying on his side, hooked up to a machine that bleeped worryingly every five seconds. The lower half of his body was completely gone; she had only taken basic medicine at school - it was another skill girls were required to learn - but she honestly wasn't sure how he'd survived. His face was bruised and broken; indeed, for a long moment, she was honestly convinced that they'd made a dreadful mistake and opened the wrong set of curtains. But he had the scar on his chest she recalled from one of their love-making sessions and his SS tattoo, on the underside of his right arm, matched the one she'd memorised.

"They tattoo our ID number and blood group so we can be treated in a hurry," Konrad had told her, once. She felt sick as she recalled the handsome young man she'd courted, the man who'd gone to war. "And it's a badge of honour..."

"Jesus," Kurt said, peering past her. "How the hell is he going to give mama grandchildren?"

"Shut up," Gudrun hissed. She couldn't help peeking at where Konrad's genitals should have been, but they were gone. Whatever had happened to him, it had taken everything below his hips. She honestly had no idea how he was still alive. "Do you think we can wake him?"

Kurt grabbed her arm. "Don't even *think* about it!"

Gudrun winced in pain, but she had to admit he was right. She didn't have the slightest idea how to wake Konrad, if it were possible. Removing him from the machine might *kill* him outright. It would almost certainly set off alarms, bringing *real* doctors and nurses running to the bed. They'd be smoked out, caught and arrested. And after that... Gudrun wasn't sure, but sending them back to their father would be far too lenient for the SS. They'd probably be exiled to Germany East. If half of the rumours were true, no one ever came back alive.

I should have married him, she thought, looking down at Konrad. It was far from illegal to get pregnant out of wedlock - the state would happily pay expectant mothers a small stipend for carrying another young German to term - but her mother would have been furious if Gudrun had allowed herself to get pregnant. *If I had...*

She swallowed, hard. Konrad wouldn't be making love to her anytime soon, let alone returning to the war. Doctors could perform miracles these days, but she doubted they could rebuild his legs, let alone his genitals. She'd heard *stories* about how sperm could be mined from a male body and then inserted into a female body, impregnating the woman, yet... she shuddered at the thought. It sounded terrifyingly unnatural. Konrad would probably die in a hospital bed, if he couldn't live without life support, or spend the rest of his life in a wheelchair like Grandpa Frank, drinking heavily and nursing his sorrows. She winced at the thought - she didn't *like* Grandpa Frank, even if he was her maternal grandfather - and then stepped away from the bed. Part of her wanted to stay with him, but she knew what would happen if she tried. The SS would take her away and...

They wanted to cover this up, she thought. Konrad was from an SS family - his father had been a trooper before retiring - and yet they'd been lied to by the state. *They wanted to conceal his wounds...*

It didn't make sense, she told herself. Konrad wasn't anyone important. His family didn't have ties to the *Reichstag*. But, instead of reporting his wounds to his family, the SS had tried to hide them. She tossed it over and over in her head, remembering what her father had said about his work as a policeman. If someone was trying to hide something, he'd said, it meant they had something to hide that *justified* the effort of hiding it. And yet, Konrad wasn't anyone important. There was no reason to hide his wounds.

Take Konrad out of the equation, she told herself. There was nothing important about Konrad, therefore no one would waste the effort *solely* for him. *And you get...*

She looked up. There had been more than two dozen names on the list - and, in the ward, there were two dozen beds, each one hidden behind a set of curtains. If each of them held a wounded soldier, and it looked as though they did, what did it mean? The news kept claiming that German troops, bringing fraternal aid to their brothers in South Africa, were winning the war. But if someone was concealing the sheer number of wounded troops... what did that say about the progress of the war? And how many troops had wound up dead in South Africa?

They're lying, she thought. She had always been dimly aware that the news services were run by the government, that nothing was ever broadcast without government approval, but she'd never fully understood what that meant. *They're lying about the war.*

She jumped as she heard someone clearing her throat. "What are you two doing in here?"

Gudrun turned. A young nurse - a *senior* nurse, judging from the gaudy rank badges on her uniform - was standing behind them, hands on hips. She looked as stern as their mother when she'd caught them in the biscuit box, back when they'd been children. Gudrun couldn't help thinking that she would have been pretty if she'd let her hair down and, perhaps, worn something a little more fitting. The uniform was just plain ugly.

"I convinced Nurse Gudrun to let me see my friend Konrad, after my own examination," Kurt lied, smoothly. It wasn't as if *Gudrun* was an uncommon name. There had been three other girls with the same name in junior school. "We served together in South Africa, don't you know? He saved my life twice."

He leaned forward. "If you're charged with his care, perhaps you can tell me how he is? I'd be most grateful..."

The nurse frowned. "You shouldn't have brought him in here without permission," she said, addressing Gudrun. "Visitors have to be cleared through security..."

"It's my fault, beautiful," Kurt said. He cocked his head. "Can I take you for a drink later?"

"Perhaps," the nurse said. She looked downcast for a long moment. "Your friend is unlikely to survive without the life support machine, sir. The brain damage was quite severe and the medical care he received in the theatre was *quite* poor. We dug quite a few pieces of shrapnel out of his flesh, but by then it was really too late. His body is still alive, if barely; his brain is dead."

Gudrun swallowed the question she wanted to ask. She didn't dare draw the nurse's attention back to her, even as Kurt flirted and the nurse - insanely - seemed inclined to respond. Perhaps, being a nurse, she didn't have many chances for romance... or, more likely, she thought a soldier would understand long hours and short tempers. Her father had once told her that policemen preferred to marry nurses...

"You escort him to the doors, then report to the security office," the nurse said, finally. "I have work to do here."

"Of course," Gudrun said. She had no intention of doing anything but walking out the doors with Kurt, removing the uniform as soon as possible and never returning. "I'm sorry..."

"Go," the nurse ordered.

"That was a close one," Kurt muttered, once they were past the guards. "But at least I got her number."

Gudrun gave him a disbelieving look. "You do realise you can't possibly call her?"

"That's not the point," Kurt said. "The point is that I got her number."

He didn't say anything else until they walked through the doors and escaped into the streets, heading towards a flat belonging to a friend. Their father would have asked far too many questions if Gudrun had returned home wearing a nurse's uniform - and, being a cop, was far too practiced at sniffing out lies. He would demand the whole story, then explode with fury at the risk they'd taken.

"You need to keep this to yourself," he warned. "If someone is trying to keep this a secret..."

"I know the dangers," Gudrun said. She had a vague plan forming in her mind, but nothing solid, not yet. And she couldn't share her thoughts with her brother. "And I know the risks."

CHAPTER THREE

Reichstag, Berlin
17 July 1985 (Victory Day)

There were times, Hans Krueger thought as he walked into the meeting room, that it would probably be easier to handle decisions if the Big Three met in private, hammered out a set of compromises and then presented it to the rest of the *Reich* Council as a *fait accompli*. It would certainly take less time, with less outraged shouting. But it was impossible. The different branches of the military would certainly want their say, the different government ministries would have their own opinions about matters and even the SS, for all it tried to present a monolithic face to the world, had its dissidents. There was no way to accommodate them all, save for inviting all the principles to the meetings.

And that tends to mean that nothing gets done, he reminded himself sourly. The only consolation was that formal protocol was practically non-existent. *By the time we're finished arguing, it's time for dinner and then we resume arguing after dinner.*

He sighed, inwardly, as he sat down and accepted a cup of coffee from the attendants. The remainder of the seats were filling up fast; the uniformed heads of the military, the ministers wearing fancy suits and the SS, clumped together at one end of the table. Hitler might have been a great man - Hans knew better than to think otherwise, even in the privacy of his own mind - but he'd never established a formal governmental structure to handle the vastly expanding *Reich*. Instead of an organised system, where power and responsibility were roughly equal, he'd presided over a hundred different fiefdoms, keeping them at loggerheads so his rule remained unchallenged. And when Hitler died, the wheels had threatened to come off the whole ramshackle structure.

And it was sheer luck that Himmler was convinced not to try to seize power for himself, Hans thought, glancing down towards Karl Holliston. The *Reichsführer-SS* would happily seize supreme power, if he thought he could get away with it. *Then, the military would have opposed the SS, purely out of instinct. Now... who knows which way everyone will jump.*

The attendants finished pouring coffee and withdrew, closing the doors behind them with a loud *thump*. Hans allowed himself a grim smile. They were in the most secure room in the *Reich* - the security team protecting the complex was the most capable in Germany - and yet, the true threat lay within. Just how many of the men at the table would make a bid for power if they thought they could succeed? Hans wouldn't - he knew how hard it would be to rule the *Reich* alone - but he had a feeling he was the only one. Everyone else? The lure of supreme power was *very* alluring.

He kept his face impassive as the *Fuhrer* rose to his feet. "This meeting is now called to order," Adolf Bormann said, turning to face the giant portrait hanging from the wall. Hans had to admit Bormann could give pretty speeches, but little else. "*Heil Hitler!*"

"*Heil Hitler,*" Hans echoed.

And everywhere else, it would be Heil Bormann, he thought, as Bormann sat back down. *But not here, not where we can't risk allowing his head to swell.*

"I move we address the war in South Africa," Holliston said, quickly. "Victory Day has, as always, given us a boost. We must take advantage of it before it is gone."

Hans exchanged glances with Field Marshal Justus Stoffregen, Head of OKW, who nodded once. The military, therefore, wanted to discuss the war too. Hans had a whole folder of economic issues that had to be addressed, but there was no point fighting an unwinnable battle against both the military and the SS. Besides, it would give him an opportunity to let Holliston make his points and then undermine the bastard. The SS man simply didn't understand the cold economic realities that were steadily undermining the *Reich*.

Holliston leaned forward. "The South African War is approaching a climax," he said, as if he hadn't said the same thing at the last four meetings of the *Reich* Council. "We have taken losses, but we are pressing the rebel insurgents hard and persistently weakening their grip on their fellow blacks. They are steadily being worn down."

He paused, waiting to see if anyone would object. Hans, who had quite a few private agents reporting to him from South Africa, could have disputed that rosy picture, but he kept his thoughts to himself. Better to let the SS man store up trouble for himself. Besides, he knew all too well what lurked behind the cold figures. Men and women killed, children rounded up and herded into concentration camps, towns and villages burned to the ground for daring to hide insurgents... no wonder the blacks were fighting desperately. They were caught between freedom and total extermination.

And thousands of our own men are dead, he thought, coldly. *The general public doesn't have the slightest idea just how many soldiers have been killed - or wounded - in South Africa.*

It wasn't a pleasant thought, he reflected. The *Reich* had no elections, no way for the civilians to express their feelings about the war. No one had quite realised just how badly public opinion, such as it was, would be shocked about the Balkan War. The public hadn't given a damn about slaughtered Jews or Muslims, of course, but telling them just how many Germans had been killed in the fighting had been a mistake. It wasn't one the SS intended to repeat.

"However, we have a major problem," Holliston continued. "Pretoria is not as enthusiastic about the war as we would prefer."

"Unsurprising," Hans commented, dryly. "We are, after all, fighting a savage war of peace on their territory."

Holliston gave him a sharp look. "We have gathered evidence that suggests the South Africans are on the verge of betraying us," he snapped. "Pretoria has been in private communications with Oliver Tambo and, apparently, attempting to come to some sort of agreement. Furthermore, Tambo and his bunch of terrorists would not have escaped if Pretoria had acted swiftly to reinforce the parachutists who attacked the bastard's territory. I believe they hesitated in the hopes that Tambo would escape."

"And succeeded, if that were the case," Field Marshal Gunter Voss commented.

"They would presumably not have wished to restart negotiations with a new leader," Hans mused. "Tambo is hardly the worst they could have had to deal with."

He scowled, inwardly. Pretoria's apartheid system had a great deal in common with the Third Reich, but the white population of South Africa made up only a tenth of the population, even though Pretoria had been working hard to lure immigrants from Spain, Italy, France and even Greece. The whites were, quite simply, badly outnumbered and every year they failed to crush the rebels, every little rebel success that helped to bleed Pretoria white, worsened their position. It was hard to blame Pretoria for looking for a way out of the war that allowed them to salvage *something*.

But Holliston, of course, didn't see it that way.

"I have two proposals," he said. "First, we double the number of German troops fighting in South Africa. We can easily spare 200,000 troops for as long as it takes to crush the blacks and bring peace to the country. Second, that we strike first and eliminate the government in Pretoria."

Hans blinked in surprise. He'd expected the proposal to double the number of troops in South Africa; it had, after all, been made before. But eliminating the South African Government? It was insane! Which planner in Wewelsburg Castle had come up with the whole idea?

Holliston pressed the idea as hard as he could. "There are factions in Pretoria who will be happy to support us, if we eliminate the current leadership," he said. "These are the factions who have been pressing for a more proactive solution to the problem..."

Hans gritted his teeth. Holliston alone couldn't commit the *Reich* to a desperate gamble, but if he dragged the military along with him... it would be hard, perhaps impossible, to head the madcap scheme off at the pass. And it *was* madness, of that Hans was sure. The *meaning* of the facts and figures might be disputed, but the facts themselves could never be.

"The last time I checked," he said, allowing his voice to drip with sarcasm, "we sent our soldiers into South Africa to support the local government. Did something change while I was sleeping?"

"Of course not," Holliston said.

"Then perhaps you can explain to me," Hans pressed, "why *supporting* the local government requires executing its members and installing a set of puppets?"

"The current government is unable to fight the war effectively," Holliston snapped. "I..."

Hans took a long breath. "Whatever we may think of the government of South Africa, the fact remains that it holds legitimacy in the eyes of the South

Africans themselves," he said, coldly. "They will not take calmly to *us* stepping in and removing their government. I dare say, given that they are of good racial stock, that they will not accept whatever government we install in its place. We will be forced to occupy South Africa ourselves, to disarm the local military and fight a multi-sided war against *two* sets of insurgents.

"Furthermore, our logistics are already problematic," he added. "Our supply lines from the *Reich* to Germany South are poor and road and rail links between Germany South and South Africa are worse, even without the insurgents taking pot-shots at our convoys..."

"We could drive the attackers away from the roads if we didn't have to humour the local government," Holliston hissed.

"And we would find it hard to make use of the local logistics network," Hans added, relentlessly. The South Africans, damn them, had chosen to licence American or British weapons rather than German, a decision that had come back to haunt them when the war began in earnest. "Indeed, the white flight from South Africa will only get worse as the war spreads into formerly safe areas. Or have you not realised just how dependent South Africa *is* on black labour?"

He allowed his voice to rise. "They use black labour everywhere, even in the military," he reminded the table. "What happens if - when - those blacks become convinced that they're ultimately doomed to go into the gas chambers anyway?"

"They're of inferior stock," Holliston snapped.

"And if they're so inferior," Hans said, "why do you need an extra 200,000 troops to fight the war?"

He kept the smirk that threatened to appear off his face with an effort. He'd argued against becoming involved in South Africa, only to be overruled by the military and the SS. Now, the SS looked grossly incompetent, grasping at straws rather than swallowing their pride and admitting they'd made a mistake, while the military were concerned about ever-increasing casualty figures. Doubling the troops in South Africa, if they could be supported, *might* end the war, but it was equally possible that it would only increase the number of dead or wounded soldiers. And who knew what would happen when *that* little fact got out?

Holliston glared at him. "And you would propose ending the war?"

"I would propose that we find a way to avoid wasting blood and treasure on a petty pointless war," Hans said. "It will not be long before the chaos starts making its way up into Germany South or French North Africa."

"The frogs can take care of themselves," Holliston growled.

"They might have some problems," Hans observed. "We place some pretty strict limits on their military, don't we?"

"Yes," Voss said, flatly. "The last thing we want is a modern tank force within striking distance of Germany."

Hans nodded in agreement. The terrain between Vichy France and Berlin was not conductive to deep strikes, but giving Vichy the power to stand up for itself would have dangerous implications. France had been in the economic doldrums for decades, despite a slow and steady advance into North Africa. The French Government might be more than willing to bend over and take whatever Berlin chose to dish out, but the French population loathed the Germans with a fiery passion. If the *Reich* ran into problems elsewhere, who knew which way the French would jump? And, to be fair, Spain and Italy didn't like the Germans much either.

He cleared his throat. "The facts and figures make it clear, gentlemen, that we need to make some adjustments in our budget," he warned. "We are spending more than we earn."

"Then print more money," Holliston said. "That's your job, isn't it?"

"That's what Weimer tried," Hans reminded him. "And what happened to Weimer?"

Silence fell. Very few of the men in the room had been old enough to understand what was going on, back when they'd been children, but they remembered how the Weimer Republic had collapsed into chaos. And yet, Hans knew that most of them didn't understand just how desperately Hitler had *needed* to keep adding new conquests to the *Reich*. It had taken years, after the end of the war, to put the *Reich* on a sound economic footing. Now, all that hard work was being wasted.

"The war in South Africa, alone, is costing us billions of *Reichmarks*," Hans said. "Both directly, in weapons and equipment lost during the fighting, and indirectly, in taking care of the wounded. The economic lifeline we've tossed to Pretoria is worse, in a way; we're simply not getting enough back from the mines in South Africa to pay for the war. But that isn't the worst of it. Our total military budget is sucking up far too much money..."

"We have to prepare to fight the Americans," Voss said. He tossed a sharp look at *Grossadmiral* Cajus Bekker. "Don't we need to build more ships?"

"We can't afford many more ships," Hans said. "A single nuclear-powered aircraft carrier, Field Marshal, costs over *ten billion Reichmarks*. Building enough to fight the Americans on even terms, which leaves the British out of the equation, will cost *two hundred billion Reichmarks!*"

"The Americans seem to be able to afford it," Holliston said. "Are you sure you're not mismanaging our money?"

"The Americans have several advantages," Hans growled. "First, they have a larger GNP than ourselves. They can afford to build more carriers, missiles and spaceships without straining their economy. Second, they have a smaller budget for their other governmental functions. Third, their weapons production is standardised, not just between the different services, but also between their allies. A British soldier can fire American bullets from his gun and vice versa. Fourth, and perhaps the most important at the moment, the Americans offer much less social benefits than ourselves."

"A mother's benefit packet is less than a hundred *Reichmarks* per week," Holliston said, tightly. The SS had been a big supporter of the scheme, although Holliston had been a lowly trooper at the time. "It is hardly a problem."

"It mounts up," Hans said. "There are roughly 1.5 million mothers in Berlin today. If each of them has two children, they can claim 160 *Reichmarks* each week from the government - and, I assure you, almost every mother in Berlin *does*. That means, each week, we spend somewhere around 240 million *Reichmarks* in Berlin alone."

He looked around the table, willing them to understand. "That's a very rough figure," he said. "Right now, the average family size is four children; six in Germany East, despite the endless insurgency. Every single one of those mothers can claim eighty *Reichmarks* per child, *per week*. The cost is staggeringly high and *we can't afford it!*"

"We need it," Holliston said, into the silence. "The *Volk* must not be allowed to vanish from the earth!"

"The *Volk* are in no danger of fading away," Hans said. "Indeed, our population is expanding rapidly. But every year we delay in dealing with this crisis, the worse it will be when it finally explodes. I can paper over the cracks for a while, but not for very long. Creative accounting will catch up with us sooner or later."

He cursed under his breath. Holliston wouldn't understand, of course. The SS was obsessed with children, to the point where it encouraged fine young German men to marry more than one wife. Hell, it had been Himmler himself who had started the original scheme. He'd noted, correctly, that cost was a major factor in bringing up children and come up with a simple idea to reduce the costs. But, like all such schemes, it had snowballed out of control and turned into a nightmare.

"We cannot make cuts," Holliston said.

"We must," Hans said. "Ending the war in South Africa alone would save a few billion *Reichmarks* per year."

"We could sell more weapons," Voss suggested.

"The world's buyers prefer British or American weapons," Luther Stresemann said. The Head of the Economic Intelligence Service looked concerned. "Our reputation for producing weapons took a pounding when the Royal Navy sank the Argentinean ships during the war."

"The brown-skinned grafters didn't know how to use them," Holliston snapped.

"It doesn't matter," Hans said. Oddly, it was one of the few points where he found himself in agreement with Holliston. "All that matters is that sales of weapons are falling and unlikely to stabilise any time soon. The only people who buy exclusively from us are our captive markets and we don't *want* to sell *them* the most advanced weapons."

"Of course not," Holliston said.

Hans sighed and glanced at the wall-mounted clock, silently resigning himself to another long and acrimonious meeting where nothing would be decided. If he could convince the military that eliminating Pretoria's government was a potential disaster, he told himself, at least that would be something...

... But, as the meeting finally drew to an end, no decisions were taken at all.

CHAPTER FOUR

Wieland House, Berlin
17 July 1985 (Victory Day)

"And where have you been all day, young lady?"

Gudrun grimaced as her mother's voice echoed out of the kitchen. She might be eighteen years old and a university student, having passed the hardest set of exams in Germany, but her mother still talked to her as though she was a little girl. It just wasn't fair, particularly when her thoughts kept returning to Konrad's broken body. But she had no choice, but to swallow it and stick her head into the kitchen.

"I've been with Hilde, watching the parade," she said. Her mother was bent over the oven, cooking something that smelt heavenly. "Watching the soldiers trooping by..."

"You should have been here to help," her mother said, straightening up. "I don't recall saying you could leave the house."

"I'm *eighteen*, mother," Gudrun said. When *she* was a mother, *she* was not going to keep her daughters locked in a gilded cage. "And..."

"And as long as you live under my roof, you follow my rules," her mother said, sternly. "I have told you, many times, that you are to *ask* before you go out, particularly this week."

Gudrun sighed as her mother turned to face her. Adelinde Wieland was tall and blonde, but her hair was slowly shading to grey after bringing up four children on a policeman's salary and what little she could claim from the government. It had often baffled Gudrun how people could compare her to her mother, although Grandpa Frank had been heard to claim that Gudrun was the spitting image of *his* wife. Her mother's face was very different from Gudrun's and her hair a shade or two lighter before it started to go grey.

"I have a boyfriend, mother," she said. She felt an odd pang at the memory. Adelinde had never really approved of Konrad, but her husband had approved the match. "I'm not going to get into trouble."

"That's what they all say," her mother said. "A soldier in a pretty uniform, perhaps a glass or two of beer... who knows what will happen?"

Gudrun felt her face heat. Her mother could be uncomfortably blunt at times; she still cringed at the memory, years ago, of having her mother explain where babies came from and why she should be very careful until she was actually married. There was a black market in contraception, she'd been told, but condoms and American-made pills couldn't be purchased unless the user already had three children. University student or not, Gudrun had no idea where she might obtain any condoms, let alone how she might convince her boyfriend to use one. Men could be such idiots at times.

She shuddered. Konrad wasn't going to recover. It was unlikely, the nurse had said, that he could survive without the machine. And even if he did, he'd be unable to do *anything* with her. Part of her even wished she'd pulled the plug on him before leaving, even though it would probably have set off alarms. Her boyfriend deserved better than to remain a vegetable for the rest of his life.

"I'm glad you're thinking about it," her mother sneered. It took Gudrun a moment to realise that her mother had seen the shudder and misinterpreted it. "Go take Grandpa Frank his dinner before your father comes home. He'll want to eat as soon as he arrives."

Gudrun groaned. "Mother, can't Johan do it..."

"Go," her mother ordered, pointing at the tray. "Now."

There was no point in arguing with her mother when she was cross, Gudrun knew from bitter experience. There were two younger boys in the house, yet *they* never had to do any cooking or washing up. It didn't seem fair, somehow; she picked up the tray, swallowing the curse that came to mind when she saw the bottle perched next to the covered dish, and headed for the door. She'd once dumped the beer down the sink, hoping it would make Grandpa Frank more pleasant, but her mother had been furious. Gudrun had never dared do it again.

She walked slowly up the stairs, stalling as long as she could. Grandpa Frank's room was at the far end of the corridor, forcing her to walk past the room shared by Johan and Siegfried and her own door before she reached her grandfather's door. Johan had complained, loudly, that he hadn't been allowed to move into Kurt's room, now that his elder brother spent most of his time in the barracks, but their father had flatly refused to allow him to take the empty room. Gudrun smiled at the memory. There weren't many advantages to living in a patriarchal household, but watching her brothers forced to share a room was definitely one of them.

"Come," an imperious voice bellowed.

Gudrun flinched - she'd never worked out how Grandpa Frank could tell when there was someone waiting outside his room - and pushed the door open, wrinkling her nose at the stench. As always, the room was an odd combination of orderly and disorderly; the bed looked neat and tidy, but there were beer bottles lying on the floor and the remains of a snack sitting on the bedside table. Grandpa Frank himself was sitting in an armchair, reading a newspaper and drinking from a half-full bottle of beer. Gudrun's stomach turned at the thought of helping the disgusting old man to the toilet, although - to be fair - he'd never seemed to have any problems staggering out of bed and doing his business as far as she knew.

"Victory Day," Grandpa Frank said. "You must be very proud."

"Yes, Grandpa," Gudrun said. She'd never been sure just who Grandpa Frank thought she was, half the time. Half of what he said made no sense at all. "But my boyfriend..."

Her voice caught. Grandpa Frank was... a cripple. No, not quite a cripple, but he needed a wheelchair if he wanted to leave the house. And Konrad wouldn't even have that, if by some dark miracle he survived. He...

"The paratrooper," Grandpa Frank said, darkly. "I heard he was planning to become a policeman. It's no place for a young man."

Wonderful, Gudrun thought. The paratrooper-turned-policeman was her father. *He thinks I'm my mother.*

She eyed her grandfather carefully as she placed the tray on the table beside him. Grandpa Frank's mood changed rapidly; she'd seen him go from maudlin, mourning his long-dead wife, to angry and raging at the world within seconds. Only his daughter could talk sense into him when he was angry; Gudrun

27

honestly didn't understand why her mother allowed the old man to stay in the house. Grandpa Frank had come alarmingly close to clobbering Johan's brains out when the younger boy had snuck up on him for a dare.

"My boyfriend didn't take part in the parade," she said, flatly. It was honest enough, to be sure. "I miss him."

"Just stay faithful to him," Grandpa Frank advised. "It's no service to a decent lad to trade him in when another one comes along."

Gudrun felt her cheeks heat. The idea of Grandpa Frank, of all people, giving her relationship advice was horrifically embarrassing. She honestly had no idea *what* he'd done in the war, but he'd had enough nightmares to make it clear that it had been *something* thoroughly unpleasant. Maybe he'd been in Stalingrad, during the brutal house-to-house fighting, or invaded Moscow towards the end of the war. He was certainly old enough...

But mother won't let us ask him any questions, she thought. *And she slapped Johan when he tried.*

"I'll do my best," she said. She stepped back from the older man, never taking her eyes off him. "I hope it's good food."

Grandpa Frank ignored her as he took a long swig from the bottle and started to mutter to himself in a dialect Gudrun didn't recognise. Careful to breathe through her mouth, she looked around the room, picked up the used plates and cutlery and headed back downstairs to the kitchen. Her mother was waiting, hands resting impatiently on her hips. Gudrun rolled her eyes as her mother pointed to the sink, then emptied the plates into the bin, put the dishes in the water and washed them hastily. Grandpa Frank never seemed to finish a meal.

Too busy drinking, Gudrun thought, as her mother started to hand out more tasks before she could make her escape. *And trying to drown his sorrows.*

She looked at her mother, who was just taking a tray of sausages out of the oven. "Why do we keep Grandpa Frank here when we could send him to one of the veteran homes?"

Her mother turned and gave her the look that generally preceded a hard slap. "When your father and I are old and grey," she said coldly, "will you look after us or will you send us to a home?"

Gudrun flinched. "Of course I'll look after you..."

"My father practically raised me since my mother died young," Adelinde said. "Whatever his flaws, and he has many, he managed to raise a daughter despite never remarrying. I cannot put him into a home to die, young lady, and you're being *thoroughly* unpleasant to suggest it."

"Yes, mother," Gudrun said, feeling tiny under her mother's gaze. "I'm sorry."

"And we get an extra stipend from the government for taking care of a veteran," a new voice said. Gudrun turned to see her father standing there, wearing his policeman's uniform. "It isn't to be sniffed at, you know."

"Herman," Adelinde said, tightly.

Gudrun gave her father a hug. "How was work?"

"Your daughter was out with a friend half the day and your eldest son has yet to return," Adelinde said, before her father could say a word. "I expect you to speak to them both after dinner."

"Yes, dear," Herman said, as he let go of Gudrun. "Gudrun, speak to me after dinner."

Gudrun nodded, hoping he couldn't see the amusement on her face. She'd been taught, in school, that a wife was to be obedient to her husband, cook his dinners, have his children and treat him like a king. Whoever had written the stupid textbooks she'd been forced to read, she was sure, was either a man with a female penname or a woman who'd never actually married anyone. Adelinde didn't even *pretend* to be obedient to her husband. The household was her realm and God help anyone who questioned her right to rule.

"There was the usual run of pickpockets and other trouble-causers," her father added, picking up a biscuit from the jar while his wife's back was turned. "A group of children ran riot in the square, but someone very high up ordered that they were merely to be sent back to school rather than face punishment. It was quite strange."

"Poor kids," Gudrun said. She'd been lucky to escape a full Victory Day parade while she'd been at school, but she'd had to stand for hours for smaller parades and, by the time they were finally dismissed, she'd been aching and sore. "Are they going to be all right?"

"Probably," her father said. "They..."

"Gudrun, take the potatoes and put them on the table," her mother interrupted. "Herman, if you're going to stand around here, take the bottles of beer and put them by the plates."

"Yes, dear," her father said. "Shall I give Johan the big mug?"

"Probably not," Adelinde said. She normally banned alcohol from the table, save for Grandpa Frank. But this was Victory Day. "I don't want him drinking too much and winding up being sick over my nice clean carpet."

Gudrun winced inwardly as she carried the potatoes out. Johan and Siegfried were already sitting at the table, looking as though butter wouldn't melt in their mouths. They might as well be twins, she'd often thought, although Johan was blonde while Siegfried was brown, taking more after their father. He was growing up quickly too, she noted; he was the baby of the family, at twelve, but he'd already lost his childlike appearance. Like everyone else at school, he'd been forced to exercise on the playing fields until he'd shed every last trace of fat from his body.

"That looks good," Johan said, eying the potatoes with interest. "You think mother cooked them in gravy?"

"Go ask her," Gudrun snapped. Johan needed to learn, the sooner the better, that she wasn't there to answer his every whim. It was a service to his future wife. "And seeing you're just sitting there, why don't you put out the knives and forks?"

"Do it," their father agreed, stepping into the room carrying a pair of bottles in one hand. "If you want to be lazy, you can go join the *Luftwaffe* and sit on your bottom all day."

"I *like* flying," Johan protested. "I'm going to sign up for the *Luftwaffe* next year."

Gudrun smiled. "You might not learn how to fly," she needled. She'd looked up the figures when one of her fellow students had started to date a pilot. "For everyone who gets accepted for pilot training, there's three or four who get accepted for work on the ground. That's not *quite* as impressive."

Johan's face fell. "But I'm a natural pilot."

"The *Luftwaffe* needs more than just pilots," their father said. He gave Gudrun a look that sent her scurrying back into the kitchen, just as Kurt arrived, still wearing his uniform. "And if you learn how to maintain a fighter jet, Johan, you will have something to build on when you return to civilian life."

"I'm going to become an astronaut," Johan said. Gudrun could still hear him, even over the sound of sizzling sausages. "If I manage to do well as a pilot, I can put in for space training and go to the moon."

Gudrun smirked as she took the sausages and carried them back into the dining room, her mother following her with the vegetables. Johan was hardly alone in wanting to fly aircraft - a third of the boys she'd known in school had had the same ambition - but the odds were against him. And if he *did* manage to join the *Luftwaffe* without actually becoming a pilot, he'd be forever branded a REMF, rather than a fighter. His chances of winning the hearts and bodies of countless girls, as he had seen on television programs, would be sharply reduced.

"This is Victory Day," her father said, once the food had been served and the beer had been poured. "Let us remember, just for a moment, how we became the most powerful nation in the world."

Now tell me, Gudrun thought. *Is that actually true?*

It wasn't a pleasant thought, but it had to be faced. The state had lied, at least once, and no matter how much she tried, she couldn't think of anything that disproved her theory that Konrad wasn't the only wounded soldier to be kept away from his family. And if the state had lied once, who knew what *else* it had lied about? How much of what she'd been taught had been a lie? She was pretty sure they couldn't have lied about basic maths - she could *prove* that two plus two equalled four - but it was a great deal easier to lie about the social subjects. Had there really been a great war?

Grandpa Frank fought in the war, she thought. He was hardly the only old man with a military background. She had several friends who had elderly relatives living with them or staying in veteran homes. *So there must have been a war. But what really happened?*

She ate her food slowly, barely tasting the sausages and potatoes as she thought. What could she do? Konrad's family might make a fuss, if she told them the truth, but it was equally possible they'd report her for sneaking into a hospital. She could keep it to herself, yet the part of her that loved Konrad wanted to do *something* about his case. But what? If she tried to protest herself, she'd wind up in an asylum, if she was lucky.

"I need to speak to you," her father said, once the dinner was over. Gudrun had been so lost in her thoughts that she hadn't noticed that the meal was coming to an end. "You too, Kurt."

Kurt gave Gudrun a sharp look as their father rose to his feet. Gudrun shrugged; their father might know they'd slipped out of the house, but he

31

didn't know where they'd been. As long as they stuck to the cover story, they'd be safe. Or so she hoped. If the nurse Kurt had been trying to flirt with reported their presence, after he stood her up, the SS might start looking for a pair of intruders. And if they got lucky, they might catch her before she could tell anyone what they'd seen.

Two more days of parades, she thought, *and then I can go back to university. And then...*

She sucked in her breath. Officially, the university was politically neutral. Unofficially, students talked all the time. They were, after all, among the smartest people in the *Reich*; many of them had worked hard to escape conscription by passing the exams and winning a place in the university. And almost all of the students would know at least one person in the military. How many students had seen a relative go to South Africa and not return?

But it wasn't something she dared discuss with Kurt. Who knew *which* side he'd take?

Talk to the students, she told herself, as she led the way into her father's office. She had a feeling her father would just tell them both off, but there was no point in dawdling. *And then decide what to do next.*

CHAPTER FIVE

American Embassy, Berlin
19 July 1985

"Well," Ambassador Samuel Turtledove said. "Thoughts?"

Andrew allowed himself a smile. Ambassador Turtledove had no time for the persistent rivalry between the Office of Strategic Services, the Central Intelligence Agency and the Defence Intelligence Agency, to say nothing of the military itself. They were, after all, right in the heart of Berlin, in the first building that would fall if war ever broke out between the North Atlantic Alliance and the Third *Reich*. There was literally no time for inter-service rivalry or disagreements. Everyone in the room was cleared to hear everything up to TOP SECRET and beyond.

"It was an impressive show," he said, as he accepted a cup of coffee from the Ambassador's aide. "I counted over thirty long-range heavy bombers in a single fly-past. They certainly *look* as though they can reach New York."

"Assuming they don't get bounced halfway there," General William Knox pointed out. The military attaché frowned down at the photographs the observers had taken during the parade and placed on the table. "We still have fighter bases up and down the east coast, despite the best efforts of Congress. The Brits have their fighters too."

"One would assume the Brits would have other things to worry about, if war broke out," Andrew said, mildly. "But I tend to agree. The long-range bomber isn't a major threat unless they build them in far greater numbers."

"Which leads to the obvious question," the Ambassador said. "*Can* they build them in far greater numbers?"

Andrew looked at Penelope Jameson, who shrugged. "The German economy is a mess, Mr. Ambassador," she said. The CIA had attached her to the Berlin Office as an expert in economics and charged her with gauging the strength of the German economy. It wasn't a task Andrew envied her. "I honestly think that most Germans are unaware of just how badly their economy is performing, certainly when compared to ours. Funding a few hundred long-range bombers would be very difficult right now."

"Particularly as they would be of limited value in South Africa," Knox said.

"Perhaps not," Andrew said. "They can fly well above the Stinger-A's range, can't they?"

He smiled as Knox - and Robert Hamilton - grimaced in unison. The OSS had been pressing the President to send Stinger-B and Stinger-C missiles to the South Africans, even though there was a very real risk that one or more units would fall into German hands and be reverse-engineered. He understood their concerns, but there was a very real opportunity to bleed the Germans white using the missiles. Shooting down a handful of heavy bombers would hurt the *Reich* more than killing a few hundred soldiers on deployment.

And if war does break out, he thought, *there will be fewer bombers to make their way to New York.*

"They're not exactly equipped for tactical support," Knox said, after a moment. "Their smart weapons are considerably inferior to our own."

"We *think*," Andrew reminded him. "The *gauchos* probably didn't know how to use their weapons to best advantage."

"They would have set up a display and shown off their merchandise if they could," Penelope said, quietly. "Their economy took a hit when the Falklands War went so badly for the side using German weapons."

"Serve them right," the Ambassador said. He cleared his throat. "Was there anything new in the parade, any potential game changers?"

"Probably not," Andrew said. "The latest tank design was a modified Panther VII, their main battle tank. I don't think we have to worry about a revolutionary new tank appearing on the battlefields in a few years."

"They also modified a handful of older Panzer XIs," Hamilton added. "It's hard to be sure, but it looks like they took off the main guns and added several machine guns to the vehicles."

"Probably for counter-insurgency work," Knox grunted. He picked up one of the photographs and held it out. "We know they've been taking losses in South Africa, Mr. Ambassador. My best guess is that they're adapting their weapons and armour to cope with the threat."

Which isn't likely to go away anytime soon, Andrew thought. *The blacks know they have to fight and perhaps die, rather than doing nothing and certainly dying.*

He shuddered at the thought. The *Reich's* population might be blissfully unaware of what had been done in their name, but everyone else knew all too well what Adolf Hitler had unleashed upon the world. He wouldn't have bet a rusty dollar that the blacks would survive for long, if the Nazis claimed the country. They'd be herded into concentration camps and brutally murdered. Indeed, there were factions in South Africa that would happily support such a final solution, heedless of the possibility that the Nazis would shove *them* into the gas chambers next.

The Ambassador cleared his throat. "Do you feel it's likely they will double down in South Africa?"

Andrew hesitated. "They made a mistake getting involved," he said. "We know that - and I suspect they know it too, now. But I think their leadership will be reluctant to retreat from their positions in South Africa. They'd see it as an admission of weakness."

He looked up at the map. The *Reich* bestrode the continent like a colossus, bright red ink soaking the land from Dunkirk to Kamchatka. And yet, their control over their vast domains was tenuous, in places. The settlements in Germany East were plagued by partisans, the Vichy French were restless and even their allies were looking for alternatives. Andrew was sure that Turkey, at least, would jump ship if there was a reasonable chance of getting away with it, while Italy and Spain wouldn't be far behind. Binding their economies to Germany had been a deadly mistake.

"Economically, they must be reaching their limits," Penelope said. "All my models suggest Germany will have to make major cutbacks within the next five years."

"Your models may not take reality into account," Knox pointed out. He'd never liked Penelope, although Andrew had never figured out why. "Surely they know how to fine-tune their own economy."

"An economy is not a military unit, sir," Penelope said. "Nor is it a piece of balky machinery that can be fixed. Fine-tuning an economy is simply impossible and trying to control it leads to disaster. The communists discovered that in 1942."

She took a breath. "My models are, if anything, optimistic," she added. "I gave the Germans every advantage I could think of, sir; I assumed a level of central understanding and control that, quite frankly, is beyond the realm of possibility. And yet, all of my models indicate a major collapse in less than five years unless something changes."

Andrew frowned. "They could be spoofing your results."

"They could," Penelope agreed. "We have always had problems gauging the true power of the German economy. However, if it was as good as they claimed, they'd have a much larger moon base and a few hundred additional spacecraft to stake their claims to the asteroids."

"True," Andrew agreed.

"It's also beside the point," Knox said. "Is the likelihood of war any stronger than it was two years ago?"

Maybe that's why he doesn't like her, Andrew thought. *He understands the machines and tactics of war, but not economics.*

"The last set of discussions I had with the Foreign Minister were unenlightening," the Ambassador said, calmly. "He lodged an official complaint about our meddling in South Africa, I lodged a complaint of my own about German weapons shipments to radical factions in Latin and South America. We had a long argument that boiled down to mutual denials that anything was actually happening."

"And so anyone on the ground will vanish, if they get caught," Andrew said.

"We do it too," Hamilton reminded him. "Any German *advisor* caught in Panama goes straight into a black prison for interrogation, not held for trade."

Andrew nodded, ruefully. The threat of mutual destruction - Germany and the United States each had over 10,000 nuclear warheads - had made it impossible for either side to risk seeking a final war to decide the fate of the planet. Instead, Germany had started running weapons and supplies to radical groups in Latin America, while America had supplied Russian, French and South African insurgents with weapons of their own. But German brutality made it impossible for them to end the war on anything other than total victory, while the United States could use a combination of hard and soft power to convince the undecided to support the Americans. Mexico was more peaceful than it had been in years; Panama, the scene of a brutal insurgency, was calming down...

But the Germans can't afford to treat anyone as equals, he thought, darkly. *They have to exterminate their enemies to win, which makes it impossible for their enemies to surrender.*

Knox looked at Penelope, sharply. "What happens if the German economy *does* collapse?"

"It's hard to be sure," Penelope said. "I think we'd be looking at something akin to the Great Depression, but probably a great deal worse. The German economy is more integrated than ours was in the thirties."

"And then they will go to war," Knox said, grimly. "Hitler saw war as the solution to Germany's woes. War will distract their people from their empty bellies."

"They'd have to be out of their minds," Hamilton said. "We have the AMERICA SHIELD, do we not?"

"The system isn't perfect," Knox reminded him. "If the Germans throw every last one of their missiles at us in a single volley, will the shield stop them all?"

"We'd certainly have a better chance of survival than *they* would," Hamilton snapped. "What the bombs didn't destroy would be wiped out by their slaves afterwards."

"And a full-scale nuclear war might well destroy the entire world," Penelope said. "Nuclear winter will finish off the survivors."

Andrew shook his head in grim horror. "Perhaps they won't see it that way," he said. "They may view mutual destruction as a victory, of sorts."

The Ambassador held up a hand. "What are their alternatives?"

"Cut their cloak to suit their cloth," Penelope said. "They'll have to make massive - and painful - budget cuts."

"Which they can't, for political reasons," Knox commented. "They're committed to trying to keep up with us."

Andrew sighed, inwardly. The Germans *had* been fearsome - and they still were - but they'd also been very good at projecting an illusion that they were stronger than they were. The CIA had yet to recover from taking some of the German claims at face value, back in the sixties, and terrifying Congress into authorising a colossal military build-up. Now, it was the Germans who were struggling to stay in the race...

Assuming we're correct, he reminded himself. *The buggers have got themselves caught in an elephant trap.*

"Maybe it would be a good time to propose limits to military spending," the Ambassador said, calmly. "Let them off as lightly as we can."

"It was tried, back in the seventies," Knox said. "We caught them cheating."

"Back when it looked as though we would lose Mexico," Hamilton said. "We faced the same dilemma the Germans are facing now. Do they cut their losses and admit defeat or up the ante?"

He shrugged. "Our ability to influence their decision-making process *is* rather limited."

"I have to speak to the President," the Ambassador said. "Do we try to take advantage of their problems or do we commit ourselves to doing nothing?"

"Unless the Germans become more reasonable, we can't really do much more than we already are," Andrew said. "We cannot trust them to honour any agreement they make; they cannot take the risk of being backed into a corner... sir, the *Reich* is hellishly unstable. If it goes down, it could easily go down into war."

Penelope leaned forward. "We could offer to mediate peace in South Africa."

"We'd have problems finding a solution everyone involved could live with," Hamilton said, darkly. "The South Africans themselves will want to remain Top Dog in the manger for the rest of eternity, while the blacks will want - at the very least - self-rule and an end to the apartheid system. And the Nasties will want to exterminate the blacks and probably add South Africa to the Third *Reich*.

"Remove the German forces and the South Africans will either have to flee the country or be brutally murdered by the blacks. Stop supplying the blacks with weapons and the Germans will probably shove them all into gas chambers - if there are any left alive by the end of the war."

Andrew shuddered. The South African Government had imposed a complete lockdown on newsmen travelling to South Africa, but a handful of intrepid reporters had made the long journey to the front. They'd sent back horrific stories and pictures, including one of hundreds of villages being fire-bombed from high overhead and refugees gunned down mercilessly. It had shocked America, particularly the black population. The President might find it politically impossible to stop sending weapons and supplies to the insurgents. He'd be deserted by every black congressman and senator in the country.

"And if the Germans do abandon South Africa, the chaos will spread to Germany South," he added. It might not be a bad thing - Germany South was the world's largest source of uranium - but it would definitely worry the German leadership. "And then it will spread upwards into French and Italian territory."

"The Germans would be wise to consolidate what they've got," Penelope said, flatly. "If they try to hold on to their entire empire, they'll likely lose everything."

"They seem to disagree with you," Knox said.

"I'd be surprised if they truly understood the problem," Penelope said, mildly. "I've met a great many political and military leaders who refused to even *try* to understand economics."

Ouch, Andrew thought, as Knox's face flushed with anger. *A palatable hit.*

The Ambassador tapped the table sharply. "I'm due to speak with the President tomorrow," he said. "Do I advise him, then, to do nothing and just wait for the *Reich* to fall apart on its own?"

"I suggest you advise him to take some extra precautions, just in case," Knox advised. "If they're planning to strike against us, they're not going to tell their own people until the rockets are in the air. Putting the air and missiles bases on alert might make the difference between survival and destruction."

"They'd just be committing suicide," Penelope argued. "It makes no sense."

She had a point, Andrew knew. The *Reich* and the NAA didn't share a border. They *might* be able to launch an invasion force across the English Channel, but getting the *Wehrmacht* to Washington DC was a fool's dream. They'd have to contend with the United States Navy, the United States Air Force, the Royal Navy and the Canadian Navy. Andrew privately doubted the Germans would get halfway across the ocean before every last one of their ships were sunk. The Germans could make America miserable - tracking down Nazi sleeper cells was a persistent headache for the FBI - but they couldn't invade and occupy territory.

"They may not realise the truth," Hamilton said. "Or they might not care. Just because they look like us doesn't mean they *think* like us."

Andrew nodded. He'd seen what passed for education in German schools. It was long on physical exercise and quasi-military training, short on teaching boys and girls how to be anything other than interchangeable cogs in a machine. He still shuddered at visiting a school, one day, and watching the children mouth their hatred of non-Aryans. The only good thing about the whole affair was that the pictures they were shown of Jews were so horrifically caricatured that the children wouldn't *recognise* a Jew if they saw one.

"See what else you can gather from your sources," the Ambassador added. "Maybe we can find a way to let them down gently."

"They'd hate us for making the offer," Knox said.

"They're already placing orders for more computers and other advanced electronics," Hamilton added. He looked at Penelope. "How long can they pay for them?"

"Unknown," Penelope said. "But the *Reich's* stockpile of foreign currency is quite low. I'd advise the sellers to make sure they get cash in advance."

Knox scowled. "Does that not present a threat to us?"

"Possibly," Andrew said, before Penelope could say a word. "But you try convincing the corporations that they shouldn't sell their outdated crap to the Germans."

The Ambassador finished his coffee and rose. "I'll see you all after I speak with the President," he said, checking his watch. It was nearly midnight. "Until then, goodnight."

Andrew smiled as he departed, followed by Knox. The military attaché would have his own report to write; Andrew, thankfully, could put his off until the following morning, when he'd had a chance to think about what he'd seen. Hamilton finished his own coffee, then headed for the door himself. Andrew watched him go, then looked at Penelope. She looked tired and cross-eyed.

"I plan to go for a walk in a couple of days," he said. He wasn't asking for a date, although he knew that some people wouldn't be able to tell the difference. "Do you want to accompany me?"

Penelope hesitated. Andrew understood. No real harm would come to them, they'd been warned when they accepted the posting, but the SS sometimes harassed American visitors to Berlin. It was no great secret that spies were based in the embassy, even though Andrew, Hamilton and Penelope herself had cover stories that should explain their activities. The SS might hope that harassing the Americans would lead them to German traitors.

"It might be fun," she said, finally. She understood what they'd be *really* doing, all right. A young couple out on a stroll would attract less attention than a man on his own. "Why not?"

CHAPTER SIX

Albert Speer University, Berlin
20 July 1985

Walking into the Albert Speer University for the first time, Gudrun recalled as she walked towards the doors, had been like taking a breath of fresh air for the first time in her life. Like every other child in the *Reich*, she had endured fifteen years of schooling where she'd been expected to regurgitate answers and otherwise do exactly as she was told. She'd quite lost count of the number of times she'd been forced to run laps around the school, stand in the corridor or undergo other humiliating punishments for daring to actually question the teacher's words, let alone the letters they'd sent home to her parents. And yet, despite that, university had seemed a more attractive option at seventeen than trying to become a nurse, a housewife or entering one of the few careers open to women. It had been a surprise when she'd been told that the traits that had got her in trouble at school were precisely the traits the university wanted from its students.

"You have not been taught to *think*," her first tutor had said, when he'd addressed the class on the very first day. It had been the first mixed-sex class Gudrun had ever had, but she'd been too fascinated to notice the presence of young men mixed in with the young women. "Here, we will attempt to teach you to *think*."

Her first year at the university had been fascinating, to say the least. She'd learned how to use a computer, one of the blocky American-made machines that were imported into the *Reich* at great expense, and dozens of other skills that made up the background for STEM courses. She knew she had to choose a major by the time she turned twenty, when she would be expected to specialise in one particular field of study, but she was honestly tempted to try to delay that as long as she could. No one had shown her anything of the sort while she'd been at school, let alone allowed her to come to her own conclusions. Hell, she'd never heard of anyone being expelled from the university for asking questions. They were all too eager to *learn* to make trouble.

"We don't take everyone," the tutor had said, a year ago. "The exams we set look for the underlying *potential* for intelligence, not *developed* intelligence. You are here because we believe we can help your minds to flourish and, in return, you will advance the *Reich*."

She took a moment to admire the statue of Albert Speer, architect, minister and one of the three guiding minds of the *Reich* after Hitler's death, then hurried into the building. As always, it was packed; students who had been given the week off for Victory Day had hurried back as soon as they could, preparing for the exams they knew to be coming in three months, exams that would determine their future. Far too many of them actually *lived* on campus, sharing rooms in university accommodation that were strictly segregated and chaperoned; Gudrun remembered, with a flicker of envy, how she'd begged her mother and father to allow her to apply for one of the university rooms. But her mother had flatly refused to allow Gudrun to live away from home.

Probably thought I'd spend all my time in bed with Konrad, she thought, bitterly. There *were* housemothers, she'd been told, but they couldn't hope to chaperone everyone. *And abandon my studies completely if I fell pregnant.*

She gritted her teeth at the thought as she hurried into the lecture hall. Some of her friends were already there, pens and paper at the ready; they knew better than to be late when a lecture was about to begin. The doors would be closed a minute after the deadline and anyone who failed to make it would be marked as absent, which would lead to a thoroughly unpleasant discussion with the dean. Gudrun had never faced the man himself, thankfully, but she'd heard rumours that anyone who missed more than two classes in a row was given a punishment so awful that no one ever spoke of it...

Which raises the question of just how people know that something happens, she thought, dryly. *The dean probably started the rumours himself, just to keep us in line.*

She took her seat and nudged Hilde Morgenstern, a dark-haired girl who'd been her friend ever since the first week at university. "Meeting in the private study room this afternoon after lunch," she hissed. "Pass it on."

Hilde gave her a sharp look - their private study group wasn't exactly a formal organisation - and then nodded, turning to whisper in Sven's ear. Gudrun hadn't been entirely sure that a group composed of both males and females could work - the handful of dances she'd endured at school had been marred by male behaviour as they grew older - but she had to admit that Sven and the others were *very* focused on their work. Sven in particular was going to be a computer designer, or so he'd said. He already had an uncanny insight into how the computers they used at university actually worked.

"I think that's everyone told," Hilde muttered, once the whispered message had gone down the row. "Isn't it a little early to be panicking over exams?"

"It's not about the exams," Gudrun muttered back. The tutor closed the doors with a loud *thud* and strode to the podium, his dark eyes searching for troublemakers. "I'll tell you this afternoon."

The lecture would have been interesting, she had to admit, if she hadn't been thinking about Konrad and everything she'd deduced. Thankfully, the tutor didn't call on her to answer questions - she'd barely heard half of what he'd said - and by the time the class finally came to an end, she'd reluctantly struck a deal with Hilde for a copy of her notes. She'd have to work extra hard, if she could muster the energy, to catch up. The tutors rarely showed any sympathy to anyone who attended the lectures and *still* needed to beg for advice and assistance.

"That's not like you," Hilde observed, as they headed for lunch. "Are you all right?"

"I'll tell you in the study room," Gudrun said. She caught Leopold's arm as he passed. "Can you bring your stereo?"

Leopold blinked in surprise. "Of course I can," he said. "I'll see you after lunch."

Hilde stuck with Gudrun all through lunch, but had the common sense to keep her questions under wraps while they joined the line for food and drink, then ate as quickly as they could at a small table. The refectory was crammed with students, some wearing uniforms from the nearby military college, others daringly wearing American jeans and t-shirts that had been either smuggled into the *Reich* or sold at an enormous mark-up in one of the few American stores in the city. Gudrun winced inwardly as she saw one girl swaying past, her jeans so tight around her buttocks that she thought they were going to split open at any moment, then followed Hilde up the stairs and into the study room. Leopold was already there, attaching his stereo to the socket.

"So," he said, as he turned on the machine. "What's all this about, then?"

"Wait and see," Gudrun said.

She sat down and waited as the remainder of the study group - five girls, seven boys - entered the room, then waved to Hilde to close and lock the door. Konrad, the one time he'd visited, had shown her where the bug was hidden, within the spare power socket. She motioned for Leopold to put the stereo next to the bug, then tapped the table for attention. Konrad might never recover from his wounds, but at least he would have a little revenge. She hesitated, knowing that a single traitor within the group would spell her death, and then took the plunge.

"This isn't about our studies," she said. "It's... it's political. If any of you are uneasy, please leave now and we won't mention it to you again."

There was a long pause. No one left.

Gudrun shuddered, inwardly. No one said anything overtly, but everyone knew that the SS had eyes and ears everywhere. *Anyone* could be a spy, anyone. Children were induced to betray their parents, if they said something against the *Reich*; wives could be convinced that their duties to the *Reich* were more important than their duties to their husbands. The university might be a lair for free-thinkers, it might have been designed to allow young Germans to think, but that only meant the SS would have more invested in keeping an eye on it. Hell, the only reason she believed Konrad had been a genuine visitor to the university, the first time they'd met, was that he'd worn his uniform.

And I will not let him down, she thought, savagely. There were some risks that had to be taken, even if the consequences were severe. She was *damned* if she was letting them get away with crippling her boyfriend and then lying to his family. *I will do whatever it takes to take revenge.*

"As you know, my boyfriend was sent to South Africa," she said. It was a nice easy way to start the conversation. "I received two letters from him after his deployment began, then nothing. His family heard nothing too. It was only through a friend in the medical office that I heard he'd actually been sent back to the *Reich*, that he is currently in hospital right here in Berlin."

She swallowed hard, then outlined what she'd done, careful not to mention that Kurt had also been involved. His CO would be furious, at the very least; Kurt would probably find himself attached to a punishment battalion and sent to clear a minefield or chase insurgents in Russia, the insurgents who'd been defeated, according to the news, several times over. The more she looked at the news with a cynical eye, the more she saw the discrepancies. If Russia was *safe*, why were so many soldiers dying there?

"They lied to us," she said.

"Konrad was nothing special," Leopold said. He'd never liked Konrad. The SS was rarely popular outside Germany East. "Why would anyone bother to cover up his wounds?"

"They wouldn't," Gudrun said, and outlined what she'd deduced. "They must be lying about more than just one wounded soldier. How many others have died, or been wounded, in South Africa?"

"The news says that only a few hundred soldiers have been killed or wounded on deployment," Hilde said. She sounded shaken. "My... my boyfriend... could he have been killed or wounded too?"

Gudrun winced. Hilde's boyfriend was a tanker who'd been deployed to South Africa a month after Konrad. Martin had never seemed a decent guy to her, but Hilde had clearly liked him, even loved him.

"I don't know," she said. "Has he been writing to you?"

"He sends letters, but they're always delayed," Hilde said. "I only get them two or three weeks after they're posted."

"They're censored," Sven said. Too late, Gudrun remembered that Sven's older brother was a soldier too. It was rare to find a German family who didn't have at least one member in the military. "The REMFs always insist on reading letters before they're forwarded to their recipients."

Hilde coloured. "But he wrote..."

Gudrun could guess. "I don't think they really care about endearments," she said. She had a feeling that Martin had written something a little more passionate than Konrad ever had, but the censors probably wouldn't care. It wasn't as if he was sending racy postcards of himself back to his girlfriend. "However, they probably do black out anything to do with the war itself."

Leopold frowned. "Do you have any idea how dangerous this conversation is?"

"Yes," Gudrun said, flatly. "Yes, I do."

"She did offer to allow us to leave," Hilde pointed out.

Gudrun shot her a grateful look. "We're being lied to," she said, bluntly. "And many of us have relatives who may already be dead or wounded - and we don't know."

"This *could* be just an absurd coincidence," Leopold said, after a moment. "Konrad" - his face twisted for a moment - "might have been caught up in a covert operation of some kind."

"This isn't a story from one of those damned Otto Skorzeny books," Sven snapped. "Konrad wasn't a superhuman commando, able to leap tall buildings in a single bound."

Gudrun hid a smile. She'd been forced to read the Otto Skorzeny books herself, at school; Otto Skorzeny, who apparently *had* been a real person, had pulled off hundreds of death-defying stunts that had reshaped the face of the world. Skorzeny had been pitted against a multitude of villains - Evil Jewish Bankers, Evil American Capitalists, Evil Russian Communists, Evil British Monarchists - and emerged triumphant every time. The books had practically drooled over how Skorzeny proved that National Socialism was the way forward; none could stand against Skorzeny, they'd claimed, because he was a true follower of Adolf Hitler.

And how many of those stories, Gudrun asked herself, *were made up of whole cloth?*

Hilde held up a hand. "If there's one, as Gudrun said, there will be others," she said. "And Martin could be among the dead."

"Let's assume that's true," Leopold said. "What do we do about it?"

"What *can* we do?" Isla Grasser asked. "It isn't as if we have any *real* power."

"The first thing we do is try and find out how widespread this is," Gudrun said. She'd need more than a single wounded SS trooper to convince people that *something* was very badly wrong. "We all know people who are serving in South Africa. I want you all to ask questions, to find out when those people last wrote to their families, to find out when they last had leave from the front. We will *all* ask those questions."

"Martin's family won't talk to me," Hilde said. "They don't think I'd make a good housewife."

Leopold snickered. "Tell them you're pregnant."

Hilde glared at him. "I've bled three times since he left," she snarled. "I don't have any way to *convince* them I'm pregnant."

Leopold turned red and started to splutter. Gudrun winked at Hilde. Sex education in the *Reich* was very limited, but they'd all been taught how their bodies worked and how to recognise a pregnancy. She'd always found it amusing how men turned deaf whenever the subject of female issues cropped up, although she was privately sure that men talked about them in private. Why not? She and her girlfriends often poked fun at male foibles.

"You can just tell them that you're worried about him," she said. "I think they'd appreciate that, you know."

"I doubt it," Hilde said. She looked downcast for a long moment. "They were trying to set him up with some brainless bitch who came top of the class in basic housewifery."

"My mother is hardly brainless," Gudrun said. "And I don't think anyone else has a brainless mother either."

"That's not very helpful," Hilde said.

Gudrun shrugged. "Are we all agreed on our first step?"

"Yeah," Sven said. "But tell me, Gudrun; what are we going to do if we discover there are *more* soldiers who've lost contact with their families?"

"Then we decide what to do," Gudrun said. She had half a plan already, but she needed them to understand what was going on before she could push them to commit to anything more than private discussions. "You can all think about it while we're gathering data and then we can decide what to do."

"Escape to America," Horst said, quietly. "My brother says he isn't planning to come back after his period in America comes to an end."

Gudrun sucked in her breath. She'd applied for the chance to become an exchange student, but she wasn't particularly hopeful. Even if she won one of the coveted slots, her parents would probably refuse to allow her to leave the country. But if she was allowed to leave... would she return? There was no shortage of whispered stories about students who tasted life in America, home of blue jeans, country music and freedom, and refused to come back to Germany.

"I don't know," she said. Without one of the slots, it was unlikely she could get to Vichy France, let alone Britain. She wouldn't have a travel permit, for one thing, and an unaccompanied teenage girl would raise eyebrows. "We are supposed to be the smartest people in Germany. I'm sure we can figure something out."

"There were stories of student protests in America," Isla said.

"Those students weren't at risk of being gunned down like rampaging *Gastarbeiters*," Horst snapped. "If we do anything with this information, we run a terrible risk."

"Yes, we do," Gudrun said. She took a breath. "Konrad was - is - an SS trooper - I know, some of you detested him for wearing the *Sigrunen* lightning bolts. But he is a brave and decent man and he has been *betrayed* by the men he serves. A dead war hero is meant to be given a hero's funeral, a wounded war hero is meant to lack for nothing. And yet, what does he have? A hospital bed in a crowded ward and no hope of recovery, while his family thinks he's still in South Africa! What will they tell his family when he is due to return from the war?"

She took a breath, looking from face to face. None of them had really known what they were getting into, not really. They certainly hadn't realised what she intended to tell them.

"I'm not going to sit on my backside and do nothing," she concluded. "We are going to find out the truth and then we're going to work out what to do with it. It is our duty to our country. *That* is what we are going to do."

CHAPTER SEVEN

Schulze Residence/SS Safehouse, Berlin
20 July 1985

"Gudrun," Liana Schulze called, as she opened the door. "Have you heard anything from my brother?"

Gudrun felt a stab of guilt as she looked at the younger girl. Liana was sixteen, on the verge of adulthood; hell, she could marry with her parents' permission, if she didn't want to finish her final year of schooling. And she'd always looked up to Gudrun, chatting happily to her about nothing in particular; Gudrun had always thought she'd make a good sister-in-law. But she didn't dare tell the younger girl the truth. She'd speak to her father and he'd report Gudrun to the authorities.

"I haven't heard anything from your brother," she said. It was true enough. "I actually came to speak to your father."

Liana's face fell. Gudrun understood. She was the only child left in the house, now that Konrad had gone to war; she'd have no one to talk to, merely chores to perform for her mother. And she had to have known, at some deep level, that Gudrun hadn't come to talk to *her*. Gudrun was eighteen and a university student to boot. Socially, they had very little in common. They'd hardly spend time together when Konrad wasn't around.

"I understand," she said. "Are you..."

Pregnant, Gudrun thought. She hadn't gone all the way with Konrad. *And it would have been obvious that I was pregnant four months ago, if I was pregnant.*

"No, but I do need to speak to him," she said. "Is he in his study?"

"I think so," Liana said.

She held the door open long enough for Gudrun to step inside and then closed it before leading the way through the living room and up to the door of Volker Schulze's study. It was firmly shut, perhaps locked; Liana tapped on the door and waited for her father to invite her in before opening the door. Gudrun stepped past her and into the study.

"Gudrun," Volker Schulze said. He lifted an eyebrow as he turned to face her. "What brings you to my house?"

Gudrun hesitated, bracing herself. Volker Schulze had always made her a little nervous, even though she had the feeling that *her* father was meant to make *Konrad* nervous. He looked like an older version of his son, his face marred by scars from a long career in the SS before he'd retired and found work as a factory foreman. His study was covered with mementos of his career, from a spiked helmet he'd salvaged from somewhere to a pistol he claimed to have taken from a British commando team in North Africa. A large chart hung on the far wall, showing the spread of the *Reich*.

And just how much of that chart, Gudrun asked herself, *is a lie?*

She pushed the question to one side. "Since we last spoke, I haven't heard anything from Konrad," she said, simply. "I was wondering if you'd heard anything from him yourself."

Volker Schulze looked pensive. "I haven't heard anything, no," he said. Gudrun trusted he wouldn't have kept anything from her, if he *had* heard something. "Do you have reason to worry?"

"I miss him," Gudrun said.

"Young men have always gone to war," Volker Schulze said, as reassuringly as he could. "I believe that young women like you have always waited for their heroes to come home."

Gudrun winced before she could catch herself. One thing that *had* been hammered into her head at school was the importance of remaining faithful. A girl who dumped a boy while he was on deployment could expect to be a social pariah, even if the boy had been abusive and beaten her while they were together. Even if there *had* been someone else, she knew, it would have been cruel to dump Konrad while he was away. She would have waited for him to come home before telling him the bad news.

"But I've heard *nothing*," she said, plaintively. Perhaps it would cover her lapse. "Where *is* he?"

"On deployment," Volker Schulze said. He stood and patted her shoulder, awkwardly. "I was often out of touch for months at a time, Gudrun. Konrad may well be in the same position."

He paused. "Are you...?"

"No," Gudrun said, firmly. She groaned inwardly, resisting the urge to rub his nose in how she *knew* she wasn't expecting a baby. "I'm not pregnant."

"That's good," Volker Schulze said. "Gudrun, I understand how you feel, but Konrad isn't choosing not to write to you. I believe he will contact you as soon as he can. He does love you and we, his parents, *approve* of you."

Gudrun felt another stab of bitter guilt. Hilde wasn't atypical; parents, particularly those who had lived through the deprivation of the war, wanted their sons to marry good housewives, women who could cook, clean and bear their grandchildren. They didn't want academics, career women or even the handful of girls who'd made a career in the military; they assumed, perhaps correctly, that such women would never let their husbands boss them around in public. Konrad's parents could easily have told him that they would never approve his relationship with Gudrun and the hell of it was that they might have had a point. Instead, they'd welcomed her into their house.

"I thank you," she said, lowering her gaze. "Have you heard anything else from the front?"

Volker Schulze gave her a sharp look. "What do you mean?"

"The news is always bland," Gudrun said, carefully. "I was wondering if you'd heard something a little more detailed."

"There are endless skirmishes with the insurgents," Volker Schulze said. It wasn't much more than she could have deduced from the news broadcasts, reading between the lines. "It may take longer than we had thought to defeat the niggers."

Gudrun blinked. "The news said it would only be a short commitment."

Volker Schulze gave her a long considering look. "There are people in my office," he said, "who don't really understand how the factory actually *works*. Therefore, they make promises they cannot keep to people who are equally in the dark about what's actually happening and rely on the managers on the ground to cover for their failings."

It took Gudrun a moment to realise what he was trying to tell her. If someone could be so out of touch in a small factory, and she had no trouble in believing it, how much *more* out of touch were the people in the *Reichstag*, the men who ran the country? Had they started the war in South Africa because they believed, honestly believed, that victory would be no harder than baking a cake?

"I believe my daughter misses you," Volker Schulze said, after a moment. "You are, of course, quite welcome to visit any time you like."

"Thank you, sir," Gudrun said. It wasn't *entirely* proper, but there would be a chaperone in the house if necessary. "And I'm sorry..."

"For not being pregnant?" Volker Schulze asked, dryly. "I respect the *Reichsführer's* feelings regarding the need to raise the next generation of German men, but I am enough of a traditionalist to believe that the happy couple should be married before they start producing children. A child should know his father."

Gudrun blushed, furiously. No one would really care if she was a virgin or not on her wedding night, not when everyone would understand her giving herself to her boyfriend before he went off to the war. The only real question would be if she'd had a child - and, if she had, what benefits the child could claim. Konrad's baby could draw an SS pension as well as state child support; hell, if she claimed he'd been planning to marry her - and his family would likely back her up - she could claim his SS pension as well. But it was immaterial. She'd never let him take off her panties, let alone go inside her...

"I agree," she said, torn between an insane urge to giggle and a growing urge to just turn and run. Talking to her mother about men had been quite bad enough. "Please will you let me know the moment you hear anything?"

"I'll call your house directly," Volker Schulze promised.

He escorted her to the door - there was no sign of his wife or daughter - and waved her through. Gudrun gave him an impulsive hug, then hurried down the steps and back onto the road that led home. She had several other people she wanted to talk to before night fell, before she was expected home to assist her mother with the cooking. And then...

His family doesn't know, she thought, as she walked past a handful of soldiers making their way to the barracks on the outskirts of the city. She'd been sure of it, but it never hurt to make sure. *They would have told me something if they'd heard anything.*

She glanced at her watch, then turned the corner. A couple of boys she'd known from her first house lived there; she'd played with them as a little girl, before they'd gone to school and emerged too stuck-up to play with girls. They too had gone to the wars. No one would mind if she asked after them, surely? And one of them had been in the same unit as Hilde's boyfriend. It would be interesting to hear what they had to say.

———

Horst Albrecht knew, without false modesty, that he was a very smart young man. Everyone had told him so, right from the day he'd entered upper schooling in Germanica and impressed his tutors with his intelligence. Indeed, his family had been so proud of him that they'd entered him into the SS Academy two years before the normal application date; the SS, somewhat to Horst's surprise, had accepted him without question. It had taken him a while to see why his superiors might be interested in a spy who was barely old enough to shave. But, by the time he'd graduated from one of the covert programs, he'd come to see the value of an agent who was *literally* eighteen years old.

"The university is a breeding ground for ideas," his trainers had told him, when he'd finally passed the course. Being a spy was far more than charging around like Otto Skorzeny, riding hot motorcycles and winning the hearts of beautiful women. "Some of those ideas will be very bad. Your task is to watch for those who spread bad ideas and report them."

It hadn't been hard, at first. Horst had entered the university with the 1984 class; he'd made friends, chatted happily to everyone and was generally well-liked by his peers. The students didn't *want* to look beyond the surface, not when they were escaping a regimented existence for the first time in their lives. Horst had no trouble making friends and generally being popular; hell, he'd even had a couple of girlfriends.

He hadn't expected *Gudrun* to be a troublemaker. Even now, hours after he'd made his slow way to the SS safehouse - it doubled as a boarding house for students from Germany East, supervised by a grim-faced matron who provided all the explanation other students needed for why they weren't invited to the safehouse - he still couldn't quite believe it. Gudrun was intelligent, true, and strikingly pretty; he might have dated her himself if she hadn't been involved with an SS trooper. Her father was a policeman, her brother a soldier in the Berlin Guard... she hardly fitted the profile of a potential troublemaker. There were few petty little resentments in her life, save for being born female...

And she could overcome most of those problems by being a good student, Horst thought, as he opened the door into his apartment. *A computer expert or rocket scientist would be worth her weight in gold, if she truly hated the thought of becoming a housewife.*

And yet, she'd said, quite clearly, that her boyfriend had been quietly shipped home, his wounds covered up. Her concern - and her anger - was quite justified.

The apartment wasn't big, although it was vastly superior to the military barracks or slave pens for the *Untermenschen* in Germanica. He dropped his bag on the bed, clicked the kettle on and prepared a mug of coffee. He'd long since grown used to the idea of never touching a drop of alcohol, even on Victory Day. Who knew *what* would come out of his mouth when he was drunk? Once his drink was ready, he placed it on the bedside table and lay down to have a bit of a think.

Technically, he should report Gudrun at once. She had doubts - and, instead of burying them, she was trying to do something, something that might easily turn out to be treacherous. Horst couldn't imagine what she had in mind - eight students or eighty, armed rebellion was unlikely to succeed and she had to know it - but it was his duty to report her to his superiors and let them decide how to handle the matter. It might come to nothing, he knew, or it might become something truly serious. His superiors might decide to quietly vanish Gudrun and her fellows, shipping them off to Germany East or merely dumping them into a slave camp; the girls, at least, would make good breeding stock.

And yet, he *too* had his doubts.

He'd liked Konrad Schulze, the first time they'd met. It wasn't something he could show, not when it would risk his cover, but he'd *liked* the older man. In some ways, Konrad had reminded Horst of *his* brother, who hadn't *actually* vanished into America and never returned. He'd been blonde, blue-eyed and muscular, so muscular that Horst had wondered if he'd been used as the template for countless recruiting posters. Horst had even used his security codes to look up the young man's file and discovered, to his amusement, that Konrad was on the short list for promotion. *Someone* thought very highly of him.

But they don't now, Horst thought, savagely. *They see him as an embarrassment.*

It was a bitter thought. Konrad had been no covert agent, no undercover operative all too aware that even the merest *hint* of suspicion would mean instant death or permanent incarceration in a black prison. He'd certainly had no reason to believe he would simply be abandoned by his superiors, if he were caught by the enemy. No, he'd worn his black uniform proudly. Konrad should have been given full honours, if he'd been killed, or brought home on a pension if he'd been badly wounded. Instead...

He didn't think Gudrun had lied, but it would be easy enough to check her story. The computers in the apartment - another reason not to let anyone who wasn't an SS operative enter the building - were linked directly to the Berlin Network. He logged on, accessed the hospital records and searched for Konrad's name. The computers were slow - they hadn't had university students fiddling with the coding to make them a little more efficient - but it didn't take him long to uncover records belonging to one Konrad Schulze. He'd been badly wounded - the file didn't go into details, suggesting that no one had told the hospital administrators very much - and wasn't expected to survive.

They should have triaged him, he thought, genuinely shocked. It was an accepted fact of military life that badly-wounded soldiers were often allowed to die so less-wounded soldiers could be saved, yet... it was clear, just from reading between the lines, that the medical staff had worked desperately to save him. And yet, the brain damage alone almost guaranteed that Konrad would never recover. The bastards could have given him a mercy killing and come up with a cover story: instead they seemed content to leave him on life support indefinitely. *A hero... and they chose to leave him a vegetable!*

Horst kept his feelings under tight control as he logged out of the hospital network, then checked the SS personnel database. Konrad's file had been marked inactive - and it wasn't the only one. Cross-referencing the database showed Horst several hundred *other* troopers who seemed to be permanently in bureaucratic limbo, marked as neither dead nor alive. And if that was true of the SS, it was very likely true of the army too.

She didn't lie, he thought, numbly. *And that means... what?*

He turned the computer off, finished his coffee and lay back on his bed. He'd been raised to worship the SS, just like everyone else in Germany East. The SS was all that stood between the settlements and insurgents who would happily kill German men, rape German women and eat German children. He'd grown up reading horror stories, all of which had happy endings when the SS rescued the women or avenged their deaths. Joining the SS hadn't been a hard decision at all. They'd been his heroes!

And now they were being betrayed, betrayed by their own leaders.

Gudrun would run into trouble, sooner or later. Horst had no doubt of it. She was intelligent, and she knew to guard her tongue around strangers, but she had no way of knowing how things worked in the world. Hell, she'd managed to invite an SS spy to her very first meeting! She couldn't get very far without help...

... And Horst, who knew his duty called for him to report her, was seriously considering offering her that help.

It was a hard choice to make. If he were caught, his family would disown him - and it probably wouldn't be enough to save their lives. It would be easy to alert the SS, to have Gudrun and the rest of the students put under surveillance, and put an end to the whole affair... but he didn't *want* to put an end to the whole affair. He wanted her to do... what? What would she do if she proved her point?

Perhaps I'll just wait and see if she has a plan, he told himself. *And if she does, I can decide what to do about it.*

CHAPTER EIGHT

Wewelsburg Castle, Germany
20 July 1985

It was blasphemy to even consider it, but there were times when *Reichsführer-SS* Karl Holliston thought that Heinrich Himmler had been a very strange man. Karl understood the value of strength - and the will to use it - as much as any other SS officer, yet Himmler's obsession with the occult had undermined the last five years of his career, allowing him to be gently nudged aside by his former subordinates. Wewelsburg Castle itself was a grand monument to that obsession; parts of the castle had been redesigned to look like something from the Grand Order of Teutonic Knights, while other parts were designed to serve as the SS's western centre of operations. There was even a monument to the Holy Grail in the lower levels, perched in the centre of a round table.

And some of Himmler's other ideas might have caught on, if he'd had longer, Karl thought. *Shrines to the old gods, grand ceremonies of might and magic...*

He shook his head in rueful amusement. Rumours of virgin sacrifices and blood oaths had hovered around the castle for as long as the SS had occupied it - and, indeed, there were some very strange cults and secret societies rumoured to exist within the SS itself. Karl had never seen anything to indicate that they even existed, but that proved nothing. The SS was a multitude of competing factions and some of them were very secretive indeed. And yet, what need did they have of the old gods? All that was needed was the will to power.

A strong will can overcome anything, Karl thought, remembering his training as a young officer. They'd been pushed to the limit, the weak falling by the wayside or dying in training; the survivors strong enough to keep going, whatever the world threw at them. It had been twenty years since Karl had seen active service, since he'd been promoted into a desk job, but he'd done his best to stay in shape. *And the will to power is everything.*

His buzzer rang. *"Herr Reichsführer, Obergruppenfuehrer* Felix Kortig is here,"* his secretary said. "Shall I send him in?"

"Yes, please," Karl said. Maria had been with him ever since he'd been promoted into high office, her status rising with his. If she had any interests outside the office, he'd never seen them. He could be rude to anyone else, but not her. "And hold all calls until I've finished with him."

He looked up as the door opened, revealing a blonde-haired man wearing a black uniform and carrying a pistol at his belt. Karl couldn't avoid a flicker of envy as *Obergruppenfuehrer* Felix Kortig strode forward and snapped out a precise salute. Kortig might be an *Obergruppenfuehrer*, but he was still jumping out of planes with the young bucks, while Karl himself was stuck in an office, playing political games with the civilians and the military.

"Herr Reichsführer," Kortig said. *"Heil Bormann!"*

"Heil Bormann," Karl echoed. "You may speak freely - and relax."

Kortig relaxed, minimally. *"Jawohl, Herr Reichsführer,"* he said. "You wished to speak with me?"

"Yes," Karl said. He tapped the papers on his desk. "I trust you have had an opportunity to study the proposals for Operation Headshot?"

"I have," Kortig said. "They're unworkable."

Karl blinked in surprise, despite himself. Very few people would tell the *Reichsführer-SS* that one of his pet concepts was unworkable, which might explain why Himmler had been able to waste so many resources on his occult research. Sending teams of dedicated researchers to Tibet, even in the aftermath of the war, hadn't been too costly, but transporting ancient artefacts all the way back to Germany had proved a major strain. The rest of the *Reich* hadn't been too pleased at the prospect of a diplomatic incident with China, even *if* the Chinese had been fighting a civil war at the time.

He pushed the thought aside, angrily. "Unworkable?"

"Yes, *Herr Reichsführer,"* Kortig said.

Karl bit down on his anger with an effort. "Otto Skorzeny plotted to jump into London in 1950 and slaughter the British Government," he said. "Wouldn't that have been a more challenging operation?"

"The operation was planned in the context of an outright invasion," Kortig pointed out, smoothly. "I have *seen* those plans, *Herr Reichsführer*; Skorzeny intended to jump into Westminster, kill as many government ministers as he could find and then escape into the streets of London. Given the lack of extraction plans, I suspect Skorzeny believed the whole operation to be a suicide mission. The best the commandos could reasonably hope for was to go to ground in London and wait for the invasion force to seize the city."

He tapped the map, sharply. "It was never envisaged, at the time the plan was drawn up, that the British would be our allies, nor that we would be trying to put a friendly government into Westminster. The understanding was that they were our enemies and their country would be ruled with an iron hand."

Karl nodded, once. Britain had been - and still was - the *Reich's* most determined enemy, one protected by a body of water that might as well have been a castle moat. Hitler had shied away from trying to launch an offensive across the English Channel, when the British had been at their weakest; in 1950, with American forces based in Britain, an invasion would have been a very chancy affair indeed. And then the British had developed their own nuclear weapons and plans for a later invasion had been abandoned. Taking London would have been pointless if Berlin had been thrown into the fire.

"Pretoria is a different case, *Herr Reichsführer*," Kortig said, his finger tracing positions on the map. "Their government is scattered, to reduce the risk of being decapitated by a suicide bomber, and we have been unable to obtain solid information on who is where at any one time. In addition, the South African troops protecting Pretoria are experienced battle-hardened veterans, men who are well used to coping with surprise attacks and driving back the attackers before they can do major damage..."

"Our stormtroopers are far better trained than black-assed terrorists," Karl said, icily.

"It won't matter," Kortig said. "At best, we may eliminate one or two senior government ministers, but I couldn't guarantee we would get them all. The South Africans would *know* we'd effectively declared war on them. These are not Italians, *Herr Reichsführer*; the South Africans will strike back at our own forces within their country. Our alliance with them will be at an end. The only people who will gain from the whole affair will be the blacks, who will no doubt sit back and watch as the whites destroy each other."

He shook his head. "South Africa is not a country that can be easily bullied, *Herr Reichsführer*," he said. "Operation Headshot is a disaster waiting to happen."

Karl gritted his teeth. He'd asked for the truth, hadn't he? And Kortig *was* an experienced officer with a string of successes to his name. If he believed the operation was impossible, he was probably right. And yet... the *Reich* needed to win in South Africa. They didn't dare lose.

"It's unlikely the *Reichstag* will agree to commit additional troops to South Africa," he said, grimly. "Do we have any other way to achieve victory?"

"Probably not," Kortig said, after a moment. "Cutting off the supply lines from America would help, *Herr Reichsführer*, but the Yankees aren't the sole problem. The blacks know they're doomed if they surrender. Fighting is the only logical choice."

"They're *black*," Karl protested.

"So were the Ethiopians," Kortig reminded him. "Just how badly did they manhandle the Italians?"

Karl grimaced. Ethiopia had nearly defeated the Italian invasion in 1935, a humiliation that had badly weakened Mussolini's government. The British had liberated Ethiopia in 1941, then - when Ethiopia had been returned to Italy by the terms of the peace treaty - left the Ethiopians with a considerable stockpile of weapons. It had taken the Italians twenty years to hammer Ethiopia into some semblance of order and large parts of the country were still restless.

"They still lost," he said, finally.

"And we may yet win in South Africa," Kortig said. "However, betraying our allies in the middle of a war will only lead to chaos."

Karl glowered. "Is there anything else we can do?"

"Find a way to stiffen their spine," Kortig said. "It isn't as if the apartheid government has anywhere to go."

"I'll see what I can find," Karl said. "Are you readying yourself to return to the war?"

"Yes, *Herr Reichsführer*," Kortig said. "However, I do have some concerns about the treatment of wounded - and the dead."

Karl cursed under his breath. South Africa had been meant to be a quick victory. The German troops would reinforce South Africa's, the blacks would be ruthlessly crushed and there would be a victory parade through Berlin to show that the *Reich* still had teeth. Instead, thousands of soldiers were dead or wounded and there was very little to show for it. For once, he was in total agreement with Hans Krueger. They didn't dare tell the *Reich* that so many fine young men had been killed or brutally maimed for nothing.

"That isn't your concern," he said. "Concentrate on finding ways to destroy the enemy."

"Rumours are spreading, *Herr Reichsführer*," Kortig said. "I've heard soldiers openly wondering just what's happening to the dead or wounded."

"Such talk is to be reported at once," Karl snapped.

"And then working with the *Heer* will become impossible," Kortig said. "We're not the *Gestapo*, *Herr Reichsführer*."

Karl scowled. The *Gestapo* had managed to wind up with egg on its face after Von Braun had defected to the United States, shortly after the Arab Uprising had begun. His predecessor had been quick to take advantage of his rival's weakness by asserting control over counter-intelligence and policing, which had led to another major turf war when the *Gestapo* had started to recover from its failure. And both services had often wound up working at cross-purposes. God alone knew what the Americans had managed to do while the *Gestapo* and the SS had been at daggers drawn.

When I am Fuhrer, there will be a reassessment, Karl thought, coldly. *The Gestapo will be folded into the SS, once the senior leadership has been purged.*

"I suppose not," he said, neutrally. "I'll see you before you depart, *Herr Obergruppenfuehrer*."

"Likewise, *Herr Reichsführer*," Kortig said.

Karl watched him go, thinking hard. Hans Krueger - damn the man - had made it clear that the civilians would never support deploying additional troops to South Africa, but the military might have other ideas. Field Marshal Justus Stoffregen was unlikely to take a stand, yet one of his immediate subordinates might be tempted into supporting the deployment, in exchange for a number of concessions. It galled Karl to have to concede anything to the military - they should know to obey orders without question - but he had no choice. The military spent more time fighting turf wars with the *Waffen-SS* than it did preparing for the final war with America.

He keyed his intercom. "Maria, please invite Field Marshal Voss to the castle," he said, slowly. He made a habit of keeping track of Voss's schedule - along with those of the other high-ranking officials - and Voss shouldn't be too far away. "Let me know when he arrives."

"Yes, *Herr Reichsführer*," Maria said. There was a long pause as she put the request through the secure computer network. "Voss's aide says he can make it to the castle within four hours, once he's finished his inspection tour."

"That will be suitable," Karl assured her. "Please let me know when he arrives."

He wondered, as he ordered dinner, if Voss was genuinely occupied or probing to see how important the matter was, but decided it wasn't worth trying to find out. Ordering Voss to the castle would make the Field Marshal dig in his heels - Field Marshals didn't like being ordered around as though they were new recruits - and probably alert the civilians that Karl was trying to make a private arrangement with the military. Kruger, to give the bastard his due, had his own network of spies and agents within both the military and the SS. But he didn't understand, he *couldn't* understand, the triumph of the will.

Our economy was poor when the Yankees blew up the global economy, Karl thought. He hadn't lived through those times, but his parents had. No wonder they'd wanted a farm, even if it exposed them to constant insurgent attacks. They'd wanted something solid under their feet. *And we still managed to create an empire greater than Alexander's.*

It was nearly five hours before Field Marshal Gunter Voss was shown into the office. Karl rose to his feet, carefully pasting a civil expression on his face. The military, for all its skill and dedication, wasn't as devoted to the will as the SS, but it had to be respected for the moment. Afterwards, when Karl held supreme power, it would be different. The military would be folded into the SS and its senior leadership removed from power. It might have been forty years since Rommel had allowed the Jews to escape Palestine, but the SS had never forgotten, let alone forgiven.

Pity Rommel died before the Fuhrer, he thought, as he shook hands with Voss. *Himmler would have given him a thoroughly unpleasant death.*

"*Herr Reichsführer*," Voss said, once they had exchanged pleasantries. "I confess I was quite curious to see the castle. I've heard so much about it."

CHRISTOPHER G. NUTTALL

"I'm afraid we don't sacrifice virgins here," Karl said. He smiled, as if to say that all such rumours were thoroughly absurd. "Nor do we bleed our men white so they are bound to us in death as well as life."

"How disappointing," Voss said. He sat on a chair and leaned forward. "I'm due to inspect the fortifications at Dunkirk tomorrow, *Herr Reichsführer*, so I really don't have much time. Can we get to the point?"

"Of course," Karl said. He disliked small talk too. Thankfully, it wasn't one of the qualifications for his post. "I want your support for deploying additional forces to South Africa."

"Chancy," Voss observed. "The logistics are going to be a pain in the ass. Any day now, the Yankees are going to start sending more advanced MANPAD weapons to South Africa, weapons capable of hitting our transport aircraft in flight. And once we start losing those aircraft in significant numbers... well, we might as well admit that the war is on the verge of being lost along with them."

"The *Luftwaffe* will certainly be horrified at the thought of having the paint on their aircraft scratched," Karl agreed, tightly.

"Scratched isn't the problem," Voss said, simply. "The problem is losing aircraft we cannot easily replace. And the road network from French North Africa to South Africa is pathetic."

Karl nodded, slowly. Millions of coolies had been pressed into working on a road and rail network to link the disparate sections of Africa together, but it was slow going. The blacks were rebellious and the French, he suspected, were deliberately delaying, fearing - perhaps - that they would lose the last vestiges of their independence once the road network was up and running. Besides, the South Africans had already lost hundreds of vehicles to IED attacks on their roads. The problem would merely spread through the rest of Africa.

Voss smiled, rather coldly. "What are you prepared to offer in exchange?"

"You're engaged in a long duel with the *Luftwaffe* over who controls the close-air support aircraft," Karl said. It wasn't a problem the SS faced, not when the *Waffen-SS* had its own fleet of CAS aircraft. "I would be prepared to throw my support behind you."

He watched Voss carefully, wondering just what the Field Marshal was thinking. The *Heer* wanted its own CAS fleet desperately, knowing that the *Luftwaffe* preferred to spend money on heavy bombers and fancy jet fighters rather than aircraft that might actually be *useful* in South Africa. And

64

yet, Goring's will still cast a long shadow over the service he'd built up from scratch. It had taken years of political infighting for the *Kriegsmarine* to get control over the aircraft it flew from its aircraft carriers...

Not, in the end, that the carriers ended up going very far from the Reich, he thought. There was nowhere for them to go, unless they wanted to run the gauntlet of British and American missiles. After what had happened to Norway, few countries would cheerfully accept a German ship paying a port call. *Sending the fleet to South Africa would be asking for trouble.*

He frowned at the thought. Might the navy actually do something *useful* and ship troops south? The rebels couldn't harm the fleet and the Americans were unlikely to start a war by attacking German ships... unless they thought they could win. Karl knew he would have started the war in an instant if *he* thought he could win outright and he assumed the Americans had the same attitude. What else could explain the steady pressure they kept on the *Reich?*

"That's a very tempting offer, *Herr Reichsführer,*" Voss said, finally. "Of course, this may put the *Luftwaffe* in the opposite camp."

"Which would put the *Kriegsmarine* in ours," Karl observed. The navy would hardly be likely to concede anything to the *Luftwaffe*. Give the flyboys an inch and they would take a mile. "We can hold them at bay."

"Let us hope so, *Herr Reichsführer,*" Voss said. "But the logistics are still a major headache."

"We can ship troops south," Karl said, and explained his reasoning. "The rebels will find it harder to interrupt *those* supply lines."

CHAPTER NINE

Albert Speer University, Berlin
23 July 1985

"I checked with a number of people I know," Gudrun said, once the room was locked and the bug was listening to bad American music. "Konrad's father is still unaware that his son is anywhere other than South Africa, while four other families have not heard anything from their children, even censored letters, for the last couple of months. Three of their children had a habit of writing at least once a week before suddenly going silent."

She took a breath. The fourth... she'd had to screw up all her courage to visit, for she'd known the father by reputation and nothing she'd heard had been good. His wife had left him shortly after the children had reached adulthood, which proved he'd treated her badly; the *Reich* wouldn't look too kindly on a wife who abandoned her husband, denying her both a divorce and the right to remarry. Two minutes of standing on his doorstep, feeling his eyes leaving trails of slime across her breasts, had convinced her that the bastard's son had every reason not to write to his father. There was no way to know if he was dead or alive.

I should have taken Kurt, she thought, although that would have been far too revealing. *He would have asked too many questions.*

"That's what I found anyway," she said. "What about the rest of you?"

"I checked with my maternal auntie," Sven said. "She told me that her eldest son has gone silent too, although his letters are always irregular. My paternal grandfather, however, said he'd received a heavily-censored letter from his middle son only last week. It wasn't very detailed, but it was *something.*"

Gudrun listened, quietly, as the remaining students offered their own observations. If they'd had doubts, she realised, they'd lost them. Too many of their military relatives had gone silent at once. Even the ones who rarely wrote home had gone completely silent. It chilled her to the bone when she considered the implications. Statistically, for a group of eight students to know over thirty soldiers who'd stopped writing to their families, the casualty rates had to be terrifyingly high.

"I came across something else," Horst said, once everyone else had finished. "My second cousin is married to a soldier on deployment. *She* got a letter from him asking after a friend who'd been wounded and sent home. So she checked with the guy's wife - she knew the lady personally - and the wife didn't know anything about it. The poor woman went to ask questions and then... nothing."

Gudrun blinked. "Nothing at all?"

"Nothing," Horst confirmed. "Someone told her to keep her mouth shut or else."

Hilde leaned forward, her face pale. "How can you be sure?"

"I can't think of any other explanation," Horst said. "They could have easily told her that her husband was fine, if he *was* fine. But they were clearly unwilling to admit he was wounded."

He looked at Gudrun. "You might want to ask the person who helped you sneak into the hospital just how many other soldiers are held there," he added. "I'd bet good money that there are more wounded distributed around the *Reich.*"

"I wouldn't take that bet," Sven said.

"Me neither," Gudrun said. She looked from face to face, bracing herself. They had already crossed the line, but it wasn't too late. "We know the government is lying to us - that it has lied to us many times before. What do we *do* about it?"

"What *can* we do?" Hilde asked. "If we start asking questions, we will get kicked out of the university."

Gudrun nodded. The one topic that was off-limits at the university was the *Reich* itself. A few students had questioned that, back in the early days, and been unceremoniously expelled. Hell, they weren't encouraged to study more than the STEM subjects. Any student who showed more than minimal interest in the social sciences was likely to run into trouble.

"Then we can't ask questions here," she said. She'd been thinking about it ever since she'd discovered what had happened to Konrad. "We need to spread the word."

"We could send messages through the computer network," Sven offered. "People like me have been sending covert messages without the SS reading them ever since the network was established."

"Or they just don't care," Horst pointed out, darkly. "What are you actually *doing* online anyway?"

Sven coloured. "Could *you* send a message without it being trapped in the filters and read?"

Horst looked back at him. "Could *you* send a message without it being traced back to you?"

"Easily," Sven said. "You just wipe the record of it being sent from the network. It looks as though the message spontaneously appeared in the recipient's inbox."

Gudrun held up a hand. "Yes, but we need to reach as many people as possible," she said, carefully. "How many people do you know who have access to a computer?"

There was an awkward pause. "Very few, outside the university network," Sven conceded, finally.

"That's true," Gudrun said. "I don't have a computer at home. Is there anyone in this room who *does* have a private computer?"

"No," Michael Sachs said. "My father would explode if I suggested spending ten thousand *Reichmarks* on an American computer."

Gudrun nodded. *Her* father would have pretty much the same reaction. It would cost much of his yearly salary, assuming he could purchase one in the first place... and, once he had it, it wouldn't be much use. Gudrun had a typewriter she shared with her younger brothers and *that* had been quite expensive enough. Buying a printer would cost another five thousand *Reichmarks* and linking it up to the national computer network would be impossible. The *Reich* wouldn't want to put such a powerful communications tool in *everyone's* hands.

"So... what do we do?" Hilde asked. One hand toyed with her hair as she spoke. "We cannot risk adding more people to our group, can we?"

Gudrun shook her head. There would be spies within the university - SS, *Gestapo, Abwehr* - and the more people she recruited, the greater the chance of accidentally bringing a traitor into the group and being betrayed. Guarding one's mouth was hard enough when one *wasn't* doing something the state would consider treacherous. Hell, the rowdier students might easily *be* the spies. They hadn't been kicked out despite skimping on their lessons.

"We can send a message through the computer network to every student in the university," Sven said. "I can make it look as though it came from outside the building. Hell, there are other campuses in other cities..."

"Yes, but they'll stamp down hard," Horst warned.

"They'd have to stamp on all of us," Sven said.

"That's one idea," Gudrun said. "But I have another."

She braced herself. "Do you recall distributing leaflets when you were in the Hitler Youth?"

"I never had to distribute leaflets," Sven said, after a moment. "Is that something *you* had to do?"

"Yeah," Hilde said. "While you boys were going camping and playing with weapons, we used to hand out papers exhorting greater efforts for the fatherland and other such pieces of crap."

"It wasn't all wine and roses," Sven objected. "They used to make us run for miles and chased us with whips."

"Poor dear," Hilde said. "At least you got to be away from home for a couple of weeks every year."

Gudrun winced in memory. The *Bund Deutscher Mädel* - the female wing of the Hitler Youth - hadn't been fun. Maybe it had had its moments - she'd always enjoyed playing sports and she'd been healthy enough to avoid the public humiliations meted out to overweight girls - but she hadn't enjoyed it. Walking around in ugly uniforms and handing out leaflets to passers-by had been annoying. Even at the time, she'd doubted that many of the recipients did anything other than use the leaflets to start fires.

"The point is that we can print out leaflets of our own," she said. "Wearing our old uniforms, we can then walk through the streets and hand them out."

"The police will notice," Sven objected.

"Not if we do it on a day when the *real* BDM is also handing out leaflets," Horst mused. "It won't take them long to discover what we're doing, but they'll have to sort you out from the younger girls."

"And they'll be having a competition," Gudrun said. "They'll have several groups of youngsters out on the streets, passing out leaflets, just to see who can hand out the most."

Sven snorted. "Why don't they just dump the leaflets in the nearest bin and claim victory?"

"Because if they get caught," Hilde said with icy patience, "they'll be forced to stand in the cold air in their underclothes, without dinner."

Gudrun shuddered. The matrons - the thoroughly unpleasant women who ran the BDM - hadn't hesitated to pit one group of girls against the others. Those who won got to watch as those who lost were humiliated in front of their fellows. And then reports were sent back to the schools and homes, just to ensure the losers received further punishment. By the time she'd grown old enough to leave, she'd been thoroughly sick of the whole organisation.

"Maybe we can get a few of the matrons into trouble," she said. *Could* they do it? Could they walk into one of the tents and exchange leaflets? God knew *she'd* never bothered to read the leaflets she'd handed out. But that would get the girls into trouble as well. "If the SS wants to ask them a few questions..."

"They'll have contacts," Horst said. "Better keep it as simple as possible."

Gudrun looked at Sven. "Can you print out copies of the standard leaflet, but with our message inside?"

"Easily," Sven said. "We have the equipment. It'll just take us some time to print them out without being noticed."

"And then we have to see when the BDM is handing out leaflets next," Gudrun mused.

"It'll be Sunday," Hilde predicted. "They always try to hand out the leaflets to people coming out of church. If we can't put together enough leaflets by Sunday, we can simply wait until the *next* Sunday."

"There'll be more of them on the streets too," Horst added. "They don't like taking the younger girls out of classes if it can be avoided."

"And to think you men had it so much easier," Hilde teased.

Gudrun coughed, loudly, before an argument could break out and turn nasty. "I have my old uniform at home," she said. Her mother had never allowed her to get rid of it, even though Gudrun had begged to be allowed to burn the ugly piece of trash. "I can probably alter it to fit me with a little effort."

"Better let me do it," Isla said. "You're not a good seamstress."

"We also need to make sure we're not recognised," Horst said. "The girls can distribute leaflets in their old uniforms, but we will find it a little harder to pass unnoticed."

Gudrun frowned. "You could wear your own uniforms," she said. "Or we could borrow some others for you..."

"No one expects to see the Hitler Youth distributing leaflets," Horst reminded her. "So we wear our regular clothes, but instead of giving leaflets to people we put them through letterboxes, as if they were advertisements. No one will think twice of it until it's far too late."

"I see," Gudrun said. She looked down at the table for a long moment. "Sven and the computer experts will send messages to everyone, the day we start distributing the leaflets. Horst and the boys ready themselves to put messages through letterboxes; I and the girls prepare to start handing out leaflets in the streets."

"Wear wigs," Horst said. "Tie your hair up and wear a striking wig, one you can remove in an instant if necessary."

He looked embarrassed for a second. "And stuff your bras too," he added. "You want to draw their eyes to your chests rather than to your faces."

Gudrun blushed. "We don't want to look *too* old," she said. "Passing for a sixteen-year-old isn't going to be easy."

"Most people won't notice as long as you look striking," Horst assured her. "Just make sure you are striking in ways you can easily remove, if necessary. If the SS start looking for a red-headed girl, you can walk past them because you're blonde."

"Clever," Sven said. "How do you know all this?"

"I was in the Hitler Youth," Horst said.

"So was I," Sven said. "And *we* were never shown anything like this."

"Of course not," Horst said, crossly. "You, you see, were in the Hitler Youth *here*. I was in the Hitler Youth in Germany East. You went on camping trips, *we* went on partisan hunts; you pretended to build fortresses, we dug trenches and sited mortars; the only danger you faced was a minor injury or a belting from the supervisors for falling asleep on watch, *we* ran the very real risk of being shot. I have more practical experience than any of you in remaining concealed."

"I'm glad you're with us," Gudrun said. She'd known that Horst was from Germany East, but she hadn't understood the implications. "Do you have any other pieces of advice?"

"Getaway vans," Horst said. "We hire a handful of vans, fiddle a little with their number plates and use them to get away from the scene. The distributors can change in the rear while the drivers get them to safety."

Leopold snorted. "And when someone makes a note of the number?"

"That's why we change it," Horst said. "Not much, not enough to make it obvious, but just enough to mislead someone watching from a distance. We return the vans in perfect condition and no one asks any questions."

Gudrun nodded. "Good thinking," she said.

"We won't have long," Horst added. He ran his hand through his hair. "I'd honestly suggest not sticking around for more than an hour, at the most. *Someone* will report the leaflets to the police and then they'll move in and try to catch us."

"Your father is a policeman," Leopold said, looking at Gudrun. His voice was thoughtful. "Is there no way you can keep track of his movements?"

"He doesn't take me to work," Gudrun pointed out, sarcastically. The very thought was absurd. Her father would have refused, she was sure, if she'd ever asked. "And how am I supposed to hand out leaflets with him right next to me?"

"We could monitor the police radios," Sven said, before Leopold could manage a sharp rejoinder. "It isn't as if it's *difficult* to adapt one of the radios to tune into their bands."

"That's illegal," Isla protested.

Horst snorted. "And handing out illicit leaflets *isn't?*"

Gudrun smiled. "Let's be brutally honest, shall we? We've already crossed the line."

"That's true," Horst agreed.

"If any of you don't want to help distributing leaflets," Gudrun said, "say so now."

She waited. Her throat was dry. Everything they'd done so far *might* be excused - they *were* among the best and brightest of the *Reich* - but actually handing out leaflets would get them in deep trouble. They'd be kicked out of the university, at the very least; it was far more likely they'd go to jail or be summarily exiled to Germany East. Or...

"I think it has to be done," Hilde said. She looked down at her hands. "I'm sick of this! I'm sick of not knowing what's happened to my boyfriend!"

"I'm sick of having to watch my words," Leopold said. "Of being worried that the next person I talk to will report me to the SS. And of being told I'm not allowed to ask questions."

"And if there are hundreds of others who feel the same way," Gudrun said, "all we have to do is get them working together."

"No," Horst said. "All we have to do is make them realise that there are others who feel the same way."

He leaned forward. "The state works hard to ensure that no one asks questions," he said, flatly. "We are taught not to ask questions from birth until death - and, because none of us ask the questions we want to ask, we never realise that there are others who feel the same way. It may be too dangerous to add more recruits to our little band, but if we can prime the rest of the population to feel the same way... others will start their own groups. The SS will be unable to keep track of us all."

"I've heard about what happens to people the SS take away," Isla said, nervously.

"It isn't pleasant," Horst agreed. "For the moment, we say nothing if we are taken into custody, nothing at all. And we don't write anything down."

"Save for the leaflets," Sven said.

"We can also pay children to take the leaflets and hand them out," Horst said.

"Too risky," Gudrun said.

"The SS wouldn't brutalise children," Leopold protested. "Their parents would never stand for it."

"They'll do whatever it takes to root us out," Horst said. His voice was very firm. "*Whatever* it takes. Once we start the ball rolling, we have to be committed to the very end."

"And, if that's true," Sven asked, "what do we want?"

"The truth," Gudrun said.

"Freedom," Hilde added.

"Free elections to the *Reichstag*," Leopold said. "Let the Nazi Party fight to win elections."

"They won't like the challenge," Horst said. He gave Leopold a long considering look. "And that is why we have to brace ourselves for the moment they push back. Because they will."

Gudrun nodded. "I think we're committed now," she said. She smiled grimly at their expressions. "I think it's time to become traitors."

CHAPTER TEN

Berlin
26 July 1985

He was committed now, of course.

Horst had no illusions. Like the rest of the little group, he'd crossed a line. In his case, he'd crossed it when he'd refrained from reporting the group's existence to his superiors. He should have reported Gudrun and her friends at once, then let his seniors decide how best to handle the matter. Instead, he'd not only kept it to himself, he'd offered Gudrun some practical advice on how best to conceal her identity when the shit finally hit the fan. If he were caught, now, he'd be sent to one of the camps, if he wasn't executed out of hand. His execution would probably be used to set an example to everyone else...

If the Reichsführer didn't want to hush the whole affair up, Horst thought. A quiet execution was the most likely outcome, even though Horst had betrayed the SS. The *Reichsführer* wouldn't want anyone else seduced into apostasy. *My family would probably be told I died in a training accident somewhere and that would be that.*

"Horst," Sven hissed. "Take these, quickly."

Horst shook himself and hastily dropped the leaflets into his bag. Sven had done a good job, he had to admit; the leaflets *looked* authentic until the reader opened them up, whereupon they would be confronted with Gudrun's message. Horst rather suspected a number of them would be covertly dropped into trash cans, unopened and unread, but enough *would* be read to allow the message to spread. And who knew what would happen then? People would talk, of course, despite the omnipresent aura of fear. And then?

I wish I knew, he thought. *And I wish I could talk to her openly.*

Gudrun, for all her intelligence, lacked practical knowledge and experience. The BDM hadn't taught her anything beyond being a good housewife; she'd certainly never applied for one of the rare female positions within the SS. Horst knew, without false modesty, that his experience was far more useful, but how was he to slip it to her without being exposed? If he told her the truth, she'd be horrified. And then...?

She either runs or tries to arrange an accident for me, Horst said. *And that will leave her without any qualified help at all.*

"Leopold is still keeping the old man busy," Sven said, as he printed out the last set of leaflets. "We spent all night devising a particularly buggy program."

Horst had to smile. Sven might be a wimp - he'd quit the Hitler Youth as soon as he could and worked hard to get into the university - but he did have a devious mind. The tutor - who wasn't as capable a programmer as some of his students - could be held up indefinitely, if someone came to him with a problem. Horst had half-expected to need to grab everything and run for his life, but so far everything had gone according to plan.

"Good thinking," Horst said. Thankfully, the computer labs were almost always deserted at this time of night, save for the tutor. He took the final set of leaflets and dropped them into his bag. "I'll see you tomorrow?"

"I'll be here," Sven reminded him. He took a breath. "Why did you want additional leaflets?"

"Just to make sure we had plenty," Horst said. "I'll stick them with a friend - better you don't know who - and distribute them later."

He sighed, inwardly. Gudrun didn't realise just how ruthless they needed to be, but *Horst* did. He had no illusions about how quickly the police would react. It wouldn't take them long to realise who was spreading the leaflets, then start rounding up all the BDM girls on the streets. Perhaps a few of the matrons *would* be in deep trouble - it couldn't happen to a more deserving bunch, if half of what Gudrun and Hilde had said was true - but the police wouldn't take long to realise that they were dealing with imposters. Something else would have to be done to distribute more leaflets.

And I will have to do it, he thought. He didn't dare trust Sven or any of the others. The only proof he had that none of them were spies was that he hadn't been arrested yet. *There's no other way to spread the word before the police catch on.*

"I meant to ask," Sven said, as they wiped the computer's memory and shut it down for the night. "Were you serious about what it's like in the east?"

"Yes," Horst grunted. "There are some parts of the region that are relatively safe, but most places can be quite dangerous. I learned to shoot when I was five years old."

Sven swallowed. "And your auntie... is she still living there?"

"Yeah," Horst said. He'd lied; he'd dug up the details of a genuine case and presented them as something that had happened to his relatives. But it was real. If he'd had doubts about helping Gudrun, they'd died when he'd looked at the files. "She used to be quite a loyalist."

"I heard that most people in the east are loyalists," Sven said. "Is *that* true?"

"Mostly," Horst said.

"Then tell me," Sven said. "How can we trust *you*?"

"I could have betrayed you by now," Horst pointed out. Thankfully, he'd had time to think about what he would say, if anyone chose to raise the issue. "As it happens, my brother left me with a great deal to think about even before I came to Berlin to study. We've been lied to constantly."

"You could be lying to me now," Sven said.

Horst kept his expression blank, thinking hard. *And why didn't you show this sort of talent in the Hitler Youth?*

He suspected he knew the answer to *that*, although he could never ask. Sven and the boys like him resented being forced into the Hitler Youth, resented being sent to camps where they learned how to march in unison. And, because they resented it, they were never very *good* at it. And, because they were never very good at it, everyone else picked on them. Horst knew the score at the camps, even though it had been minimised in Germany East. The strong bullied the weak, those who couldn't keep up.

Maybe it would have been better if Sven had been allowed to carry weapons, he thought, ruefully. *He might have dealt with a bully or two by shooting the asshole in the head.*

He gathered himself. "If I wanted to betray you, Sven," he said, "I would have done it by now. None of you are particularly important. You know how it works. A single report is quite enough to get you all in hot water. Instead, I'm doing my best to help keep you all alive long enough to do something effective, just as *you* are using *your* skills to help us. Is that not good enough for you?"

Sven looked rebellious, but subsided under Horst's stare. Horst wondered, absently, if *Sven* was another spy, trying to divert suspicion, yet he knew it was unlikely. The logic that kept *him* from being declared a spy worked for Sven too. Spy-Sven should have reported the group at once, incidentally landing Horst in trouble too. Unless Sven had decided to switch sides as well...

And that way lies madness, Horst thought. *The entire group cannot be made up of agents who decided to switch sides.*

He scowled as he picked up the bag and led the way to the door. He'd tried looking up the names of other SS agents within the computer files, but they had been classed as well above his security clearance. *Sven* could probably hack into the files, given the access codes, yet that would be far too revealing. All he could do was keep an eye out for suspicious behaviour, particularly when the computer messages started making their way through the network. Sven claimed to have rigged the system to keep the messages going, even when the first set were wiped from the nodes. Horst believed him. Sven was an odd duck, someone who would probably be happier in America, but he knew computers.

Maybe I should give him my access codes after all, he thought. *I could always threaten him into silence... or try to steal someone else's codes.*

"I got the van parked outside," he said, as they left the building. "We'll be ready to get into place on Sunday morning."

"I'll have the radio ready by then," Sven said. "Just make sure no one sees the leaflets."

"Of course not," Horst said. "No one will see them until Sunday."

———

It had taken months of arguing before Gudrun's parents had agreed to let her put a lock on her door. Gudrun had pointed out that she was a growing girl, that she didn't want her brothers walking in on her while she was changing and that she deserved some privacy. Her parents had finally agreed, then imposed so many rules - most notably, that she couldn't close or lock the door when Konrad was visiting - that she sometimes wondered if there had been any point in trying to get the lock in the first place. Her mother, after all, had one of the spare keys. But, right now, her mother was shopping and her brothers were out of the house. She had time to prepare for Sunday.

She opened the bag Isla had given her and carefully placed the BDM uniform on the bed. No one had to *pay* for their uniforms, which was a relief; it was hard enough scrabbling with her mother over what clothes she was allowed to buy for herself without having to endure her mother's outrage over buying the uniforms too. A white shirt, loose enough to conceal the shape of her body, a long black skirt that stopped barely a centimetre above the ground, a long brown coat and a pair of ugly black shoes that made it impossible to run. It was, she had to admit, an improvement on the BDM sports uniform, but not much of one. And to think she'd hoped to throw the whole thing out when she'd finally been allowed to quit the BDM.

Gritting her teeth, listening carefully for signs of life from Grandpa Frank, she stripped down to her underwear, donned a pair of jeans and a tight American t-shirt, then pulled the uniform over it. Thankfully, Isla had loosened the skirt so it was no longer so tight around her rear end; she studied herself in the mirror and decided, after a little adjustment, that no one could tell she was wearing a whole additional layer of clothing underneath the uniform. Bracing herself, she tore the uniform off as quickly as she could without tearing it and checked, again, in the mirror. She might just get told off by a policeman for wearing revealing clothes in public - her mother's reaction would be downright murderous - but she certainly didn't *look* like a BDM girl. And that was all that mattered.

She dressed again, then tried on the wig. She'd never worn a wig before; it took her several tries at fiddling with it before it looked convincing, the long dark hair tied into two ponytails that made her look several years younger. If nothing else, she reflected ruefully, it was one thing to thank the BDM matrons for; they'd been so insistent that the young girls in their care had to have their hair in ponytails that it would be easy enough to hide, just by tearing them down or removing the wig. Finally, she opened her shirt and stuffed her bra, trying hard to make it look convincing. She honestly didn't know where Horst had found the nerve to suggest that she and the other girls use padding to make their breasts look bigger, although she had to admit it was a good idea. The policemen wouldn't know where to look if they caught her.

And let's hope father doesn't catch me, Gudrun thought, as she slowly undressed and packed the uniform away in her bag. She doubted her mother would want to see it in the next couple of days. *He'd kill me if he caught me dressed like a common tart.*

She sighed, inwardly, as a slip of paper fell out of the skirt and landed on the floor. One of the matrons had made her write the lines out, time and time again, until her hands were aching, a punishment for some offense she no longer remembered. The lines of the poem urged her to forget about being anything other than a housewife and mother... she shuddered in bitter memory. How often had she been told she wouldn't ever be anything else? And if Konrad had remained unwounded, would she have been allowed to be a computer engineer or would she be expected to be his housewife?

"Take hold of kettle, broom and pan," she muttered. "Then you'll surely get a man!"

She remembered, now. She'd asked one of the matrons why she was unmarried - and why she was allowed to have a job teaching girls that all they could expect to be in the future were housewives and mothers. The fat ugly woman - they'd joked that no amount of kettles, brooms or pans could win her anything other than an ugly Jew - had been *furious*. Gudrun suspected, sometimes, that the only thing that had saved her life was the crone's awareness that Gudrun's father was a policeman. As it was, her hand had been sore for *days* after she'd copied the poem out a thousand times.

"And she still didn't get a man," she muttered, as she pulled her working clothes back on and headed for the door. The leaflets would be stored in the vans until Sunday, whereupon they'd start their act of defiance. "No one mourned for her when she had a heart attack and died."

Gudrun groaned as she heard the sound of Grandpa Frank ringing his bell, demanding immediate attention. She considered, briefly, ignoring the sound, but it would be just like the old bastard to recall that Gudrun had been in the house and report her to her mother. Getting grounded would be bad enough at any time; now, when she needed to be with her friends on Sunday, it would be disastrous. Bracing herself, she walked down the corridor to Grandpa Frank's room and peered inside. He was lying in his bed, looking thoroughly drunk. The stench of beer was bad enough to make her recoil in disgust.

"Fetch more beer," he ordered. "And bread!"

"Yes, Grandpa," Gudrun said. Who knew? Maybe there was no beer in the fridge and she'd have an excuse to refuse. "I'll bring it for you as quickly as I can."

She picked up a number of empty bottles, then hurried downstairs and dumped them in the bin before opening the fridge. The cranky machine - it was the best her father could buy on his salary - was unreliable, but typically it had managed to keep a few bottles of beer chilled and ready for the drunkard. Gudrun took them out of the fridge, added beer to the list of things her mother had to buy and then carried the bottles and bread back upstairs. Grandpa Frank was already in bed, caterwauling a song she didn't recognise. It certainly wasn't one of the ones she'd learned in the BDM!

"You're a good girl," Grandpa Frank said, as she put the bottles beside his bed. "Just like your mother."

My mother keeps you in this house, you disgusting old man, Gudrun thought. She knew what her mother had said, time and time again, but she still didn't understand. *And if I behave like this to my children, if I ever have them, I'll deserve to be kicked into the streets to die.*

"Thank you," she said, instead. "And now, if you don't mind, I have to go work on my studies."

"Nothing good ever came of women studying," Grandpa Frank called after her. "You need to marry a man and have his children..."

Gudrun slammed the door as she left, but his laughter followed her as she headed down the corridor into her room. She hated him. She *hated* him. How could her mother give such a disgusting old man a home, even if he *was* her father? Surely, Gudrun's own father wouldn't be such a nightmare if he moved in with her after he retired. And if they had to put up with him, why couldn't her mother handle him personally?

She worked on her studies for an hour, then heard her mother opening the door downstairs and entering the house. Gudrun stood, checked her bag was out of sight, and hurried downstairs to assist her mother to unpack her bags. Not entirely to her surprise, one bag was full of new bottles of beer. Grandpa Frank could continue drinking himself to death if he wished.

He's too disgusting to die, she thought, morbidly. Her mother was in a cheerful mood, twittering away about a warning from her friend at the shop that the price of fruit and vegetables was apparently on the rise. *He'll still be alive after we're gone.*

She looked up, sharply, as something her mother said penetrated her mind. "Prices are going up?"

"Yes," her mother said. "The beer cost more than double what it cost last week."

"Perhaps we should stop buying it," Gudrun said. Her mother gave her a dark look, but said nothing. "And the meat cost more too?"

"Yes," her mother said. "I don't know what we're going to do if prices keep rising, Gudrun."

I might have to get a real job, Gudrun thought. *And then...?*

She pushed the thought aside as her mother ordered her into the kitchen to start chopping the vegetables. Sunday was only two days away, after all.

But it felt as though Sunday would never come.

CHAPTER ELEVEN

Berlin
28 July 1985

"So, we're agreed," Aldrich said. "You'll supply an extra five hundred computers at a thousand dollars apiece."

"That sounds acceptable," Andrew Barton said, trying not to let the tiredness sink into his voice. It had been a long negotiating session and tempers had frayed on both sides. "I trust we will receive payment in advance?"

"Half in advance," Aldrich said. "We'll want to check the machines before we make the final payment."

He paused. "My superiors would be happy to pay more for the latest computers," he added, slowly. "And there might be a commission in it for you."

Andrew made a show of glancing at Penelope, who scowled at him. "I'm afraid my superiors have been unable to convince Congress to make an exception to the export restrictions," he said. Aldrich had cheerfully tried to bribe him the first time they'd met, back when Andrew had been establishing his cover as an electronics salesman, and hadn't seemed put out by his failure. "It's a major hassle, having to certify that exports don't breach the law, but what can we do about it?"

Aldrich shrugged. "It is of no matter," he said. Given that he'd repeated the unsubtle offer of a bribe every time they'd met for negotiations, Andrew rather doubted he was telling the truth. "My superiors will be happy with what they get."

And unlucky for you if they're not, Andrew thought, as they exchanged copies of the contracts. He had few illusions about the *Reich*. Those who failed were lucky if they weren't exiled to Kamchatka. *Your superiors won't be that happy with outdated computers they don't entirely trust.*

He smiled as he rose to his feet. "You'll join us for drinks, won't you?"

"Of course," Aldrich said. "I have even booked a table in the pub."

Andrew smiled, winked at Penelope and then allowed Aldrich to lead them out of the Finance Ministry and across the road to the pub. It was a Party establishment, Aldrich had told him when they'd first met; the SS and the military rarely entered, save on official business. He'd also assured Andrew that the pub was swept regularly for bugs, just to keep the security services from spying on private conversations, but Andrew suspected the Economic Intelligence Service kept a sharp eye on everyone who entered the building. Perhaps it was fortunate, he told himself, as Aldrich ordered three beers. If the *Reich* stopped spending so much time and effort spying on its own people, it might pose a greater threat to America.

"Drink up," Aldrich urged, as a comely waitress placed three large glasses of beer in front of them. "There's nothing but the best in this place."

"German beer is always good," Andrew agreed, taking a sip. It was true, but he knew better than to drink any more, not while he was on duty. "I must order some bottles for myself."

"I'll have a crate sent over to the embassy," Aldrich told him, cheerfully. "You can think of me every time you crack open a bottle."

"I will," Andrew assured him. Aldrich was odd, at least by American standards; he was scrupulously honest while handling his ministry's work, but also deeply corrupt in his private life. Andrew wouldn't have given two cents for his chances if the SS ever caught him with his pants around his ankles. "And your shipment of jeans will be on their way tomorrow."

"Thank you," Aldrich beamed. He switched his attention to Penelope. "And would you like a private tour of Berlin, my dear?"

"Alas, I have to write reports," Penelope said. "My superiors have enough trouble believing I can handle my job without me taking time to sightsee."

"A shame," Aldrich said. "There's a lot I could show you in Berlin."

Like your bedroom ceiling, Andrew thought, darkly. Aldrich wasn't married, but he'd had a string of lovers, including a number of married women whose husbands had been away at the front. *You wouldn't show her any of the truly interesting sights.*

He leaned back in his chair and took another sip of beer, carefully survey-ing the pub. A half-drunk musician was butchering a tune on the piano, while a singer was trying hard to belt out a popular song, a task made harder by the musician changing the tune every so often. No one seemed to be listening; they were babbling away, chatting so loudly that it was impossible to pick out a single conversation amidst many. If there was anyone listening in, Andrew hoped, they'd find it hard to hear anything worthwhile.

"My superiors are worried," Aldrich said, after Penelope politely declined his third attempt at a pass. "They're not sure they can meet their budget for the year."

"Raise taxes," Andrew suggested, mischievously. "And put out a new cam-paign about how everyone must sacrifice for the good of the *Reich*."

"The people who need to pay taxes are the ones who are protected by the state," Aldrich commented, crossly. "They pay nothing while smaller busi-nesses are crushed under the weight of taxation."

Andrew nodded, thoughtfully. The Third *Reich* had a thoroughly unhealthy relationship with big business, dating all the way back to Adolf Hitler. Corporations had supported the Nazi Party in exchange for tax cuts, a ban on unions and police support if the workers got out of line. Now, they were so deeply embedded in the *Reich* that taxing them was almost impos-sible, which forced the *Reich* to raise taxes on businesses without powerful patrons to protect them. But *that* ensured that the smaller businesses would never be profitable, if they survived at all. Andrew had a feeling that the *Reich's* economy was weaker than anyone dared suppose.

He looked at Aldrich. "Do your superiors have a message for me?"

"They want to make cuts in the military budget," Aldrich said. He'd passed on messages before, although most of them hadn't come to anything. "They're looking for a way out of South Africa."

"Just leave," Andrew pointed out. "The South Africans aren't going to keep you there if you want to leave."

"They need a face-saving excuse to leave," Aldrich said. He leaned for-ward. "I heard a rumour that the SS and the military are banding together to send more troops to South Africa."

Andrew studied him for a long moment. He'd worked hard to build up a relationship with Aldrich, even to the point of supplying him with

American-made items he could sell on the black market, but he would be a fool to *trust* the man. Aldrich's superiors knew, of course, that he was talking to an American; they used him to pass on messages that couldn't be officially acknowledged. But it was very hard to tell if Aldrich was passing on information he'd collected on his own or information his superiors wanted the Americans to have.

It would be a great deal easier if I had something on him, Andrew thought. Unfortunately, Aldrich was neatly covered by his superiors. *He's playing both sides of the field.*

"I see," he said, finally. "Do they think they can win?"

"I think they're unwilling to pull out," Aldrich said. "My superiors would like to find a way to abandon South Africa and withdraw the troops without losing face."

Andrew considered it, thoughtfully. Given everything he knew about the *Reich*, he would honestly advise the Germans to abandon Germany South and concentrate on rebuilding their economy. But he knew the *Reich* would never consider it. Hitler himself had said, in 1942, that territory claimed by the *Reich* could never be surrendered, even for a brief tactical advantage. Even if the United States managed to offer a face-saving formula, it was unlikely that the German military or SS would accept it.

"I'll forward it to my superiors," he said, finally. "But I don't know what they'll say."

"*My* superiors are very concerned," Aldrich said. "They'd like to end the arms race."

Andrew exchanged glances with Penelope. "I see," he said. "And what sort of guarantees do they propose to offer?"

———

Tourists rarely saw the outskirts of Berlin, Horst reminded himself, as he parked the van outside a long grey building surrounded by barbed wire. The grandiose buildings designed by Albert Speer and constructed by slave labour had long since given way to very basic houses, warehouses and barracks for the *Gastarbeiters*. He checked his borrowed uniform in the mirror, then picked up the heavy bag, climbed out of the van and locked the door. Crime was minimal at the heart of Berlin, he knew from his briefings, but rampant in the outskirts. The police rarely interfered as long as *Gastarbeiters* were the ones in trouble.

He showed his fake ID to the guard, then stepped through the gate and headed towards the building. There were no windows, nothing to allow the occupants to look out of their barracks while they were resting. The *Gastarbeiters* had been brought to Germany on long-term work contracts and they weren't allowed to do anything else, not even have a single day of rest. Chances were, Horst knew, most of them would wind up dead before they were permitted to return to France, Spain or Italy. And those who completed their contracts would probably still be cheated of their pay by their owners.

The door opened as he approached, allowing him to step into the office. He'd had dealings with slave labour commissions before, in Germany East, but dealing with a purely-civilian commission was new. On the other hand, it wasn't exactly unknown for pureblood Germans to take a contract for something, pass the work on to the *Gastarbeiters* and keep most of the money for themselves And this particular commission had a reputation for not asking many questions. Reading between the lines, Horst rather suspected they supplied women for the brothels on the outskirts of Germany.

And they're probably tied to criminal gangs, he thought, as he stepped up to the desk. A grim-faced woman was sitting there, a riding crop resting on the desk beside her; her face was ugly enough to suggest she'd been deemed too sadistic to work for the BDM. Horst had seen her type before; male or female, they took their anger at the world out on the unfortunate *Gastarbeiters* under their command. *She won't hesitate to use her riding crop on any of the poor bastards who disobey orders.*

She looked up at him, reluctantly. "Yes?"

Horst gave her his most charming smile. "I wish to hire some workers for a task," he said, reaching into his pocket and dropping two hundred *Reichmarks* onto her desk. "It needs to be done today."

The woman took the money and counted it with practiced ease, then looked up at him and smiled. "What needs to be done?"

"I need these leaflets posted through as many letterboxes in the city as possible," Horst said. It was a shame he couldn't spread the word to other cities, but he hadn't been able to think of a way to do that which would also allow him to be with Gudrun in Victory Square. "They're advertisements for my services."

"That will be an additional three hundred *Reichmarks*," the woman said, picking up the bag and wincing at the weight. She probably thought he was a criminal, rather than a small businessman trying to advertise his services, but it hardly mattered. Horst and the others had spent hours folding the leaflets so that they couldn't be unfolded without making it obvious that someone had looked at them. "I will have them handed out this afternoon."

"That will be quite sufficient," Horst said. He counted out the rest of the money and dropped it on the desk. His superiors would be less than amused if they found out what he was doing with his discretionary funds, although *that* was the least of his worries. They'd have problems deciding which one of his crimes to put on the execution warrant before they stuck him in front of a firing squad. "If this works as well as I expect, there will be more advertisements in the future."

He concealed his amusement as he walked out to the van, waving a cheerful goodbye to the guard at the gate. The woman hadn't bothered to ask for ID, even though it was a legal requirement; she'd *definitely* assumed he was a criminal. She certainly hadn't realised what he was doing, let alone the prospect of getting in deep trouble when the SS tracked her down. And the description she'd give of him, under threat of torture, would be quite misleading. There was an art to disguise, after all, and he was a practiced master. If there had been a camera in the office, and it was a possibility, it wouldn't help them.

Starting the engine, he drove back onto the road and headed into the city. The streets were starting to fill up with traffic, forcing him to slow down. There were hundreds of similar vans on the road, hiding him as neatly as a piece of straw in a haystack. He'd been told, years ago, that only two corporations were allowed to manufacture civilian vehicles - and both of them produced only a handful of models, none of which were totally reliable. It might keep the mechanics gainfully occupied, but it was also immensely frustrating.

I just need to find a place to change, then meet up with Gudrun and start handing out leaflets, he thought. It had crossed his mind that it would be better to let the *Gastarbeiters* distribute the first set, but Gudrun would have asked too many questions. He wasn't the only student with an expense account, yet hiring the vans alone had been quite costly. *And then wait and see what happens.*

He smiled to himself as a small Volkswagen overtook him, heading towards the centre of Berlin. Sunday wasn't just a day for Church; it was a day for taking one's children around the city, visiting parks, admiring the buildings and bathing in the glories of the *Reich*. There would be so many people around them that the tiny band of rebels would pass largely unnoticed, at least until the police set up barricades. And *that* would do more to give credence to the leaflets than anything else.

As long as we don't get caught, he reminded himself. He'd done his best to prepare the group for what would happen if - when - one or more of them were caught, but he knew that his preparations were lacking. The Hitler Youth didn't offer lessons in how to comport one's self after being taken prisoner. *If someone is caught, they may talk...*

... and if they talk, we're dead.

———

Gudrun let out a sigh of relief as Horst parked next to her van, then tapped on the door and stepped inside when she opened it for him. He was wearing civilian clothes, looking rather like an engineer, the type of man who would drive a van to his next port of call. Horst nodded to her politely, then looked her up and down. Gudrun felt her face heat under his scrutiny before he pronounced himself satisfied.

"You don't look anything like yourself," he said. "And you don't look profoundly unnatural - or suspicious. That's the important thing."

"I had a look before we started to change," Gudrun said. "There's a lot of BDM girls out there, as always."

"Good," Horst said. "Where are the others?"

"Hilde and Isla are in the next van," Gudrun said. "Hedy and Genovefa are on the other side of the road. I'm going to wave to them as I walk past and then start distributing leaflets."

"Don't go too close to any of the matrons," Horst reminded her, sternly. "They're the ones who are most likely to recognise that something isn't right about you. And don't go too close to the policemen, when they show up. Hand out leaflets for twenty minutes, then come back to the van and we'll head off. There's no point in pushing our luck too far."

"We did discuss this," Gudrun reminded him, tartly.

"This is not the time to forget," Horst snapped. "If one of us gets caught, we're in deep trouble."

Gudrun nodded, grimly. Horst had told them all, in great detail, precisely what they could expect if they were scooped up by the SS. The only hope for escape was to keep their mouths firmly shut, but if they were caught with the leaflets there would be no point in trying to pretend they were innocent bystanders. Even being caught in their BDM uniforms would be bad enough, although they had devised a cover story about a student prank. Somehow, Gudrun doubted the SS would believe a word of it. All of a sudden, she wanted to run home and forget everything she'd planned.

But I can't forget Konrad, she thought. *And every other wounded soldier who has been packed off to hospital while their families are left in the dark.*

She gritted her teeth, pulled on the white gloves and picked up the leaflets. Most of them would probably be dumped as soon as the bearer was out of sight, but a few of the leaflets would be read. And then all hell would break loose.

Horst met her eyes. "Are you having second thoughts?"

Gudrun glared at him. She'd always been told she wasn't expected to be anything more than a housewife and a mother. Girls weren't brave; girls were meant to keep their mouths shut and just do what they were told. And it had always gnawed at her. Horst, she was sure, wouldn't think any less of her for backing out, simply because she was a girl!

"No," she said. "Just be ready to drive off when I come back."

"I'll move Leopold into my van, once he gets back," Horst said. "And I'll be ready."

"So will I," Gudrun said. "The policemen won't even get a *look* at me."

Bracing herself, she stepped out of the van and onto the street.

CHAPTER TWELVE

Victory Square, Berlin
28 July 1985

Gudrun had always found Victory Square a little intimidating.

It had been designed, she'd been told, to showcase the victories of the Third Reich. There were dozens of statues, each one representing a hero of Nazi Germany, and plinths representing battles fought and won by German armies. Every day, thousands of men, women and children thronged through the square, admiring the relics, visiting the museums and donating small change for wounded soldiers. Gudrun had donated some of her pocket money every time she'd visited the square with the BDM - she hadn't been given a choice - but now she wondered where the money actually *went*. Did it really go to the soldiers or was it stolen by some corrupt government official?

She pushed the thought aside, straightened her shoulders and started to look for her first target. There was an art to handing out leaflets, she'd been taught as a child; she had to make eye contact, using the motion to make it absolutely clear that the target *had* to take the leaflet. As an adult, she suspected that the targets only took the leaflets because they knew better than to refuse, but right now it hardly mattered. She walked forward with the gait she'd learned in the BDM and started to hand out the leaflets. As she'd expected, the targets took the leaflets without hesitation and shoved them into their pockets.

Maybe we should have handed out advertisements instead, she thought, as she kept moving, neatly avoiding a BDM matron on the prowl. The crone wouldn't recognise her, of course, but that might not stop her trying to issue orders. *Something that would stand out from the normal BDM leaflets.*

She smiled at a pair of young soldiers and passed them a couple of leaflets each, then made a gesture towards the matrons when one of them started to try to flirt with her. He was handsome enough, she had to admit, but there was no time to waste. Besides, even though she knew it was unlikely Konrad would ever recover, she was damned if she was cheating on him until she *knew* he was dead. She spied a young couple, the woman carrying a small boy on her back, and gave them a leaflet, smiling at the child as she walked away. Who knew what sort of world the child would inherit?

A pair of older men wearing workers overalls leered at her; she smiled charmingly at them both and handed out a pair of leaflets. They took them and looked her up and down, their eyes locking on her padded breasts. Gudrun flushed, then hurried past them towards the next group of prospective targets. The workers, at least, wouldn't be able to say anything about her beyond the fact she'd had an impressive chest. And, once she pulled out the padding, they wouldn't have anything to go on. She glanced at her watch - ten minutes left - and moved onwards.

She jumped as a hand fell on her shoulder and spun around to see one of the matrons. "You," the matron growled. "This section belongs to my girls!"

Gudrun lowered her eyes, pretending to be scared. It wasn't hard.

"Matron told us that..."

"I don't give a damn what your matron told you," the woman snapped. Her breath stank so badly Gudrun rather suspected she never bothered to brush her teeth. "This is our section, so clear out!"

"Of course, of course," Gudrun said.

She turned and hurried away, wondering just what had got into the older woman. Had someone complained that the BDM weren't handing out their quota of leaflets? Or was she just enjoying the chance to boss a younger and prettier girl around, scaring the life out of her all the while? She dismissed the thought - it didn't matter - and walked around the square before she started handing out more leaflets. It wasn't as if she had a matron of her own to complain to.

A handful of men were coming out of a pub, facing the Ministry of Finance. Feeling daring, she hurried forward and started to hand out leaflets. One man and woman looked odd - there was something about them that puzzled her - but they took a pair of leaflets anyway. Gudrun walked past them and slowly started to make her way back to the vans. No matter how she looked at it, time was running out. It wouldn't be long before someone *read* one of the leaflets and gave it to a policeman...

———

"That is a very odd man," Penelope said, once Aldrich had headed back to his office. "Why was he being such... such a creep?"

Andrew smiled. "You've never encountered anyone like him in America?"

"No," Penelope said. "Certainly no one so... crude."

"He's a government official in the most deeply corrupt government in the world," Andrew explained, as he took a final sip of his beer. "A man in his position, with a little ingenuity, can do almost anything, as long as he doesn't offend his superiors. I wouldn't put it past him to refuse to issue permits without a bribe or some other... *considerations*. He's certainly in a good position to sell my gifts and make a tidy profit for himself."

Penelope gave him a sharp look. "And no one dares to complain?"

"This isn't America," Andrew said. "In America, a government official who acts like an asshole can be arrested, put in a courtroom and jailed. Here? Anyone who dares complain will probably wind up on the wrong side of the law and wind up in deep trouble. All Aldrich has to do is mention their name to the security services and watch the rest from a safe distance."

"I see," Penelope said. She looked as if she had some other questions, but kept them to herself. "When can we go back to the embassy?"

"I was going to propose a walk around the square," Andrew said. He understood her feelings - this was her first time in Nazi Germany - but he couldn't afford to allow her to indulge them. The sooner she grasped - truly grasped - the nature of the Third *Reich*, the better. "It might help get some of the taste of corruption out of your mouth."

He waited for her to visit the ladies, then led the way out of the pub and onto the roadside. A BDM girl in a strikingly ugly uniform gave them a long look - she could tell they were foreigners, although he doubted she could peg them for Americans - and then gave them each a leaflet. Andrew took his, put it in his pocket and shook his head as the girl walked onwards, leaving them behind. It really *was* a strikingly ugly uniform.

"And to think I thought the girl scouts was bad," Penelope muttered. "That poor girl..."

She glanced at him. "What do we do with the leaflets?"

"We pass them to the desk officer at the embassy," Andrew said. The girl would probably wind up in trouble if the leaflets were simply dumped, particularly as the police couldn't do more to the Americans than escort them back to the embassy. "They'll inspect the leaflets to see if there's anything new, then discard them into the recycling bin. We may as well get *some* use out of them."

"Like lighting a fire," Penelope said.

"Good use for them," Andrew agreed. He caught sight of another pair of BDM girls and steered Penelope away from them. There was no point in collecting more leaflets. "But for everyone here... being caught using them for anything other than propaganda is a good way to get into trouble."

———

Horst knew himself to be a brave man. He'd had no doubt he could handle himself since the first time his settlement had come under attack, when he'd been seven years old. His training in the Hitler Youth, then the SS had only honed his edge. He'd never truly doubted he could handle anything he faced. But now he was worried. Gudrun and the other girls were out in the square, handing out the leaflets, yet he could do nothing to help them. He listened to the police band with one ear - Sven had done a very good job, he had to admit - but if the police started to hunt for BDM imposters, there was nothing he could do to alert the girls.

We really need some small radios, he told himself. *And a few other pieces of covert gear.*

He scowled. He'd given the matter a great deal of thought, but he honestly couldn't imagine how to *get* the equipment, at least not without raising too many questions. Besides, even if he *could* obtain a few radio sets they wouldn't be useful for very long. A handful of American spies had been caught because the SS had tracked their transmissions, pin-pointed the source and sent in the stormtroopers. He didn't want Gudrun and the others to go the same way.

The radio buzzed. Horst felt a chill run down his spine as he listened to the message, then relaxed as he realised it had nothing to do with the girls.

Someone had stolen a car and all policemen were to be on the lookout for it. Horst smirked - the car must have belonged to someone important - and then dismissed the matter. Anything that tied up the Berlin Police was useful, as far as he was concerned. He took another look at the timer and winced. Time was running out.

He reached instinctively for where his pistol should have been when he heard the sound of someone opening the rear door. Cursing - he hadn't been allowed to take a pistol to the university - he glanced back, groping frantically for a heavy axe as the door opened and Gudrun stepped into the van. Letting out a sigh of relief, he let go of the axe as Gudrun closed the door behind her and smiled at him.

"Ready to sell your life dearly?"

"Yes," Horst said, flatly. No matter what he'd told the group, he knew he wouldn't survive once he was arrested. Those who went into the *Reichssicherheitshauptamt* - the Reich Main Security Office - never returned. Fighting - and perhaps forcing them to kill him - seemed the better option. "How did it go?"

"No trouble," Gudrun said. She sounded pleased. "The others are back. I think we'd better go."

"Understood," Horst said. He turned back to the wheel and started the engine. "You get the uniform and wig off once we're on the move. We really don't want to be caught now."

"Of course not," Gudrun said.

Horst allowed himself a tight smile as he guided the van out onto the streets, then headed down the nearest road out towards the suburbs. The others would go in different directions, meeting up again near the university campus. If they were *really* lucky, they'd be able to return the wigs to the amateur theatrical group before anyone thought to look for them. He kept a sharp eye out for police cars as they slipped onto the main road and then gunned the engine. As long as they looked harmless, they would merge seamlessly with the whole and remain unnoticed.

The radio crackled. "This is Callsign Blue," a voice said. Horst tensed; Callsign Blue was the Berlin Security Office. It didn't sound as though the speaker was used to issuing orders over the radio. "All policemen within sectors one and two are to round up BDM girls and their matrons; I say again, all policemen within sectors one and two are to round up BDM girls and their matrons. Reinforcements have been dispatched."

"They caught on," Gudrun said. "Someone must have taken a leaflet to a policeman."

"It certainly sounds that way," Horst said. "Have you finished changing?"

He wasn't particularly worried. Unless something had gone *very* wrong, all four vans were going to be well out of sectors one and two by the time the police started putting up barricades. He'd assumed the SS stormtroopers charged with defending the *Reichstag* would get involved, but it sounded like the police were taking the lead. Probably not a mistake on their part - the stormtroopers had live ammunition and were trained to use it - yet it only gave the group more time to make their escape.

"I have," Gudrun said. She giggled, nervously. "I sure hope my father doesn't see me like this."

Horst glanced back, briefly. Gudrun's shirt and jeans were almost painfully tight. He could see the outline of her bra against her shirt.

"I think your father will have other things to worry about," he said, as he hastily turned his attention back to the road. "Did you see him while you were handing out leaflets?"

"I didn't," Gudrun said. She giggled, again. "We got away with it!"

"Don't get overconfident," Horst warned. "We haven't even *seen* their official response to our leaflets."

———

He was right, Gudrun knew. The police were acting faster than she'd feared, but they weren't going to catch anything beyond a few hundred innocent girls. Chances were they'd confiscate the leaflets from everyone caught within the barricades, not keep the girls behind bars for very long. Who knew how their parents would react after finding out that their daughters, some as young as twelve, were being held by the police?

She found herself giggling, once again, as she realised just what they'd done. They'd walked through Victory Square itself, handing out seditious leaflets, and no one had noticed in time to try to stop them. That matron was going to be in deep trouble when she confessed she'd seen Gudrun and done nothing... and, if she gave the SS an accurate description of what she'd seen, it would lead them in entirely the wrong direction. Who knew? Maybe someone would assume the BDM itself had been handing out the leaflets, perhaps a rogue matron with a grudge against the state. It might even sound plausible...

"I feel funny," she said. It reminded her of when she'd drunk a little wine the day she'd turned sixteen. Her head had felt strange for hours and she'd giggled like a little girl at everything, even unfunny jokes. "Is that normal?"

"It's fairly normal," Horst said. He parked the van in a lay-by, clambered out of his chair and came into the rear. "Did you hand out all of the leaflets?"

"Yep," Gudrun said. She had to fight to hold down another fit of giggles. "Everything's gone."

Horst nodded, then opened a bag and packed the remains of her BDM uniform away. Gudrun was too giggly to help him, even though she hated leaving the task to him. His eyes swept the vehicle, looking for anything else that might prove incriminating. But there was nothing, save for the radio itself. Gudrun watched as he packed it into another bag, then placed both bags near the door.

"I'm going to drop you off near your house," he said. "Take your uniform and return it to wherever you kept it. You probably shouldn't be carrying it around at all."

"I'd sooner burn it," Gudrun said. "Can't we just toss it into the fire?"

"Safer not to risk your parents noticing," Horst said. He glanced up at her. "There's no point in taking risks. I'll give the radio to Sven and he can break it back down into its component parts before it occurs to them to search the university."

Gudrun nodded, feeling suddenly sober. They'd done it. They'd crossed another line, one that would lead rapidly to jail if they were caught. She didn't understand how Horst managed to remain so calm, when they'd thoroughly compromised themselves. Her entire body began to shake as it hit her, suddenly, just how far they'd gone. And how far they had yet to go, if they weren't caught.

"It's all right," Horst assured her. He put a hand on her shoulder as she shook. "You've done fine, really."

Gudrun leaned forward and kissed him, hard. There was no conscious thought in it, just a desire to feel someone pressing against her. For a second,

Horst kissed her back and then he pulled away, gently holding her at arm's length. Gudrun stared at him, her emotions spinning madly. For all she'd done with Konrad - and the thought of her boyfriend added an extra stab of guilt to the mix - she'd never felt the simple burning *need* for his touch. Part of her wanted to slap Horst for not kissing her as hard as he could, the rest of her felt ashamed. This was neither the time nor the place.

"It's a natural reaction," Horst assured her, gently. "You just want to feel *alive*."

Gudrun stared at him, trying to wrap her mind around his refusal to kiss her back, let alone go further. She'd been told that a man would go as far as the woman would let him - and further, if he thought he could get away with it. And yet, Horst was gently refusing her unspoken offer. They could have made love in the back of the van and no one would have been any the wiser.

"I'm sorry," she said, finally. "I..."

"Ask me afterwards, if you like," Horst said. "But right now, Gudrun, you're not thinking straight."

"Bastard," Gudrun muttered.

Horst climbed back into the driver's seat and restarted the engine. "I'll drop you off in two minutes," he said. "Remember to come into university as normal tomorrow, but be careful what you say and do. There's no way to know how the government will react."

"I understand," Gudrun said. She removed a small mirror from her pocket and inspected her face carefully. She looked normal, thankfully. "And thank you."

"Thank me afterwards," Horst grunted. "Not before."

CHAPTER THIRTEEN

Victory Square, Berlin
28 July 1985

"They want us to do *what?*"

"Round up the BDM girls," Caius said. "All of them."

Leutnant der Polizei Herman Wieland blinked in surprise. The *Ordnungspolizei* rarely had anything to do in Victory Square, although they were required to keep a strong presence near the *Reichstag* to make sure nothing happened to the tourists. It made a change from patrolling the darker and grittier streets on the edge of Berlin - or, for that matter, being stationed in Germany East. Herman had heard too many stories from policemen who'd gone there, after being offered bonuses that would allow them to retire early, to feel willing to go there himself.

He shook his head in disbelief as he looked over at the nearest group of girls. They were young; the oldest was at least a year younger than Gudrun. And yet, he was to round them up? He knew how to handle rioting *Gastarbeiters*, he knew how to handle drunken soldiers celebrating their last few days of leave, but arresting young girls? How the hell was he supposed to handle *them?*

"Get them into the centre of the square," he ordered, finally. Orders were orders - and besides, such innocent girls wouldn't be in any real danger. "You keep an eye on them once I get them there."

He strode over to the nearest matron and frowned at the expression of fear, mixed with indignation, that flickered across her face. He'd never liked the BDM matrons, particularly the one who'd written outraged screeds about Gudrun. Herman had never been one to spare the rod for *any* of his children, but there were limits. Gudrun's hand had ached for weeks after she'd been forced to write thousands of lines and Herman would have happily arrested the matron, if there had been any grounds to throw her in jail. His daughter might have lost the use of her hand for the rest of her life.

"This is a police emergency," he said, fighting down his annoyance. There was no point in frightening the girls, no matter how much he wanted to frighten the matron. "Get the girls into the centre of the square and wait there."

The matron stared at him. "But..."

Herman met her eyes - he could have sworn she was growing a moustache - and cowed her into silence. The girls tittered, nervously. They had to know that *something* was wrong, but watching their matron taken down a step or two had to delight them. Herman felt a flicker of sympathy - the matron would take her embarrassment out on the girls once they were alone - and made a mental note to have a few words with her before she was released. The youngest girl in the group couldn't be more than ten years old.

"Get the girls into the square," he ordered, coldly. "Now."

The matron hurried to do as she was told. Herman watched her for a long moment, then turned and walked over to the next set of girls. Their matron, at least, seemed a little more reasonable; she listened to him politely, then started to steer the girls into the square. Herman moved from group to group as more policemen flowed into Victory Square, some keeping a sharp eye on the girls while others were collecting leaflets and examining them with grim expressions.

"Herman," Caius called. "Take a look at this!"

Herman took the proffered leaflet and read it in growing disbelief. The outside was normal - another set of exhortations to sacrifice for the good of the *Reich* - but on the inside... he stared in horror as he realised that it was seditious. A writer, an unknown writer, was claiming that thousands of soldiers had been killed or wounded in South Africa, despite the claims that the war was nothing more than a simple police action. And if that wasn't bad enough, there was a call for action, a call for free elections to the *Reichstag* and an end to the omnipresent terror. Herman shuddered, suddenly unwilling to even *touch* the leaflet. How many of the damned pieces of crap had been handed out?

"Someone was given this by a maiden," Caius said, very quietly.

"Shit," Herman muttered.

He looked at the girls - and their matrons. They were scared, he saw; whatever humour they'd seen in watching their matrons bossed around by the policemen had faded as the remainder of the square cleared rapidly. Berlin hadn't seen a major police action since the *Gastarbeiter* riots in the sixties, but few Berliners were prepared to stand around and risk being arrested. The girls... he swallowed, hard. It was impossible to believe they'd handed out the material wittingly, let alone willingly, but the SS might be harder to convince.

And, as if his thoughts had been enough to summon them, a handful of SS stormtroopers headed into the square, carrying weapons and looking dangerous.

Herman winced, inwardly. Technically, the Order Police and the SS were separate organisations, both reporting to the RSHA, but he knew better than to think he could stand up to the SS. The SS had lost its grip on the police after Hitler's death, yet they were still very much the senior service. If they wanted the girls, they could take the girls and no one could stop them.

"Herman, Caius, get over here," his superior bellowed. "You're needed on the barricades!"

Herman took one last look at the girls, then did as he was told. They'd just have to fend for themselves.

———

"Andrew," Penelope said. "Is this normal - or have I just forgotten how to read German?"

Andrew turned to look at her. She'd unfolded her leaflet and was reading it, carefully. Her German was perfect - German was the second global language, after all - and Andrew would have been surprised if she'd had any trouble reading it, yet she sounded as if she didn't quite believe what she was reading. He took the leaflet when she offered it to him and stared in disbelief as he read the words.

"No, it's not normal," he said. The British had had some links with the German underground, he'd heard through the grapevine, but the underground had largely gone dormant since the end of the war. He'd always assumed that its members had made their peace with the regime or had been quietly purged. "It isn't remotely normal."

He swore under his breath as he heard shouting ahead of him. A line of policemen had appeared out of nowhere and were hastily setting up metal barricades, trapping the two Americans - and hundreds of Germans - within Victory Square. He looked behind him and saw a number of young girls, wearing the same strikingly ugly uniforms he'd seen on the girl who'd given them the leaflets, being herded into the centre of the square. There would be no point in trying to go back, he was sure. The Berlin Police would have sealed off all the exits by now. If the girl they'd seen was trapped within the square, she was dead.

"I can hide the leaflet in my pants," Penelope said. "I..."

"They may check," Andrew said. He had to smile. He hadn't expected Penelope to suggest hiding the leaflet anywhere intimate, although it was pointless. "And if they find a hidden leaflet, they will try to make life uncomfortable for us."

Penelope blinked. "They can't do that, can they?"

Andrew frowned. "You should have read your briefing notes," he said. He put both of the leaflets in his pocket and gave her a wink. "They have been known to take Americans into custody if they think they have good cause. It's happened to me before."

He gritted his teeth at the memory. In theory, the policemen should either wave them on or provide an escort back to the embassy; in practice, they might be taken into custody and held until their credentials were checked against the Foreign Ministry's records. The Berlin Police might be relatively gentle, but the SS would insist on a strip search, perhaps even a cavity search. They'd *certainly* insist on a full search if they thought Penelope was hiding something in her underwear. The embassy would protest, of course, and there would be a series of unpleasant exchanges, but nothing effective would be done.

"Remain calm and let me do the talking," he said. Thankfully, they *did* have a legitimate reason to be in the square. "If they split us up, remember your instructions and *follow them.*"

Penelope nodded, her face pale. Embassy staff, even the ones who rarely left the building during their entire term in Germany, were carefully briefed on what to do if they were arrested or otherwise taken into custody. Cooperate, within limits; inform the Germans, at once, that holding an embassy staffer prisoner would cause a diplomatic incident; don't sign anything, no matter what the Germans said. Andrew hoped she'd be fine; there were limits, unfortunately, to just how far training could actually *go*.

They joined a line of civilians waiting to go through the barricade and watched, grimly, as the policemen frisked the civilians, sometimes removing copies of the leaflets, before allowing the civilians to go onwards. A couple of middle-aged men were sitting on the ground in handcuffs, although Andrew couldn't tell what they'd done to get arrested. He braced himself as the line moved sharply onwards, then met the policeman's eyes when his turn came.

"My card," he said, holding up his diplomatic ID. "We're attached to the embassy."

The policeman's eyes narrowed sharply. Andrew could practically *see* the internal debate behind his eyes. If he frisked them both and the embassy complained, his career would be sacrificed to avoid a diplomatic incident. But if he let them go and his superiors found out, his career would be smashed flat. It wasn't a surprise when the policeman motioned the two Americans to stand aside and called his superior on the radio. Moments later, a grim-faced man in an SS uniform arrived. Andrew was surprised to realise that he didn't have any rank insignia at all.

He glared at Andrew, then addressed him in heavily-accented English. "Why were you in the square?"

"We had a meeting with Mr. Aldrich of the Ministry of Finance," Andrew said, calmly. "We are currently heading back to the embassy to file the paperwork for the latest trade deal."

And if you treat us badly, the deal may be wrecked, he added, silently. He was sure the officer would pick up on the subtext. *You should let us go right now.*

The officer's mouth worked for a long moment before he said anything. "I will check it with the Ministry," he said. "Wait."

Andrew gave Penelope's hand a reassuring squeeze as the officer lifted his radio and called the Ministry of Finance. Aldrich, he was sure, would tell the officer that there *had* been a meeting and an important trade deal, encouraging the officer to just let them go without further ado. But if someone had pulled off a coup in the middle of Berlin, handing out leaflets to hundreds of people, who knew what would happen? The SS might even try to arrange accidents rather than risk the news getting out.

"Mr. Aldrich vouches for you," the officer said, finally. He waved to a pair of policemen, who strode over and scowled at the two Americans. "Escort these two back to the American Embassy and ensure they don't get lost along the way."

"*Jawohl, Mein Herr*," the policemen said.

"Come on," Andrew said, as the policemen motioned for the two Americans to follow them past the barricade. "We need to get back home before it's too late."

Penelope looked as if she wanted to ask questions, but thankfully she had the sense to keep her mouth shut. Andrew had no doubt that the policemen would overhear anything they said and report back to their superiors. They could discuss the leaflets once they got back to the embassy and then decide what, if anything, they should do about them. He tried to remember what the girl had looked like, but - if he were forced to be honest - he'd paid more attention to her uniform than her face.

It could have been worse, he told himself, firmly. Crowds were already gathering past the barricades, staring into the square. *It could have been a great deal worse.*

———

"There's a crowd gathering," Caius muttered. "Word is spreading."

Herman looked past the barricade and swore, inwardly. Frisking everyone and then letting them leave might have been a mistake. By now, word was spreading through Berlin that the police were holding nearly fifty BDM girls in the square and worried parents were heading to the centre of the city, despite the risks. And what would happen, he asked himself, if the SS insisted on taking the girls away for further interrogation?

No one would care if they were a bunch of Gastarbeiters, he thought. It was perfectly true, after all. *But young German maidens... their parents will be up in arms!*

He cursed the leaflet-writers under his breath. Whoever they were, they'd neatly put a finger right on the *Reich's* weak spot. The SS couldn't take the girls, he told himself; there'd be riots, mutinies, even an uprising. He honestly wasn't sure what *he'd* do, if Gudrun had been among the girls who'd been arrested.

Hell, there were at least a dozen policemen he knew who had daughters in the BDM. What if *they'd* been arrested?

His radio buzzed. "The girls don't seem to have any of the leaflets," a voice said. "We're letting them go with a warning."

Herman allowed himself a moment of relief as the girls were released, heading back to their parents, then found himself dragged into helping to pick up the leaflets and dump them into rubbish bags. They'd be transported to the RSHA, where the SS would pick over them in the hopes of finding something - anything - they could use to track down the writers and arrest them. Herman rather doubted they'd find anything. Whoever had written the leaflets wouldn't leave fingerprints; hell, gloves were part of the BDM uniform. He gritted his teeth in anger as he tossed the final bag into the SS truck. Bringing the leaflets to the centre of the *Reich* had been madness.

"We'll be working late tonight," Caius commented. "The Captain was saying we might be staying on duty until nine."

"I'll miss my wife's dinner," Herman muttered. He wasn't fool enough to say it any louder, not when his superiors might hear. "She won't be pleased."

"I dare say she doesn't have a choice," Caius said. "And neither do the rest of us."

———

She kissed me, Horst thought, as he returned the van to the garage. The owner examined it quickly, checked the gas in the tank and then grudgingly returned the deposit. *She kissed me.*

He couldn't help feeling excited, even though he knew it was probably nothing more than a reaction to stress and then the relief of knowing they'd managed to get clean away. Gudrun had a boyfriend. She'd think better of what she'd done in the morning, after she had a chance to sleep. She'd...

Sure, his own thoughts mocked him. *How likely is it that Konrad will recover?*

Horst was no doctor, but he'd read Konrad's medical report - and the summery - very carefully. It was quite likely, when his family were informed about his condition, that they would be urged to pull the plug, cutting off his life support. The damage to his legs was quite bad enough - Horst had shuddered when he'd read the description - but the brain damage was worse. Konrad would be a drooling imbecile for the rest of his life. How long would Gudrun stay faithful when she knew, deep inside, that her boyfriend was gone?

And yet she doesn't know what you are, he reminded himself. *What will she say when she finds out the truth?*

It wasn't a pleasant thought. Sure, Gudrun had accepted Konrad - but Konrad had never tried to hide the fact that he was an SS trooper. Horst had; no, Horst had done a great deal worse, even though he was now trying to help Gudrun and her friends. He'd come to her, pretending to be a student, and befriended her, intending to betray her if she did anything worth reporting. How could she forget that, if she found out?

He sighed. He was no virgin. There were brothels near the Hitler Youth camps in Germany East - another feature that wasn't present anywhere else - and he'd been taken there by the older boys once he'd plucked up the nerve to ask. The women there had been *Untermenschen*, sterilised just to ensure they didn't become pregnant and give birth to half-caste children. They'd done whatever they'd been told...

Gudrun is different, Horst told himself. *She'd never just roll over for anyone.*

He cursed his own feelings as he started the walk back to the university. He'd never tried to court a girl in Germany East, not when he'd known his duty would lead him elsewhere... and besides, he'd had to remain unattached at the university. He couldn't allow himself more than a brief affair. Now, he found himself unsure of how to proceed, or even if he *should* proceed. He couldn't help cursing his own training. He'd been so sure that Gudrun was just reacting to her relief that he hadn't been able to bring himself to give in. And yet he'd *wanted* to give in...

And how much of that, he asked himself, *is driven by your own relief?*

It was a pointless argument, he told himself firmly. Gudrun probably wasn't *really* interested in him - and even if she was, it would be unwise for them to become involved until the whole affair was over. And yet, Horst knew just how likely it was that they'd all be arrested, tortured and executed. They might as well enjoy themselves while it lasted...

Confused and tired, Horst slowly made his way home.

CHAPTER FOURTEEN

Wieland House, Berlin
28 July 1985

Gudrun had received her first surprise when she'd returned home and opened the door. A leaflet - a copy of *their* leaflet - lay on the table, having been pushed through the letterbox and brought into the dining room by her mother. The second surprise had been Grandpa Frank sitting in an armchair, watching her mother as she fretted over the leaflet. He was holding a bottle of beer in one hand, but he seemed surprisingly sober.

"Don't touch that leaflet," her mother snapped, when Gudrun reached for it. "I'm going to show it to your father."

"It's one of the leaflets we had to hand out as children," Gudrun said, pretending to be perplexed. "It's nothing..."

"Don't touch it," her mother snapped. "Go upstairs and change into something *proper* and then come back down and help me with dinner."

Gudrun nodded and hurried up the stairs, puzzling over the leaflet. She'd known that some of the boys were going to post them through letterboxes, but *her* letterbox? Had they thought it would help her avoid suspicion? Did they even know where she lived? She'd taken Hilde and Isla back to her home a couple of times, but Konrad had been the only boy who'd visited since she'd turned thirteen. Horst only knew where she lived because she'd had to tell him where to drop her off.

She closed and locked the door, then unpacked the BDM uniform and hid it at the back of her wardrobe. Hopefully, her parents wouldn't demand to see it in the next couple of days. She *was* expected to do the washing on

Wednesday, when she had no classes at the university; she'd insert it into the washing pile before anyone had a chance to look at the uniform.

And for once it's a good thing the boys aren't expected to do anything around the house, she thought as she changed into a skirt and blouse. Her father would have a fit if he saw her in tight jeans and an American t-shirt, even if he had other things to worry about. She had no way of knowing where he'd been stationed, but he would probably have been called to Victory Square to help round up the BDM girls. *He'll be hopping mad when he comes home from work.*

She walked back down the stairs, almost running into her mother as she helped Grandpa Frank stagger back upstairs to his room. The drunkard looked surprisingly bright-eyed; he was normally drunk out of his mind when Gudrun came home. Her mother pointed to the kitchen; Gudrun nodded and hurried down the rest of the stairs, looking around for the vegetables she knew she'd have to chop. There was no sign of the leaflet.

And what, Gudrun asked herself, *will mother do with it?*

She worried over it as she donned an apron and set to work. They'd been told at school, time and time again, that seditious literature had to be handed in to the police at once. Gudrun remembered, at the time, trying to decide what counted as seditious; the definitions they'd been given were very broad, too broad to understand. Her mother would show the leaflet to her father and then... and then what? Who knew *what* her father would do?

The door opened. Gudrun looked up, just in time to see Kurt sneaking into the kitchen and making a beeline for the cookie jar. She hissed at him threateningly - their mother would be furious if he spoiled his appetite before the main meal of the day - and chased him back out of the kitchen. He raised his hands in mock surrender as he retreated; Gudrun was tempted to ask him why he wasn't in the barracks, but swallowed the thought as she realised he might well have seen the leaflets too. Who knew what the soldiers had made of them?

And he might guess I had something to do with them, she thought, as she put the chopped vegetables into water and put the pot on the stove. *He knows Konrad's a cripple - and unlikely to survive.*

Her mother came back downstairs, muttering under her breath, and bustled into the kitchen, issuing orders with all the determination of an army officer. Gudrun pushed her fears out of her mind and set to work following them, silently grateful that her mother was doing her fair share of the work. One of her friends who'd married young had told her that the mother-in-law did nothing, apart from issuing instructions and moaning when they weren't followed to the letter. Gudrun had privately determined she wouldn't be marrying *anyone* unless they moved into a private home, well away from the in-laws. She hadn't been looking forward to the argument with Konrad...

She sagged against the table as it struck her, again. There wouldn't be *any* arguments with Konrad; there wouldn't be *anything* with Konrad, ever. He'd die in a hospital bed, his life support cut off, or he'd remain a cripple for the rest of his life. The nurse had talked about brain damage. Gudrun was no doctor, but she knew that brain damage could be impossible to repair. His body was still alive, yet his soul might have fled long ago.

"Gudrun," her mother snapped. "What's got into you, girl?"

"I'm sorry," Gudrun said, pulling herself upright. "I... I'm just tired."

Her mother gave her a considering look. "You had better go to bed early, after you've taken Grandpa Frank his dinner," she said, finally. "You'll be useless if you go to the university without a good night's sleep."

Gudrun was tempted to protest that she worked hard at home *and* at the university, but she kept that thought to herself as she heard the front door open. The one time she'd complained about having to do all the chores herself - her brothers were allowed to get away with leaving their rooms messy - her mother had pointed out that *she* needed to develop the skills to be a good wife and mother. There was no point in having the same argument a second time.

She looked up as her father entered the kitchen. He was wearing his green uniform - he normally changed at the station - and looked grim.

"I'm going to have to go back to the station tonight," he said, after he gave his wife a hug and kiss. "The captain wants us all on duty."

"I've got something to show you," his wife said. She looked back at Gudrun. "Get the food on the table, please."

"Yes, mother," Gudrun said, feeling a chill running down her spine. "Beer?"

"No beer," her father said, quickly. "Just coffee, please."

Gudrun nodded and turned away before her father could see the guilt written all over her face. He'd always been good at spotting their lies, when they'd been children; Gudrun and her brothers had learned long ago that it was pointless to try to deceive their father. Did he know, she asked herself, that she was worried about *something*? Or was he too wrapped up in his own troubles to worry about *hers*?

"I told you not to read it," her mother said, loudly enough for Gudrun to hear her even though the walls. "I told you..."

She picked up the pan and carried it through the door, into the dining room. Kurt was standing at one side of the table, the leaflet in his hand; their parents were standing at the other side, glaring at him. Gudrun kept her eyes lowered as she put the pan on the table, then looked up to see Kurt holding out the leaflet. She took it, only to have it snatched out of her hand by her father.

"*Father*," Kurt said.

"I will not have this... this seditious crap in my house," her father snapped. He stuffed the leaflet into his pocket and glared at his son. "And showing it to your sister was unwise..."

"It concerns her," Kurt said, calmly.

Gudrun looked up at him. "What does it say?"

"None of your business, young lady," her mother said. "Go back and bring in the meat!"

"It says that soldiers who have stopped writing are crippled or dead and the government is covering it up," Kurt said. "Soldiers like Konrad..."

Gudrun felt her mouth drop open in shock. Kurt had guessed. He *had* to have guessed... and he'd given her a cover she could use to protect herself, if she wished. Now she'd have an excuse for knowing about Konrad's injury.

She turned to her father. "Konrad is wounded?"

"His name isn't mentioned," her father said, crossly. "Whoever is passing out these leaflets used BDM girls as pawns. They're monsters."

"Show me the leaflet," Gudrun demanded, angrily. It wasn't a tone she would have normally dared to use, but she felt she could get away with it now. "I need to see."

"No, you don't," her father said. "Everyone who sees one of these leaflets is going to be in deep trouble."

"Including us," Kurt said, coolly. "Where did it even come from?"

"I found it in the letterbox," their mother said. "I don't know who brought it here!"

"Whoever they are, they will be tracked down and punished," their father snapped. He stamped his foot angrily. "They're telling lies!"

"I haven't heard anything from Konrad in months," Gudrun said, careful not to look at her father. He might see the lie written on her face. "His family hasn't heard anything from him either."

"He would hardly be the first young man to be more interested in fighting than writing," her father said. He sounded as though he was trying to be reassuring, but couldn't quite pull it off. "Why, when I was a soldier, there were times when I didn't write to your mother for weeks. The postal system was so disorganised that I sometimes got three or four letters from her in a single packet and had to be careful to read them in order..."

"And father was less than pleased you weren't writing," her mother added. "He told you off for it when you came home on leave."

"Konrad promised he would write to me every week," Gudrun said, feeling a sudden lump in her throat. "And then he just stopped!"

"Maybe he found someone else," Siegfried said.

Gudrun blinked in shock. When had *he* entered the room?

Kurt slapped the back of his head, hard. "Shut up," he snapped. "Or I'll make damn sure that the only girl who will ever look at you will be an ugly old bitch..."

"*Kurt*," their mother thundered.

Gudrun felt tears welling at the corner of her eyes. She knew Konrad was crippled, not cheating on her... but she couldn't say that out loud. Siegfried... had all the innocent malice of a child; he didn't know just how badly his words had hurt her. Their father banished Siegfried from the room, promising him that he wouldn't have anything to eat until the following morning.

"A little hunger will teach you a lesson," he shouted after his youngest son. "And I don't want to hear a peep out of you for an hour!"

"It's going to be ok," Kurt said, reaching out to take Gudrun's arm. "Konrad..."

"... Is perfectly fine," their father said, turning back to them. "Just because he hasn't written to you in months doesn't mean he's dead, or wounded, or looking elsewhere. He's a stormtrooper, Gudrun. They're sometimes barred from sending home letters until their operation is completed."

"He'd have told me something," Gudrun protested. She *had* to see the leaflet before she said something she couldn't justify. "Please! Show me the leaflet!"

"It's none of your concern," her father said, sternly.

"Father," Kurt said quietly, "ignorance won't protect her..."

Their father glared at him. "Knowledge won't save her either."

"Fetch the rest of the food," Gudrun's mother ordered. "And put some aside for Siegfried."

"I said he wasn't to have any food until tomorrow," their father snapped, rounding on his wife. "He's going to learn a lesson!"

"And he will need to eat a proper meal for breakfast tomorrow," their mother said. She'd never disagreed with any of their father's punishments, but she'd sometimes acted to moderate them. "He's got school in the morning and Hitler Youth in the evening. He doesn't need a bad fitness report from his teachers."

Gudrun winced as she hurried back into the kitchen, wiping the tears from her eyes. A bad fitness report could be disastrous, particularly if Siegfried wanted to get into the air force or the navy. It was at least four years before he could join, but if the recruiters had too many volunteers they might look as far back as the Hitler Youth to decide who should be given a chance. Siegfried had always been a little nastier than her other brothers - she dreaded to think of what would happen if he ever worked out that she'd helped write the leaflets - yet he didn't deserve to have his life ruined by being too hungry to march, run or play football with the other children.

She put enough food aside for him, then carried the rest of it back into the dining room and placed it on the table. Kurt and their father were seated, staring at each other, while their mother was standing behind their father, wringing her hands together. Gudrun didn't really blame her for being worried. There had been arguments before, of course, but *then* her children had been *children*. Now, Kurt was an adult with his own life, Gudrun was old enough to marry and Johan would be going into the army next year, unless he passed the university entrance exams. Only Siegfried was still a child and he was growing up fast.

Kurt waved cheerfully to Johan as he entered the room, then took a potato from the pan and leaned forward. "What happened at work?"

"Those damnable leaflets were being handed out by young women in BDM clothes," their father said. "We had to round up every girl in the square, which naturally brought dozens of parents to mass on the other side of the barricades..."

"The girls were handing out the leaflets?" Kurt asked. He made a show of stroking his chin thoughtfully. "How... *strange.*"

"As I said," their father snarled, "the girls handing them out wore BDM uniforms, but they were apparently not BDM."

"And yet they wore those uniforms voluntarily," Kurt mused. He winked cheerfully at Gudrun. "They must have escaped from the madhouse."

Gudrun kicked him under the table. Her mother smacked her on the head, then sat down and started to ladle food onto her plate. Gudrun ate quickly, trying to follow the argument; Kurt seemed more inclined to wonder at how many soldiers hadn't been writing home, while her father flatly refused to consider the matter. The leaflet itself was nowhere in sight; she guessed her father had shoved it into his pocket, then buttoned it up.

"The discussion is closed," her father said, finally. "There will be no more talk of it within my house."

Kurt scowled at him. "How many soldiers haven't come home?"

"The discussion is closed," her father repeated. "When are you going back on duty?"

"We're supposed to start prepping for deployment in a month," Kurt said, shortly. "I'm not sure where we're going yet, but the CO is insistent we get ready for intensive training."

Gudrun felt her blood run cold. "South Africa?"

"Probably," Kurt said. He didn't sound pleased. "We may be stationed in Germany Arabia, but South Africa or Germany East sounds likelier."

"You'll do fine, wherever you go," their father said. He gave Kurt a look of approval that twisted Gudrun's heart. What did *she* have to do to earn her father's approval? "I'm proud of you."

"You might die - or be wounded," Gudrun said. She shuddered as the full implications struck her. Kurt could wind up as badly wounded as Konrad - or worse - and they'd never know what had happened. "What would it mean if *you* stopped writing...?"

"That will do," her father snapped. He fixed Gudrun with an icy glare that rooted her to the spot. "The university has done nothing for your mind, young lady. It's high time you and Konrad were married and started raising children."

Gudrun stared at him in shock. She'd known her father was a traditionalist, but she'd always thought he was proud of her university career. The exams she'd passed to enter were among the hardest in the *Reich*. Once she graduated, she'd be in a good position to make a professional life for herself, rather than becoming just another housewife.

"Father..."

"I mean it," her father said. His eyes never left her face. "I should never have agreed to let you go to the university when you had a perfectly acceptable suitor. Young girls..."

"My boyfriend is a cripple," Gudrun shouted, feeling her temper snap. "There won't be a marriage!"

"You don't *know* he's a cripple," Kurt said, quickly. He looked at their father, clearly trying to draw his wrath away from Gudrun. "You should have let her see the leaflet."

Their mother slapped the table, hard. "Gudrun, take Grandpa Frank his dinner," she ordered, as silence fell like a hammer. "And then go to your room. Your father and I will discuss your future when this affair is over."

Gudrun swallowed. If Kurt hadn't covered for her, she might have revealed far too much to their father. "I..."

"Go," her father ordered. His voice brooked of no objection. "I'll speak to you before I go out."

"Yes, father," Gudrun said. There was no point in arguing. She'd be lucky, after the shouting match, if they allowed her to go into the university tomorrow. "I'll be waiting."

CHAPTER FIFTEEN

Wieland House, Berlin
28 July 1985

I shouldn't have lost my temper like that, Gudrun thought, as she walked slowly up the stairs, the tray balanced neatly on one hand. *Father is not going to be pleased.*

She shuddered as she reached the top of the stairs. Her father was the master of the house, as far as he was concerned, and even his adult children couldn't defy him without punishment - if, of course, he considered her an adult at all. She was, after all, a girl... she'd pass straight from her father's authority to her husband's without ever having any true freedom of her own. Konrad had seemed willing to accept her as anything but a housewife, yet would that have lasted once they were married? He might have changed his mind when his comrades starting mocking him for having a wife who actually *worked.*

Gudrun gritted her teeth in helpless fury. She wasn't scared of her father's punishments, even the threat of his belt, but she *was* scared of being told she couldn't go back to the university and study. Even if she hadn't been involved in the... whatever they came to call their little group... the threat would have scared her. She needed her father's permission to study at the university and, no matter how clever she was, they wouldn't allow her to stay if her father changed his mind. The *Reich* wouldn't allow the university to call into question a husband's or father's role as head of the household. Hell, she knew girls who had been withdrawn a few weeks after entering the university because their parents had thought better of it.

I'm not going to let him take me out, she thought, grimly. But what could she do? Her father had ultimate authority over her, as long as she was unmarried. And it wasn't as if she could marry Konrad tomorrow. *What do I do?*

She paused outside Grandpa Frank's door, feeling beaten and defeated. It wasn't *fair!* She knew she was smarter than her brothers, she knew she was a better student than half the boys at university, yet the mere fact of being born a girl hampered her future. She'd never be truly free, she'd never be truly independent; she'd never even be able to get married without her father's consent. Unless, of course, she allowed herself to get pregnant out of wedlock, which would have its own complications. Her parents would be furious and her in-laws wouldn't be very pleased either.

Rapping on the door, she pushed it open. The stench of beer and smelly old man seemed weaker, somehow; Gudrun wondered, savagely, if her mother had given the room an airing out while her grandfather had been downstairs, then dismissed the thought as she stepped inside, closing the door behind her. Grandpa Frank was sitting up in bed, reading a small leather-bound book; he looked up at her, then slipped the book under the sheets. Gudrun guessed, as she put the tray down and cleared away the remains of his lunch, that it was a dirty book. A handful of French books had been passed around at school before the teachers confiscated them and they'd been very explicit indeed.

"Here's your dinner," Gudrun said shortly, as she picked up the tray and put it on the bedside table. "Mother will be up later..."

She broke off as Grandpa Frank's hand lunged out with terrifying speed and caught her wrist, pulling her towards him. Gudrun struggled, trying to pull free, but his hand felt like a band of steel. She couldn't understand how he was so strong, when he spent most of the day in bed, yet it hardly mattered. All that mattered was that she was trapped.

"Sit down," Grandpa Frank hissed. "Don't make a noise."

"Let go of me," Gudrun said. If she shouted... what did Grandpa Frank *want?* Her imagination supplied too many possibilities. "Please..."

"It was you," Grandpa Frank whispered. "You helped write those leaflets."

Gudrun stared at him in shock. "How do you...?"

"It was written all over your face when you saw the leaflet on the table," Grandpa Frank rasped. He pulled her into a sitting position on the bed, then met her eyes. It struck her, suddenly, that he sounded surprisingly sober. "You *knew* what it was before you opened it, before your mother snapped at you for even trying. I hope your father didn't read *that* on your face."

"I hope so too," Gudrun said, trying to keep her voice level. She'd feared her father somehow guessing her involvement, she'd suspected *Kurt* would deduce her involvement... but Grandpa Frank? He was a drunkard. She'd assumed he wouldn't pay any attention to anything beyond the next bottle of beer. "How...?"

"I read the leaflet," Grandpa Frank told her. "Not a bad piece of work, really."

"Thank you," Gudrun said. He hadn't let go of her wrist and it was starting to ache. "I... Grandpa... let go of me?"

"I have something to tell you," Grandpa Frank said. He met her eyes. "Promise you won't run?"

"I won't," Gudrun said. What choice did she have? Maybe her father wouldn't believe Grandpa Frank, but if he took one look at her former uniform the game would be up. "What do you want to tell me?"

Her grandfather let go of her wrist. "I never told anyone this," he whispered, hoarsely. "Not even your grandmother, may she rest in peace. She knew I had nightmares - your mother knows I have nightmares - but she never knew why. There are... *things*... I never wanted your mother to know."

Gudrun shivered. She'd been woken, sometimes, by Grandpa Frank screaming in his sleep, calling out names of people she didn't recognise. Her father had said that it was a legacy of the war, but he'd refused to say anything more and forbidden her from talking to her grandfather about it. No doubt he knew something about his father-in-law's military service - he'd have needed Grandpa Frank's permission to marry his daughter - yet he'd never seen fit to share the secret. In time, Gudrun had decided that there was *no* secret.

Her grandfather sat upright and pulled up his right sleeve, revealing a blue tattoo. Gudrun stared; she'd seen Konrad's tattoo, more than once, but Konrad hadn't had a skull and crossbones over his ID number. She'd never even *heard* of anyone having anything more than a number, as long as they were in the military. Kurt had once asked for a tattoo and his father had bawled him out for even thinking of it before he completed his time in the Hitler Youth, let alone the military.

Gudrun tried to think about what it meant. "You were an SS stormtrooper?"

"I was *Einsatzgruppen*," Grandpa Frank said. "Do you know what that means?"

He answered the question before she could find the words. "Of course you don't know what that means," he said, bitterly. He gave a harsh little laugh that chilled her to the bone. "We were the *Reich's* dirty little secret. You don't know, none of you know, just what the *Reich* did to secure itself. How can you know? You've been lied to from the very start."

Gudrun swallowed. "What secret?"

"I drink to forget," Grandpa Frank said. He eyed one of the bottles - an unopened bottle, she noted with some surprise - and then shook his head. "I always wondered why they didn't round us up and kill us all, Gudrun. It wasn't as if we could have stopped them from exterminating us. The secret would have died with us."

He caught her wrist again, holding it tightly. "You weren't there," he said. "You couldn't understand. I joined the SS when it started; I helped purge the SA when the *Fuhrer* decided their leader had gone a little too far." He snickered. "But you won't have heard of them, will you? Röhm is an unperson now, serves the bastard right. I did well in my work, too well; they offered me a chance to transfer to the *Einsatzgruppen* when they were founded and told me there was a promotion in it for me if I did well. And they were right. I did very well.

"We went into Poland and Russia behind the armies, Gudrun. We rounded up soldiers, political leaders, everyone on the hit-list... we marched them into the camps, at first, and then we killed them. Hundreds of thousands of men, women and children were killed - and, after they were dead, we stripped them bare; we even stole their *teeth*. The bodies were dumped in unmarked mass graves, which were soon wiped from the records. I watched as entire villages were given to the flames, their populations destroyed so that new German settlers could be moved eastwards. Germany East is *built* on a giant mass grave."

Gudrun stared at him. She'd been told, at school, how Hitler had taken Russia as living space, but she'd never thought through the implications. What had happened to the original inhabitants? They'd been subhuman, she'd been taught; they'd deserved to be displaced...

"But it was in Warsaw that it happened," Grandpa Frank said. "It was 1944; the Americans had invaded Japan, the Russian armies were being destroyed and we were clearing the city of Jews. I was in charge of one block... there was a Jewess living there. She was the mother of a little girl, but she was pretty. I made sure she got to remain there as long as she was my lover."

"A Jewess," Gudrun repeated, shocked. The pictures she'd seen of Jews had all shown misshapen figures, so dirty and filthy they could hardly pass for human. "You started an affair with a stinking *Jewess?*"

Her grandfather squeezed her wrist, hard. "You've been lied to," he said harshly, as she winced in pain and tried to pull away. "They were *human*. They didn't have horns, or cloven feet, and they certainly didn't stink. You couldn't tell the difference between a Jew and a German if you met them in the streets. Tell me - how could the misshapen monsters you're taught to recognise at school possibly pass for Germans?"

Gudrun swallowed. She'd never thought about it.

"That woman... I was her lover for nearly a year," Grandpa Frank said. "Her child... she started to call me *papa*. I used to bring her little gifts as well as ration packs; I even fiddled the records so she'd be classed as a Pole, rather than a Jew. It wasn't much, but I thought it would keep them alive for longer. Maybe it did. But in the end they found out."

He laughed harshly. "They weren't too pleased at me sticking it in a Jewess, I can tell you," he said, darkly. "I might have sired a child on her, you know; a half-German child. *That* really would have upset the Race Classification Bureau. They might even have had to class the child as something other than a Jew. But I didn't get her pregnant. My CO told me that I had to take her to the camps myself. I had to sentence her to death to save myself. And I did, Gudrun. I bound her hands, put her in the car and drove her to the camps. All the way, the little girl was asking me where we were going, what had happened to her mother..."

"No," Gudrun said.

"Yes," Grandpa Frank said. "They took them both at once, of course; they added them to the next batch for extermination. I was forced to watch as they were both stripped naked and marched into the showers, accompanied by dozens of other Jewesses. And then the gas started pumping into the chamber and they started to die. The little girl kept looking at me, as if she couldn't believe what I'd done to her, until she collapsed and died. And after they were dead, we had to burn the bodies..."

He shuddered, violently. "Do you understand why I drink?"

Gudrun stared at him. She'd never imagined, not in her worst nightmares, that the state could do anything of the sort. Everything she'd been told had been curiously hygienic, as if the natives had merely disappeared after the Germans had arrived. And yet... it never occurred to her to doubt his words. They had the ring of truth and they chilled her to the bone.

She found her voice, somehow. "What happened to you?"

"Oh, they never trusted me after that," Grandpa Frank said. "I had betrayed the *Volk*, you see, by making love to a Jewess. There was no hope of promotion. I took early retirement and went back to Berlin. Your grandmother was kind enough to marry me; I never told her the truth, of course, even when my nightmares drove her out of bed. We had the nastiest arguments before she fell pregnant and left her job. And then she died four years after your mother was born. I brought her up on my own. Never married again, either."

He let go of Gudrun's wrist. "Every time I close my eyes, I see *her* face," he muttered, reaching for the bottle. "If I remain drunk all the time, it helps... I keep thinking about killing myself, but what good would that do?"

"I don't know," Gudrun said. It had been easy to dismiss Grandpa Frank when he'd just been a disgusting old man. Now... now she wasn't sure *what* to think. "But what else *can* you do?"

"I was taught that suicide was a mortal sin," Grandpa Frank said. "And yet, surely what we did in the *Einsatzgruppen* was even worse.

"We told ourselves that they were subhuman. We told ourselves that we were strong and they were weak and the strong had rights to use the weak as they saw fit. We told ourselves that their mere existence was a threat to the *Reich*, that they had to be destroyed to save ourselves from certain destruction. And yet, after what I did, I can no longer believe it..."

His voice trailed off. "You wrote that leaflet," Grandpa Frank said. "And you could possibly pass for a BDM girl if you wore your uniform and kept your eyes downcast."

"I did," Gudrun confirmed. There was no point in trying to deny it. "Grandpa..."

"The state isn't going to let you get away with it," Grandpa Frank hissed. "They've buried so many would-be reformers over the years. Don't ever underestimate how far they're prepared to go to root out all opposition to their rule. But don't stop. Don't let them get away with it."

He leaned back in his bed. "I told myself there was nothing I could do," he whispered, as he closed his eyes. "And at the time, maybe I was right."

Gudrun waited, her heart pounding in her chest, but he said nothing else. She checked his breathing - for a moment, she thought he'd finally let go of life and surrendered to death - and then relaxed as she realised it was stable. Rising to her feet, she walked out the door and headed down to her room. Suddenly, the threat of her father's anger seemed unimportant, compared to what she'd been told. She felt sick to even consider her grandfather having an affair with anyone...

But he wasn't an old man at the time, she told herself, as she closed the door behind her - there was no point in locking it - and sat down on the bed. *He wouldn't have been much older than Kurt.*

Her thoughts were so jumbled up that it was a relief when she heard someone tapping at the door. She braced herself, grimly prepared to take whatever punishment her father decided to mete out, then blinked in surprise as Kurt opened the door and stepped into the room. He was holding the leaflet in one hand.

"You may as well read it," he said, as he closed the door. "I managed to talk father out of beating you, but it would probably be better if you didn't show your face until tomorrow."

Gudrun swallowed. "Thank you," she said, as she took the leaflet. It was identical to the leaflets she'd handed out only a few hours ago. "What did you *say* to him?"

"Told him you'd jump to the worst possible conclusion, because that's what girls do," Kurt said. He ignored the rude gesture she aimed at him. "And that you probably thought Konrad was mentioned by name."

He lowered his voice. "You're playing a dangerous game, Gudrun."

"I know," Gudrun said. She looked up at him. "Are you going to betray me?"

"How could I without revealing that I sneaked into the hospital beside you?" Kurt asked, dryly. "You couldn't have done it without me."

That was true, Gudrun knew. But betraying the person who'd helped write and distribute the leaflets would probably have won him forgiveness.

He wasn't a student, after all; he was a Berlin Guardsman who was probably bound for South Africa soon...

"Thank you," she said, instead. "I'm not going to stop."

"I know," Kurt said. "You're as stubborn as father."

"And if I wasn't a girl, he'd have something to be proud of," Gudrun snarled.

"He's had a bad day," Kurt reminded her. "The girls he had to round up would have been very like you - some of them might only be a year or two younger. He didn't join the police for *that*."

Gudrun shrugged as her brother patted her on the shoulder and rose, heading for the door. As far as she could tell, the Order Police were *intended* to push people around. Why else would anyone join up?

"Get some rest," Kurt advised. "You have to go back to university tomorrow."

"I know," Gudrun said. "Thank you."

CHAPTER SIXTEEN

Reichstag, Berlin
28 July 1985

It was not, Hans Krueger decided, going to be a particularly pleasant meeting.

He'd been expecting a vote on the deployment of additional troops to South Africa - his sources had told him that the SS was trying to strike a deal with the military - and had been preparing for a long argument when the news about the protest leaflets reached the Ministry of Finance, followed by an urgent demand for an immediate meeting. He'd obtained one of the leaflets from the security office, read it while walking to the *Reichstag* and made his way up to the central meeting room. The others had already arrived and were seated around the table.

"This is a crisis," Karl Holliston said. The *Reichsführer-SS* had one of the leaflets unfolded in front of him and was glowering down at it. "Someone spread seditious propaganda in Berlin itself and escaped!"

Hans took a seat, forcing himself to remain calm. The SS - and the other security forces - would be embarrassed, if not humiliated, by the whole affair. He didn't blame them. It was physically impossible for them to patrol the entire *Reich*, let alone maintain a level of omnipresence second only to God's. Their control rested on fear, rested on the population believing that they might be under surveillance at any moment, that anything they said might be recorded and used in evidence against them at a later date. To have someone - or a small group of traitors - pull off such a coup in the centre of Berlin would call their capabilities into doubt.

"Let us not turn this molehill into a mountain," he said, as he dropped his own copy of the leaflet on the table. "Annoying as this is, it is a very minor issue."

"Any defiance of the *Reich* is a major issue," Holliston snapped. "By now, copies of this damnable tissue of lies are spreading through the city!"

Hans frowned. "They are?"

"*Yes,*" Holliston said. "Apparently, a number of copies were dropped into letterboxes all over Berlin. We've had at least a dozen handed in to the local police. This is not an isolated act of protest, but a calculated strike against the authority of the *Reich!*"

"So we track down the people responsible and eliminate them," Field Marshal Justus Stoffregen said. "That should not be too difficult."

"It may not be that easy," Hans said. He hadn't had long to think about the implications, but he *was* a veteran of countless political wars. "We need to treat this very carefully."

"We need to stamp on these traitors as hard as we can," Holliston insisted.

"It isn't that simple," Hans said. "How many leaflets were *not* handed in to the police?"

He pressed on before anyone could try to answer an unanswerable question. "This leaflet urges people to ask questions about other soldiers who have dropped out of contact, neither writing to their families nor returning home on leave," he said. "How many civilians in Berlin have relatives in South Africa, relatives who have seemingly vanished because we have not told their families about their conditions? It will not be long before people start putting together the full story."

"They are not encouraged to ask questions," Holliston said.

Hans gave him a sharp look. "You plan to keep two mothers from talking about their children? Or two housewives from worrying about their husbands? Right now, I imagine, word is spreading, no matter what we do about it. There is no way we can deny everything and expect to be believed."

"Radio Berlin can tell the *Reich* that the leaflets are talking nonsense," Holliston insisted.

"But they're *not* talking nonsense," Hans snapped back. "And the population will *know* they're not talking nonsense."

"Then we tell the population that the soldiers died in a good cause," Holliston said. "We shift our policy to honouring the dead and tending to the wounded!"

"That would add credence to the leaflet's claims," Field Marshal Gunter Voss said. "It would also make it look like we were allowing these... these *rebels* to dictate our actions."

Holliston scowled at him, angrily. "And they also want free elections to the *Reichstag*," he said. "Are we going to tamely surrender power?"

"We could give them what they want," Hans pointed out. "The *Reichstag* hasn't had any real power since 1944."

"The Nazi Party has governed this country since 1931," Holliston said. "In fifty-four years, we have risen to a position of global dominance our forefathers couldn't possibly have imagined. Our armies are the strongest in the world; our settlers are turning the wastelands of Russia and the Middle East into new civilisations. There is no reason to give power to a bunch of whining civilians who have done *nothing* to earn it."

Hans frowned, inwardly. There *was* a certain degree of social mobility in the *Reich*, either through the military, the SS or the Nazi Party bureaucracy. He'd started out as a young bureaucrat, after all, and Holliston - to give the devil his due - had been a brave stormtrooper who'd seen genuine action. But the odds of *anyone* reaching the *Reich* Council were staggeringly low and, by the time they actually reached high office, they would be so thoroughly ingrained with the ideals of their particular branch that they'd have trouble seeing anyone else's point of view. There were far too many bureaucrats, after all, who couldn't understand why small businesses were complaining about the tax burden.

"I think we have to admit," he said slowly, "that everything has just changed."

He tapped the leaflet with one finger. "We have been using trickery to hide the fact that the death rate in South Africa is alarmingly high - and that isn't the only thing we've been trying to hide. The state of our economy..."

"To hell with the economy," Holliston thundered.

"That's precisely where it's going," Hans said, mildly. "We have been robbing Peter to pay Paul for the last decade, using the loot from our conquests and our captive markets to paper over the cracks in the system. Now, we are running out of time; now, people are going to be asking questions; now, our *reaction* to those questions will only give the charges against us" - he tapped the leaflet again - "more credence. You know as well as I do that people talk, that word is going to spread through the *Reich*..."

He forced himself to calm down with an effort. "And *you* ordered the BDM girls to be corralled in the square," he added. "Just how many mothers do you think you panicked when they heard that their little girls were under arrest?"

"Those girls were helping to spread these damnable leaflets," Holliston said.

"There isn't a shred of evidence that the *official* BDM girls were doing anything other than handing out the standard propaganda leaflets," Hans said. *That* might have been a lucky break; he'd long suspected that no one actually bothered to *read* the leaflets, no matter what they might have been told at school. "They're not Jews, Karl. You can't arrest - even for a couple of hours - fifty-seven schoolgirls and expect no one to comment on it."

"I suggest," Voss said, "that we focus on the issue at hand. Do we have any leads at all?"

"We're working on it," Holliston said. "There have been some... *clashes* between the different organisations involved in securing Berlin. The SS should take the lead, but the *Gestapo* and the Order Police think differently. I propose that the SS should formally take command of the counter-rebel operation."

Hans frowned. The SS had lost control of the Order Police in the fifties, after Himmler had overreached himself. *No one* outside the SS - and quite a few factions within the SS - had been keen to see Himmler in sole control of the security services. And he wasn't blind to the implications of handing Karl Holliston so much power. He'd take what he could and then make it permanent, perhaps even using it to boost himself into supreme power. Had he even started handing out the leaflets in the first place? Hans wouldn't have put the thought past him.

And he may think I started it, he thought, morbidly. *But neither of us really wants to undermine the Reich itself.*

"We can discuss that later," he said. "What do we know?"

"The leaflets were distributed by at least three girls, all wearing BDM uniforms," Holliston said. "Only a couple of the witnesses were paying close attention; one reported a girl with long dark hair, another insisted he'd seen a blonde with a very large chest."

"The witness was a teenage boy, I assume," Voss said.

Hans fought to hide his smile. "It could easily have been a middle-aged man," he pointed out. "Was it?"

"It was a soldier, home from the wars," Holliston said, curtly. "As far as we can tell, all of the BDM girls who were trapped within the square were linked to matrons, so we believe that the fakes left the square before the alert was sounded and made their escape into the city. So far, we do not have any leads on just who spread the rest of the leaflets, but we are working on it. There aren't, however, many places the leaflets could have been printed."

Voss took the leaflet from the table and inspected it. "The paper is softer," he said. "Not absorbent enough to be useful, unfortunately, but it isn't a *perfect* copy."

Holliston gave him a sharp look. "A small printing shop could have done it," he said, "and we will follow them. However, the most likely place where the leaflets were produced is the university."

Hans swore under his breath. Holliston had always hated the university, hated how it brought American ideals into even a relatively small population of students. And yet it was necessary. No one knew better than Hans just how badly the *Reich* was falling apart, just how desperately they needed to reinvigorate their technological base. The students might be the only thing capable of saving the *Reich* from itself.

"We shut the university down," Holliston continued, "and investigate all the students for seditious leanings."

"That would do a great deal of damage to our already weakened economy," Hans pointed out, tartly. "The computer network alone would be badly hampered if we refused to allow university-taught experts to work on it. And without that..."

"Our forefathers didn't have a computer network," Holliston snapped.

"They weren't facing anyone who did, either," Hans countered. "The Americans have been leveraging their computer network and using it as the base for a whole new series of technological developments. If we shut our network down, as sparse as it is compared to the American design, we might as well shoot ourselves in the head and save time!"

"And yet we have to buy computers off the Americans," Holliston said. "How do we know we can even *trust* them?"

"The university will give us better computers in time," Hans said. It was an old argument, but the truth was that the United States had moved far ahead. Reverse-engineering some of the more advanced machines the *Reich* had... *obtained* from the US had proved impossible, while what computers the *Reich could* produce were unsellable outside the *Reich's* captive market. "We just need to give it time to flourish."

"You've been saying that for five years," Holliston reminded him.

"And what use," Hans asked, "could one get out of a five-year-old child?"

"I think we're moving away from the point," Voss said. "We don't have time to bicker when we need to come up with a response to these leaflets."

"That is correct," Field Marshal Stoffregen said. "Allow me to suggest a compromise."

Hans exchanged a look with Holliston, then nodded.

"Finding these rebels and rooting them out is a priority," Stoffregen continued, smoothly. Military officer or not, he wouldn't have reached high office without being a skilled politician. "At the same time, we have no proof that the university is involved in the affair - and we *do* need the university. Therefore, I propose that we do not act overtly against the university, but we also place control of the affair in the hands of the SS. This would, of course, be a short-term measure."

"That would be acceptable," Holliston said, after a moment. "But we do need to tighten up security, both on the university campus itself and the streets."

And you'll do your level best to make it a long-term measure, Hans thought, coldly. The hell of it was that he doubted he could argue against the suggestion. They would leave the university in peace, at least for the moment, in exchange for a short-term surrender of power to the SS. *And you can use that to take over the university or shut it down, given time.*

"Putting additional policemen on the streets might be a good idea," he said, carefully. "I would insist, however, that your people within the university be carefully trained in recognising the difference between student chatter and actual sedition."

"There's no time to train up additional agents," Holliston said. He leaned forward. "A strong and *visible* presence may deter students from *joining* the movement, even if it doesn't lead to any of the ringleaders."

"Who may not even be students at all," Hans snapped. He didn't fault Holliston for jumping to such a conclusion, but there was no proof. A cell within the Nazi Party itself could have produced the leaflets, then arranged to have them handed out. It wasn't beyond belief that some of his subordinates had actually decided to take matters into their own hands. "It was hard enough to build the university, Karl. We don't want it wrecked overnight."

"There is no need to import *Americanisms*," Holliston sneered. "We have always been at our strongest when we go back to basics."

"There's nothing *basic* about a Panzer tank," Hans snapped. "There's nothing basic about a radio, or vaccinations, or man-portable antiaircraft missiles. And the Americans are already ahead of us! How long will it be before they come up with something that gives them an unbeatable advantage?"

"You don't know that will happen," Holliston said.

"I doubt Fredrick the Great could have predicted the arrival of panzers," Hans pointed out, sharply. "And even if he had, could he have stopped a dozen panzers from ripping his army into little pieces?"

"We need to vote," Field Marshal Stoffregen said, before Holliston could come up with a biting retort. "All those in favour?"

———

It was, Karl Holliston conceded afterwards, a bitter victory.

He was not fool enough to believe, despite the prospects for winning the endless struggle for power in the *Reich*, that Hans Krueger was responsible for the leaflets, or for aiding and abetting their producers. Krueger, whatever his faults, wouldn't risk the fundamental balance of power that controlled the *Reich*. And that, Karl was sure, was true of everyone else who had a seat on the *Reich* Council. They simply had far too much to lose if social upheaval swept through the *Reich*.

But they were soft. And that softness was going to get them killed.

It *had* to be the university, he was sure. The SS, the military, even the party bureaucracy... none of them would tolerate the kind of free-thinkers it would take to gather the evidence, produce the leaflets and then distribute them to the masses. They'd have problems even recognising that the masses could be politically important. Hell, they *weren't* politically important. What did it matter if some workers wanted to form an independent union, or some housewives started demanding more rights, or schoolchildren wanted an end to the harsh discipline and relentless tutoring? There was nothing they could do about it, was there?

Karl had studied universities in America, back when he'd been mustering his objections to the whole concept. Yes, they did encourage the development of new technological ideas - he'd never tried to deny that - but they also encouraged the spread of *political* ideas. And some of those ideas could be very dangerous. The current racial melange that made up the United States was partly the work of American students, who'd fought to embrace *Untermenschen* to their bosom. Good German girls wouldn't even *think* of allowing themselves to be sullied by an *Untermensch*; American girls didn't think twice about dating and even marrying *Untermenschen* men. The Americans didn't even seem to realise just how badly they were damaging their own society...

And Japan is the worst of America, Karl thought. It still made him shudder, every time he thought about just how deeply the races had blended together, just how the once-proud white stock that had tamed America had been diluted by the intrusion of Japanese blood. *They will not be allowed to spread their perversions over here.*

But it had to be the university students, he told himself. No other group in Germany could combine an awareness of their surroundings with a political naivety that would urge them to try to spread the word. There was simply no one else so foolish, so free of the ever-present listening ears - and besides, if students could cause long-term political damage in America, perhaps they would think they could do the same in the Third *Reich*.

He kept his face expressionless as the meeting finally came to an end, giving him the chance to hurry back to his office. The *Gestapo* and the Order Police, for once, would have to take orders from the SS, orders that would lead them right to the rebels. And if the rebels proved harder to find than he expected...

It might be time to start coming up with some contingency plans, he thought. Silently, he started drawing up some possible concepts. *Plans that will stamp on the rebels once and for all.*

CHAPTER SEVENTEEN

Berlin
29 July 1985

"Do you all understand your objectives?"

Leutnant der Polizei Herman Wieland nodded hastily. He'd gone into the station after the acrimonious family dinner, only to be told to bed down in the barracks and wait for orders, along with the rest of his squad. By the time they'd been awoken and told to shower, shave and get into fresh uniforms, it was the following morning; oddly, he was almost relieved that he wouldn't be going home until he'd had a chance to find out what was actually going on and, perhaps, find out if he should hand over the cursed leaflet to his superiors. But the briefing hadn't been very detailed and, according to rumour, the one policeman who'd made the mistake of admitting receipt of one of the leaflets had been hauled out of the station and interrogated by the SS. Herman had quietly promised himself that he'd dump the leaflet he'd left at home as soon as he returned from work.

"Get into your vans," the captain ordered, curtly. "Go."

Herman hurried out of the station and clambered into the van, followed by a dozen other Order Policemen who were checking their pistols, truncheons, handcuffs and radios as they readied themselves for the operation. There was no talking in the rear of the vehicle as the engine roared to life; they knew, all too well, that they might be running straight into an ambush. Herman was old enough to remember the *Gastarbeiter* riots and the last gasps of the French Resistance, when thousands of people - the innocent along with the guilty - had been rounded up and marched to the camps. The leaflet-writers knew they couldn't expect mercy from the *Reich*. They'd be more likely to try to kill as many policemen as possible before being gunned down themselves.

He shuddered, inwardly, as he checked his own weapons. The briefing had asserted that the leaflets had been spread by *Gastarbeiters*, men and women who had come to Germany to work. It was unlikely a *Gastarbeiter* had actually *written* the leaflet - for once, Herman was inclined to agree with the SS officer who'd briefed them - but that didn't absolve the *Gastarbeiters* of their role in the scheme. They should know better than to cross the authorities, he reminded himself; they had no rights, no legal protections, if a pureblood German swore out a complaint against them. A *Gastarbeiter* who ran into trouble with the law would be lucky if he was *only* dispatched to the east and put to work building the giant *autobahns* that were slowly opening up eastern Russia to German settlements.

The vehicle lurched violently as the driver turned on the siren, clearing civilian traffic out of their way as they drove into the suburbs. Herman gritted his teeth - he preferred driving to sitting in the back of the van - and tried not to think about what might be lying in wait for them. But his thoughts kept straying to Gudrun, to the beautiful and clever daughter he didn't really understand. Marlene and Hanne - his sisters - had been content to marry well and become housewives, tending the house and bringing up a small flock of children, but Gudrun? She wanted to be something more, something *masculine*. Herman would have forbidden her from attending the university, he knew now, if he'd realised just what it would do to her. She was trying to slip away from becoming a wife and mother and...

... And what? It would only bring her heartbreak.

Herman winced, inwardly. There were few jobs for women in the *Reich*, particularly young and fertile women who could have married and had children instead of trying to compete with the men. Gudrun's only real hope lay in computers - the strange devices imported from the United States - and, even then, the big companies would be reluctant to hire a young girl who wasn't married. The only fields completely open to women were nursing and the never-to-be-sufficiently-damned BDM. He tried to imagine Gudrun as a BDM matron and shuddered at the thought. His daughter was too sweet, too caring, too compassionate to develop the sadism required of a matron. Gudrun would never bully young girls, he was sure; she'd never force overweight girls to stand in the centre of the room and hold back tears as they were mocked by their fellows. The very thought was absurd.

And if she graduated, he asked himself, *who would want to marry her?*

It was an odd thought, but true. What sort of man would want to marry a woman who had more qualifications than himself? Gudrun might be doomed to permanent spinsterhood merely by having a useless scrap of paper, a qualification she couldn't use because she was a woman. Herman had approved of Konrad - he didn't have the arrogance that typified SS stormtroopers - but would he still want Gudrun after she graduated? And what would she have done if Konrad had refused to allow her to work? It was his right, as her husband, to decide if his wife *could* work. What would Gudrun have done if he'd told her to stay at home and have his babies?

I shouldn't have let her go to the university, he thought, as the vehicle lurched again. *She will only think she can be more than a housewife...*

Caius tapped his shoulder. "We're going to be there in two minutes," he said. "Wake up!"

"I wasn't sleeping," Herman muttered, as he sat upright. The other policemen looked as tired and wary as he felt. "Are you ready?"

"They should have sent in the stormtroopers," Caius said. "God knows what we might encounter."

"Politics," Fritz said. He had relatives in high places, Herman had heard, although they clearly couldn't be bothered to boost Fritz's career. "They don't want to put the SS in *complete* control of the investigation."

Herman fought down the urge to roll his eyes like a child. It was flatly illegal for a *Gastarbeiter* to own a gun - and gun control within the *Reich* was strict - but there had been a thriving trade in weapons shipped in from France and Russia for decades. They might just run into a terrorist cell with rifles and machine guns... and, as the terrorists would have nothing to lose, they'd sell their lives dearly. Putting the thought aside, he checked his pistol as the vehicle came to a halt, then followed Fritz and Caius though the metal doors and into the cold morning air. The *Gastarbeiter* barracks were right in front of them, a pair of armed guards at the gatehouse staring at the policemen in surprise.

"Arrest them too," the Captain ordered. "And then get the *Gastarbeiters* under control."

"Here we go," Caius commented.

Herman gave him a sharp look as the armed policemen hurried through the gates and down towards the barracks. It was a solid building, reminding him of his military service; indeed, the only real difference between the army barracks and the *Gastarbeiter* barracks was that there was only one set of doors, right at the front of the concrete building. The *Gastarbeiters* would have problems getting out, if there was a fire, but no one really gave a damn about their safety. They were hired for grunt labour, nothing more; there was an infinite supply of Frenchmen and women who would come to work in the *Reich*, even though the pay was poor and the conditions were dreadful. Herman wouldn't have given two rusty *Reichmarks* for their future. Vichy France wasn't about to complain if a few hundred *Gastarbeiters* were unceremoniously shipped east so they could be worked to death.

They passed through a small office - the corporation that controlled the *Gastarbeiters* had a habit of hiring them out for private commissions - and opened the metal door that led into the barracks itself. Herman wrinkled his nose at the smell of too many men in close proximity - the *Gastarbeiters* didn't have regular showers, unlike the men in his former unit - and then cocked his pistol as the *Gastarbeiters* jumped up, some of them cracking their heads on the upper bunks. Their eyes were wide with fear.

Untermenschen, Herman thought. He couldn't help noticing that some of the men were so poor they had to sleep in their work clothes - or in the nude, despite the cold. Many of them were scarred, suggesting they'd been whipped at some point in the non-too-distant past. He relaxed, slightly, as he realised there wouldn't be a fight. *Men without the spirit to try to resist.*

"GET UP," the Captain bellowed, as the policemen spread out. "HANDS IN THE AIR; HANDS IN THE AIR!"

Herman watched, feeling his hands grow sweaty around his pistol. If there was going to be any resistance, it was going to be now... but the Frenchmen showed no signs of being willing to fight. He smirked, remembering his father's stories of how the *Wehrmacht* had marched through France, sowing their oats in the wombs of French maidens as they passed. His father had told him that Frenchmen were always cowards and Herman hadn't seen much, in his military and police career, to suggest differently.

The Captain barked more orders. Herman, Caius and Fritz got the job of stripping, handcuffing and searching the *Gastarbeiters* one by one, while other policemen searched the barracks or headed off to find the corporate officials responsible for supervising the *Gastarbeiters*. There was no resistance, even when Herman used a knife to remove clothes and pushed the prisoners out into the cold morning air, where they squatted on the ground and awaited their fate passively. The only moment of excitement came when a policeman found a small packet of German chocolates hidden within a bedroll, probably stolen from a German shop. Herman was almost disappointed with the lack of action by the time the prisoner vans arrived from the station. The *Gastarbeiters* were herded into the vans, their hands still cuffed, and told to sit down. No one would care if they suffocated inside the vehicles before they reached the station.

"You'll be escorting them to the processing camp," the Captain said. "The SS will take them from there."

"Understood," Herman said.

He nodded to Caius and led the way to the nearest van, where they clambered up beside the driver. The stench of unwashed bodies was strong, despite the air conditioning; he forced himself to breathe through his mouth as the driver started the engine and drove back onto the streets. So early in the morning, there was almost no traffic in the suburbs. He smiled to himself as they drove past another set of barracks - they'd be having their own visits from the police soon enough - and then past one of the brothels. A handful of bleary-looking soldiers were staggering out of the door, clearly somewhat the worse for wear. The sight brought back happy memories of his own premarital days.

"They'll be in deep shit when they get back to the barracks," Caius predicted. "I bet you ten *Reichmarks* they overslept in the arms of a whore or two."

"No bet," Herman said.

His lips curved into a smile. Soldiers were allowed to slack off for a few weeks after Victory Day - it was why Kurt was still at home, rather than in the barracks with his unit - but there were limits. He suspected that some *Oberfeldwebel* would make them regret they'd ever been born after they staggered back through the barracks, if they were lucky. Being officially charged with desertion would probably get them sent to a punishment battalion somewhere in the east.

"Approaching the camp," the driver said. "You want to get out first and check the prisoners?"

Herman nodded as they passed through two sets of gates and came to a halt beside the entry building. A handful of SS stormtroopers were already waiting, one of them eying the police vehicles with barely-concealed contempt. Herman shook his head - there was little room for elegance in police transports - and clambered out of the cab, jumping down neatly to the hard concrete ground. The SS stormtrooper threw a sharp salute and nodded to the rear of the transport.

"These the *Untermenschen?*"

"Yes," Herman said. As if *regular* prisoners were ever brought to the SS camps. "They're cuffed and naked."

The driver flicked a switch in the cab, unlocking the rear of the van. The SS troops threw open the doors, then recoiled at the stench. Several of the prisoners had fouled themselves, clearly convinced they were going to die. Others were lying on the floor, seemingly unconscious or dead. Herman sighed inwardly - dead prisoners would mean more paperwork when he got back to the station - and watched as the stormtroopers ordered the living prisoners to climb out of the van, one by one. Naked, bound; they were prodded through the gates by rifle barrels and into the building, where they would be processed and then made to wait until their fates were decided.

Untermenschen, he thought, again. None of the prisoners seemed capable of offering even the slightest resistance - and a handful were crying. *There isn't a real man amongst them.*

Caius elbowed him as another van passed through the gates and came to a halt. "You think we can slip back to the station once the prisoners are handed over?"

"We might have to wash out the van first," Herman muttered, resentfully. Prisoners fouling themselves was not unusual - and no one really cared if a couple died on the way to the jail - but it wasn't as if *they* had to clean up the mess. "You just *know* who'll inspect the vehicles this evening."

Caius opened his mouth to answer, then stopped and stared as the second van was opened and the prisoners marched into the camp. They were all women, as naked as the day they were born, their hands cuffed behind their backs. Herman stared, despite himself; they looked to be maids, young women hired to assist German housewives after they turned out their fourth child and earned the *Mutterkreuz*. Adelinde had flatly refused to allow one in her house, even though she was technically qualified to have one; Herman didn't know if his wife feared *he* might fancy the girl or if Adelinde's father would play games with her...

And what sort of message would it send to the children, he asked himself, *if I played around with the maid right in front of their mother?*

"*Untermenschen*," the SS stormtrooper said. "Such whores can never be good Germans."

Herman nodded. It wasn't safe to disagree. Besides, back when he'd been in the military, there had been strict regulations banning relationships with *Untermenschen* women. He'd regarded them as a killjoy - far too many other soldiers had felt the same way - but the Race Classification Bureau had made it clear that good German genes were not to be introduced to the Slavs. There were so many Slavs that even a small handful of German-Slav hybrids might allow them to fight and win a war against the *Reich*.

He pushed the thought to the back of his mind as he scrambled back into the van - once the last of the girls was through the gates and into the processing centre - and they were driven back to the station. He'd hoped for a break, but instead he was ordered to supervise a handful of German prisoners - the corporate officials who owned the *Untermenschen* - and watch as they were interrogated by the SS. Herman couldn't help feeling a little sorry for them, even though they were unwilling participants in treason. They might be released, if they weren't guilty of actually writing the damn leaflets themselves, but it would cast a long shadow over the rest of their lives. They would probably find themselves exiled to the east.

"Get a bite to eat," the Captain said, when the last of the prisoners was finally escorted down to the cells and locked in. "And then report to my office in thirty minutes."

Herman and Caius exchanged looks, then hurried down to the canteen and hastily ate a quick snack before heading back up to the Captain's office. There were hardly any policemen in the corridors as they walked up the stairs. It looked, very much, as though most of the policemen attached to the station were out on the streets or supervising prisoners. Herman shuddered inwardly at the thought of one of them searching his house - he reminded himself, again, to destroy the leaflet as soon as he returned home - and knocked on the

Captain's open door. The Captain was sitting behind his desk, examining a set of folders, while Fritz was sitting in front of him.

"Come in," the Captain said. "I have a specific job for you."

Herman nodded and took the proffered seat. Caius sat next to him.

"We have not learned much," the Captain said, shortly. "The *Gastarbeiters* were apparently hired to hand out the leaflets by a person who remains unidentified. There are no pictures available of this individual and the descriptions we have are so imprecise that it is impossible to narrow down the field. Most of the fingerprints on the leaflets belong to the *Gastarbeiters* or the Germans who handed them in. However, we may have had one lucky break. One of the fingerprints matched an individual on file."

Herman leaned forward, feeling his heart starting to race. Fingerprints were not altogether reliable, but if they'd matched one fingerprint to the files... they might just have caught the ringleader. And that would mean promotion...

"*Herr Doctor Professor* Claus Murken," the Captain said. He picked up one of the files and passed it to Herman. "Professor of Computer Studies at Albert Speer University."

Caius smiled. "And you want this man arrested, *Herr Hauptmann?*"

"I do," the Captain confirmed. "Arrest him and bring him to the station, now."

CHAPTER EIGHTEEN

Albert Speer University, Berlin
29 July 1985

Gudrun had been relieved when she'd woken up and discovered, as she helped her mother make breakfast, that her father had had to stay at the station overnight. It wasn't common - her father normally worked from nine till five and then headed straight home - but it was a relief. Kurt might have spoken to their father for her, yet she'd been dreading their next meeting. Walking out of the house, carrying her bag of university books, had left her with the sensation that she was escaping a destiny mapped out by someone else. By the time she reached the university itself, she felt almost as if there was nothing she couldn't do.

Horst met her by the gates. "There's a lot of chatter," he said, as Gudrun flushed with embarrassment. She'd kissed him - and she would have gone further, if he'd let her. "Just remember to be careful what you say."

"Of course," Gudrun said, a little tartly. Part of her would have been relieved if she'd never seen Horst again, even though she was sure he wouldn't tell anyone about the kiss. But she needed to ask him and the others why the leaflets had been distributed far more widely than she'd expected. "Can we sneak up to the meeting room?"

"Better to wait for a while," Horst said, as they stepped through the gates. "The entire university is buzzing."

He was right, Gudrun discovered. Students were talking in small groups about the leaflets, comparing notes about soldiers who'd gone to South Africa and dropped out of contact; fathers, brothers and friends who seemed to have vanished. Gudrun listened, careful not to say too much, as the chatter grew stronger; hundreds of students, it seemed, were realising for the first time that they'd been told lies by the state. And, the more they compared notes, the clearer the picture became.

They can't arrest everyone, she told herself. She had no idea if that was actually true, but there were over two thousand students in the university itself, all with friends and family who would be upset if they were arrested. *They can't take us all away, can they?*

She shuddered, remembering Grandpa Frank's words. The *Reich* had slaughtered untold millions - perhaps billions - of human beings, men and women who weren't so different from the Germans themselves. It was a crime so vast as to be almost beyond her comprehension, an atrocity so stagger-ing that it would be easy to believe it had never happened. And yet, reading between the lines, it was clear that it *had* happened. Grandpa Frank might have told her what he'd seen, but... but she'd read the books and noted carefully what they *didn't* say.

"My father wasn't too pleased," she muttered to Horst. "He was demand-ing to know when I'd get married and out of his house."

Horst shrugged. "Fathers are like that," he said. "Mine certainly told me I'd be expected to marry as soon as I decently could, no matter what I did with my life."

Gudrun shook her head, tiredly, as they made their way to the classrooms. Konrad was unlikely to recover, but her father didn't know that. Not yet. As long as he thought she was engaged to Konrad - or close to engaged - he wouldn't insist that she looked for another suitable husband. But once he found out the truth, he would tell her to find someone or to allow him to suggest potential candidates. Her stomach turned at the thought of who her father would consider suitable. A boring man, she was sure; a man who'd want a housewife and nothing more. And her father would keep shoving candidates at her until she gave in...

She looked at Horst, thoughtfully. He was handsome enough, she sup-posed; strong, smart - he'd have to be to get into the university - and all-too-aware of what she was doing instead of studying. Marriage to him wouldn't be too bad, but she'd have to go to the east once she finished her studies... unless he decided to stay in the west with her. She opened her mouth to ask him what he'd do, then dismissed the thought. It was unlikely in the extreme that they'd live long enough to get married and make a future together.

Horst gave her an odd look. "Are you all right?"

"It's just... it's just the *excuse*," Gudrun lied. They'd called their periods *the excuse* in the BDM. Horst frowned, then blushed with embarrassment. Gudrun couldn't help smiling, despite her own embarrassment. Konrad had affected a selective deafness whenever female issues were mentioned. "I'll be better soon, I'm sure."

"I'm sure of it," Horst agreed. He gave her a bland smile. "Gudrun, I..."

He broke off as a rustle ran through the students behind them. Gudrun turned and saw a trio of green-clad Order Policemen making their way through the crowd, their mere presence parting the students as effectively as Moses had parted the Red Sea. Horst caught her arm and gently pulled her out of the way, slipping down a side corridor as the policemen walked past their position. Gudrun tensed as she realised one of them was her father. Had he come to look for her? Or had he been called to the university on other business?

"That's my father," she breathed. Panic started to bubble up within her mind. "Horst..."

"Remain calm," Horst whispered. Students were scattering in all directions, unwilling to risk doing anything that might draw attention from the policemen. "Just..."

He looked around, then drew her into an alcove. "We need to see what they're doing here," he added, at her bemused look. "Or do you want to run and hide?"

Gudrun, stung, drew herself up to her full height. "If he's here for me," she said, "is there any point in hiding?"

"Probably not," Horst said, after a moment. "But if he *was* here for you, why would he bring two of his friends?"

———

Herman had never set foot in the university before, not even when Gudrun had been accepted as a student. Parents weren't meant to supervise their children's education and, while the university had thrown out many traditions, it had made sure to keep *that* one. Indeed, Herman had only visited his children's schools after the teachers had complained about their behaviour. Kurt had often been in trouble for fighting and Johan, it seemed, was going the same way.

Good for him, Herman thought, as he made his way through the corridors. He'd never been in the building before, but there were helpful signs everywhere. *A fighter is better than a coward.*

The university struck him as *odd.* It was nothing like a school; indeed, the mandatory portraits of Hitler and the Reich Cabinet were at a bare minimum, while the walls were covered with bright maps, abstract paintings that looked as though someone had splashed ink randomly on paper and photographs of spacecraft, space stations and the tiny base on the moon. Kurt had wanted to be an astronaut, Herman recalled; he'd been disappointed for weeks after he failed to get into the air force, the first step towards flying into space. Johan had been talking about being the first man on Mars too...

And this place is where they design the next generation of spacecraft, he thought, as he paused in front of a drawing of a massive space rocket. It looked too big to be realistic, unless there was something special about the rocket drive; the tiny image of a teenage boy, a sea captain and a bald professor at the bottom caught his eye for a long moment. *Maybe Johan will fly that rocket into space.*

He pushed the thought aside as they walked on until they reached the computer labs and stepped through the door. Inside, there were fifty computers lined up in neat rows, dozens of students sitting in front of them tapping on keyboards. Their eyes went wide as they saw the policemen, guilt written all over their faces. Herman smirked inwardly - everyone, it seemed, remembered guilty secrets when they saw a policeman - and raked the room with his eyes, searching for *Herr Doctor Professor* Claus Murken. The Professor was standing behind a female student - Herman was irrationally grateful it wasn't Gudrun - one hand resting on her shoulder as he explained something to her.

"*Herr Doctor Professor* Claus Murken," he said, as the policemen stepped forward. Murken didn't *look* dangerous, but they had strict orders to bring him in alive and relatively unharmed. "You are under arrest."

Murken's eyes widened in shock. He offered no resistance as he was roughly searched and his hands were cuffed behind his back. Herman had been curious to discover what a professor of computer studies might carry in his pockets - he'd tried reading one of Gudrun's books and found it completely beyond his understanding - but Murken wasn't carrying any-thing apart from a pair of pencils, an American-made pocket calculator and a tiny device Herman couldn't identify. He bagged everything, then nodded to Fritz and Caius, who frog-marched the professor through the door and out into the corridor.

Herman braced himself as they marched past a number of students. Many of them had their faces frozen in the expressionless masks they learned as children, when showing the wrong emotion could lead to a beating or worse, but a number were staring in horror - and hatred, even though it could be dangerous. Herman was tempted to snap and snarl at them as they passed, or to drag them in for interrogation, yet he knew it would be pointless. Instead, he merely ignored the students, counting on their uniforms to clear a pathway for them. It worked; no one barred their way as they half-carried the shocked professor through the corridors and out through the gates. They'd get Murken back to the station, where the SS would interrogate him harshly.

"I didn't do anything," Murken said. "I didn't..."

"I'm sure," Herman snapped. He felt a flicker of guilt as they walked past a pair of female students, both of whom stared in horror. Murken wasn't big enough to justify carrying him around like a drunken soldier. But he knew they had no choice. "The SS will be the judge of that."

———

Gudrun had *liked* Professor Murken. He was always friendly, always willing to explain some of the more difficult concepts and, unlike some of the other pro-fessors, never seemed willing to assume that a girl was automatically nowhere near as capable as a boy. She'd hoped he'd tutor her when she entered her second year of computer studies. But now, her father and two burly policemen were carrying him out of the university, in cuffs. She felt sick as she watched them go by, her father bringing up the rear... she shrank back into the shadows as they passed, hoping and praying that her father didn't see her.

They came and took the professor, she thought, numbly. She'd half-expected to be arrested herself, or to watch helplessly as some of her friends were marched away; she'd never expected to see Professor Murken arrested by her father. *Why did they arrest him?*

"They arrested him," she muttered, once the policemen were out of earshot. If her father had seen her, and he might have done, he'd shown no sign of it. "Why did they arrest him?"

"I don't know," Horst muttered back. "But we'd better get into class."

Gudrun gave him a nasty look as they made their way down the corridor. "How can you be so calm?"

"There's nothing to be gained by panicking," Horst pointed out. "The professor knows nothing and he's quite valuable, so I'm sure he will be released soon enough."

"I hope you're right," Gudrun said. "But if you're wrong..."

She left the thought unfinished. They'd poked the authorities in their collective eye - and now they were angry. Her father might be the *face* of authority - and he had complete authority over *her* and her siblings - but he wouldn't be the one making the *real* decisions, not after her little group had embarrassed the entire state. The Reich Council would be angry and humiliated and... and who knew what they'd do? They might consider the professor an acceptable scapegoat for the leaflets - or they might genuinely believe that he'd been involved in the plot.

And we sent copies of the leaflets through the computer network, she thought, as her blood ran cold. *They might well have good reason to blame the professor.*

Classes, not entirely to her surprise, were a joke. The professors were clearly nervous; the students were chattering away in small groups, telling one another what they'd seen when the policemen had entered the university. Gudrun did her best to keep her head down by reading her book, waiting for a chance to meet up with her friends after lunch. The professor dismissed class early, to her mingled dismay and relief. They'd learned nothing - and they had exams coming up in a matter of months.

Not that exams will matter that much, she thought, as they ate lunch and headed for the study room. *If we get caught, I'll be lucky if I get exiled to the east.*

"They must have taken the professor's fingerprint from one of the leaflets," Horst said, once the door was closed and the bug was neutralised by bad American music. "He was the one who loaded the printer, I suspect. They took his fingerprint and assumed it was one of ours."

Gudrun swallowed. "Is there anything we can do about that?"

"Not unless you want to be arrested yourself," Sven said. "We should just count ourselves lucky that the professor knows nothing."

"But he's innocent," Gudrun protested.

"They'll find that out while they're interrogating him," Horst reassured her, again. "But for the moment, we can only consider our next move."

Sven took a breath. "We sent copies of the leaflet to every email address in the *Reich*," he said, "and worked additional copies into some of the more complex computer programs in existence. They may wipe the first set from the network, but the second set will be resent every Sunday until a genuine computer expert removes them completely. It will take some time for them to even realise there is a problem."

"A week, to be precise," Isla added.

"More or less," Sven said. "There have been some covert messages exchanged on the network, Gudrun, and promises to share the leaflets widely across the *Reich*."

"I heard that copies were found on trains and aircraft," Günter said. "Word is spreading, is it not?"

"Yes, it is," Gudrun said. "How did the leaflets get so far?"

"I believe some people took them, read them and dumped them," Horst said, calmly. "And the more people who read them, the better."

"We did ask readers to pass on the leaflets as quickly as possible," Sven agreed. He sounded surprisingly cheerful. "They might just be taking us at our word."

"That's good," Gudrun said. She held up a hand. "What do we do now?"

"Nothing," Horst said.

Günter stared at him. "You think we should do *nothing?*"

"Yes," Horst said, unabashed. "Right now, the security services will be on the alert. I would be surprised if we don't get a few dozen new spies inserted into the university, now they think they can pin everything on poor Professor Murken. Anything we do may be noticed and lead back to us. We keep our heads down and wait for an opportunity to spread the word still further."

Gudrun frowned. "But shouldn't we strike while the iron is hot?"

"We're more likely to be struck," Horst countered. "Besides, what are we going to do?"

"We don't have any weapons," Leopold pointed out. "But we could get some, couldn't we?"

"We'd be smashed flat in an instant if we tried an armed uprising," Horst said, curtly. "I thought you would have learned that in the Hitler Youth!"

"So we keep pressing the issue," Gudrun said. "I could go to Konrad's father and ask him about the leaflets, convincing him to go demand answers about the fate of his son..."

"It might be dangerous," Horst warned her. "He could report you to your father - or the SS."

"We've already crossed the line," Gudrun snapped. "If we can't do anything spectacular, Horst, we can at least try to do something on a smaller scale."

"I suppose," Horst said. "But, right now, they *will* be wary. We need to be wary too."

He was right, Gudrun knew, but it galled her. She didn't want to admit it, yet she had a sense that time - her time - was running out. Maybe, just maybe, it would be better *not* to go visit Konrad's family, not to ask his father to demand answers. Because, once they *got* an answer, Gudrun's father would start insisting she looked for another potential husband...

He could at least give me time to mourn, she thought, bitterly.

"We could talk to our mothers," Hilde offered, shyly. "My mother hosts bake sales and dozens of other activities. She's involved in *everything*. She might well start asking questions of her friends."

"That's a possibility," Gudrun agreed. Hilde's mother was the kind of person who pulled *everyone* into her orbit. "My mother might be interested, if she were invited... so might Konrad's mother."

Horst nodded in agreement. "The SS would have problems if they tried to round up mothers running bake sales," he said. "There'd be a riot."

Gudrun nodded. "But be careful," she warned. "Not all of our families are going to be happy when we start asking questions - and suggesting that *they* ask questions."

"Everyone knows about the leaflets now," Sven said. "The risk may not be as great as you think."

"I hope you're right," Horst said. "But be careful. Be *very* careful. Because if we are caught, we will be killed."

CHAPTER NINETEEN

Reichssicherheitshauptamt (RHSA), Berlin
30 July 1985

"You're late."

"Yes, *Mein Herr*," Horst said. The summons to the RHSA had come at an inconvenient time and he'd been forced to come up with an excuse on the spur of the moment. "I offer no excuses."

"I'm pleased to hear it," *Standartenfuehrer* Erdmann Schwarzkopf said, sarcastically. "There is nothing more important than serving the *Reich*."

"Yes, *Mein Herr*," Horst said. "However, if I were to act suspiciously, the other students might regard me as a potential spy."

Schwarzkopf eyed him for a long moment, then nodded and turned to lead the way down the corridor. Horst followed him, feeling nervous; he hadn't been summoned to the RHSA since he'd first come to Berlin, a year before he'd entered the university for the first time. Any citizen of Germany would feel worried at the thought of entering the building, knowing that the doors could slam shut at any moment, but Horst knew he had reason to be afraid. If his superiors had figured out what he'd done, he'd die slowly and painfully.

They don't know anything, he reassured himself, as they entered the interrogation section and walked past a handful of unmarked doors. *If they knew something, I would be in one of these rooms already.*

"We interrogated the professor quite extensively," Schwarzkopf said. "He knew nothing, it seems. It was a dead end."

Horst kept his face impassive, even though Schwarzkopf was in front of him. Who knew *who* was watching through a hidden camera? "The professor was quite an important man," he said, flatly. "Killing him will have unfortunate consequences."

"The professor will not be returning to the university," Schwarzkopf said, coldly. "His future is none of your concern."

"Yes, *Mein Herr*," Horst said. There was no point in pressing the issue. As a good son of the east, he was meant to disdain computers and other American toys. "I…"

"Officially, he will have retired," Schwarzkopf added, cutting Horst off. "No one will know any differently."

They reached a small office and stepped inside. Schwarzkopf shut the door firmly, gestured to a chair and sat down on the other side of an empty desk. It wouldn't be his real office, Horst knew; it was just a place to talk to the agents he handled, a place they'd never be able to describe if they ran into trouble. Personally, Horst thought Schwarzkopf was uncomfortably paranoid, but even paranoids had enemies. Besides, it *was* good tradecraft.

"The students know, of course," Schwarzkopf said. It wasn't a question. "How are they taking it?"

Horst took a moment to compose his answer. *He* wouldn't be the only spy, of course; there would be others monitoring the university and if his answers didn't match theirs, he would be in deep trouble. The only evidence that he was the *only* spy in Gudrun's group was the simple fact that none of them had been arrested yet, not after they'd started distributing leaflets. Horst rather doubted that anyone, even Schwarzkopf, would allow a tiny rebel group to get that far.

"They are asking questions, *Mein Herr*," he said, finally. "Many of them have family or friends who are currently serving in South Africa and quite a few have dropped out of contact with their relatives. They thought nothing of it until they realised that other families had had the same experience. *Then* they started wondering what *else* they might have been told that was also a lie."

"Questions," Schwarzkopf repeated. "You *have* attempted to distract them, of course?"

"I have tried," Horst lied. "However, *Mein Herr*, the public arrest of a popular professor has only given the leaflets credence. I do not believe there is any way to stop the spread of the rumours."

Schwarzkopf's face darkened. "That is not good."

"No, *Mein Herr*," Horst agreed. "However, the students need to focus on passing their exams. They may well lose interest if the matter is allowed to die."

"Perhaps," Schwarzkopf said. He didn't sound convinced, unsurprisingly. "Do you know who might have written the leaflets?"

"*Mein Herr*, there are too many students with relatives who are in South Africa," Horst said, seriously. "I have no proof that any of them are responsible for writing the leaflets, let alone passing them out in the streets. I will, of course, keep my ears open."

"You'll do more than that," Schwarzkopf said. "First, we expect you to find and infiltrate the rebel group. We believe a small cabal of students was behind the leaflets."

That, Horst had to admit, was frighteningly accurate. He'd assumed they would deduce as much, to be fair, but... he couldn't help feeling a shiver running down his back. Gudrun might be in more danger than she knew. And yet, with a policeman for a father and an SS boyfriend, she didn't actually match the pattern of a rebellious student. Horst himself fitted the pattern better than she did.

And I am a rebel, he thought, with a flicker of wry amusement. *The pattern fits.*

He cleared his mind as he looked up at his handler. "Why a small group of students?"

"A large group would be easy to notice," Schwarzkopf pointed out, dryly. "We're looking, I suspect, for three or four students, close friends or family. Probably students with relatives in South Africa. We expect you to find that group and root it out."

"I will do my best, *Mein Herr*," Horst said. He'd have to seriously consider betraying a handful of uninvolved students, if only to give himself cover. By now, he was sure, there would be hundreds of other small groups in the university. "If the group can be found, I will find it."

"Good," Schwarzkopf said. "Your second task, however, is harder. We intend to insert more agents into the university. You will be responsible for assisting them to blend into the student population."

Horst kept his face expressionless with an effort. "It isn't easy to blend in with the other students," he warned. "I only fit in so well because I *am* a student. Anyone else would have problems fooling any of the other students."

Schwarzkopf's eyes narrowed. "Why?"

"You were trained as an SS officer," Horst said, carefully. "From the moment you entered Wewelsburg Castle as a new recruit, you were steeped in the history and traditions of the SS, everything from songs to precisely how to stand when inspected by a superior officer. You aren't posing as an SS officer, you *are* an SS officer. Every little detail confirms your identity as one of us. Could a civilian, even one with the correct uniform, mimic you so precisely that they'd fool a *genuine* SS officer?"

"Of course not," Schwarzkopf said, flatly. "They wouldn't be quite *right*."

"Nor would your agents," Horst said. "The university isn't a parade ground, *Mein Herr*, or an army barracks. Your agents would stand out like a nude woman in the middle of the Victory Day parade. The only way to pass as a student is to *be* a student."

"You could prepare them," Schwarzkopf said.

"Not in less than six months," Horst said. "They'd need to unlearn a great deal, *Mein Herr*."

"But we have orders to insert more agents," Schwarzkopf said. "You'll just have to try your best."

"Associating with them may blow *my* cover," Horst warned. Unless he was underestimating the SS agents, Gudrun and the other students would have no difficulty identifying the spies and isolating them. Newcomers in the middle of term would raise more than enough eyebrows. "I'd have to be put in a position where I would be forced to work with them."

"That can be arranged," Schwarzkopf said. "Now, here's what we want you to look out for..."

———

"He knew nothing," the interrogator said.

Reichsführer-SS Karl Holliston peered through the one-way mirror. *Herr Doctor Professor* Claus Murken sat in a metal chair, his naked body strapped to the metal and his face battered into a bloody pulp. The interrogators had been quite precise, as always, combining physical torture with a brutal beating that rarely failed to drag answers out of uncooperative suspects. But it seemed as though it was nothing more than a waste of effort.

Either Murken had the ability to fool a pair of experienced interrogators or he was innocent all along.

Karl turned to look at the interrogator. "You're sure?"

"He was practically pissing in his pants as soon as we strapped him into the chair, *Herr Reichsführer*," the interrogator said. "It took us some time to actually focus on the leaflets because he wanted to confess to fucking two of his female students. But he knows nothing about the leaflets."

"I see," Karl said.

He gritted his teeth. It was possible that the professor was concealing something - he might have given up one piece of information to keep the rest hidden - but he had faith in his interrogators. Besides, he rather doubted a pampered university professor, a man who hadn't experienced real pain since the Hitler Youth, could have endured a torture session without breaking. The man really was disgustingly unfit. Karl took a look at his chest and shuddered at the thought of him huffing and puffing over a nubile young German maiden. No doubt he was on the verge of a heart attack every time he took off his trousers.

Torture worked, he'd been told, *if* the interrogators were careful to convince their subject that they would always be able to detect a lie. A proper session could take hours, with the interrogators confronting their subject - their *victim* - with what they knew about him, just so he would lose the habit of lying before they reached the questions they couldn't verify. But it could be maddeningly imperfect if the victim retained his presence of mind. The fact that the professor had confessed to seducing not one, but two students was a good sign he hadn't managed to keep himself under control, yet Karl knew he'd always have doubts. What if the bastard *had* managed to fool the interrogators?

"Take him to the cells and have the medics see to him," Karl ordered, finally. He could have killed a rebel out of hand - or handed him over to the *Reichstag* for a show trial - but there was no point in killing someone who had been scooped up by accident. "And make sure he knows he won't be returning to the university."

He strode out of the torture chamber before the interrogator could reply and headed up to his office, barely noticing the uniformed officers who saluted as he walked past. It was frustrating. The only lead they'd had was the fingerprint and that had turned into a damp squib. Whatever the professor was guilty of - and Karl was sure that everyone was guilty of *something* - it wasn't being involved with the rebels. And that meant... what? The professor's fingerprints being on the leaflet suggested the rebels studied under him, but there were over two thousand students at the university. Tracking down the true rebels would take a long time...

... But Karl was no longer sure they *had* time.

He stepped into his office and closed the door behind him, then sat down and forced himself to think. There *had* to be a way of locating the rebels quickly, before word spread further... if, of course, it hadn't already spread right across the *Reich*. The computer network was a security night-mare because it allowed instant communications right across the whole continent - the Americans had offered to link their network into the *Reich's* network, a thought that had made the SS have a collective fit - and word could spread to every email address in the country. And who knew where it would go after that?

His intercom buzzed. "*Herr Reichsführer*, the Territories Minister requests an interview at your earliest convenience," Maria said. "What would you like me to tell him?"

Karl frowned. "Tell him I'll see him in twenty minutes," he said. He had no idea what the Territories Minister would want with him, but it would dis-tract him from his thoughts about the future. "And have a pot of coffee sent in when he arrives."

"Yes, *Herr Reichsführer*," Maria said.

And so another lead is gone, Karl thought, as he skimmed through the reports from the earlier interrogations. The *Gastarbeiters* had known nothing, of course, and they were now on their way to the great slave labour camps in the east. Their masters had taken the commission without checking it care-fully - let alone reading the leaflets - and had very little to offer to mitigate their crimes. They'd probably wind up in the camps themselves once the Reich Council met to confirm their fate. *And so we are left blind.*

He was still mulling it over when Marie showed Philipp Kuhnert, the Territories Minister, into his office. Kuhnert was an odd duck, caught perma-nently between the Finance Minister, the Foreign Minister and the SS; Karl respected Kuhnert, even though he didn't particularly like the man. It was his job to keep Germany's satellites in line, obedient to the will of the *Reich*, without provoking them into futile rebellion.

We should just take over, Karl thought, as he rose to his feet. The Ministry of Territory was no match for the SS, but its master was not to be despised. *Just make the French do as we tell them.*

"*Herr Reichsführer*," Kuhnert said, as Marie poured coffee for them both. "Thank you for seeing me at such short notice."

"It was my pleasure," Karl said. Marie retreated through the door, which she closed firmly behind her. "What can I do for you?"

"The leaflets have spread to France and Norway," Kuhnert said, flatly. "I don't expect trouble from the Norwegians, but the French may become a problem."

Karl swore under his breath. "The computer network?"

"Someone printed them off at the far end, then started to pass them around in a dozen cities," Kuhnert said. "Vichy caught a couple of distributors, but they escaped before they could be taken for interrogation."

"They escaped?" Karl asked. Losing prisoners was rare. It almost always spoke of gross incompetence - or a deliberate decision to allow the prisoners to flee. "How?"

"The French aren't saying," Kuhnert said. "But from what I picked up from my sources, they were simply allowed to escape by the security forces. Deliberately."

He leaned forward before Karl could say a word. "That's not the only problem," he added, grimly. "There's a rumour going around France that we're planning to send French troops to South Africa."

Karl let out a harsh bark of laughter. "Do they really expect us to send cowards to fight in a war?"

"The French lost - and lost badly - in 1940," Kuhnert said, calmly. "But they were betrayed by their leaders, not their fighting men. And now there are many Frenchmen wondering if the chance of freedom is worth the risk of death."

"Every time we have fought the French," Karl countered, "we have beaten them. We would have crushed France in 1914 if the British hadn't intervened and the Jews hadn't stabbed us in the back. They are not fool enough to lift a hand against us now."

"I'm not worried about them fighting us," Kuhnert said. "Vichy knows what will happen if they challenge us and yes, they will do whatever it takes to root out their own rebels so we won't do it for them. I'm more worried about the economic effects such rumours will have on our industry."

"You sound like Krueger," Karl said.

"The French supply us with various raw materials, foodstuffs and a considerable amount of manpower," Kuhnert said, ignoring the jibe. "Their production level has been poor ever since the sixties, when they realised they weren't going to get out from under our thumb. Why should they produce anything when nine-tenths of what they produce goes straight to the *Reich*? They're still on pretty low rations and they resent it. Far too many of the best Frenchmen are immigrating to North Africa or fleeing to Britain."

Karl frowned. "So?"

"Their government is, if anything, more repressive than ours," Kuhnert continued. "The workers in France haven't been allowed a proper trade union for years, ever since we defeated them in 1940, and the worker associations they do have are more concerned with pleasing the government than assisting the workers. There have long been rumours of plans to set up secret unions and demand change..."

"Which we will crush," Karl interrupted.

"They may no longer care," Kuhnert said. "The Spanish and Italians have the same problem, *Herr Reichsführer*. Their populations have long resented slaving for us. Now... they are starting to wonder what would happen if they simply refuse to work."

Karl scowled. "And what *will* happen?"

"We'll start having supply problems of our own," Kuhnert said. He nodded towards the map hanging on the wall. "These issues aren't going to fade away in a hurry, *Herr Reichsführer*."

"I see," Karl said.

He gritted his teeth in frustration. The only French department he'd thought the *Reich* could rely on was the Vichy government itself. Massively unpopular, caught between the *Reich* and its own people, it was hellishly effective at sniffing out trouble. But if the French security forces were starting to rot, if the French military thought it would be sent to fight in South Africa, Vichy might lose control. And who knew what would happen then?

We have contingency plans, he reminded himself. *We could get the Panzers rolling into France within hours of trouble breaking out in Vichy... except those forces are earmarked for South Africa...*

His blood ran cold. *And if the Americans start to meddle in France itself...*

"Thank you for letting me know," he said. Something would have to be done, but what? "I will consider your concerns."

"Thank you, *Herr Reichsführer*," Kuhnert said. "I appreciate it."

CHAPTER TWENTY

Schulze Residence
31 July 1985

"Gudrun," Liana said, as she opened the door. "How are you?"

"Well enough," Gudrun said. It was hard to disguise her nervousness, but she had to try. "Are your parents in?"

"Father is in the living room, talking to mother," Liana said. She gave Gudrun a wink. "I think they're discussing my marriage."

Gudrun blinked in surprise. Liana was sixteen, barely old enough to marry; hell, Konrad had been twenty and *he* hadn't been married before he'd gone to the war. But Konrad's father was a traditionalist, far more of a traditionalist than Gudrun's own father. He'd want his daughter married off as soon as possible, after he presented her with a list of possible candidates. She winced in bitter sympathy. Liana could only hope that the list included someone she might like and grow to love, in time.

"They might have something else to discuss," she said. "Can you tell them I'm here?"

"They're always pleased to see you," Liana said, catching Gudrun's arm and hauling her into the small house. "Come on."

Gudrun nodded and followed Liana into the living room. Konrad's father was sitting in an armchair, holding court, while Konrad's mother was seated on a sofa, her arms crossed under her breasts. She didn't *look* very happy, Gudrun noted; she had a feeling that Konrad's mother might never contradict her husband in public, but it would be a different story in private. God knew the BDM had told her, time and time again, that she should never argue with her husband publicly. Male pride didn't like it.

"Gudrun," Gerde Schulze said, rising to her feet. "How lovely to see you again."

"Thank you," Gudrun said, flushing in embarrassment as the older woman gave her a tight hug and a kiss on the cheek. She'd always liked Konrad's mother, but Gerde was a little too tactile for her tastes. "Can we talk privately?"

"Of course we can," Volker Schulze said, gruffly. "Liana, go to your room."

Liana gave Gudrun a betrayed look, then turned a pleading gaze on her father. "Father, I..."

"Go," her father ordered. "I'll speak to you later."

Gudrun winced inwardly as Liana turned and stalked out of the room, holding her back ramrod straight. She hoped the girl didn't try to argue with her father later, but she knew Konrad's sister had always been impetuous. Volker Schulze sighed out loud as Liana's footsteps echoed through the house as she stamped up the stairs, then waved Gudrun to a seat facing him. Clearly, he didn't think Gudrun had come to see Gerde alone.

He always was perceptive, Gudrun reminded herself. *And if his loyalties haven't changed, I may be putting my head in the noose.*

She braced herself and looked up, meeting Volker Schulze's eyes. "On Sunday, someone handed out thousands of leaflets in Victory Square," she said. She had no idea if Volker Schulze had received a copy of his own through the letterbox. "Have you seen them?"

Volker Schulze's eyes narrowed. "I have seen the leaflets," he said, neutrally.

Gudrun swallowed. Volker Schulze *was* a former SS officer, after all. If he decided his loyalties still lay with the SS...

"The leaflets claim that wounded or dead soldiers have been concealed by the government," she said. She tried to put a pleading tone into her voice. "Is there any way you can check up on Konrad? Ask what happened to him? You must have contacts..."

"Most of the people I knew have retired or moved on to other posts," Volker Schulze said, carefully. His face was completely expressionless, denying her any chance to glimpse his emotions, but his wife looked worried. "It wouldn't be easy to get any information on Konrad's current location..."

Gerde leaned forward. "But you are going to try," she said, sharply. Gudrun had never heard her speak in such a tone before, even when she'd been asking questions about Gudrun's family and future prospects. "Just for our peace of mind, if nothing else."

Volker Schulze gave his wife a sharp look. "There's no proof that Konrad is wounded or dead," he said. "And I..."

"We should have been told if he was dead or wounded," Gerde insisted. "My father was visited by two officials when my brother was killed in the Middle East. If Konrad has been wounded, or killed, we should have been told."

"But we haven't been told anything," Volker Schulze said, irritated. He couldn't be pleased with Gerde arguing with him, not in front of a visitor. "Konrad is fine."

"Konrad used to write to us every third day," Gerde said. "Even if it was just a short note saying he was fine, he'd write to us. We haven't heard anything from him for months."

"Nor have I," Gudrun said, quietly.

"Konrad would hardly have stopped writing to his girlfriend," Gerde snapped. "He wouldn't have wanted to lose her through neglect."

"Asking questions could also get us in trouble," Volker Schulze reminded his wife. "Do you really want to risk our family...?"

"Konrad *is* our family," Gerde snapped. "And Gudrun is going to marry him. She's practically part of the family already!"

Gudrun winced, inwardly. Volker Schulze wasn't looking happy at all. She understood his refusal to ask questions - he had a wife and daughter at risk - but she *needed* him to ask questions. And he wouldn't be very pleased with his wife afterwards. Gudrun hoped - prayed - that they wouldn't have a colossal fight after she left. She wasn't sure she could bear the guilt of splitting up Konrad's family as well as concealing the truth from them.

"I just want to know what's happened to him," she said, lowering her eyes and trying to sound plaintive. "I *miss* him."

"We do understand, my dear," Gerde said. "We miss him too."

"Konrad knew he would be parted from his friends and family for months, if not years," Volker Schulze reminded her, sternly. "We knew there would be a long separation when he graduated."

"But we also knew he'd be writing to us," Gerde reminded him. "He was raised to stay in touch, was he not? So where are his letters? The censors might have covered the pieces of paper in black ink, Volker, but they wouldn't destroy them altogether."

Volker Schulze rose to his feet. "I shall contact an old comrade," he said, stiffly. He gave Gudrun a sharp look that made her cringe. "And if Konrad is fine, young lady, your conduct will be reported to your parents."

"Her worries are understandable," Gerde said. "Volker..."

"There are limits," her husband snapped. "And I think she's crossed them."

He stalked out of the room before his wife could reply. Gudrun watched him go, feeling a yawning despair opening within her heart. Her father would be angry, if Volker Schulze carried out his threat, but her mother would be *furious*. Gudrun knew she'd probably spend the rest of the week in the kitchen, barred from leaving the house, if her mother found out what she'd said to Konrad's parents. And yet, she knew she'd had no choice. The only way to ensure that Konrad's parents knew what had happened to him was to make his father use his contacts to check up on his son.

"Don't worry," Gerde said, reaching out to squeeze Gudrun's hand. "Volker may try to put a brave face on it, but he's worried too."

"You got one of the leaflets," Gudrun said. She hadn't had one sent specifically to Konrad's house, but whoever had been distributing them had clearly stuffed one through their letterbox. "I... I worry about him."

"That's the curse of being a grown woman, my dear," Gerde said. She patted Gudrun's hand gently. "We bring the men into the world, we marry them, we bear their children... and then we have to stay at home when they march off to war, knowing that they may never come home - or, when they do come home, that a demon might come back with them."

Like Grandpa Frank, Gudrun thought. *He was so horrified by what he'd done that he tried to drown himself in drink.*

She shuddered. Grandpa Frank wasn't the only one who'd gone off to war and come back a changed man. She'd heard horror stories, filtered through the grapevine at school and then at university, about men who woke up screaming, fathers who beat their children bloody, husbands who bragged to their wives about how they'd slept with whores while at the front... she'd wondered, at the time, why *anyone* would want to get married to a soldier. And yet, *her* father was strict, but he wasn't a drunken monster - and nor was Volker Schulze.

Mother must have had a hard time of it, she thought. She wasn't quite sure how the dates added up, but she suspected that Grandpa Frank had come back from the wars shortly before he'd married, long before his daughter had married Gudrun's father. *How did Grandpa Frank treat his wife and daughter?*

Gerde cleared her throat. Gudrun realised, suddenly, that Konrad's mother had been speaking... and she hadn't heard a single word.

"I'm sorry," she said, softly. "I was miles away."

"I understand," Gerde said. "I was wondering if your brother is still unmarried."

"None of my brothers are married," Gudrun said. Gerde couldn't be planning to marry her daughter to Kurt, could she? Johan would be a better fit, if only because they were the same age. "I don't think Kurt plans to marry in a hurry."

"Handsome young man like him?" Gerde asked. "Doesn't he have a girlfriend?"

"If he does, I don't know about it," Gudrun said. She didn't really want to *think* about Kurt having a girlfriend, let alone a wife. "Why do you want to know?"

"Liana needs a man," Gerde said. "And your brother is already an established soldier..."

Gudrun shook her head, sadly. "I don't know what he'd want," she said. The thought of *her* brother marrying *Konrad's* sister was... icky, even though it wouldn't be technically illegal or immoral. But she knew now she wasn't going to marry Konrad. He'd be lucky if they didn't turn the life support off in a few weeks, if he showed no signs of recovery. "You'd have to talk to my parents."

She felt a sudden flicker of envy. *Kurt* could refuse, if pressed; *he* didn't have an obligation to listen to his parents when it came to choosing a wife. He had a career, he had a life... he could marry a whore from the brothels if he wanted and no one could say no. But Gudrun herself? *She* had to listen to her parents when it came to getting married.

"I will," Gerde said, briskly. "And..."

She looked up as her husband returned, his face very pale. Gudrun took one look and knew what he'd been told. Volker Schulze looked like a man who had been punched in the belly, repeatedly.

"Konrad is in hospital," he said, numbly. "He's not expected to survive."

Gerde gasped. "How? Why?"

"There was an ambush, apparently," Volker Schulze said. He sounded shaken; Gudrun watched with growing concern as he walked over to the cabinet, produced a bottle of expensive imported whiskey from Scotland and poured himself a glass. "Konrad was badly wounded. They did what they could to keep him alive, but... but there was apparently some brain damage. He's not expected to survive."

He swallowed the whiskey in one gulp and poured himself another glass. "Gerde, I..."

"My son," Gerde said. "Where *is* he?"

"I couldn't find out," Volker Schulze said. He downed the second glass of whiskey and refilled it once again. "My contact couldn't open the entire file. It seems that certain parts of Konrad's dossier have been sealed. They don't want anyone to know where he is."

"He may already be dead," Gudrun said, shaken. How long had it been since she'd seen his torn and broken body. "They..."

"They'd have listed him as dead and closed the file," Volker Schulze said, sharply. He stared down at his glass, but didn't drink. "Konrad... they should have told us."

"Then the leaflets are correct," Gudrun said. "Konrad isn't the only soldier to be wounded or killed in South Africa."

"They told us it would be a walkover," Volker Schulze said. He glared at the radio as if it had personally offended him. "That only a handful of soldiers would be killed in the fighting."

"And if they lied about Konrad," Gerde added, "how many others have also been killed or wounded?"

Gudrun looked at her. "So what do we do about it?"

"*You* do nothing, young lady," Volker Schulze snapped. He swallowed the whiskey, then returned the bottle to the cabinet. "You cannot, obviously, marry my son. I wouldn't expect you to honour your commitment, such as it was, under these circumstances. I shall speak to your father and inform him that the arrangement has to be cancelled."

"He isn't dead," Gudrun protested. She'd come to the same conclusion herself, but somehow, having it put so bluntly *hurt*. "I could still..."

"He is a cripple with brain damage," Volker Schulze snapped. The raw anger in his tone shocked her to the bone. She'd never seen Konrad's father drink before, let alone lose his temper. "He is certainly no longer capable of fathering children. You would be condemning yourself to life as a permanent nursemaid, assuming he could ever be taken off the machine and go home. I would not ask you to marry him under those conditions."

He looked down at the empty glass in his hand. "I may have to ask them to turn the machine off and let him die," he added, sadly. "What sort of life could he have after... after..."

Gerde rose and embraced her husband, holding him tightly. Gudrun looked away, torn between embarrassment and guilt. She'd stripped away the lies they'd told themselves, the hopes they'd clung to... and now, Volker Schulze was drinking and his wife was crying. It was her fault.

But they would have found out sooner or later, she thought, as she rose herself. *They would have guessed the truth after Konrad remained silent...*

She could feel her own eyes tearing up. If she'd allowed herself to cry for Konrad earlier... she pushed the thought aside. She'd avenge her boyfriend if it was the last thing she did.

"I will speak to your father," Volker Schulze said, stiffly. "And it would not be proper for you to visit again."

"Volker," Gerde snapped.

"I understand," Gudrun said. As Konrad's girlfriend, she could go to his house even when he wasn't present; as an unmarried girl, it wouldn't be proper for her to visit. "Please tell Liana that I am sorry I won't be able to speak to her again."

"You can talk to her outside the house," Gerde said, sharply. She made a visible effort to calm herself. "If you want to sit here for a while, you can..."

"I'd better go," Gudrun said. She had no idea what she'd started. What would Konrad's parents do, now they knew their son was a brain-damaged cripple? Volker Schulze was a stubborn man, one experienced in the ways of the SS. What would he do? "And... I'm sorry."

"So are we," Gerde said. "You would have made a good daughter-in-law."

Perhaps, Gudrun thought. *Or perhaps you would have found me a tiresome girl who wanted a career of her own.*

She pushed the thought aside as she strode out of the room and out onto the streets, silently grateful that Liana was nowhere in sight. Gudrun wasn't sure she could have faced Konrad's sister, not now. And to think Gerde wanted to try to marry Liana to *Kurt*! Was there a reason they wanted to marry their daughter off at such a young age? What age had Gerde been when she'd married Volker Schulze?

Gudrun was so wrapped up in her thoughts that she was barely aware of her surroundings until she was standing in front of her door, fumbling for the key. Her mother opened the door before she could get the key into the lock, then pulled Gudrun into a hug. Gerde must have called her, Gudrun realised, as she allowed her mother to hold her tightly. Her father probably wouldn't be home from the station until the evening, unless he came home especially for her. It didn't seem likely, somehow.

"I'm sorry," her mother said, as she helped Gudrun into the living room. "I know you loved him."

Gudrun shuddered, feeling tears welling up in her eyes. "He... he deserved so much better," she said. "I loved him. We were going to marry and..."

"I know," her mother said, wrapping an arm around Gudrun's shoulders. "You and he would have been good together."

We would have been better than good, Gudrun thought, miserably. She'd bottled up her tears, knowing she dared not cry without a reason she could tell her mother, but now she let them flow freely. Konrad wasn't dead, yet his life was effectively over. *We would have lived together, built a life together and...*

"Hey, cry-baby," Siegfried called, peering into the room. "What's..."

"Get up to your room and wait until your father gets home," his mother snapped. Siegfried recoiled in shock. Their mother rarely told off her youngest child. "He'll have more than a few words to give you."

She turned back to Gudrun as Siegfried fled up the stairs. "I do understand, my darling," she whispered into Gudrun's ear, rocking her like a baby. "Cry all you like. Let it out. There's nothing else you can do."

But there is, Gudrun thought, bitterly. The leaflets were just the beginning. *We can make the state pay for what it's done.*

CHAPTER TWENTY-ONE

Berlin, Germany
4 August 1985

My sister is playing a very dangerous game, Leutnant Kurt Wieland thought, as he stepped into the barracks. *And who knows what will happen when something goes badly wrong?*

It wasn't a pleasant thought. No one else seemed to have realised that *Gudrun* was responsible for the leaflets, but *Kurt* knew all too well that Gudrun had means, motive and opportunity. She might have been a girl, yet she'd been brave enough to sneak into a secure hospital just to visit her boyfriend. Kurt couldn't have asked for more from the soldiers under his command.

"*Leutnant*," *Oberfeldwebel* Helmut Loeb said. "The CO has called a briefing in ten minutes."

"And I'm expected to attend," Kurt said. Loeb was an NCO, old enough to be Kurt's father; he'd forgotten more about war than Kurt had ever known. "I'll be there."

He placed his knapsack in the locker, then hurried down to the briefing room. The ordinary soldiers had an additional two days of leave, while their officers and NCOs received their orders from their superiors and planned how best to carry them out. Kurt had a nasty feeling that the Berlin Guard was going to be deployed away from Berlin for the first time in quite some time, perhaps as a complete unit. Individual companies had been rotated through Germany East, Germany Arabia and Germany South to give their officers and men some valuable experience, but the Berlin Guard as a whole hadn't left Berlin for years. Their battle honours had been allowed to lapse.

But we weren't meant to face real trouble in South Africa, Kurt thought. He remembered feeling envious of the soldiers who'd been sent to South Africa. It might not be a proper war, but at least it was some action. *Now, if the rumours are accurate, the war in South Africa may blaze on for years with no end in sight.*

He pushed the thought aside as he entered the briefing room. It was pleasantly informal while the soldiers were still on leave; the CO was standing in front of a podium while his subordinates were pouring themselves mugs of black coffee and sitting down on hard metal chairs in front of him. A large map of South Africa hung from the wall, suggesting that Gudrun had been right and the Berlin Guard *was* going to the war. Kurt couldn't help a flicker of fear and dread as he poured himself coffee and sat down; he knew he was brave, but the thought of ending up like Konrad, his body a mangled wreck, was terrifying. He would sooner die.

And my family might not know what happened to me, he thought, grimly. He wasn't quite sure how Gudrun had found out where Konrad was, but after the leaflets had started to appear it was unlikely her source would dare tell her anything else. *They'd have a sudden end to my letters and nothing.*

It was a bitter thought. He prided himself on being faithful - he'd always been faithful, right from the moment he'd first entered the Hitler Youth. He'd enjoyed himself; singing songs, marching in unison and practicing with guns, even as some of the more sensitive souls had found the Hitler Youth a foretaste of hell. And yet, if someone as faithful as Konrad - and an SS officer, no less - could simply be discarded, it could happen to *him.* How could he be loyal to the Third Reich when it was clear that the Third Reich was not loyal to its fighting men?

Kurt had no illusions. People died on military service; hell, he'd watched in horror as a boy died on the ropes, back in the Hitler Youth. The teenagers had been told that the boy had effectively been an *Untermensch,* that he'd *deserved* to die through sheer incompetence; in hindsight, Kurt wondered if it had been wise to force the poor boy to try to climb slippery ropes when his skill at climbing ropes was minimal. But even if the masters had been right, it didn't justify hiding the dead and wounded and then lying about it. Didn't Konrad's family deserve some closure?

I'm sorry, Gudrun, he thought, as the CO tapped the podium for attention. *I wish I was there for you.*

That too was not a pleasant thought. Kurt would happily have beaten his younger brother to a pulp for daring to make fun of Gudrun's grief, but he had no idea how to comfort a stricken soul. Gudrun had known Konrad had been badly injured, yet she'd been able to cling to hope until Konrad's family had formally terminated the engagement. It wouldn't reflect badly on her, Kurt was sure, but it had still been shattering. And, given what *else* she was doing, she really didn't need the stress.

"Our new deployment orders have finally arrived," the CO said, after the standard *Heil Bormann*. "The Berlin Guard - all 5000 of us - is going to be deployed to South Africa in the next three months, where we will be reinforcing troops already on the ground. We will commence tactical exercises as soon as the troops report back to barracks, focused around convoy protection, aggressive patrolling and counter-terrorism operations. This is an opportunity for us to be blooded as a unit, rather than as a handful of individual companies."

And an opportunity to wind up crippled, Kurt thought, sardonically. He wasn't fool enough to say that out loud. *Who knows what will happen if one of us winds up dead or wounded?*

He listened, carefully, as the CO ran through the first set of assignments. Moving a military unit from Germany Prime to Germany South would be a logistical nightmare, even though the *Kriegsmarine* seemed confident it had the shipping to move thousands of troops and their equipment from Berlin to the ports in Africa. After that... it would be worse, he suspected, when he looked at the briefing notes. The news claimed that Germany South was safe, but they wouldn't have been ordered to prepare to defend their convoys if there wasn't a risk of being attacked. And afterwards...

The population map made the problem far too clear. South Africa had fifty-seven million people within its borders, a mere *five* million of whom were white. It looked, very much, as though the South Africans were either refusing to breed or fleeing the country, no matter what their government had to say about it. Even if one counted the relatively small Indian and Chinese populations as white, it was still clear that the white population was staggeringly outnumbered. The CO might insist that one good German was worth ten black men, but Kurt had the uneasy feeling that the blacks *could* afford to trade ten of their men for one German and still come out ahead. And if there were parts of Russia that were still dangerous, even forty years after the conquest, who knew how long it would take to pacify South Africa?

"This could take a while," *Leutnant* Bernhard Schrupp muttered.

Kurt winced inwardly, hoping desperately that the CO hadn't overheard Schrupp's rather sarcastic comment. Schrupp wasn't a bad person, not really, but he had a tendency to grumble and ask pointed questions. Indeed, Kurt had often wondered how Schrupp had managed to win promotion in the first place. As far as he knew, Schrupp didn't have any relatives in high places.

"A number of officers who have served in South Africa will be arriving at the barracks tomorrow," the CO concluded. "You will have a chance to learn from their experiences and prepare exercises for the troops. Dismissed."

Kurt saluted, then rose with the other officers. There were briefing papers to read, then officers to interrogate; he needed to be ready by the time the troops returned to their barracks and readied themselves for war. And yet, there was a gnawing feeling in his chest that all was not right, that going to South Africa might be the last thing he'd ever do. It just didn't seem right...

We might not be able to win, he thought, taking a long look at the map. *How do we crush a rebellion that has over ninety percent of the population on its side?*

Schrupp followed him back to the barracks, then into one of the small offices they were allowed to use for their paperwork. "I read the leaflets," he said, once the door was firmly closed. "We might be going to our deaths."

"That's always a risk," Kurt pointed out, trying hard to keep his face impassive. One day, Schrupp would go too far and wind up hauled off by the SS for interrogation. "We're not *sailors,* you know."

"My brother is a sailor on the *Graf Zeppelin,*" Schrupp said. "He says that life on the ocean waves can be just as dangerous as life in the *Heer.*"

Kurt snorted. It was an article of faith among the soldiers - and the *Waffen-SS,* he suspected - that the *Kriegsmarine* sailors did nothing more than sit in port, scrub their decks and try to look good in their fancy uniforms. And it might even be true. The sea could be rough - he'd enjoyed sailing with the Hitler Youth, once he'd managed to recover from an unexpected bout of seasickness - but it wasn't as dangerous as being shot at by insurgents.

"But that isn't the point," Schrupp added, after a moment. "What happens to us when we get wounded in South Africa?"

"Good question," Kurt said. "Why don't you ask the CO?"

Schrupp gave him a sardonic look. "Do you think he'd give me a straight answer?"

He turned and headed out of the tiny office before Kurt could formulate a response. Kurt watched him go, trying to understand what Schrupp was doing. Grumbling was one thing, but doing something - anything - that could be taken as trying to prepare the ground for a mutiny was quite another. Kurt could report him right away and Schrupp's career would come to a screeching halt, even if he avoided anything worse than the punishment units in Germany East. It was Kurt's *duty* to report him. And yet, betraying Schrupp would ensure that no one ever trusted him again...

Maybe I should just leave him to get on with it, Kurt thought.

But the thought kept nagging at his mind. He'd be leading a platoon into combat in South Africa, with a number of men under his command, men he'd be responsible for. What would happen when one of them died while under his command? Would the dead man's family be informed or would they just be left in limbo?

He shuddered. Perhaps it would have been better if he hadn't accompanied Gudrun to the hospital, if he'd reported her to their father as soon as she asked for his help. But he hadn't and now he had to deal with his own doubts about the *Reich*.

And we're leaving for South Africa in three months, he reminded himself. *By then, something may change...*

———

Volker Schulze knew, from hard experience, that life could be painful. He'd joined the SS as a young man, gone through a brutal training program that killed a handful of new recruits every year and served as a front-line *Waffen-SS* soldier for fifteen years before retiring and going to work in a factory. He had no illusions about the world; it was a brutal place and the Third *Reich* needed brutal men to dominate it. Loyalty had been hammered into him from birth.

And yet, he was angry.

He'd known that Konrad could end up dead or wounded. He had accepted that the moment Konrad insisted on following in his father's footsteps and applying to join the *Waffen-SS*; Konrad might die in training, let alone in the field. Volker had accepted that, he told himself, and yet... he'd believed that his loyalty would always be returned. The SS would have told his parents if *he* had died, he was sure, and they should have told him when his son was brutally wounded, permanently crippled. But they hadn't. They'd lied to him. And even his contacts within the bureaucracy hadn't been able to locate his son.

The thought had nagged at his mind ever since he'd discovered the truth. He'd given the best years of his life to the *Reich*. His son, it seemed, had lost *his* life for the *Reich*... and yet, the *Reich* hadn't even *tried* to honour his death. Konrad should have been allowed to die with dignity, his family by his side, his body laid to rest in the ground. Instead, he was trapped on life support, eternally suspended on the brink of death, his hopes and dreams smashed along with his body. And they'd lied to him.

He mulled the feeling over as he made his way slowly into the giant factory complex, nodding to a handful of men he recognised along the way. The giant complex produced vehicles, ranging from the handful of publicly-available cars to lorries and small armoured patrol vehicles for the military. He'd been proud to work in the factory, once upon a time; it had seemed a chance to make use of his experience even though he was no longer a *Waffen-SS* stormtrooper. Now... now it had all turned to ashes in his mouth.

"Volker," the secretary said, as he entered the office. "What can I do for you?"

Volker sighed, inwardly. The secretary had never served. He'd gone straight into the corporate sphere as soon as he'd graduated from school, instead of volunteering for active service. Volker had always disliked him, but now... now he wished Konrad had chosen to do something - anything - else to prove he was a man. At least he'd still be alive.

"I want you to arrange a meeting of everyone who has a relative in the military," he said. The secretary would have no trouble putting together a list, just by consulting the files. "Have them assemble in the cafeteria after the next shift."

The secretary frowned. "I could only ask the workers on the current shift," he said, after a moment. "Unless you wanted to put it off for a couple of days, so that everyone could be informed."

"Just inform as many as you can," Volker said. "I intend to find a way to honour our serving men."

He turned and strode out, confident his orders would be obeyed. The secretary wouldn't defy him on such a minor matter, even though he'd probably report the meeting to higher management. He doubted his superiors would care, as long as he wasn't pulling workers away from their duties. Besides, corporate events honouring the troops were popular and suggested the corporation cared about the fighting men.

Not that they do, Volker thought. He still shuddered at the thought of having to ride in one of the new jeeps a corporation had produced for the soldiers. They'd been so unprotected that a lunatic with a single pistol could do real damage. *All they care about is money.*

The thought was a distraction, so he turned it over and over in his mind as the whistle blew and he went to work. They'd been working longer hours recently, turning out fewer civilian cars and more military vehicles; reading between the lines, he had a private suspicion that meant that the losses in South Africa were far higher than expected. Panzers would probably make short work of the insurgents, if the insurgents were fool enough to stand and fight. The Arabs had tried that in their rebellion and it had ended very badly, for them.

He wasn't sure how many workers would turn up for his meeting, but when he entered the cafeteria he was relieved to discover that over fifty workers had attended. Chances were that some of them had thought attendance was compulsory - the secretary had probably made it so - and weren't too keen on anything other than getting home to their wives and children, but the meeting wouldn't take long. He strode over to the jukebox, turned on a recording of one of Wagner's longer compositions - the only music they were allowed in the factory - and turned to face his audience. Thankfully, he knew most of them personally.

And some of them have been grumbling over the increased hours, he thought. *And about how little say we have in our own affairs.*

It was a risk, he admitted privately; he could be sacked on the spot for trying to form a non-governmental union, let alone discussing what had happened to Konrad. His bosses might be pleased with his work, but they wouldn't tolerate anything that smacked of worker power. It would threaten *their* grip on power...

"I'm sorry for asking you all to attend," he said, curtly. Liana was too young to understand what was happening, but he *had* discussed his plans with Gerde and she'd agreed that they had to take the risk. "There is a matter I need to discuss with you."

He took a breath, then pulled one of the leaflets out of his pocket and held it up. "This is true," he said. "My son is one of the wounded. My son was shipped back home to a hospital somewhere in Germany - and they never told me what happened to him. Now, I find out through my own contacts that he will probably never recover. There is nothing I can do."

A low rumble of anger ran through the cafeteria. Volker might have been an SS officer, once upon a time, but he was a popular and reasonable foreman who'd gone to bat for his subordinates more than once. None of his workers believed he deserved to lose a son...

"It gets worse," Volker added, once several workers had added their own stories. "The demands on our time are likely to increase."

He braced himself as he took the plunge. "I think it's time to take our fate into our own hands."

CHAPTER TWENTY-TWO

Morgenstern Residence, Berlin
5 August 1985

Hilde Morgenstern would never have admitted it, at least not outside the privacy of her own mind, but there were times when she envied Gudrun and many of her other girlfriends. Their mothers might be strict, their mothers might insist that dinner and house chores came before their studies, their mothers might be willing to slap their faces if they talked back or disobeyed... and yet none of them came close to *Frau* Morgenstern for sheer overbearing obnoxiousness, let alone a burning desire to climb the social ladder until she was the mistress of Berlin's social scene.

"Hilde," her mother called. "Bring out the refreshments!"

Hilde groaned inwardly as she picked up the plate of homemade cakes and biscuits - she'd had to turn them out herself, while the foreign-born maids cleaned the house thoroughly even though there hadn't been a speck of dust in sight - and carried them into the dining room, where her mother was holding court in front of a gaggle of middle-aged ladies who had money and time on their hands. They eyed her doubtfully as she passed the plate of cakes around, then resumed their discussion. Hilde was only marginally surprised to hear that the topic of the discussion was the leaflets.

"I've located seven families who have a son who has dropped out of touch," one middle-aged lady said. Hilde had never tried to remember their names, if only because they came and went so quickly. "My husband says that one of the foremen at his factory has also lost a son, a son who was actually sent back to Germany - and no one told him!"

"Shocking," *Frau* Morgenstern said. "And what are we going to do about it?"

Hilde found a seat and listened as the discussion raged around the table, genteel politeness mixed with a strange kind of fear and excitement. *Frau* Morgenstern and her friends did everything; they baked cakes for bake sales, they organised school trips for needy children, they even collected money for wounded soldiers or war widows. Hilde had long since learned to dread the days when her mother came up with another idea for poking her overly long nose into someone's affairs; making friends had never been easy when her mother had seen Hilde's friendships as just another foot in the door. She would have done anything to live on campus, as Sven and the boys did. At least she'd be a long way from her mother.

"We need to support the mothers and wives who have lost sons and husbands," *Frau* Morgenstern said, finally. "But we also need to learn the truth about what's actually happening."

"The leaflet says that the government is lying to us," one of her friends pointed out. She was someone important - her husband was a big wheel in the Ministry of Finance, Hilde had been told - and wasn't particularly scared of the SS. "We need to force them to tell the truth."

"So we need to get thousands of women to work with us," *Frau* Morgenstern said. Her eyes were glinting with inspiration. "A full-sized protest movement, just like they have in America."

Hilde swallowed. She had no way to know for sure what happened in America, but she *did* have a good idea how the SS would react to a public demonstration. The women would be greeted with clubs, whips and machine guns. And yet, would the SS dare to fire on German womenfolk when German men had been taught it was their duty to protect the women? The SS might start a riot or mutiny just by giving the order to fire.

"We already have strong ties to the Sisters of Mercy," *Frau* Morgenstern added, after a moment. "There's no reason we can't use this to attract more people to the cause."

And get yourself some more power, Hilde thought, cynically. *You don't give a damn about the dead or wounded soldiers, you just want to use their fates for your own purposes.*

She scowled, inwardly. Her mother thought in terms of power and influence, rather than anything more feminine. No wonder her father spent as much time as he could at the office, working for the Ministry of Industry. When his wife wasn't building her own power base, she was nagging her husband to work on his. Hilde was *sure* that her mother's pestering had been what had turned her father's hair grey before his time.

And yet, her mother's concept might actually *work*. *Frau* Morgenstern sat in the centre of a spider's web of tiny organisations, each of which might provide a core of women willing to help force the government to change. She smiled at the thought of her mother nagging the *Reichstag* - *Frau* Morgenstern was a hellishly efficient nagger - and then considered the possibilities more carefully. Gudrun and the rest of their tiny group might have started the ball rolling, but it was clear that events were already moving out of control.

Which is a good thing, isn't it? She asked herself. *We have to keep our heads down for a while, so if someone else takes up the cause...*

She rose as her mother gestured to her, then hurried back into the kitchen to pick up the next tray of snacks. One of the maids was hastily pulling another cake out of the oven, her pale face marred where *Frau* Morgenstern had slapped her hours ago. Hilde felt a stab of pity - no one would give a damn if the maids were beaten to death - but she knew there was nothing she could do. The poor girls were *Untermenschen*. If they died while working in the *Reich*, her mother would just be able to get a couple more from the *Reich* Labour Commission.

And they have to sleep in the outhouse, Hilde thought, guiltily. She'd looked into the outhouse once, when she'd been younger. It was dark, dank and smelly; the maids had to take showers before they were allowed to enter the house. *Mother can't even give them a proper bedroom.*

She picked up the tray and hurried back into the dining room. The discussion had turned into a working party, *Frau* Morgenstern taking ideas from her friends and working them into a coherent whole. Hilde would have been impressed if she hadn't been so worried about just what her mother would do, once she had her protest groups organised. Or, for that matter, just what would happen if the SS arrested the women before they could do anything. Hilde had no illusions about her mother's backstabbing tendencies and she had a nasty feeling that one or more of the well-dressed women sitting in the room shared them. A single word to the SS would be enough to bring *Frau* Morgenstern and her husband before a tribunal. And who knew what would happen then?

A hand touched her shoulder. She flinched and looked up. A maid was standing just behind her, looking terrified.

"My Lady, your father has returned home," the maid said. Her voice was so quiet that Hilde had to force herself to listen just to make out the words. "He requests your presence in his study."

"I understand," Hilde said. At least it was an excuse for not listening to the older women for the next few hours. "Thank you."

She saw a disapproving expression flicker across her mother's face as she rose - one did not thank *Untermenschen* - and knew she'd be in trouble later, but she did her best to ignore it as she hurried out of the room and headed up the stairs. Her father rarely talked to her - Hilde was sometimes surprised that her parents had managed to produce a single child - and she was torn between a surprised delight and a gnawing fear at the sudden summons. Bracing herself, she tapped on the door and stepped into her father's office.

"Hilde," her father said, looking up from his ledgers. "Sit."

Hilde nodded and sat down, resting her hands on her lap. She'd never been entirely sure of what her father did for a living, although she *did* know it was a high-paying job somewhere in the tangled web that made up the Ministry of Industry. And it granted social status as well, she knew, enough to turn her mother into a power on the social scene. It wasn't the kind of life Hilde wanted for herself - she hadn't gone to the university to become yet another gossipy housewife - but at least it made her mother happy.

She studied her father thoughtfully as he reached the end of the page and closed the book with a resounding *thud*. Unlike her big mother, Arthur Morgenstern was actually quite a small man, with a tacky suit, greying hair and a face that - she thought privately - resembled a weasel. She had wondered, from time to time, why her father hadn't hired someone to give him a makeover, but she supposed he was rich and important enough not to need one.

"Hilde," Arthur Morgenstern said. "I trust your marks are as high as always?"

Hilde hesitated, just for a second. Her father wasn't a strong man, not in her opinion, although in some ways that was actually a blessing. She'd had friends with strong fathers and *they* had all been married off as soon as they'd reached legal age, practically given to men their fathers had chosen. And he had never tried to discipline Hilde, leaving all such matters to her mother. She sometimes wondered if he really cared for either his daughter or his wife.

"My marks are high," she said, finally. "I'm still planning to study computers if I can get into the classes."

"Good, good," her father said. He looked up suddenly. "I hope you were not playing games with your tutors."

Hilde coloured. She'd heard the rumours about Professor Murken - she had no idea who'd started them or why - but she had never touched or been touched by any of her tutors. Hell, as far as they knew, she hadn't even had a boyfriend! Being with Martin had been fun, but she knew her parents would have hauled her out of the university if they suspected, even for a second, that she was having an 'unsuitable' relationship.

"No, father," she said. "They have been nothing but proper to me."

"Good," her father said. He cocked his head, slightly. "I've heard a vague rumour that the leaflets came out of the university, Hilde. Would you care to comment?"

"I have heard the same rumour," Hilde said. He didn't suspect her, did he? She had no idea how he *could* have suspected her. Her parents practically treated her as an extension of themselves. "Father, I know no one at the university who would dare write such leaflets."

"Your mother apparently received a copy," her father said. "Did you give it to her?"

"No, father," Hilde lied. If he knew already, if one of the maids had reported her slipping it into the pile of letters for her mother, she was doomed. He'd pull her out of the university and send her to one of the finishing schools in Switzerland, where young female brains were turned into mush. It wasn't as if her parents couldn't afford the fees. "I wouldn't dare pass on one of *those* leaflets."

"A sensible attitude," her father said, blandly. "Should you discover who happened to write the leaflets, Hilde, you will inform me at once."

"Yes, father," Hilde said. She knew better than to argue openly. She'd just keep her mouth shut and pray the group was never uncovered by the SS. "May I ask a question?"

"You may," her father said, after a moment. "I do not, of course, promise to answer."

Hilde took a breath. "Are the claims in the leaflets true?"

"Of course not," her father said, too quickly. "They're lies, lies put about to weaken the *Reich*. We had similar problems in the sixties with radicals who were influenced by American ideals. They were rapidly crushed."

He shook his head. "The fools who wrote and distributed these leaflets may think they're doing the right thing," he added, after a moment. "They're young, of course; only a youngster would have the conceit to believe they could change the world by distributing leaflets. But they're wrong. They're *very* wrong. They're undermining the *Reich* itself, Hilde."

Hilde couldn't bring herself to meet his eyes. "Is that wrong?"

Her father gave her a sharp look. "You studied Rome, didn't you?"

"Yes, father," Hilde said. She'd found history boring, but she remembered a few details. "I had to read about the Romans for school."

"Brutus killed Julius Caesar," her father said. "Do you recall that part of the story?"

Hilde shrugged. Her lessons had centred around the great Teutonic heroes who'd brought down the Italians and established, once and for all, that Germans would never be slaves as long as they stood united. She recalled Julius Caesar, but only in passing.

"Brutus and his comrades had no plan for what would happen after Julius Caesar was brutally murdered," her father said, after a moment. "He had no idea how to capitalise on his success, so he did nothing as events slipped out of hand. And so, instead of the successful restoration of the Roman Republic, Emperor Augustus rose to power."

"I see, father," Hilde said.

"Go," her father said. "I have a meeting now, but I'll see your mother and yourself at dinnertime."

Hilde nodded, rose and left the room. It might have been an accident, but her father had given her something to think about. And something, she knew, she would have to discuss with the rest of the group as soon as possible. Who knew what would happen if the *Reich* came apart at the seams?

———

"You weren't seen, were you?"

"I don't believe so," Andrew Barton said. Walking through the richest part of Berlin was far safer than trying to sneak through the suburbs. "As long as the papers you provided are in good order, I shouldn't have been in trouble even if I had been stopped by the police."

He smiled as Arthur Morgenstern sat back in his chair. The man was deeply corrupt - and desperate for ready cash. Slipping him a few hundred thousand dollars had been more than enough to turn him into a source, although - as always - Andrew had to remember that the SS might be playing him, rather than the other way around. Morgenstern was genuine, as far as he could tell, but there was always a quiet nagging doubt.

"That's good," Morgenstern said, after a moment. "There have been developments."

Andrew took a seat and leaned forward. "What sort of developments?"

"Threats of a new set of trade unions in various corporations," Morgenstern said. "And people whispering about those damnable leaflets. Even my *wife* knows what they are."

"I'm sorry to hear that," Andrew said, sincerely. *Frau* Morgenstern would have made an excellent source, if she hadn't been more determined to build up her own power base than assist the United States. "And your daughter?"

"Denies everything," Morgenstern said. He looked up, suddenly. "Could you offer her a scholarship to Caltech?"

"I could arrange for her to be selected, if she puts her name on the lists," Andrew said. The university would kick up a fuss - and the FBI wouldn't be any happier - but the OSS had more than enough clout to make sure that Hilde Morgenstern was safely out of the *Reich* for a couple of years. "Does she have genuine potential?"

"Her marks are good," Morgenstern assured him. "I'm sure she could pass the entrance exam."

That proved nothing, Andrew knew. Caltech would try to reject her if she *didn't* pass the exam - and they'd be furious if Andrew's superiors insisted on allowing her to attend anyway. But competition was fierce at Speer University, he had to admit. Hilde Morgenstern wouldn't have managed to get as far as she had if she hadn't had genuine talent along with her family's connections.

Morgenstern sighed, loudly. "First we had problems in France, now we have problems in the *Reich* itself," he added, leaning back in his chair. "I don't like the idea of new trade unions."

"I suppose you wouldn't," Andrew agreed. "I thought they were banned."

"Oh, they are," Morgenstern said. "And the workers should know it. There are government unions to take care of their requirements. But they're ignoring the rules."

Andrew wasn't surprised. The only hint of socialism in Nazi Germany lay within the Nazi Party's name - National Socialism. In reality, the corporations made big donations to the *Reich's* government and, in exchange, all independent trade unions were banned. Anyone who tried to found one could expect to be fired and jailed, perhaps exiled to the east, in short order. And yet, as the *Reich's* economy tightened and pay checks grew thinner, it was harder and harder for the bosses to intimidate the workers into silence.

"That could be a problem," he agreed, dryly. "What have your masters decided to do about it?"

"Nothing, as yet," Morgenstern admitted. "I think they're hoping the whole problem will just go away."

"They thought that before the Great Depression too," Andrew reminded him. "But it didn't."

"No, it didn't," Morgenstern agreed.

He was frightened, Andrew realised. Given his position in the Ministry of Industry, he had good reason to know the full scale of the problem. Andrew hadn't been sure what, if anything, to make of the leaflets, but if *Morgenstern* was worried...

"And if it doesn't go away," he said carefully, "what do you think they'll do?"

"Something drastic," Morgenstern said. "And I want my daughter out of the *Reich* before that happens."

Andrew nodded. "We'll see what we can do," he said. "But she will have to pass the exams, *Herr* Morgenstern. Anything else would be far too revealing."

CHAPTER TWENTY-THREE

Wieland House, Berlin
6 August 1985

Gudrun lay on her bed, staring up at the ceiling.

Her parents hadn't been particularly demanding, much to her relief, ever since Konrad's father had called *Gudrun's* father and had a long - and private - discussion with him over the telephone. Gudrun hadn't been sure how her father would react - particularly if he realised that she'd known Konrad was crippled *before* his father had found out - but he'd largely left her alone, while her mother had only given her a handful of chores to do when she got home from the university. In some ways, it was a relief, but she had a nasty feeling that the *Reichmark* was about to drop. How long would it be before her father started nagging her to find a husband - or presented her with a list of suitable candidates?

And Konrad was going to die.

She'd known he wasn't going to recover completely, if he ever made it off the life support machine, but she'd dared to hope that they might have a life together. Now, she could no longer cling to the illusion. Konrad's father would turn the machine off, once he actually *found* his son; he wouldn't leave his son's shattered mind trapped in a crippled body. It wasn't fair, Gudrun's thoughts mocked her; no one had seriously considered telling Grandpa Frank that it was time to die, to go on to the next world, even though he was a disgusting old man. But what had Konrad done to deserve such injuries? He'd been young and strong and the world was at his feet.

And it killed him, she thought, bitterly. How many times had he sat beside her on the bed, sneaking kisses despite the open door? She wasn't sure she could bring herself to kiss anyone, ever again; she'd practically betrayed Konrad by kissing Horst, even though it had been in the heat of the moment. *Konrad did everything right and he was still betrayed by his own government.*

She wanted to sit up, she wanted to do something, but she couldn't muster the energy to do anything more than lie on the bed. There were chores she needed to do, she was sure, and homework she needed to finish before going back to the university, yet it was so hard to focus her mind. If her father saw her latest set of marks, he'd blow a fuse; Gudrun knew, without false optimism, that her grades had slipped badly. And yet, between the knowledge of what had happened to Konrad and her own work with the leaflets, it was hard to focus on her studies. What sort of future did she have if nothing changed?

There was a tap on the door. She looked up. Her father was standing there, looking worried; Gudrun sat upright hastily and beckoned him into the room. She couldn't keep her heart from pounding, although she was fairly sure she wasn't in trouble. Her father rarely entered her room unless she *was*. It was her mother who normally inspected it each weekend and snapped at her to clean up her mess, place clean clothes in the drawers and wash her dirty outfits in the sink.

"Gudrun," her father said, sitting on the bed next to her. "I am truly sorry."

"Thank you," Gudrun said. She wasn't used to her father being sympathetic - or understanding. Even when he'd bawled out the BDM matron, he'd given Gudrun a look that promised she'd be in hot water as soon as she got home. "Konrad... Konrad meant everything to me."

"Your mother means everything to *me*," her father said, uncomfortably. "But if she died, she wouldn't want me to just give up."

Gudrun stared down at her hands. "I'm not feeling suicidal, father."

"Good," her father said, dryly. "I'd hate to have to take you to hospital."

Gudrun flinched. A person who showed suicidal tendencies could be committed to a mental health institution and held indefinitely. Gudrun had heard enough horror stories about what happened behind their locked doors to know she never wanted to step into one, certainly not while there was breath in her body. She *had* heard of a couple of students who'd committed suicide under the pressure, but it was very rare. Students at the university weren't encouraged to wallow in self-pity.

"I just don't want to think about anything else at the moment," she said, carefully. "He was proud of me, father. I don't want to let him down."

"I'm proud of you," her father said.

You don't understand me, Gudrun thought. Her father had always gotten on better with his sons, taking them to play football and camping in the hills while Gudrun had stayed with her mother. *You would have been happy if I'd been born male too.*

"I approved of Konrad," her father said, after a moment. "SS he might have been, but he was a good lad and would have taken care of you."

"I don't need a man to take care of me," Gudrun snapped. "I'm not... I'm not going to be a housewife."

Her father gave her a long considering look. "And if you graduate with the highest marks in your class," he said, "what will happen then?"

"There aren't enough computer experts in the *Reich*," Gudrun said. She allowed a hint of sarcasm to run through her voice. "I may be a weak and feeble woman, father, but they won't be able to dismiss me because I was born the wrong gender."

"I hope you're right," her father said. "But you do need to consider finding a new husband."

Gudrun stared at him. It was easy to sound horrified - and tearful. "Konrad isn't even *dead* yet!"

"But he will be," her father said, wrapping an arm around her shoulders. "And even if they keep him on life support, he will not be a suitable husband. He will not be able to father children."

Gudrun shuddered. She did not want to have *that* discussion with her father. Her mother had discussed how babies were made when she'd bled for the first time - she remembered that it had almost been a relief, because she'd been convinced she was desperately ill - and the BDM had explained it in clinical detail, but discussing it with her father would be far too embarrassing. She recalled Konrad's bandaged body, lying in the hospital bed, and shuddered again. His genitals had been blown off by the blast.

She took refuge in anger. "Father, is having children the sole purpose of my life?"

Her father frowned. "You are a young woman," he said. "The longer you wait before having children, Gudrun, the harder it will be to get pregnant and bring the child to term. If you wait too long, you simply won't be *able* to have children."

"And if I do," Gudrun said, "I'll be trapped in the house."

"Your mother rules the house," her father pointed out.

"But she is trapped," Gudrun countered. "She has to look after three little brats who don't do anything to help..."

"You had your own bratty stage," her father said, sarcastically.

"That's not the point," Gudrun said. "Kurt, Johan and Siegfried do nothing around the house - they don't even pick up the trash in their rooms. Johan and Siegfried threw a fit when mother told *me* to clean their room, but they weren't willing to do it for themselves. And even if mother goes back to work when Siegfried turns eighteen and gets a job of his own, she'll have given up the best years of her life."

Her father's face darkened. "If she *hadn't* had children," he said, "you wouldn't exist."

"I know," Gudrun said. It was true, after all. There was no point in trying to deny it. "But I want to be something more than a housewife and mother, endlessly picking up after my children."

"You're a young woman," her father said. "You were *born* to be a mother."

"It doesn't seem fair," Gudrun objected. How could she expect her father, the lord and master of the household, to understand? "Why do *I* have to be a mother?"

Her father gave her a long look. "No one would expect you to go to work," he said, after a moment. "You are not expected to go to war, or work in a factory, or do anything to bring in money for your family. Your husband, Gudrun, will be considered a failure if he *doesn't* ensure you have everything you need. He will be roundly mocked if his wife is in rags and his children are naked..."

"And then he will get drunk and take it out on his wife," Gudrun said. She'd never seen her father hitting her mother, but she'd known a couple of girls in school who'd had terrifyingly violent fathers. No one had cared when they'd come to school sporting nasty bruises they refused to talk about, let alone show to the matrons. "And the wife has no rights at all."

She looked down at her hands. The BDM matrons had gone over the responsibilities of a wife in some detail, assuring their charges that a *proper* housewife was loyal, obedient and never complained, let alone committed adultery. If she did, Gudrun had been told, she could expect to lose custody of the kids, if she didn't wind up in jail. Gudrun recalled asking just why the husband was allowed to commit adultery, if his wife didn't have the same rights, and being forced to write lines as punishment. Her mother hadn't found it very amusing when Gudrun, her hand aching, had been sent home with a note. In hindsight, Gudrun couldn't help wondering if her mother's angry reaction had been fuelled by her awareness of her own helplessness.

"That's not always true," her father said. "There have been men who've defended battered wives..."

"But the wives don't get to defend themselves," Gudrun said. Something would have to be done, she was sure. Women's rights were just another issue for the next leaflets, once they readied themselves to distribute a second set. "They may not be lucky enough to have defenders."

"You'll have me," her father said. "And your brothers. They won't hesitate to come to your defence."

"Siegfried might," Gudrun muttered. Her little brother blamed her for the thrashing he'd received from their father, five days ago. "He hates me."

"He'll get over it," her father assured her. "I thought I hated my sisters too, once upon a time."

He cleared his throat. "I understand that you are in mourning," he said, "and I will give you as much time as I can, but you do need a husband."

Gudrun shook her head, mutely.

"I'm not going to let you run free without a man," her father said, firmly. "You are young, beautiful and intelligent. You'll have no trouble finding another boyfriend."

"Widows get at least a year before they're expected to remarry," Gudrun muttered.

"You're not a widow," her father pointed out. "And you're not pregnant."

Gudrun rolled her eyes, even though she knew it would annoy him. The whole system was strange, at least when she applied logic and reason. She knew she wasn't supposed to have sex before marriage, but her father wouldn't have objected if she became pregnant out of wedlock, provided she married her boyfriend before she started to show. No one would be particularly surprised when a bride proved able to produce a child quicker than a properly-wedded wife.

But then, producing the next generation of Germans is an important goal, she thought, recalling the BDM's lectures. It was their duty, as maidens, to marry, have children and raise them to become good little servants of the *Reich.* A handful of girls becoming pregnant before marriage, as long as there *was* a marriage, was hardly a problem. *They just want us to have babies and raise them.*

Her father gave her a brief hug. "I know this is hard for you," he said. Gudrun rather doubted that he *did* understand. "But your time is running out."

And if I don't find someone, Gudrun thought nastily, *you'll find someone for me.*

Her father rose and headed out the door, leaving her behind. Gudrun shook her head tiredly, then rose herself. There were chores to do, after all, and they would keep her from thinking about her prison. Find a man, any man... or accept her father's choice. Who knew what sort of young man he'd consider suitable? A policeman? Or a soldier? Gudrun wasn't sure she could bear the thought of being married to a soldier, not after what had happened to Konrad. What was the point of building a life together if it could be snatched away in the blink of an eye?

Maybe I should ask Horst, she thought, as she headed downstairs. He was smart, after all, and unlikely to be sent into danger. The *Reich* didn't have enough computer experts to risk losing one on the front lines. *At least he'd understand why I had to keep spreading leaflets around...*

"Gudrun," her mother called. "Can you go clean Grandpa Frank's room?"

You should go do it yourself, Gudrun thought, rebelliously. Perhaps she'd refuse to take her parents in, once they were no longer capable of taking care of themselves. But she knew her mother wouldn't allow her to escape the job. *You don't want to handle your father yourself.*

Gritting her teeth, she hurried back up the stairs and knocked at Grandpa Frank's door, then opened it to peer inside. The old man was sitting in the armchair, reading the newspaper; he looked surprisingly active, for someone who drank several bottles of beer a day. And yet, when she started to scoop up the bottles, she discovered they were full. Her grandfather hadn't drunk *any* of his ration of alcohol.

"Pour them down the sink," Grandpa Frank ordered. He sounded sober, too. "Or just stick them back in the fridge."

185

Gudrun eyed him. "You're sober."

Grandpa Frank gave her a sarcastic look. "Would you rather I was drunk?"

"No," Gudrun said, after a moment. Grandpa Frank *knew*. If he got drunk, if he blurted it out in front of her parents, she was dead. Her father would drag her out of university, marry her off to some knuckle-dragging moron and deny he'd ever had a daughter. "But I thought you needed the drink..."

"I find that confession unburdens the mind," Grandpa Frank said. He put the newspaper down on the table and smiled at Gudrun, rather unpleasantly. "Not that I ever set foot in a church after I returned from the war. I had the impression I'd be violently rejected after everything I'd done."

Gudrun nodded, although she didn't really understand. The *Reich* didn't encourage church attendance; indeed, families who *did* attend church regularly could expect to be asked some pretty harsh questions. She knew very little about organised religion, save for what she'd been taught in school - and much of what she'd been taught, she suspected, was outright lies. Had the great Christian, Jesus Christ, really been killed by the evil Jews? Or was there something more to the story? And just what had *really* happened on Christmas Day?

She finished cleaning the room - thankfully, a sober grandfather meant less mess - and piled the rubbish into a small bag. Her mother didn't seem to have noticed that her father was sober, although *that* proved nothing. Gudrun hadn't been paying attention to much of anything over the last few days. She gave her grandfather a sidelong look, then took a breath and leaned forward. If he was sober, maybe he could answer a question or two.

"Father wants me to marry soon," she said. "Is there any way I can dissuade him?"

Grandpa Frank shrugged. "You're a healthy young woman," he said, after a moment. "It is natural for you to have a husband. Your father won't be there to look after you for the rest of your life."

"I don't want to get married," Gudrun said. "Not... not like this. I want to finish my education and get a proper job."

"You could always have four children very quickly," Grandpa Frank suggested. "You'd be able to apply for a maid once you won the *Mutterkreuz*. And then you could go back to your studies."

"I don't think I'd be allowed to let the maids raise the children," Gudrun said. Only very wealthy families could afford to hire *German* maids. "And my husband might start eying the maids."

"Standards have slipped," Grandpa Frank agreed, dryly. "Make sure you get the maids fixed before you allow them to sleep in your house."

Gudrun shuddered. She didn't want to *think* about her future husband, assuming she ever had one, sleeping with the maids.

"But you have other problems," Grandpa Frank added. "Have you done anything else?"

"Not yet," Gudrun said. The university was buzzing with talk, but most of it was nothing more than talk. "I don't know how to proceed."

"You need to make alliances outside the university," Grandpa Frank told her, curtly. "If there's just a handful of you, the SS will find it easy to isolate and crush your little band."

"I see," Gudrun said. She shook her head. "But every time we try to make contact with someone else, we run the risk of being uncovered."

"Then make the invitation public," Grandpa Frank said. "You need to concentrate on leaderless resistance, not establishing a strict hierarchy. That's what did in the French Resistance."

Gudrun nodded, slowly. "Thank you, Grandpa."

Grandpa Frank shrugged. "Bring me some coffee," he said. He waved his hand dismissively. "And see if you can fill a couple of bottles with water for me."

"I'll do my best," Gudrun said. Coffee was growing more expensive, according to her mother. "At least water is still free."

CHAPTER TWENTY-FOUR

Aĺbert Speer University, Berĺin
7 August 1985

If Horst had been genuinely interested in rooting out dissidents, he would have filed a whole series of complaints about the 'transfer students' he was forced to supervise. They were laughably underprepared for their roles; indeed, they fitted in so badly that he couldn't help wondering if his superiors had deliberately intended to make their watching eyes so noticeable that even a rank amateur would have spotted them before they opened their mouths. Maybe their *real* goal was to divert attention away from Horst and his fellow agents, the men and women who actually blended into the university's population... it was, he felt, the only explanation that suggested his superiors weren't terrifyingly incompetent.

And no one pays any attention to us, he thought, *while the goons make their way through the university.*

It was clear, astonishingly clear, that none of the new students had any real experience with academic life, let alone passed the exams necessary to attend the university as new students. No one could possibly mistake them for *real* students - and, if that wasn't bad enough, they were crashing through the classrooms, asking so many dumb questions that Horst was tempted to report them as potential dissidents. He couldn't help wondering if some of the other spies, the ones who *weren't* charged with supervising the assholes, had already reported them. It wouldn't be the first time that an intelligence operation had been ruined by two different people working at cross-purposes.

At least they know not to bother me on campus, he thought, as he left the lecture hall and headed up to the meeting room. *That would have blown their cover as well as my own.*

He caught sight of one of the spies, looming over a young girl and sighed inwardly. Of all the people they had to send, did they really have to send someone so... so *entitled* that he thought he could press his attentions on a student? Horst had met his kind before, the men who thought that being in the SS gave them licence to harass any woman they liked; he had no doubt that the idiot would blow his cover sooner rather than later. After all, the poor girl would probably report him to the university authorities, who wouldn't be able to expel him because of his connections...

Idiot, he thought. He briefly considered reporting *that* to his handlers, then dismissed the thought. A corps of visible spies was more useful than a handful of agents who genuinely blended into their surroundings. Unless, of course, the visible spies were meant to distract attention from the *invisible* spies. *And if the game was that easy, anyone could play.*

He pushed the thought out of his mind as he walked up the stairs and stepped into the meeting room. Half of the group - it struck him, suddenly, that they still didn't have a proper name - was missing, unable to get away from classes or practical work to attend. Horst understood; there were just too many outsiders tramping through the university for them to risk doing anything out of the ordinary, even though the meetings were important. Sven sat at one end of the table, next to Hilde; Gudrun sat at the other end, looking tired and wan. Horst couldn't help feeling a flicker of concern. Unlike him, she hadn't been trained for long periods of stress, with the risk of capture permanently looming over her shoulder.

"We should be safe now," he said, once he'd closed the door and turned the jukebox on, deafening the bug with American music. He had no idea if someone - anyone - was actually *listening* through the bug, but better safe than sorry. "There are at least nine new spies within the student body."

"I noticed," Gudrun said. She sounded vaguely amused. "That Rudolf has never touched a computer in his life. He sat next to me in the lab and stared at it before the professor showed him how to turn it on."

Horst smiled. "That isn't uncommon in the east," he said. "Computers? What can you do with a computer that you can't do with a gun, farming tools and a great deal of grit, spunk and determination?"

"Play computer games," Sven said, wryly. "Send messages across the entire continent in the blink of an eye. Access files everywhere and change them, if necessary."

"True," Horst agreed. German bureaucracy was famed across the entire world for sheer bloody-minded thoroughness. There were copies of SS files right across the *Reich*; he knew, if he walked into an office in Germany South, the officers on duty would be able to access a copy of his file and confirm his identity with ease. "But they rarely see anything more advanced than a tank or a CAS aircraft."

He shrugged as he sat down. "There have been other developments," he added. "Have you heard about the unions?"

Sven smiled. "My father's a member at the plant," he said. "He's been bitching for months about having to work longer hours for less pay; now, he's banding together with most of his fellows to demand higher pay and shorter work hours."

"I'm not sure he'll get anywhere if he demands more money for less work," Hilde said, quietly. "My mother has been organising protests through her network of female organisations. She's even been gathering information from the Sisters of Mercy. The crisis is far worse than we assumed."

"Things are moving faster," Gudrun said. She didn't sound as enthusiastic as Horst would have expected. "How do we make them slow down?"

"We don't," Horst said. "The government isn't going to slow its response to suit us."

Hilde leaned forward. "Are we doing the right thing?"

"*Yes*," Gudrun snapped.

"My father said that we were weakening the *Reich*," Hilde said, after a moment. "That we were fools who were threatening order and stability..."

"That's an interesting argument," Horst said. He'd actually expected the government to use a similar line to dismiss the leaflets, even though it would have been a *de facto* confession that the leaflets actually existed. "But tell me... will anything change if we do nothing?"

He took a breath. "The government got us into a war that seems to be unwinnable, the government is lying to us and the government has no reason to change," he added, after a moment. "We have to force them to change before the whole edifice breaks apart and shatters."

"So what do we do," Hilde asked, "if we win?"

"We worry about it when we win," Horst said, dryly. The leaflets might have upset the government, but they hadn't really threatened its grip on power.

"You do realise the odds of us ending up hanging from meat hooks are alarmingly high?"

"True," Gudrun said. She sounded more cheerful, although it was apparent that something was bothering her. "So... what do we do about the unions?"

"I can use the computer network to spread the word," Sven offered. "The corporations are quite dependent on computers, these days, and their security is terrible. Blinking messages through the network shouldn't be *that* hard."

"Then do it," Gudrun said.

"Do more than that," Horst said. He smiled, rather coldly. "Put out rumours as well, rumours that will be believed. The corporations are about to cut wages, again; the demand for production is about to skyrocket... rumours that will be believed by the people at risk."

"Perhaps even add a suggestion that hundreds of workers are going to be fired," Gudrun offered. "Maybe even replaced with *Untermenschen*."

Sven looked doubtful. "They wouldn't believe that, would they?"

Horst snorted. "What makes you think the corporations *wouldn't* replace their labour force with *Untermenschen* if they thought they could get away with it?"

"Write out a list of rumours and start spreading them," Gudrun said.

"We need more than that," Horst said. "People will only move if they believe that they will not move alone, Gudrun. We need to create a legend. We need something people will believe in, an organisation that unites all the disparate interest groups against the government."

"A brotherhood," Sven said.

"A super-union," Horst agreed. "We need a name for ourselves and a figurehead."

Gudrun frowned. "The Reich Reform Commission?"

"I'd have thought something more striking," Horst said. "The Valkyries, perhaps. And their leader, Sigrún."

"That might work," Gudrun said, thoughtfully.

"You'd be Sigrún," Horst told her. There were few Germans alive who wouldn't be aware of the name's origins. They'd all been forced to study the Norse myths in school. "We'd issue proclamations in your name, using them to create an impression of vast numbers - and, in doing so, make them true."

"That would tell the government that our leader was a girl," Sven objected.

"They'd be unlikely to believe it," Horst assured him. "Why *would* they believe it? They don't think much of women."

"My mother is likely to take advantage of that," Hilde observed. "She's already starting new groups."

"We need to work on women's rights too," Gudrun said. "Get all of the women on our side."

Horst nodded. "Shall we work on the first proclamation?"

He'd been told, years ago, that a committee was the only animal in existence with multiple bodies and no brain. It wasn't something he'd really understood until the four of them had put their heads together and drafted out the first set of demands: free elections, freedom of speech, freedom of the press, freedom of association, an end to the war in South Africa and, above all, an end to the climate of fear. Horst had to admit, as he read the prelude, that Gudrun knew how to turn a phrase. She might lack the polish of the writers who wrote the regime's propaganda, but that only made it stronger. Her words came from the heart.

"Upload it onto the network," Gudrun said, when they were finally finished. "And, for God's sake, don't let any of the spies see you typing it into the computer."

"We'll need to print out more leaflets too," Horst observed. "And then start scattering them around the city."

"Maybe we can hide them around the university," Sven said, "with notes asking the finders to hand them out. They wouldn't have any direct link to us if they got caught."

"True," Horst said. "But be careful this time, understand. *No fingerprints!*"

He threw a look at Gudrun as Sven and Hilde left the room, motioning for her to stay. She looked oddly reluctant - he wondered if she was still embarrassed about the kiss - but remained seated, studying her fingertips as if they were the most fascinating thing in the universe. Horst checked the door, then sat down next to her. If anyone glanced inside, they'd hopefully assume that Horst and Gudrun had found a private place for some alone time. He just hoped the spies didn't see them together.

"Konrad's father is involved with the unions," he said, flatly.

Gudrun's eyes went wide. "Are you sure?"

"I have a... friend who's just joined up," Horst lied. In reality, his handler had told him that Volker Schulze had already been tagged as a union leader by the SS - and ordered Horst to watch for anyone at the university who might have a connection to him. "Volker Schulze may not be the *sole* leader, but he's definitely involved. Tell me... your engagement to Konrad ..."

"Is over," Gudrun said, bitterly. "His father terminated it."

Horst hesitated, unsure what to say. He *liked* Gudrun - if things had been different, perhaps he would have courted her himself. And there had been that kiss... the nasty part of his mind was almost tempted to applaud. But Gudrun had loved Konrad and he hadn't deserved to wind up a cripple, alone and helplessly dependent on a life support machine. *She* certainly didn't deserve to lose her boyfriend so casually, to have her relationship dismissed by his father. The only consolation was that it wasn't a declaration that she wasn't suitable as a prospective bride.

"I'm sorry to hear that," he said. He practically swallowed his tongue to keep from pointing out that Gudrun and Konrad would never have been able to have a normal life together. A young man as badly wounded as Konrad was nothing more than a drain on the *Reich*. Some bean-counting bureaucrat who had never met him would order the life support turned off, sooner or later. "But I need to know. Was your engagement ever formalised?"

"Not really," Gudrun admitted, after a moment. "We'd exchanged letters, of course, but we hadn't registered the engagement."

Horst let out a breath he hadn't realised he'd been holding. "So there's nothing formal to tie you to Konrad?"

"No," Gudrun said, miserably. She looked up, suddenly. "Do you think they might draw a line between myself and Konrad's father?"

"It's a possibility," Horst admitted. He'd gone through the files as thoroughly as he dared, but he hadn't been able to tell if anyone had reported an intruder visiting Konrad's bed. The SS already believed that the leaflets had come from the university; if they knew about Gudrun and Konrad, they'd certainly have grounds for hauling Gudrun into the RSHA for a long interrogation session. "You need to consider the prospect of someone asking you a few questions."

"Konrad wasn't a student," Gudrun objected.

"They know the leaflets came out of the university," Horst said. He covered for his slip instantly. "There wouldn't be so many spies in the building if they *didn't* know. They must have figured out that the professor they arrested was innocent - or, at least, that he had nothing to do with the leaflets."

Gudrun snorted, rather sourly. Horst understood. He had no idea who'd started the rumours about the arrested professor sleeping with some of his students, but they just wouldn't go away. It was a standard tactic - undermining the professor's reputation to make it harder for anyone to defend him - and it seemed to be working. The students were still discussing the leaflets, but very few of them still respected the professor.

"I'll watch myself," Gudrun assured him, finally. "And I won't tell them anything."

"Just stick to the basics," Horst said. He had no illusions. If the SS had good reason to link Gudrun to the leaflets - to the *Valkyries* - it was unlikely she would be able to hold out for long. There were plenty of ways to make someone suffer without ever laying a finger on them. "And try to say as little as possible when they ask questions."

"I'll try," Gudrun said. She took a nervous breath. "Do your parents think you should get married?"

Horst blinked in surprise. "That's... an odd question," he said, finally. "They do want me to find a nice girl and move back east, but I don't think I want to give them the satisfaction."

Gudrun looked up at him. "Why not?"

"The east... is very strict," Horst said, carefully. "If you were born there, you'd probably be a farmwife. You would live and die on the farms, while the menfolk go off to war or man the ramparts against terrorists. There is very little to do beyond working on the farms. I was lucky - very lucky - that I was able to sit for the exams."

"I know," Gudrun said.

"I might be expected to marry two women," Horst said. "Or more. I knew men who had three or four wives, women who'd been married before only to have their husbands killed on deployment. I'd bring up a flock of children and watch the girls marry soldiers and the boys march off to war. And heaven help anyone who asked questions."

"You make it sound awful," Gudrun said, after a moment.

"It does have some compensations," Horst admitted. What he'd said was true enough, but incomplete. "People are more... connected in the east, Gudrun. Everyone knows everyone else. You know who you can rely on in the settlements, who you can trust with a gun at your back. And the SS is much less overbearing in the east, even though it is far more numerous. But I wouldn't want to spend the rest of my life there."

He cleared his throat. "Why do you ask?"

"My father spoke to me yesterday," Gudrun said, slowly. "He wants me to marry soon, to choose someone even though Konrad is still alive. I wanted to know if you faced the same pressure."

"I do," Horst admitted. "But it's a little different for me."

"They don't seem to nag *Kurt* to marry," Gudrun said. "It isn't *fair*."

"Kurt's a young officer," Horst pointed out. "He might be in position to marry a girl with excellent family connections."

Gudrun shook her head. "I don't know how long I can keep putting it off," she said, reluctantly. "It could turn nasty if father finds someone for me..."

"Say you need at least six months to mourn Konrad," Horst said. Part of him was tempted to push his luck, but it would only make her hate him. "As far as they know, you only just found out what happened to him. After that, you can start looking for someone suitable and promise to let your father offer suggestions if you don't find someone within a year."

Gudrun blinked. "A year?"

"We may be arrested and brutally executed tomorrow," Horst said. Maybe, after six months had passed, he'd feel better about courting Gudrun himself. "Or we may win. Or the horse may even learn to sing."

"My father's singing is a deadly weapon," Gudrun said, wryly.

"And if that isn't enough, find someone willing to pretend to be your boyfriend," Horst added, after a moment. "They'll understand you rejecting someone after a few weeks of casual courting."

He glanced at his watch, then rose. "I have a lecture in ten minutes," he said. He watched as she rose and unplugged the jukebox. "I'll see you later."

"You too," Gudrun said.

CHAPTER TWENTY-FIVE

Reichstag, Berlin
8 August 1985

Hans Krueger wrinkled his nose as he stepped into the council chamber and took his seat at one side of the table, facing the *Reichsführer-SS*. Several ministers and military officers were smoking, a sure sign of their agitation, while the *Fuhrer* was looking around as if he thought he was actually expected to direct the meeting. Hans gave Adolf Bormann a nasty look, then eyed the *Reichsführer-SS*. Karl Holliston had called the meeting and, judging by the papers in front of him, it was going to be a long one.

"The meeting is now called to order," Holliston said, taking control as soon as the last councillor was in his seat. "*Heil Hitler!*"

"*Heil Hitler*," the councillors said, in unison.

Holliston didn't give anyone else a chance to override his control of the meeting. "It's spreading," he said, simply. "Our failure to put a stop to this right from the start" - he threw Hans a nasty look - "has encouraged others to defy the *Reich*."

"You speak of the trade unions," Hans said, calmly. *Someone* had to be the voice of reason at the table. "Or is there something I've missed?"

"The trade unions are not the only problem," Holliston snapped. "There are hundreds of little groups springing up everywhere, discussing the leaflets and comparing notes. We have this piece of shit" - he took one of the papers from the table and waved it in the air - "to tell us just what imprudent demands these... these Valkyries demand!"

"The Choosers of the Slain," Hans mused, as he took the sheet of paper. "Odd choice of name for a dissident group."

"It's a deliberate insult," Holliston thundered. "Something must be done!"

"We know who the ringleaders are, at least in the factories," Luther Stresemann said. The Head of the Economic Intelligence Service leaned forward. "We could round them up and arrest them - or simply order them fired."

"The problem isn't that simple," Hans warned. "Each of these... *ringleaders* is a symptom, not the disease itself. We're pushing our industrial base to the limit and our trained workers are finally pushing back."

"Forming a union without government permission is flatly illegal," Holliston sneered. Hans would have privately bet good money that Holliston was feeling the heat from industrialists who were closely connected to the SS. "Every member of each and every union should be thrown into the camps."

Hans resisted, barely, the temptation to sneer back. "You are talking about arresting two-thirds of our trained workforce," he said. "Good luck getting the damned *Gastarbeiters* to run a modern manufacturing plant!"

"The *Gastarbeiters* are not permitted to do more than dig ditches and plant crops," Holliston pointed out. "Such jobs are reserved for good Germans!"

"Yes, the Germans you're talking about throwing into the camps," Hans said. Holliston was right; the training for industrial jobs was reserved solely for Germans, although a handful of non-German Aryans might be allowed to join if they showed promise. "You put even a tenth of our total workforce out of work and our economy will go straight into the shitter."

Holliston took a moment to gather himself. "We cannot allow them to defy the government like this," he said, in a markedly calmer tone. "And that set of demands" - he jabbed a finger at the paper in front of Hans - "is unthinkable."

Hans looked at the paper and was tempted to agree. Some of the demands were reasonable - he would happily have agreed to end the war in South Africa if he could - while others... others were impossible to grant without undermining the *Reich* beyond hope of repair. The whole concept of free elections was absurd. It wouldn't be long before the population started electing politicians based on who could make the best promises, not on practical matters like experience, understanding and common sense.

"And we cannot act against them openly, either," he said. "If even the most optimistic report is accurate, *Reichsführer*, word is spreading too far too fast. The unions can bring the country to a halt just by going on strike."

"Then we clobber them," Holliston snapped.

"And who will run the industries afterwards?" Hans snapped back. "We're going in circles!"

"This is all your fault," Holliston said. "Bringing in *American* ideals…"

"We had an industry before the start of the war," Hans pointed out, smoothly. "Those Panzer tanks that smashed Poland, Denmark, France and Russia didn't just spring into existence, you know. And we had to do whatever we needed to do to keep up with the Americans. A Panzer III wouldn't last two seconds on a battlefield facing the latest American tank!"

He took a breath. "This situation has gotten badly out of hand," he said. "Right now, our falsehoods about the war have been exposed and so the population no longer trusts us. They are forming private groups and discussing discrepancies between our words and reality. It will not take them long to find other times when we lied to them."

"For their own good," Holliston said.

Hans met his eyes. "We tell ourselves that," he said, although he doubted it was true in Holliston's case. "But I don't think they agree with us."

"I will not see us going all the way back to the days when Germany was stabbed in the back by the Jews and Americans and stamped into the ground by the French and British," Holliston said. "And I will not hand power over to a bunch of anarchists who don't have the faintest idea of how to form a government, let alone make the hard decisions!"

"So tell me," Hans said. "What *do* we do?"

He looked around the table, silently trying to gauge support. So far, most of the other councillors were content to watch and wait for a clear victor to emerge, or to see who would make the best offer for their support. It was frustrating, but in some ways it was almost a relief. At least he'd be able to make his case without being interrupted or shouted down.

"The French were supposed to pay us their tribute on the 1st of the month," he said, after a moment. "That tribute has been grossly reduced because the French are having their own labour problems. The stockpiles of food and raw materials they were also supposed to be sending to the *Reich* have also been delayed."

"Send in the troops," Holliston offered. "Take the foodstuffs by force, then lay waste to the fields to teach them a lesson."

Hans chose not to respond directly. "Because of that, we have a cash shortfall," he added, wondering how many of them would understand. "We've been sailing too close to bankruptcy for years; now, without the French cash, we may well cross the line and find ourselves faced with massive painful budget cuts. We simply have too many commitments and not enough cash to meet them. For example, we owe the Americans millions of dollars - dollars, not *Reichmarks* - for our recent purchases."

"So we delay paying," Holliston said.

"And so they delay supply," Hans said. "The Americans are not the French, *Herr Reichsführer*. They will not accept a promissory note drawn on a bank they know to be failing. Worse, perhaps, they will not supply us with anything *else* until they are paid in full."

"We don't need anything they can send us," Holliston insisted.

"That's not the only problem," Hans continued. "Where do we make our budget cuts? The military? The war? The support payments we make to mothers with more than two children or the pensions we grant to veterans?"

There was a long pause. "We could cut back on our purchase of war materials," Holliston mused, finally. "We don't need more tanks."

"But we do need vehicles designed for counter-insurgency operations in South Africa," Field Marshal Gunter Voss snapped. "We spent years building up the largest tank force in the world, which is next to completely useless in South Africa!"

"And we can't stop making payments to veterans," Field Marshal Justus Stoffregen added, coldly. "We made them *promises*."

Which we haven't been keeping for a long time, Hans thought. There had been a commitment, a honourable commitment, to look after the dead and wounded. But that commitment had been broken in South Africa. Trust in the government, never high at the best of times, was almost certainly gone. *But there will be riots if we start cutting the support payments.*

Hans tapped the table. "We can cancel some of our long-term procurement," he said. "The planned sixth carrier can be placed on hold, if necessary" - he ignored the squawk from *Grossadmiral* Cajus Bekker - "and we can scrap the planned development and purchase of a replacement main battle tank. We already have more than enough nuclear missiles to give the American ABM system a very hard time indeed, if it comes down to total war, and the Americans are unlikely to launch an invasion of the continent. Our security is unlikely to be put at risk.

"The problem, however, is that this will have dangerous knock-on effects," he added, wondering just how many of them would understand. "If we stop paying for new tanks..."

"We would have more money," Holliston snapped.

"Yes, and the corporations we would be paying *wouldn't*," Hans said. "They would wind up with a cash shortfall, so they would either have to cut wages - again - or sack hundreds of trained workers. And *that* will cause more social unrest at the worst possible time."

"They could go east," Holliston offered. "We need more farmers..."

"There's no shortage of farmers," Hans snapped. "They're trained and experienced industrial workers. We *cannot* afford to lose them."

He looked down at the table. "But even if we do, it will not fix the hole in our budget," he warned. "The really big expenses are the ones we don't dare risk cutting. Keeping the garrisons in position to monitor the French alone is quite costly; keeping Germany South a going concern is staggeringly expensive. And the support payments may be the single worst item on the list. We have *got* to stop handing out money to every woman who has more than a single child!"

"But we need to keep our population from decaying," Holliston insisted. "How will the women have children if they cannot afford to keep them?"

"Our population is not in danger of falling," Hans said.

It wasn't entirely true, he knew. Industrial societies - and Germany Prime *was* an industrial society - had significantly lower birth-rates than farming societies. America had had a baby boom after the war with Japan, then the birth-rate had dropped sharply over the following decades. The *Reich* had escaped the same fate through passing laws that made it easier to afford more children, both through support payments and public honours for women with many children. But now, simply paying the women their monthly allowance was a major strain on the public purse. Who knew what would happen, apart from massive civil unrest, if the payments were ever cut?

"The *Untermenschen* breed like rabbits," Holliston said. "We have to keep up with them."

"The *Untermenschen* are unlikely to pose a major danger, at least for the foreseeable future," Hans countered. "Our current problems lie with the so-called Valkyries."

"The corporations will not allow any independent trade unions," Friedrich Leopoldsberger said, coldly. The Industries Minister was their creature, Hans knew; the Ministry of Industry was, perhaps, the most deeply corrupt ministry in the *Reich*. "There are corporate-sponsored unions to handle the workers and their concerns."

"Unions which do nothing more than identify and marginalise trouble-makers," Hans pointed out. "Can the corporations afford to lose half of their workforce?"

"They will come crawling back after a couple of weeks of unemployment," Leopoldsberger said. "Let them experience life without a regular salary. Let them see what it is like to be without money, without hope of employment. Where else can they go?"

"That would work," Holliston said.

"And how long would it be," Hans asked, "before the entire workforce goes on strike?"

He scowled at Leopoldsberger, who scowled back. "You're thinking in terms of a handful of little men," he said. "And yes, a handful of bad apples can be isolated and kicked out of the bunch. But thousands of workers, all of whom are already feeling the pinch? You might just start a whole series of strikes if you sacked them... and if that happens, you will find it impossible *not* to surrender. There are no replacements for trained workers."

"We could train others," Leopoldsberger pointed out.

"In time?" Hans asked. "God knows our training system has been having problems too. Or are you planning to bring in the military to run the plants?"

"We couldn't," Voss said.

"We could at least try to break their morale," Holliston said. "If they resist... we're no worse off than we already are."

"We'd have allowed them to see their strength," Hans said, exasperated. "And *that* will undermine us more than the financial crisis."

He gave Holliston a long considering look. "It may be time to start considering other ways to save money and put the *Reich* on a firmer footing," he added. "Perhaps it is time to bring the war in South Africa to an end."

"Out of the question," Holliston thundered. "If we leave, Pretoria will go under and the niggers will rule South Africa. And then Germany South will fall. And then the French, Italian and Spanish empires will fall. And then there will be a black tide washing at the southern coastline of Europe!"

"It's rather more likely that they'll have a civil war," Stresemann said. "The blacks are split into multiple different factions. Several of them are centred around tribes that are only working together because they see the Afrikaners as a worse threat. If the war comes to an end, if they win their freedom, they might start killing each other instead of threatening our borders."

"The black population of Germany South will take heart from our surrender," Holliston insisted. "And it *will* be a surrender! Adolf Hitler *himself* insisted that not one jot of German land was to be surrendered to the barbarians."

"Hitler *did* understand the value of a tactical withdrawal," Stoffregen reminded him. "It isn't as if the land won't be recaptured one day."

"This isn't a limited tactical withdrawal to buy time," Holliston said, coldly. He held up a hand before any of the military officers could correct him. "I know; we often fell back when the Russians lunged at us during the war, just to allow their advance time to stall before we counterattacked and retook the territory, destroying their forces as we advanced. But here, we would be abandoning a government that shares our ideals. Our enemies will not hesitate to take notice.

"Vichy France is already under pressure from its own people. If we abandon South Africa, the French will assume that we will abandon the Vichy Government and rise up against it, forcing us to intervene. The war in South Africa may be bad, but it will be far worse if we have to fight an insurgency in the south of France. Fighting will spill over into our territories and the results will be disastrous. And Spain, Italy and Greece will go the same way. To surrender South Africa risks surrendering the entire *Reich*.

"And the Americans will not hesitate to take advantage of our weakness. They will ship weapons into France, allowing the French to shoot down our aircraft and destroy our tanks; they may even slip weapons into Germany itself, passing them on to the *Gastarbeiters* in their camps. We cannot give up now or we will lose everything!"

So we go in a circle, Hans thought. *We cannot arrest the rebels, nor can we grant their demands. What the hell do we do?*

"We use pressure to convince the trade unionists to give up," Holliston said. "And we pull out all the stops in searching for this... this *Sigrún*! We launch a full-scale propaganda campaign to convince the population that the Valkyries will eventually lead Germany to its doom. We make it damn clear that the war in South Africa is *necessary*!"

"That would force us to admit that we underestimated the situation," Hans pointed out, smoothly.

"Then let us make that admission," Holliston snapped. "Let us admit to the mistake, let us put our justification in front of the people and let the true Germans see what has to be done."

Hans frowned. "And if they reject the arguments?"

"We control the mass media," Holliston said. "The Valkyries have to sneak around the computer network and leave their damnable leaflets in libraries or hidden under seats on the trains. We've even arrested a couple of idiots carting them around the city. They cannot compete with us when it comes to speaking to the people."

"And yet the people are more likely to believe them," Hans said. "We were caught lying, Karl. It's hard to regain trust when you lose it so roughly."

"Then we tell them why we lied," Holliston said. "Because there's no other way to tackle the problem."

Hans sighed, inwardly, as the councillors started to vote. Holliston, damn the man, had offered them an alternative to either making massive budget cuts or surrendering some of their power. They believed him because they *wanted* to believe him, because they hoped there was a way out of the crisis without tearing the *Reich* apart. And nothing he could say would make a difference.

He cursed under his breath as Holliston flashed him a look of triumph, once the voting was over. Who knew? Maybe Holliston *was* right. But the figures didn't lie. No matter how he looked at it, there was no way to avoid a major budgetary crisis forever. Indeed, he suspected the crisis would be impossible to hide in less than a month...

... And who knew what would happen then?

CHAPTER TWENTY-SIX

Berlin, Germany
12 August 1985

"The manager wants to see you," the secretary said curtly, as Volker Schulze entered the factory. "You're to go straight to him. No detours along the way."

Volker Schulze nodded. He'd expected to be hauled up in front of the factory's manager sooner rather than later. Indeed, he was surprised it hadn't already happened. There was always some ass-licking bastard willing to rat out his fellows for money or a chance at promotion. But, given the sheer number of workers in the new union and the rumours spreading through the grapevine, he suspected that management was passing the buck higher and higher up the chain. The manager of the factory couldn't even muster the initiative to wipe his own ass without orders in triplicate from *his* superiors.

"I'll be along in a moment," he said. His eyes found Joachim as he entered the factory and gave him a significant look. They'd had a week to come up with contingency plans for when management finally decided to do something about the union and they were, he suspected, about to find out just how good they were. "I'll have to leave my coat in the cloakroom..."

"Now," the secretary said. Someone must have bawled him out for his role in helping to arrange the first union meeting, even though he hadn't had the slightest idea what had actually been going on. Volker Schulze would have felt sorry for him if the secretary hadn't been such a pissy little man. "The manager wants to see you at once."

Volker Schulze mouthed orders at Joachim, then turned and allowed the secretary to lead him up the stairs to the management offices. He'd only entered them twice before, back when he'd been a loyal foreman; he'd had to defend two workers who had been on the verge of being fired for problems beyond their control. He couldn't help feeling a flicker of doubt as he passed through a solid wooden door that was normally locked, even though he'd made his plans and discussed them with his wife. If he'd misjudged the situation - and he knew all too well just how ruthless the government could be - he was in deep trouble.

They can't afford to punish all of us, he reassured himself. A week had given him time to spread the idea of independent unions far and wide. *His* was still the best-organised, but others were growing in size and power. *They need us to man the factories and produce their guns and butter.*

"Wait here," the secretary said.

Volker Schulze snorted, rudely, as he leaned against the wall. It was intimidation, childish intimidation. It might work on a young boy who'd been kicked out of class and told to report to the headmaster, but not on a grown man with genuine combat experience. The secretary had none, as far as he knew; he'd been too cowardly to volunteer for military service and lucky enough to escape conscription. And he would be surprised if his managers had any experience themselves. He'd be more worried if he was getting called for an interview with his former CO.

He was midway through a silent recitation of SS *Adolf Hitler's* battle honours when the secretary returned, looking as if someone had crammed a rod up his butt. Volker kept his face under control as the secretary motioned for him to step through the door, into the manager's office. Not entirely to his surprise, he noticed as he entered, the factory manager was absent, his place taken by two men in fancy suits. He recognised one of them as a senior official within the factory's parent corporation - there had been an article on him in the corporate newsletter - but the other was a complete stranger.

"Foreman Volker Schulze," the official said. Volker had to think hard to recall the man's name. Leonhard Crosse, if he recalled correctly. "You have formed a union, in defiance of both your contract with the corporation and *Reich* law. Do you have anything you wish to say in your defence?"

"Yes, sir," Volker said. He adjusted his posture, trying hard to present a picture of a man who was both willing to compromise and yet determined to stand his ground. "The current working conditions are appalling and they're only going to get worse. There have already been a number of deaths over the last two months, caused by increased demand for production combined with poor maintenance. We simply cannot go on like this."

It was worse than that, he knew. Four men had died only two months ago, after the piece of machinery they were working on had exploded. That had been bad enough, but their families - unfortunate enough to live on corporate property - had been immediately evicted, on the grounds that their relatives no longer worked at the plant. In hindsight, Volker suspected, they should have taken *that* incident as an excuse to form an independent union. There had been so much anger on the factory floor that it would have been easy to start a strike.

"Your conduct is inexcusable," Crosse said. If he'd heard a single word Volker had said, he didn't give any sign of it. "You are accordingly dismissed from your job. Your appeal has already been reviewed by the labour commission and rejected. You will be escorted to the gates and evicted. As you have admitted to forming an unregulated union, you will not be paid your final paycheck."

Volker kept his face expressionless. He hadn't expected anything else. The 'appeal' - the appeal he hadn't even made - was nothing more than a mere formality, a meaningless statement designed to suggest that there had been a form of due process. He could have put forward any excuse, he knew, and they would have rejected it. Forming a union, challenging the corporate managers directly... it was an unforgivable sin. But it was far too late for them to crush the union by firing its founder. The union was already out of control.

He glanced behind him as the door opened, just in time to see two burly men step into the chamber. Corporate security, he noted dispassionately; they carried themselves like thugs, not real soldiers. He offered no resistance as they grabbed his shoulders, spun him around and marched him through the door. The secretary, standing outside, sneered at Volker as he was pushed through the outer office and down the stairs. A number of workers were waiting at the bottom. Volker smiled to himself as the security guards hesitated, suddenly unsure of themselves. They were good at pushing individuals around, but they didn't have the bravery to face an entire group.

"Strike," Volker announced, loudly. "STRIKE!"

He yanked his hands free as the workers swarmed forwards. Joachim had already briefed them, he knew; the guards had no time to resist before they were grabbed, searched and shoved into an office to wait until they were released. They made no attempt to draw their pistols and fight back before it was too late. Volker took one of the pistols and checked it - he dreaded to think what his training officers would have said if they'd seen the weapon - and then started to bark orders. The unionists took up the cry of strike, sending advance parties running through the factory. Volker himself turned and led another team back up the stairs, into the outer office. The secretary, no longer sneering, had scooped up a telephone and was frantically dialling a number. Volker resisted the temptation to shoot the device out of his hand - he honestly wasn't sure if the pistol would fire when he pulled the trigger - and instead motioned for the secretary to put the telephone down.

"Wimp," Joachim commented, as Volker motioned for the secretary to stand up and move away from his desk. His trousers were stained with urine. "Honestly. He should try working on the shop floor."

Volker wrinkled his nose in disgust. He'd pissed himself too, the first time he'd gone into battle, but he'd been up against a *serious* enemy. They'd known what would happen if they were captured by the Arabs and every man in the unit had privately resolved to save one bullet for themselves, rather than fall into enemy hands. The secretary, as priggish as he was, had nothing to fear as long as he behaved himself. But then, he probably thought the workers on the factory floor were barbarians. He'd certainly never spent any time with them.

"Keep an eye on him," he ordered, as he led the way into the inner office. "I... ah."

He snorted in annoyance as his eyes swept the fancy office. He'd hoped to capture the managers, but their chamber was already deserted. They'd sneaked down the rear stairs to the loading bay and probably run into the streets. It might not be a bad thing - the government might feel less inclined to negotiate if there were hostages in the factory - but it was still annoying. He'd been looking forward to the chance to show Crosse just how it felt to be at another's mercy.

"The factory is ours," another worker reported, as they made their way back to the lower levels. "Most of the workers have joined us."

"Tell anyone who wants to leave now that they can go," Volker ordered. There was no point in trying to keep the secretary and the rest of the administrative staff. Besides, there was too great a chance of someone beating hell out of the bureaucrats and making it harder for the workers to come to a peaceful settlement. "And round up a handful of volunteers to deliver messages."

Joachim gave him a sharp look. "We need to spark off other strikes, don't we?"

Volker nodded. A single factory had a *mere* three thousand workers, most of whom had either joined the union when it was announced or would join now that the union had proven itself capable of effective action. But they really needed the other factories to go on strike too or the government would isolate them, seal off their lines of supply and wait for the strikers to starve. It didn't seem to have occurred to them - yet - that mistreating trained and proud men might not be a wise idea.

"Yeah," he said. "Put it out on the computer network, then start making telephone calls before they cut the lines. We need the strike to spread as widely as possible."

And hope that Gerde and Liana get out of easy reach, he added, mentally. The strikers had planned as best as they could, but no battle plan ever survived contact with the enemy. If he was in the RSHA, he'd try to bring pressure to bear on the families of the strikers. *If they don't get into hiding in time, they may be arrested.*

———

Gudrun had never really liked eating meals at school - every student was served the same meal and the teachers were quite happy to punish anyone who failed to eat every last bite - but she rather enjoyed eating in the university cafeteria. There was a wide selection of choices, tables and chairs were scattered everywhere instead of being placed in neat little rows, while students could sit anywhere they wanted rather than being tied to a specific chair for their entire year. Just being allowed to choose her own food, instead of choking down something that smelled suspiciously like manure, was enough to make her actually enjoy herself.

"They say university fees are going to rise," Hartwig was saying, loudly. He was a year older than Gudrun, a blonde boy with a reputation for chasing women as well as scoring high marks in all of his classes. She would have liked him if he hadn't been loud and boastful as well as intelligent. "We may have to start paying to attend."

She smiled, inwardly, as she ate her meal. *That* was one of the rumours the Valkyries had started, a suggestion that the students would soon have to actually pay to attend the university. It was a terrifying thought. Of all the students she knew, only Hilde's family was wealthy enough to afford the prospective fees. Three-quarters of the student body would have to leave if they found themselves being charged to attend.

"That's outrageous," Lin said. She was Hartwig's current girlfriend, a girl as blonde as Hartwig or Gudrun herself. Gudrun sometimes wondered if she had paid someone to take her exams, because she seemed to lose half her IQ whenever Hartwig smiled at her. "I couldn't afford to attend!"

Idiots, Gudrun thought. One of the spies wasn't too far away, listening intently. Hartwig and Lin might find themselves in trouble, if the spies couldn't find anyone more significant. Or was Hartwig's family important enough to escape the consequences of their son having a big mouth and no brain cells? *You'll get yourselves in hot water.*

She glanced up, sharply, as Tomas charged into the cafeteria. "There's a strike," he bellowed, as everyone turned to look at him. "The workers are going on strike!"

Gudrun listened, surprised, as he babbled out an explanation. Seven factories had gone on strike? How many workers had believed the rumours the Valkyries had started? And how many more would go on strike before the affair came to an end? And what would the government do?

"We have to go help them," Hartwig said. He rose. "Come on!"

Gudrun hesitated. The spy had already started to hurry towards the edge of the room, clearly planning to find a telephone and alert his superiors. And not every student looked enthusiastic about leaving the campus and hurrying down to the factories before it was too late. But Hartwig was drawing dozens of students in his wake, pointing out that the government would never dare harm young men and women. Gudrun hoped, as she rose to follow him, that he was right.

She jumped as a hand caught her arm. "You shouldn't be going," Horst muttered. "Gudrun..."

Cold logic told her he was right. She'd *started* the Valkyries; she'd started the rumours and proclamations that had probably helped spark off the strike. If there was a riot, if she was arrested or killed, the entire movement might fall apart. And yet, she couldn't let her fellow students - and the strikers - go into danger alone. She owed it to her conscience to share the same risks.

"I have to go," she muttered back, confident that the student babble would make it hard for any listening ears to overhear. "Tell Sven to start sending out messages encouraging others to join the strike."

Horst gave her a worried look. "I can go with you..."

"Don't," Gudrun said. She brushed off his arm and turned towards the door. It was a risk, but it was one she had to take. "We can't *both* be caught."

———

"There's a *what?*"

"A strike," Holliston said, with heavy satisfaction. Hans couldn't help wondering what he was so pleased about, not when he would have bet good money that Holliston's policy had started the strike in the first place. "Twelve factories have gone on strike, so far, and rumours are spreading across the entire city."

Hans swore under his breath as Holliston outlined the situation. There was no time to check with his own sources, no time to do anything but rely on the *Reichsführer-SS's* version of the tale. He doubted Holliston would actually *lie* to the Reich Council - his career wouldn't survive a deliberate lie - yet he would definitely paint the situation as darkly as possible. A strike, right in the heart of Berlin...

"You tried to fire someone for forming a union," he said, when Holliston had finished. "And that led to an immediate strike."

He groaned as the full implications struck him. Attacking the striking workers would weaken the economy at the worst possible time, but conceding their demands would be even worse, as Holliston's corporate allies had probably pointed out. The strikers would be emboldened; they'd demand more and more until they hit something the *Reich* literally could *not* give them. And then...? The *Reich* would not be in a good position to put a stop to the whole affair.

"We have to take action," Holliston said, curtly. "I have two battalions of military police on alert, ready to handle the strikers."

"So you do," Hans said. "And then what?"

"We move in, arrest the strikers and then dictate terms from a position of strength," Holliston insisted, firmly. "They're breaking the law by forming an independent union."

"Yes, I know," Hans said. "And are you going to arrest *all* of them?"

"The ringleaders will be executed," Holliston said. He thumped the table with his fist. "And the others will go back to work."

Hans glared at him. "And what if they don't?"

"Then we'd hardly be in a worse position," Holliston snapped. He looked up, his gaze skimming around the table. "I call for a vote. Do we send in the police or try to 'negotiate' with law-breakers? We cannot allow the strikes to spread."

"They will," Hans said.

He forced himself to keep his voice calm. "There's a saying I heard from my son, who went to work in China," he said. Helping the Chinese Nationalists build up their industrial base might have been a mistake, in hindsight; China might pose a threat to Germany East in the next few decades. "There was a Chinese ruler who punished everything with death. One day, a bunch of men discovered that they were late for work. If they arrived, they would be executed. But the punishment for revolting against the ruler was *also* death. What did they have to lose?"

"We cannot let law-breakers get away with it," Holliston said. "I call for a vote."

Hans sighed. Put like that, the result was a foregone conclusion. The strike would be brutally crushed and the strikers would be arrested. And then...?

He kept his face impassive. It might be time to start coming up with some contingency plans of his own.

CHAPTER TWENTY-SEVEN

Berlin, Germany
12 August 1985

Herman stared at the Captain. "They want us to do what?"

"Seal off the factory district," the Captain ordered. "There's a strike, apparently, and friends and family of the strikers are hurrying to their side."

"A strike," Herman repeated.

He shook his head in disbelief. There were no strikes in the *Reich*. The French might strike at the drop of a hat - he'd heard stories about French workers downing tools because someone had said an unkind word - but the German worker was made of sterner stuff. And besides, strikes were illegal. The workers might wind up being dispatched to one of the less comfortable settlements in Germany East, if they were lucky.

The Captain ignored him. "I want barricades set up here, here and here," he said, tapping a number of road intersections. "If anyone tries to get past you and into the sealed zone, turn them back; if they're persistent, arrest them and we'll process them later. Anyone trying to get *out* of the sealed zone is to be arrested. These are German citizens so use the minimum necessary force, consistent with your personal safety."

"Shit," Herman muttered.

Caius stuck up a hand. "Sir? Who's going to assist the strikers?"

"Their friends and families," the Captain said, in some irritation. He hated repeating himself. "And, apparently, some students from the university. Turn them back; arrest them if they won't go."

Herman swallowed. Students from the university? Could *Gudrun* be going? He hoped not - she wouldn't be sitting down for a week if he caught her trying to bring aid and comfort to the strikers - but she'd certainly have friends and fellow students heading to the sealed zone. If he'd had time, he would have called the university and ordered Gudrun to go home at once, yet he knew the Captain would never allow it. His superiors would be breathing down his neck, ordering the police to get into position before the situation got completely out of hand.

If it isn't already, he thought, as he hastily donned riot gear and readied himself, as best as he could. They were trained in handling criminals and *Untermensch* who rioted on the streets, but they'd had very little training in handling civilian rioters gently. *If they've planned for a riot, they'll be ready for the gas and water cannons...*

He pushed the thought aside as he hurried down to the vans, following the rest of the policemen. Caius held the door open for him, then slammed it closed and barked orders to the driver, who started the engine and drove the vehicle out of the parking lot. Herman winced as the howl of the sirens echoed through the air, warning civilian traffic to get out of the way; he hoped - prayed - that the radio would be telling civilians to go home and stay there. If they were lucky, perhaps the strikers would see sense when they saw the police setting up barricades...

They're committed, he thought, grimly. He'd always hated trying to arrest criminals who *knew* there was no hope of escaping a life sentence to the camps - or death. They simply had nothing to lose. Why *not* try to kill a policeman so they'd have company in hell? *They're striking - and striking is illegal.*

It was an unpleasant thought. Konrad's father - he rather liked the man, even though he'd gone straight into civilian life rather than serving as a policeman - was an experienced military officer, while many of the strikers would have at least *some* military experience. They might even have weapons - retired soldiers and SS stormtroopers were often quietly allowed to keep their personal weapons - and they wouldn't back down at the slightest hint of trouble. Indeed, some of them would be very well versed in ways to use the terrain - and improvised weapons - to their advantage. Berlin might be turned into a battleground.

The driver clicked on the radio. "... Is an emergency announcement," a grim-sounding speaker said. "All civilians are ordered to remain in their homes or

CHRISTOPHER G. NUTTALL

workplaces until further notice; I say again, all civilians are ordered to remain in their homes or workplaces until further notice. If you are on the roads, pull over and remain there until further notice; I say again..."

"Nice speech," Fritz said, sarcastically. "Do you think anyone will listen?"

Herman shrugged as the driver pulled up at their destination. It had been a decade since the last nuclear attack drill, when the *Reich*-wide emergency broadcasting system had been tested. Few civilians would know what to do if all hell broke loose, let alone a riot in Berlin or an American attack. It was possible that most people would obey orders, but if even ten percent of the city's population *failed* to obey orders...

He gritted his teeth and followed the rest of the policemen out of the van. Civilians were scattering in all directions, some clearly trying to get out of the sealed zone and others trying to sneak in. The policemen ignored the civilians until they had the barricades firmly in place, then started warning intruders to turn back. Thankfully, most of the civilians trying to get *into* the sealed zone seemed willing to obey orders. It was the ones trying to leave who caused the worse problems. Half of them seemed convinced they were so important that, instead of trying to arrest them, the police should drive them immediately to the *Reichstag*.

And some of them probably are important, Herman thought, as the number of handcuffed prisoners started to rise sharply. *But we don't know how to tell the difference.*

———

Reichsführer-SS Karl Holliston was angry and he didn't care who knew it. Report after report was coming into the RSHA, warning him that the government was on the verge of losing control of the industrial zone. Thousands of civilians were even trying to support the strikers, despite increasingly harsh emergency broadcasts. The treachery had sunk so deeply into the *Reich* that even the corporate managers, the men who'd been first in line to demand immediate action, were hesitating.

He glared down at the map, silently considering how best to proceed. Attacking the factories themselves was dangerous as hell - Hans Krueger and his cronies would make a terrible fuss if pieces of expensive machinery were destroyed - but the marchers in the streets could be handled without risk-ing serious trouble. Who cared if a few hundred idiots got banged up by the military police? And the prospect of teaching some of the students - he knew several dozen had managed to get into the industrial sector before the police had set up barricades - a sharp lesson was delightful. Hans Krueger would have to work overtime to come up with excuses after the little bastards were caught in the act.

"*Herr Reichsführer?*"

Karl allowed himself a tight smile as he looked up. "Clear the streets."

———

"Andrew," Clyde Marshall said. "Are you sure we're safe here?"

Andrew shrugged. "I wouldn't count on it," he said, after a moment. "But I do think we're *reasonably* safe here."

He smiled at Marshall's expression. The *Reich* hadn't quite figured out that he was a reporter, rather than a press attaché - or that he'd happily accompany Andrew into the teeth of possible danger. There hadn't been any real trouble in Berlin since the sixties, as far as anyone knew; the growing mass of workers, students and civilians was unprecedented within the *Reich*. Thankfully, unlike some of the uglier riots in the US, it seemed to be reason-ably peaceful.

"Keep taking and uploading photographs," he ordered, instead of adding more empty reassurances. "They'll probably smash the camera if they arrest us."

"That girl looks very photogenic," Marshall agreed. A young girl - she couldn't have been older than eighteen - was perched on top of a burly worker, waving her shirt in the air, her breasts wobbling dangerously in her bra. "What keeps that bra on, do you think?"

"The eyes of every young man in the vicinity," Andrew said. "But she isn't the most important person here."

He couldn't help feeling a flicker of sympathy for the girl. It was unlikely she'd be molested, at least by the workers and her fellow students, but she might well be expelled from the university. The *Reich* had yet to embrace topless protests. Indeed, there were laws against revealing too much flesh in public. Even men were expected to wear knee-length shorts during the hotter months.

He frowned, inwardly, as they made their way down the street. It had been sheer luck - and a tip-off from a contact within the Ministry of Industry - that had got them into the factory complex before the police arrived and started to seal the whole area off. Andrew honestly wasn't sure what the authorities would do next, particularly if the strikers refused to back down... and he suspected they *couldn't* back down. Strikes were illegal, after all; the workers were expected to accept whatever their corporate masters saw fit to hand out. And then...

"Don't start taking notes," he warned, as he caught sight of Marshall reaching for his notebook. "They'll just be taken away if we get arrested."

Marshall paled. "I should have volunteered to go to South Africa instead," he said. "This place is shit."

"Just be glad you don't live here," Andrew muttered.

And that the Reich hasn't yet realised the power of digital cameras, he added, silently. *They may arrest us, they may smash the camera, but the photographs will get out. And then...?*

———

Gudrun had never enjoyed marching in unison, not in school and not in the BDM. It was so... rigid, so controlled; children were punished for stepping out of line, for speeding up, for slowing down, for doing anything other than obeying orders without question. By the time she'd turned eighteen, she'd been so indoctrinated that it had taken her months to stop walking like a schoolgirl or jumping to attention whenever someone spoke to her in the voice of authority. Individuality was not encouraged.

But the protest march outside the factory gates was different. People - workers, students, civilians - milled around, chatting happily as they wandered backwards and forwards. A handful of men were trying to make speeches and protesters were listening or not as they chose. There was no compulsion, there was no threat of force... the crowd was brimming with a strange energy, a sense that they were free, that they could do anything. Gudrun knew she should be trying to speak herself, even though it would be far too revealing, but instead all she wanted to do was enjoy the sensation of acting out as part of a crowd. There were just too many of them to be arrested.

And if we'd all stood up to the matrons, she thought, *perhaps the BDM would have been more fun.*

It was a galling thought. She could see, with the advantage of hindsight, just how carefully they'd been indoctrinated into the organisation, which had been preparing them to be good little housewives and civilians. Those who had been different - the fat, the questioners, the dissidents - had been separated from the herd, then publicly punished and shamed in front of their peers. No one had wanted to stand up for them and take the risk of being punished too, even though the matrons would have had problems handling a mass rebellion.

Or they would just have sent us home with notes, she thought, sourly. Her parents would have been furious - and afraid - if she'd stood up to the matrons. Who knew *what* sort of attention it would muster? *And our parents would have punished us for them.*

She smiled as someone produced a jukebox and plugged it into the factory's power supply, producing an American jazz song that was technically banned. The crowd looked shocked, then laughed; the sense of freedom was almost intoxicating. A dozen students began to dance, some of the girls pulling the male workers onto the streets and into the dance. Gudrun felt a flicker of bitter guilt - she'd only ever danced with Konrad, outside the stiffly formal dances they'd been forced to endure at school - and then pushed it away as a young worker held out a hand, inviting her to dance. Grinning, she took his hand and allowed him to lead her into the swing. It felt as though she was casting off a pair of invisible shackles.

And I am, she thought. *Together, we can do anything.*

———

Herman winced as a line of black vans appeared, driving down the road towards the barricades. The military policemen stopped just outside the roadblocks and scrambled out, brandishing their clubs and shields as they formed up into lines. A trio of armoured vehicles followed them, bristling with water cannons. He hoped desperately that the set of tubes on top of the vehicles were designed to launch gas canisters, rather than mortars. The crowds within the sealed zone were seemingly unarmed.

"Open the barricades," their CO ordered. He was a grim-faced man who looked ready to do anything to restore order. "And stand ready to receive prisoners."

Herman nodded and hurried to obey. It was hard to see their faces, under the black helmets they wore, but it didn't look as though the military policemen were worried about what they were going to do. They looked ... *enthusiastic*. It struck him, suddenly, that they would normally handle captured POWs and their families. German civilians would be a great deal safer than prisoners who *knew* they were going to the camps.

"This is going to be messy," Caius predicted, as the military policemen marched through the barricade and down towards the factories. "Very messy."

"I know," Herman said. He had no sympathy for the strikers, but there were hundreds of innocents caught in the sealed zone. "God help them."

———

Gudrun came to an embarrassed halt as the jukebox simply died, followed by the factory lights. She stared at her partner in shock for a long moment, then realised - as murmurs ran through the crowd - that someone must have turned off the electricity. She'd heard her father moaning about the cost of power often enough to know that the mains could be cut off in a power station, rather than at home, but she hadn't realised it could happen to a factory too...

And then she heard a rattling sound echoing from the police barricades.

"Get into the gates," someone shouted. "Get into the gates!"

It was too late. The striking workers were already closing the gates, readying themselves - she saw now - for an assault. She turned, realising in horror that the sense of freedom had vanished as the crowd started to scatter. The sound of armoured vehicles - and the steady rattling - was growing louder, bearing down on them from all directions. She heard a popping sound in the distance, followed by screams... what the hell were they *doing*? They weren't shooting, she was sure... or were they? Maybe the government had just decided to gun down the strikers rather than try to negotiate.

She gritted her teeth, then turned and ran, pushing her way through the crowd towards the brick walls. She'd be safer there, she thought, but the sound was growing louder. The crowd recoiled around her; she saw, as she broke free, a line of black-clad men advancing towards them, banging their clubs against riot shields. They'd been paying attention in the Hitler Youth, her mind frantically noted; they might have been walking towards a panicking mob of civilians, but they were banging their shields in perfect unison. White mist surrounded them, blowing towards the crowd. Her eyes started to water as the mist surrounded her.

The policemen stopped, still banging their shields. She stared, just for a moment, then blinked in surprise as she saw an armoured vehicle advancing slowly behind the policemen, who opened ranks to allow it to crawl forward. Gudrun wondered, in shock, if they were about to be mown down with machine guns, just before the water cannons started to spew water towards the crowd. She had no time to duck before ice cold water slammed into her, sending her falling to the ground. Her clothes were so drenched that it was hard to move; she found herself shivering helplessly as the policemen resumed their advance. She tried to crawl backwards, although she was sure the police were advancing from all directions, but it was too late. Strong hands grabbed her, shoved her down to the tarmac and yanked her hands behind her back. There was no time to object before she was cuffed and helpless.

"Stay there," a voice growled. She felt a hand hastily frisking her, then giving her bottom a hard squeeze. "Don't move a muscle."

Gudrun tensed, expecting to feel hands slipping into her bra or panties - or worse - but instead her captor just walked away. The cuffs were tight, so tight her wrists were rapidly beginning to ache; she strained against them for a long moment before realising that it was hopeless, that there was no way human muscle could break free. Instead, she turned and saw hundreds of people - strikers, students - lying on the ground, being steadily rounded up and cuffed. The factory gates were still shut, but it was no consolation. It wouldn't be long before the policemen smashed them down and arrested the rest of the strikers.

She shivered as a cold wind blew over Berlin. They'd talked about what would happen if they were caught, but she'd never really believed they would be caught. And now she had been caught, as a protester rather than one of the Valkyries...

... And her luck had finally run out.

CHAPTER TWENTY-EIGHT

Berlin, Germany
12 August 1985

"They're clearing the streets," Joachim said.

"Looks that way," Volker agreed.

He cursed under his breath. The policemen - they looked like military policemen to him, although it was hard to be sure - had handled everyone trapped on the wrong side of the gates with brutal efficiency. Now that the gas was fading away, they were rounding up the protesters and marching them towards a line of black prisoner transports. God alone knew what would happen to them, but he doubted it would be anything pleasant. And, once the impromptu street party had been smashed, the policemen would turn their attention to the strikers.

"The generator is up and running," Joachim offered. "But they've definitely cut the telephone and computer landlines."

"And now we're isolated," Volker said. Twelve factories had joined the strike, but now, with the policemen blocking the roads, each factory was on its own. "This could get messy."

"Yeah," Joachim agreed. "But I don't regret anything. Do you?"

Volker shrugged. The policemen hadn't yet tried to batter down the gates or come over the walls. They had to know the strikers had very few weapons; giving Volker's people time to improvise a few nasty surprises would be a dangerous mistake. Very few people realised just how easy it was to produce weapons, given the right tools and materials... and the strikers had plenty of both. But they wouldn't be enough to keep the policemen out forever.

"Make sure we keep the food strictly rationed," he ordered. If the policemen didn't intend to storm the gates, it could only be because they thought starvation would do the job. And they were probably right. There was a vast stockpile of food in the building, but it wouldn't last for more than a few days, even if the cooks stretched it as much as possible. "We'll see if they're more willing to talk after a few days of no production."

He smiled, rather wanly. Losing even a day's work would cause knock-on effects further down the line. The longer the strike lasted, even if it was broken and the workers put back to work once it came to an end, the more damage it would cause the *Reich*. And if half the workers were killed or arrested, it would be impossible to restore the production lines. In their place, he would have tried to negotiate some sort of compromise.

But the SS isn't known for compromise, he thought. He ought to know. He'd been an SS officer. *They may be plotting to strike without realising that they're striking at the heart of the Reich.*

"Get on your feet," a policeman snapped. "Now!"

Gudrun could barely move. She was almost grateful when a policeman caught hold of her arm and half-dragged her to her feet. Her wrists ached; her face hurt where she'd hit the roadside when she'd been knocked down by the water cannons; her drenched clothes clung to her skin, revealing every one of her curves. Gritting her teeth, reminding herself that it was likely to get a good deal worse, she looked around in horror as the policemen pushed her into a long line of prisoners. The street looked like a nightmare. A handful of dead bodies - including four children - lay on the ground, while hundreds of men and women were being pushed towards the transport vans.

"Keep your mouth shut," one of the policemen snapped, when a young man tried to ask a question. The speaker recoiled, too late to avoid a punishing blow from a truncheon. "Say nothing unless you are spoken to."

The policemen seemed to be organised, Gudrun admitted ruefully, as she was finally prodded into a prisoner transport van. It smelled bad, worse than Grandpa Frank's room after a particularly bad night; she heard a number of her fellow prisoners gagging as they were shoved roughly into the van and told to sit on the hard metal floor. Gudrun was almost relieved it was dark inside, save for a handful of air slits too high to reach even if she *hadn't* been cuffed by the police. The doors were banged shut once the van was full - there were so many people in the vehicle that she couldn't help feeling claustrophobic - and the engines roared to life. She tried to guess where they were going, but rapidly found it impossible. The RSHA itself? A camp outside the city? A makeshift detention centre? Or would they simply be dumped on the far side of Berlin and told to make their own way home? She clung to the final thought, even though she knew it was unlikely. The government would hardly be content with drenching her and the others...

But they don't know anything, she thought. As far as she knew, she was the only one of the Valkyries who had gone to the factories. Horst knew she'd gone, of course, but no one else did. They might never know what had happened to her... and yet they'd worry that she'd tell her captors everything. She knew the names and faces of everyone who'd joined the original Valkyries. *What happens if they make me talk?*

The thought chilled her to the bone as the vehicle lurched. Someone was crying softly - it sounded like a young girl - but what did *she* have to worry about? *She* was innocent of everything apart from being in the wrong place at the wrong time. *Gudrun*, on the other hand... if someone connected her to Konrad - and perhaps Konrad's father - they might start wondering just what *else* she was connected to. They'd check her records, identify her as a student and then wonder if she was involved with the Valkyries. It wouldn't take them long, if Horst was right, to break her. Unless, of course, they didn't believe their luck.

She flinched as someone spoke into the darkness. "What are they going to do to us?"

"Kill us," someone else said. "Or put us in the camps."

Gudrun shuddered. There had always been dark rumours, even before she'd started the Valkyries; there had always been suggestions of what happened to those who failed to fit into the *Reich*. And, after what Grandpa Frank had said... they might be driven to a camp, forced into a gas shower and exterminated. She thought - she still thought - that the *Reich* wouldn't dare harm so many Berliners, in plain view of the entire city, but it was hard not to fear the worst. Her family might never know what had happened to her.

Tears welled at the corner of her eyes as the vehicle lurched one final time, then came to a halt. She would have given anything to see her parents one last time, to make her apologies in person, to ask them if they were proud of her... hell, she would have given up her university career. And yet, Konrad and the hundreds of others like him had never had that option. Surrendering now would mean that they'd died - and been wounded - for nothing, that the government had got away with its crimes. She flicked her head, forcing the tears away as she heard the door slowly being unlocked. There would be a chance to escape, she told herself, and if she saw it, she would take it.

"Climb out of the vehicle and walk straight through the door in front of you unless you are drawn aside," a voice ordered. Gudrun flinched away from the light pouring in through the open door. "Sit down on the floor, then wait. Do not speak to your fellows."

Gudrun looked around as she was helped out of the van, then pushed towards the door. They were in a garage, she thought; a chamber large enough to house several giant prisoner transports. A policeman was standing by the door, eying her with cold blue eyes; she forced herself to keep her head up straight as he held up a hand to stop her, then frisked her with brutal efficiency. She was tempted to point out that she'd already been frisked once, but she suspected there was no point. Inside, there was another large chamber, totally bare save for a large portrait of the *Fuhrer*, looking unrealistically stern. The painter had done something to the image, she realised as she sat down on the hard floor; the eyes looked as though they were following her around the room. It should have been funny, but it was actually alarmingly intimidating.

No men, she realised, as she looked around carefully. The only prisoners in the room were female. *They must have been sent to a different room.*

She forced herself to try to remember what her father had said, back when he'd been trying to interest Johan in joining the police force rather than volunteering for the military. The policemen on the streets handed prisoners over to the policemen in the station, who processed them and determined their fate. It all seemed rather slapdash to her, but if her father was to be believed, prisoners were rarely *innocent*. The only real question was if they would be sent to jail or transported east to help make Germany East safe for German citizens. She shuddered bitterly, remembering what Horst had said, then forced herself to relax as best as she could. The long wait, in handcuffs and freezing cold clothes, was probably just another attempt to wear her down before the interrogation began.

The door opened. A grim-faced policeman entered the room, picked a girl at random and marched her back through the door, which closed behind them with a loud thud. Gudrun wondered briefly what the girl had done to deserve being picked first, then decided it didn't matter. She had a feeling she'd go through the whole process herself soon enough. The door opened again, revealing a different policeman who took a different girl. Gudrun almost giggled as her dazed mind wondered if the girls were being taken for a dance.

Her blood ran cold. There were horror stories - darker horror stories - about girls who went to semi-legal dances and raves. Her father had never let her go, even with Konrad; she'd never dared to defy him, not when many of her friends were also forbidden to attend. And the policemen were taking the girls... she suddenly felt very vulnerable and helpless. They *wanted* her to feel that way, she was sure, and yet... it was working.

Patience, she told herself firmly, as the door opened again and a policeman walked towards her. *Konrad went through worse. You can get through this.*

The policeman helped her to her feet with surprising gentleness, then escorted her into a corridor and down towards a large metal door set within the stone wall. It opened with a series of clicks - Gudrun couldn't help wondering just how many locks had been worked into the door - revealing another cold chamber. It was bare, save for a single metal table; two stern-faced men sat behind it. The table - and their chairs - were firmly fixed to the floor.

"You are under arrest," one of the men said. The policeman who'd escorted her to the room stepped backwards until he was standing in front of the door. The *only* door. There was no hope of escape. "If you cooperate, it will be noted. Do you understand me?"

Gudrun nodded, feeling her heartbeat starting to race. Any hope she'd had of escaping, of vanishing into the streets, was gone. She fought to keep her breathing under control, knowing it was a losing battle. This was worse, far worse, than being forced to write lines, or having her hand swatted with a ruler...

"Good," the man said. "Name?"

"Gudrun Wieland," Gudrun said.

It was hard to speak. Her thoughts ran in all directions. She hoped her parents wouldn't get into trouble. She'd known some parents who *had* got into trouble because their children were little brats, but the kids had been much younger than eighteen. Gudrun was old enough to be accountable for herself, yet she was also a girl - an *unmarried* girl. Her father could be punished if she stepped too far out of line.

"Noted," the man said. His voice was flat, utterly atonal, but there was a hint of something unpleasant in it. "There are checks we have to perform. If you cooperate, everything will go smoothly and swiftly; if you refuse to cooperate, we will carry them out by force and you will find them thoroughly unpleasant. Are you going to cooperate?"

"Yes, sir," Gudrun said.

"Remove the cuffs," the man ordered.

Gudrun let out a sigh of relief as her hands were released. She brought them around and stared at her wrists. The skin was badly bruised; she rubbed them frantically, trying to get some sensation back into her hands, but she felt nothing. She couldn't help wondering if she'd lost all feeling in them for good. The policeman let her have a moment to work her hands, then tapped the table impatiently. Gudrun couldn't help feeling a flicker of amusement as she realised there were three men guarding her, as if they considered her a deadly threat. She knew, without false modesty, that she couldn't hope to beat even one of them in a fight.

One of the policemen produced an ink pad and a pad of paper. Gudrun had had her fingerprints taken before, the day she'd entered school; she recalled, with a hint of bitter shame, that she'd considered it fun. Now, it was terrifying. Her anonymity was being stripped from her, piece by piece. If there was a single fingerprint of hers anywhere on the leaflets, they'd know who she was. And then it would be over.

"Very good," the policeman said, once the whole process was complete. His companion removed the fingerprint paperwork, then produced a small metal box from under the table and put it on the top. "Now, I want you to remove your clothing, piece by piece, and pass each item to me."

"I can't," Gudrun objected. She hadn't taken off her clothes in front of a stranger since her last medical examination - and the doctor had been female. Even Konrad had never seen her naked. "I..."

"You can either undress on your own, in which case the clothing will eventually be returned to you, or you will be cuffed and your clothing will be cut away," the policeman said. He didn't show any hint of anticipation, but his companion was clearly looking forward to the display. Gudrun shivered as his eyes crawled over her body. "There will be no second chance to cooperate."

"They'll want to degrade you," Horst had warned, back when he'd talked about how prisoners were treated. "They'll want to make it clear that you are no longer in control of your own life."

Gudrun shuddered. She'd never been allowed to wear something revealing, not even when she'd been at home. Tight jeans had shown off her curves, but not her bare skin... her cheeks burned with shame at the thought of being so exposed. And yet, she knew they weren't joking. If they stripped her themselves, it would be far worse. Gritting her teeth, she undid her shirt slowly, trying to pretend that she was undressing for bed. She was damned if she was going to give them a strip show.

She was grimly aware of their gazes - one lustful, one cold and dispassionate - as she removed her trousers and stood in front of them, wearing only her bra and panties. Bracing herself, she slowly removed her last protections and stood naked in front of them. The policeman by the door was breathing heavily; she wanted to curse him, even as the policeman inspected her last few articles of clothing and dropped them into the box, covering her breasts with one hand and the crack between her legs with the other. She wanted to run, but there was nowhere to go; she wanted to cry, but she didn't dare admit weakness. It would be disastrous.

"Hands on your head," the policeman ordered.

Gudrun hated him in that moment, hated him with a helpless fury she hadn't felt for anyone else, not even the worst of the BDM matrons. But she did as she was told, trying not to look at them studying her. She had never been so exposed in her entire life. Their eyes were trailing over her breasts, drinking in every detail. They had to know she was completely clean. Where could she hide anything now she'd been stripped naked?

"Turn around," the policeman ordered, coldly. He rose to his feet and walked around the table. "Bend over and grab your ankles."

Gudrun stared at him in disbelief, but there was no point in trying to argue. All she wanted was to get it over with as quickly as possible. She turned and bent over, grimly aware that they were seeing far too much of her. Cold hands gripped her buttocks and pulled them apart... she cringed, half-expecting to feel a finger poking up inside her most private parts, before she was released.

"Stand," the policeman ordered. He was already walking back around the table, as if violating Gudrun's most intimate parts was nothing. "Cuff her, then take her to the holding cell."

It *had* been nothing, Gudrun realised, as the policeman snapped the cuffs back on, trapping her hands behind her back. They didn't know who she was, or what she'd done; they were just showing off their power. It was crude, it was effective...

... And yet it had failed. They hadn't broken her.

You don't know who I am, she thought, as she was pushed into a small holding cell. She might be naked, she might be cuffed, but she felt as though she had won. *You don't know who I am and that means I still have a chance.*

CHAPTER TWENTY-NINE

Berlin, Germany
12 August 1985

"Ah, *there* you are," *Frau* Morgenstern said, as Hilde stepped into the room. "I trust you are ready to go out?"

Hilde looked up, surprised. "Mother?"

"They're arresting children on the streets," *Frau* Morgenstern said, tartly. "Children who could be you, if things were different. Something has to be done."

She went on before Hilde could say a word. "I'm heading straight to Silgan's house," she added. "The telephones are no longer working, so I want you to take a note to several others. We're going out onto the streets in protest."

"Mother," Hilde protested. "You could wind up in jail..."

"So could you," her mother said. "This is the one chance we have to make our voices heard, to ally ourselves with others who want change. And so I'm leading the way onto the streets."

She picked up a sheet of paper and started to scribble a quick note. Hilde stared at her, unable to quite believe what was happening. Her mother had been holding dozens of meetings, some more civilised than others, but it was hard to imagine her bossy mother leading a small army of women onto the street like common workers. And yet, her mother *had* been outraged at the suggestion she was still under her husband's thumb. The chance to insist on greater rights for women was not to be missed.

"Once you've delivered the note, I want you to come straight back home and wait," *Frau* Morgenstern added, as she folded the sheet of paper and passed it to Hilde. "You are not to go onto the streets yourself or leave the house for any reason at all. The maids will take care of you until your father comes home."

Hilde swallowed. She had no idea what her father would say, if he discovered his wife was leading the protests on the street, but she had a nasty feeling he'd take it out on her. He couldn't stand up to his formidable wife, after all. Hilde had no idea why her father had even married her mother, unless there was money and a name involved somewhere. His career had probably benefited from her mother's quiet politicking on his behalf. Maybe it had benefited enough for him not to want to discard his wife.

"I understand," she said, finally. "Be careful..."

"They won't shoot us," *Frau* Morgenstern said, firmly. "Each and every one of the women in the group has a powerful husband or family."

"Yeah," Hilde said. "Just make sure the police know that."

She glanced at the note - it was nothing more than a handful of lines, telling the recipients to assemble at the predetermined spot - and headed for the door. There hadn't been any incidents in *their* part of Berlin, as far as she knew, but that was about to change. God alone knew what would happen when the wealthy and powerful women started marching in support of the strikers - and their list of demands.

Bitterly, half-wishing she'd never heard of Gudrun or allowed herself to be lured into the Valkyries, she hurried though the door and down the drive to the gates. She could be arrested, if the police saw her on the streets; she could be taken into the RSHA and tortured until she confessed everything. The emergency broadcasts had taken over everything, even the handful of privately-owned television sets. There was no excuse for being caught outside the home. But the thought of her mother's anger - and her own position - drove her on.

They won't be patrolling the streets here, she told herself, hoping desperately that she was right. Her father's house - it was effectively a mansion - was in the safest part of the city, where the wealthy and powerful lived. The men who owned these houses were among the chief supporters of the regime. *They'll be sending the police to the industrial zones...*

But she knew she wouldn't feel safe until she was back home, praying her mother returned safely.

"They arrested Gudrun?"

"It looks that way," Leopold said. "I didn't get a good view from my vantage point, but they were arresting and cuffing just about everyone on the streets. I'm pretty sure I saw Gudrun being manhandled into a police van. The factories are sealed off and isolated."

"Write down a list of names," Horst ordered. The telephone lines might be down - some bright spark in the RSHA had turned the civilian network off - but the computer network had barely been hampered. There was no way the state could cripple it without rendering it useless to themselves, as well as the Valkyries. "Make sure you only list the students you *know* were taken into the vans."

He thought fast. Gudrun *had* said she was going down to the factories, along with hundreds of other students, so it *was* likely she'd been arrested. He didn't think any other Valkyries had joined the protest - Leopold had found a place to watch, rather than go all the way into the sealed zone - yet there was no way to know for sure. It was unlikely Gudrun would be given any *special* treatment, once she reached the processing centre, but being strip-searched would be so outside her previous experience that it might break her. And if she provided a list of names to the SS, Horst and the other Valkyries would have bare hours to live.

It would be simple enough to run, he knew. He'd been trained in escape and evasion; he could make it to the American Embassy, if he tried, or head south to Switzerland. Or head west to Vichy France. It wouldn't be too hard to steal a fishing boat and flee to Britain. And yet, leaving now would mean abandoning all his hopes and dreams - and Gudrun. He didn't want to leave her in the *Reich's* clutches.

Particularly as she might have kept her mouth shut, he thought. Gudrun might not have endured the worst of the Hitler Youth, but the BDM matrons had been thoroughly unpleasant, if not outright sadists. *She knows to say nothing and hope.*

"Here," Leopold said. "These are the students I know were arrested."

Horst glanced at the list. It was shorter than he'd expected, but in all the confusion a great many students would have been arrested or injured without anyone noticing. The police would have refrained from using lethal weapons, he was sure, yet tear gas alone could be nasty if the protesters were unprepared for its use. He'd have to make sure the next message that went out on the computer network included instructions for dealing with it.

"Put it on the net," he ordered. Sven took the list and hastily tapped it into the computer, then uploaded it. God alone knew how many people it would reach - the regime could turn off the power in most of Berlin, simply by pushing a switch - but they had to try. "And see who you can send to their homes. Tell them that their children have been arrested."

"I can ask someone from downstairs," Leopold said, after a moment. "But that might be too revealing."

"Be careful," Horst advised. Whatever happened in the days and weeks that would come, a line had been crossed. "And watch your back."

There was a knock on the door. Horst swore inwardly as Sven hastily blanked the screen, then brought up a computer game he'd written himself. He'd told Horst that he had high hopes of selling millions of copies; Horst, privately, suspected it would be pointless to try until there were more than a handful of computers in civilian hands. Pushing the thought aside, he leaned over Sven's shoulder as the door opened - he'd rigged the doorknob to be harder to open quickly - and pretended to watch the game.

"Horst," a gruff voice said. "There's a telephone call for you."

Horst had to fight to keep his expression under control. He'd never thought highly of Krabbe - the would-be spy was suitable for nothing more than cannon fodder - but this was a new low. The telephone lines were down and everyone knew it. Krabbe might just have blown his cover in one stupid moment. And even if there was a telephone line that was isolated from the rest of the landlines, which was technically possible, some of the students would still wonder.

He could have said there was a message for me and it would be less revealing, he thought, straightening up. Something would have to be done about Krabbe. Horst's handler would probably be annoyed if he beat the idiot to within an inch of his life, but a careful report might see the stupid bastard reassigned to mine-clearing duty in Germany East. *And now I have to come up with a cover story.*

"I'm coming," he said. It was rare for parents to ring the university - and if they did, it was almost always an emergency. He glanced back at Sven, hoping the computer expert wasn't paying close attention. "I'll see you later."

CHRISTOPHER G. NUTTALL

Somehow, he resisted the temptation to punch Krabbe as soon as they left the computer lab and headed down the stairs. There were only a handful of students within earshot, but fighting in the corridors would be enough to get them both expelled - or, if their superiors intervened, raise yet more questions about why they *hadn't* been expelled. Horst silently wrote the report in his head, then decided it would be better not to write it. Krabbe was an idiot, but an idiot would be safer than someone competent. Unless, of course, he was a decoy...

"You're wanted at the main office," Krabbe said, as soon as they were alone. "Take one of the cars from the accommodation block and drive there."

"And get arrested by the police, no doubt," Horst sneered. What had happened to the sterilisation camps? People like Krabbe shouldn't be allowed to breed. "None of our cars have any special plates to keep the police from flagging them down."

He shook his head. Being close to Krabbe was killing his brain cells. "I'll walk," he said, firmly. "And you can go back to the apartment block and stay there."

Gritting his teeth, he hurried towards the gates. It could be a trap, he knew; his superiors might have reasoned out his role in the whole affair and called him in for interrogation. But Krabbe didn't seem to be trying to follow him. If *Horst* had wanted to arrest someone on suspicion, *he* would have made sure the suspect didn't have a chance to saunter off into the backstreets and escape. A public arrest would be easy enough - and, he was sure, it would arouse no comment. Unless that was what he was *meant* to think.

It makes no sense, he reassured himself, firmly. *They wouldn't ask me to visit if they knew what I'd been doing, they'd grab me before I could escape. And so... whatever they want me for, I'm not in trouble myself.*

Hoping to hell he was right, he headed onwards through nearly-deserted streets.

———

The sound of the riot - or protest march, or whatever the hell it was - quietened alarmingly, much to Herman's relief, as the military police took over the sealed zone and marched the hundreds of prisoners away to an uncertain destination. Herman was relieved just to see the back of some of the prisoners,

232

particularly the ones who just would *not* shut up about how important they were and how the policemen would be shovelling shit in Germany East tomorrow if they didn't release their prisoners immediately. Let the military police handle the assholes, Herman told himself, and take whatever punishment was due.

"We're to head back to the muster point," Caius said. The radio network had been having hiccups. Some idiot back at the station, according to rumour, had scrambled all the channels for some silly reason. "The military police are to take over the barricades."

Herman shrugged. The barricades were no longer necessary, now that most of the watching civilians had gone back home as soon as the military police arrived. God alone knew what they were saying, what rumours were spreading through the city, but for the moment he found it hard to care. The buildings within the sealed zone had either been locked up tight by the strikers, who were now trapped, or emptied by the military police. Herman rather doubted that anyone taken into custody by the military policemen would be enjoying the experience.

He followed Caius back to the van and scrambled inside. The vehicle roared to life; he sat back and forced himself to relax, despite the tension. He'd expected worse, somehow, than merely putting up the barricades. But then, the military policemen had done the real job...

And it isn't over yet, Herman thought. *The strikers will still have to be handled, somehow.*

"We're being diverted," the driver called. "There's a new crowd of people spilling out onto the street."

Herman said nothing, but he worried as the van lurched. The strikers were bad enough; who *else* was joining the protests and why? Caius and several of the other policemen hurled questions at the driver, but he didn't know anything more than what he'd already said. All they could do was wait, checking their weapons and equipment, until the van came to a halt one final time. The door opened, revealing a residential street... and hundreds of women of all ages marching down it, wearing their finest clothes.

Caius gasped. "What the hell...?"

Herman could only agree. He'd been prepared for rampaging students or workers, perhaps even *Gastarbeiters*, not women. Many of them were middle-aged, the same age as his wife, wearing outfits that cost more money than he cared to think about. They all looked to be respectable German womenfolk, wives and mothers; indeed, some of the women were even carrying their children in their arms or pushing prams. He knew how to handle rioters, but women? The thought of charging them, of using tear gas to break up their ranks, was unthinkable. And then his blood ran cold as he saw his wife in the throng.

"Adelinde?"

"Your wife?" Fritz asked. "You'd better get her out of here before all hell breaks loose."

Herman nodded, then hurried away from the clump of uncertain policemen. At least he had something to focus on, besides absolute confusion and unwillingness to treat the women as just another bunch of rioters. The Captain would have to be insane to order the police to attack the crowd, not when it was so clearly composed of women and children. Herman knew he would go deaf if the order was ever given... and, if his superiors were wise, they'd accept it rather than risk triggering a mutiny.

"Adelinde," he said, as his wife looked up at him. "What are you doing here?"

"Marching," Adelinde said. She'd never argued with him in public before, even though she ruled the household with an iron hand. "They've arrested our daughter."

Herman staggered backwards. *Gudrun* had been arrested? Of course she had, his thoughts yammered at him. It wasn't as if he had any *other* daughters. And yet... he hadn't seen her among the prisoners, but that proved nothing. Hell, Adelinde could be wrong. It wouldn't be the first time she'd jumped to the wrong conclusion and stuck to it in defiance of all logic and reason.

"You have to go home," he said. He was the man of the house, damn it! His wife shouldn't be embarrassing him, let alone defying him, in front of his comrades. "Adelinde..."

His wife tilted her head, looking alarmingly like his strong-willed mother. "Our daughter is under arrest," she said, "merely for being a student. I'm not going home when she's in danger."

Herman found himself unsure what to say, let alone do. Adelinde had *always* defended her children, even as she meted out strict discipline. He pitied the teacher who'd sent home a note accusing her children of atrocities. But coming out onto the streets, risking arrest or worse... he felt sick as he realised what Gudrun might have gone through already and what might be waiting in her future. His daughter was no criminal, no *Gastarbeiter* bitch with no rights; she was a good little German girl, smart enough to be a university student, old enough to be a wife and a mother.

His wife read the expression on his face. "She's your daughter," she hissed. "Start doing your duty as a father and *find* her!"

"We're not going home," an older woman said. She was well-dressed enough that Herman had no trouble believing that her husband was both wealthy and *very* well connected. God knew she certainly *sounded* snooty enough to believe herself above rebuke, let alone punishment. "We want change."

"We want our sons home," another woman said. A dozen other women took up the cry. "We want an end to the war."

Defeated, Herman could only turn and walk back to the other policemen, uncertain what he could say to them. Women were meant to obey their menfolk, first their fathers and then their husbands. But Adelinde had defied him, publicly. And, if she was right about Gudrun being arrested, he couldn't blame her.

Fritz eyed him as he rejoined the small clump of policemen. "Well?"

"I have to make a few calls," Herman said. "Until then, we do nothing."

And hope to hell our superiors don't do something stupid, he thought, privately. Almost every policeman he knew was married. How many *other* wives and daughters of policemen had joined the marching women? He was *damned* if he was firing on a crowd that included his wife, the mother of his children. *But what do we do if we are ordered to fire?*

CHAPTER THIRTY

Berlin, Germany
12 August 1985

"This is getting out of hand," Hans said. He glanced at his watch, meaningfully. It was late at night and dusk was slowly settling over Berlin. "The troubles are threatening to spread to a dozen other cities."

"Then we clamp down on them," Holliston insisted. The *Reichsführer-SS* hadn't given up, not yet. "We should crush the strikers in their lairs."

"If we kill the strikers, we lose part of our pool of trained labour," Hans said, wearily. The argument had been going in circles for hours, as more and more reports flooded in from all over the *Reich*. "If they have time to damage or destroy the machinery in the factories, we will have to replace it... and that will put yet another hole in our budget. And if we order the police or the troops to open fire on the women... we'll have a mutiny on our hands."

"He's right," Field Marshal Justus Stoffregen said. The Head of OKW leaned forward, his face pale. "There are already rumours spreading through the Berlin Guard, *Herr Reichsführer*. If they are sent in to clear the streets of *women*, I believe they will refuse to obey orders."

"So arrest them for mutiny," Holliston snapped.

"There hasn't been a mass mutiny since we were stabbed in the back in 1918," Stoffregen said. "A single coward could be arrested easily - his own barrack mates would hand out some rough justice if he wasn't arrested quickly enough - but a collective mutiny would be much harder to suppress. The soldiers might turn their guns on the arresting officers."

Holliston let out an angry hiss. "This is what you get for not indoctrinating soldiers properly!"

"Not all of us believe in the doctrines preached by the SS," Stoffregen said. "We want our soldiers to take advantage of fleeting opportunities, not wait for orders while the moment slips away."

Hans held up a hand. Normally, he would have enjoyed watching the military and the SS at loggerheads, but they didn't have time to continue the pointless argument. They'd played the only cards they could - firing unionists and clearing the streets - and both had failed. The strikers were still holding out, thousands of others had come onto the streets in support and Berlin, as day turned to night, had ground to a halt. Even if the strike ended at midnight and the city went back to normal, it would take months - if not years - to repair the damage.

"This argument is immaterial," he said, flatly. "We have to admit, right now, that we are on the verge of losing control."

He repeated the facts, once again. "There are rumblings of trouble right across the *Reich*," he said, firmly. "I suspect we will see more strikes tomorrow - I believe that some corporations are already considering closing their plants for the duration of the crisis, which will only provoke their workers further. Our police have refused to disperse the women in the streets; our soldiers are unlikely to fire on the women if ordered to do so. We have pushed matters as far as we can, without causing serious damage, and we can go no further. The population no longer trusts us, the workers no longer expect us to defend them against their corporate masters, the *Untermenschen* see their chance for freedom and even the police and soldiers are restless. Our *Reich* rests on a knife-edge."

"We can fight," Holliston said.

"We can try," Voss muttered, "but there won't be much of a *Reich* left afterwards."

Hans nodded in agreement. "The Americans are already moving ahead of us," he reminded the council. "A long period of civil unrest in the *Reich*, even if we manage to keep a grip on power, will give them the chance to make their lead insurmountable. And then the legacy of the *great* Adolf Hitler will be lost forever!"

He willed them, desperately, to believe. The American ABM system was bad enough - if the Americans thought that they could stop ninety percent of the *Reich's* missiles, they might decide that they could survive a nuclear war - but their steady advance into space was worse. The Economic Intelligence Service was already predicting the next generation of space-based weapons, concepts right out of American science-fantasy movies that, if turned into reality, would render most of the *Reich's* armed forces obsolete. The *Reich*, already dangerously behind the United States, could not allow itself to lose any more ground. If they did...

If they did, we might as well call Washington and ask President Anderson for terms, he thought, sourly. *We couldn't possibly win if they deploy space-based weapons against us.*

"I agree," Stoffregen said. "It's time to put an end to the matter."

"And how," Holliston asked icily, "do you intend to do that?"

"We concede most of their demands," Hans said. "Let them have their unions, for the moment; let them have their freedom of speech and assembly. Let them even start offering independent candidates to the *Reichstag.*"

"Out of the question," Holliston snapped.

"It makes no difference," Voss said, amused. "The *Reichstag* is powerless."

"Unless these... *independent* candidates start voting to block our proposed budgets," Holliston pointed out. "What do we do then?"

It was, Hans had to admit, a good question. Technically, the *Reichstag* was responsible for approving laws and budget proposals. None of the proposals put forward by the *Reich* Council had ever failed to pass, of course; the *Reichstag* knew it had no power to do anything other than rubber-stamp the proposals. But if there were independents elected to the *Reichstag*... who knew what would happen then?

"We control the bureaucracy," he said, finally. He tried to make his tone as reassuring as possible. "Let them make their speeches, if they wish. It will make no difference. The important detail is that we will be buying time."

"We cannot end the war," Holliston snapped.

Hans nodded, although he knew the war couldn't be allowed to continue for long. But the military might not support him if he proposed otherwise, not when Holliston - damn the man - had been making private deals with the senior officers. The war would have to continue for a few months, at least. By then, he'd know just how badly the budget needed to be slashed to keep the *Reich* afloat.

"We *can* shift responsibility onto the South Africans," Voss offered. "If we provide training and equipment - even a handful of units of French volunteers - we can slowly draw down our own commitment. Let the bastards fight for their own country."

They are, Hans thought. The Italians hadn't put up much of a fight when the Arabs revolted - and the French hadn't done much better - but the South Africans were tough. They were just outnumbered so badly that only superior training and their foes disunity had kept them from losing the war within the first year. *And maybe they will be glad of a few hundred thousand French volunteers.*

"Then we offer to concede most of the demands," Hans said. "And release the prisoners as a gesture of good faith."

"They're guilty of unauthorised political activity," Holliston insisted. "They cannot simply be let free."

"So is most of Berlin, now," Hans countered. "Do you want to put the entire city in the extermination camps?"

"This isn't Warsaw or Moscow," Voss agreed.

"*Germanica,*" Holliston snapped.

Hans winced, inwardly. Moscow - Stalin's capital - had been battered to rubble by savage street fighting as the Germans forced their way into the city. Half of the population had died at their posts; the remainder had been rounded up, marched into a concentration camp and starved to death. The city had been rebuilt shortly after the end of the war - it had been the hub of the USSR's road and rail network - and renamed Germanica. These days, it was an SS stronghold, the core of Germany East.

"Let them go," he said, gently. "It will help to buy us time."

"Very well," Holliston snapped. "Let it be done."

———

"You're late," *Standartenfuehrer* Erdmann Schwarzkopf observed.

"I had problems convincing the police of my identity," Horst said, shortly. He was *sick* of being told he was late. "They did not believe me at first."

He scowled at the humiliation of admitting that he'd practically been arrested by his own side. If he'd had an SS card, getting past the policemen would have been simplicity itself, but the card would have been far too revealing if Gudrun or another student had seen it. As it happened, he'd had to let them take him to a processing station and speak to an SS officer there - and, by the time he'd been processed himself, several hours had passed.

Schwarzkopf shrugged. "These are not easy times."

"No," Horst agreed. He bit down the urge to lodge a complaint against Krabbe. "I never expected to see the streets of Berlin filled with whining women."

"Me neither," Schwarzkopf said. He sounded, for once, just a little unsure. "A number of students were arrested, mostly in front of the factories. I need you to review their files and mark any that require special attention."

Horst frowned, inwardly, as he took the set of folders. Every student had a dossier, kept within the RSHA; he had no doubt that the SS's bureaucrats were hastily updating them even now, at least for the students who'd been arrested. They might be released - computer experts were invaluable - but being arrested in such a compromising position would haunt them for the rest of their lives. And yet, they were the lucky ones. Someone without their training would be halfway to Germany East by now.

The first batch of students were largely unfamiliar to him, although he vaguely recognised one of the young men as a braying fool who'd bragged of his family connections to anyone who'd listen. One of the young girls - his eyes lingered on the photos of her processing for longer than he knew they should - had a brother who'd gone to war and never returned; he hoped, as he returned the first stack of files, that her loss wouldn't be held against her. She had an excellent motive for joining the Valkyries.

"That young man is a loudmouth," he said, tapping his folder. "But I don't think he's a real troublemaker. He has too much to lose."

Schwarzkopf eyed him, sharply. "Two of the other spies have classed him as a potential dissident."

Horst forced himself to keep his voice level. "*Mein Herr*, he talks too much," he said. He was tempted to drop the idiot in hot water, but that would be cruel. "A dissident would be quieter, I believe."

"His talk is already seditious," Schwarzkopf pointed out. He picked up the next set of folders and held them out. "And these?"

The first two folders showed boys he didn't recognise, but the third folder belonged to Gudrun. He glanced at her photographs first, hoping that his superior would think he was admiring her body if he showed any reaction, then checked the rest of the file. Thankfully, Gudrun seemed to have been classed as someone who'd been in the wrong place at the wrong time, rather than a potential dissident. The bureaucrats hadn't known she'd been engaged to Konrad before he'd been sent to South Africa. Having a policeman for a father probably told in her favour, although she also had a tie to the SS. Horst made a mental note to consider that later, wondering what the tie actually *was*. Gudrun's elder brother was in the Berlin Guard, not the *Waffen-SS*, and her other brothers were still in the Hitler Youth. It was unlikely as hell they were already marked down as potential SS recruits. Only bad fiction for impressionable young men involved children serving as full-fledged secret agents charged with hunting down spies.

"I know her from my classes," he said. He made a show of looking back at the pictures. "I was planning to court her."

"I can understand why," Schwarzkopf said. "Pretty, definitely; her bloodline shows no trace of non-Aryan blood."

Horst flushed on Gudrun's behalf, silently praying she never found out that he'd looked at her naked photographs, then frowned as the implications struck him. If she'd wanted to marry an SS officer, she needed a certificate of racial purity, a confirmation that her parents and grandparents had been of pure German blood. He wondered, suddenly, why someone had looked up Gudrun's bloodline - it wasn't normally done outside the SS - but the file provided no answer. There had to be a connection between Gudrun and the SS he wasn't seeing.

"I may still do so," he said. He put the file back and took the next one. "Unless it would impact on my career..."

"It probably wouldn't," Schwarzkopf assured him. "She doesn't seem to be one of the ringleaders."

And let us hope you're telling the truth, Horst thought, as he checked the next file. *If a competent spy saw us together, you might wonder...*

"Another loudmouth," he said, dismissing the subject. The male student was two years older than him and completely unconnected to Gudrun. "This one, however, was involved with inciting students to go to the factories."

Schwarzkopf frowned. "Are you sure?"

"He wasn't the only one," Horst said. He would have preferred not to mention it, but the idiot just *had* to shoot his mouth off in public, where one of the other spies would definitely have heard. Better he ended up in an interrogation chamber than Horst himself. "There were a couple of others I don't know so well."

"Several students are also dead," Schwarzkopf said. "They may have hoped to be killed."

"Only the Arabs charge into battle praying for death," Horst said. The SS praised death before the dishonour of running away, but even the most fanatical unit understood the value of a tactical retreat. "I don't think the students would have enough bravery to make a fight of it."

"This one did," Schwarzkopf said. He held up another file. Inside, there was a picture of a brutally-wounded young man. "Do you recognise him?"

"Hartwig," Horst said. He hadn't liked the young man - he'd lured Gudrun into danger - but he hadn't deserved to die so savagely. "Hartwig Rhineland. Another loudmouth."

"Noted," Schwarzkopf said. They ran through the rest of the files quickly. "Do you know any of the students personally?"

"A few," Horst said. Thankfully, he knew more than just Gudrun and the Valkyries. "I have classes with them."

"We have orders to release them tomorrow morning, save for a handful who merit further investigation," Schwarzkopf said. "Do you want to drive any of them home?"

Horst kept his expression blank with an effort. He needed to talk to Gudrun - and he needed to do it before she vanished into her home. Her father was a policeman, after all; he'd be embarrassed when he discovered that his daughter had been arrested, even if it didn't blight his career for the rest of his life. Horst knew what *his* father would have done if *he'd* gotten into real trouble and he doubted Gudrun's father would take it any better. But then, Gudrun was a girl. She might just be grounded for the rest of her life instead.

But if he showed any interest in any of the girls, his superior might wonder why... unless, of course, he gave them a good reason.

"I can drive Gudrun home," he said, pasting a smile on his face. "She might appreciate it."

"She might," Schwarzkopf said. "We're asking students to drive the arrestees home, rather than allow their parents to collect them in a body. Listen carefully to what she says as you drive her home. If she happens to say any-thing actionable, report it to us."

"I will," Horst said. He'd check the car overnight, just to make sure no one had added any new bugs. Disabling the one he knew about and making it look like an accident would be easy, but disabling a new bug would raise eyebrows. "Will you inform her parents she's going home?"

"I believe there will be a formal announcement," Schwarzkopf said, casu-ally. "For the moment, however, I suggest you wait. The streets are not safe at the moment."

Horst managed to keep himself, barely, from making a sarcastic remark. The police, instead of arresting strikers or rioters, had managed to dump an SS agent into a processing centre. If they'd known what he'd done, it would have been a great success, but as it happened it had merely been a minor hic-cup. But when his superiors complained, the police would be less willing to take suspects into custody, even ones who were clearly breaking the law...

"Yes, *Mein Herr*," he said, instead.

———

Volker listened to the radio broadcast in some disbelief. The government was... *surrendering?* The strikers were to be forgiven? The fired workers were to be allowed to return to work? The union was to be legalised - along with many of the other rights they'd demanded when they'd taken over the factories? It sounded almost too good to be true.

And it probably is too good to be true, he thought, darkly. He'd been *in* the SS, after all; they might concede ground when it could not be held, but they refused to simply let it go permanently. *They'll start preparing for the next round.*

"We won," Joachim said. He sounded as surprised as Volker himself. "Didn't we?"

"For the moment," Volker said. They'd have to move fast to capitalise on their success before the government recovered its balance. "But this is only the first round. I imagine they'll do what they can to undermine us."

He sighed. "And they haven't agreed to end the war, Joachim," he added. "They're making concessions, not surrendering. We have to be ready for their counterattack."

CHAPTER THIRTY-ONE

Berlin, Germany
13 August 1985

Gudrun had endured a naked and uncomfortable night.

The cell hadn't been as unpleasant as she'd feared - it certainly smelled better than Grandpa Frank's room - and once a policeman had removed the cuffs she'd been able to move around freely and drink water from a tiny nozzle, but it had been boring. When she'd been grounded as a young girl, she'd been able to read books even if she hadn't been allowed out of her room, let alone into the garden or onto the streets. There was simply nothing to do in the prison cell, save for trying to sleep and fretting about what would happen to her. She wasn't even sure just how long she'd *been* in the cell. Her watch, along with everything she'd been wearing or carrying, had been taken from her during processing and the light bulb never dimmed.

She was half-asleep, dozing fitfully, when someone knocked on the metal grating that ensured she had absolutely no privacy. The noise jerked her awake; she hastily covered her breasts and crotch with her hands as she sat upright, blinking. Her head hurt; it occurred to her, suddenly, that she hadn't eaten anything for hours, perhaps days. How long had she been a prisoner in the cell? How long could someone survive on water alone? She didn't know.

"Eat," the guard said, slipping a tray through the bars. "And then be ready."

Gudrun scowled at him. "Ready for what?"

The guard ignored her and walked onwards, pushing a trolley to the next cell. Gudrun stood, brushed her hair out of her eyes, and picked up the tray carefully. She had no idea what went into the stew, but it didn't smell anything like the stew her mother made, while the piece of bread was hard enough to threaten her teeth. There were no knives or forks, let alone salt and pepper. It tasted, when she placed a piece of meat in her mouth, like pork on the verge of going bad. Her stomach rebelled at the thought of eating it, but she knew there was no choice. She forced it down her throat with plenty of water and pushed the tray back out of the cell. No doubt the ghastly food was yet another form of torture.

She looked up as the guard returned, jangling his keys as he stopped in front of her cell and peered in at her. Gudrun covered herself as best as she could, knowing that nothing would stop the guard if he decided to open the grate and have some fun with her. She promised herself that she'd fight, that she'd put a knee between his legs before she let him rape her, but she knew she was too tired and hungry, despite the food, to hold out for long. It was a relief when another guard arrived, spoke briefly to the first guard and then tapped on Gudrun's grate. When she looked up, she saw he was holding a pair of handcuffs.

"Turn around and give me your hands," he ordered.

Gudrun considered refusing, but she knew it was pointless. She turned and allowed him to cuff her, then shrank backwards as he entered the cell. He caught her arm in a vice-like grip, pulled her out of the cell and through a solid metal door that looked as though it should belong in a battleship. It banged closed behind her as she was shoved down the corridor and into another room. A familiar box, marked with her name and a number she didn't recognise, was positioned neatly on the floor.

"Get dressed," the guard ordered, as he removed the cuffs. He sounded bored, despite her nakedness. Perhaps he saw naked prisoners every day. "Make sure everything you had on you when you were arrested has been given back to you."

Gudrun blinked at him. "I'm to dress?"

"Yes," the policeman said, shortly. "Get dressed. Someone is on their way to pick you up."

She fought down her surprise as she opened the box, reminding herself that it might just be a trick. But all of her clothes were inside, neatly folded; she shuddered at the thought of policemen pawing them before deciding it didn't matter. She pulled on her panties and bra, then her trousers and shirt, feeling better with every piece of clothing she donned. By the time the box was empty - she hadn't been carrying much, save for a couple of pens and a set of house keys - she felt almost human again.

The policeman snapped on the cuffs again, then marched her through another series of corridors into what she guessed was a waiting room. He removed one of the cuffs, locked it to a chair and walked off, leaving her alone. Gudrun scowled after him - did they really think she was that dangerous? - and then started to wonder who was coming to pick her up. Her father? Her brother? Either one might - might - have been able to get her released. There were no other prisoners in the room... maybe she was the only person being allowed to go free. It wasn't a comforting thought. Her father would probably forbid her from returning to the university; he'd probably tell her to find a man within the next week or marry his choice, whoever it turned out to be.

She looked up as the door opened to reveal another female prisoner. The policeman escorting her cuffed her to another chair at the far end of the room, then left the two girls alone. It was impossible to talk without shouting, so Gudrun settled for sending the newcomer a reassuring look and waiting to see what happened. She didn't seem to have any other choice, beyond demanding to be allowed to go to the toilet... and the toilet in the cell had been unspeakably vile.

It's a prison, stupid, she reminded herself. *It's not a holiday camp.*

It felt like hours before yet another policeman arrived, released her from the chair and marched her out of the room, into a lobby. *Horst* was standing there, looking nervous; Gudrun flushed with embarrassment as she realised he could see her in cuffs, then blinked in surprise as she tried to work out what he was doing there. He wasn't her father, her brother or her boyfriend... why was *he* coming to pick her up? Did he think their kiss gave him a claim on her? Or...

"You are free to go," the policeman said, removing the cuffs for the final time. Gudrun rubbed her wrists. The cuffs hadn't been as tight as they'd been yesterday, but they'd still been uncomfortable. She had a feeling she'd be sore for days. "Go."

"Come on," Horst said. "I've got the car just outside."

Gudrun followed him, feeling numb. "Where are we?"

"A police station on the outskirts of Berlin," Horst said. He opened the door; Gudrun blinked and hastily covered her eyes as the sunlight shone down. "They wanted students rather than parents to pick up the prisoners."

That sounded odd, Gudrun thought; every time she or her brothers had managed to get in trouble at school, their parents had been summoned to pick them up. Perhaps it was different for the police... or, perhaps, the police hadn't wanted to make a fuss. Her father was a policeman, after all. Who knew what he would have said to the officers who'd processed his daughter?

"It should be safe to talk in here," Horst said, once they were in the car. He started the engine as Gudrun buckled herself into the passenger seat. "Quite a bit has happened since you were arrested."

Gudrun listened in growing disbelief as he outlined the end of the strike. "They just... they just surrendered?"

"I very much doubt it," Horst said. "They *were* surprised, of course, when mothers and wives came out onto the streets in a mass protest. So many people walked away from their jobs that the city literally ground to a halt. The government might have had to make concessions, just to get the city moving again, but they won't let it rest."

"No," Gudrun agreed. "They've been humiliated."

"A bit more than *merely* humiliated," Horst said. He gave her a sidelong look. "How did they treat you?"

Gudrun felt her body starting to shake. They'd stripped her naked, seen her most private places... they could have done worse, far worse, and she knew it. She'd been helpless, defenceless, she could have vanished into the prison system and never been allowed to emerge... she could still feel their hands on her, turning her into a helpless piece of meat. She was barely aware of Horst parking the car as she curled up in the seat, then flinched in surprise as he wrapped an arm around her shoulders, trying to give what comfort he could. But he couldn't understand what she'd been through. How could he?

"Badly," she said, finally. She wanted to keep it to herself, but she had a feeling that talking about it would help her to overcome the sense of bitter helplessness. "They stripped me, inspected me... like a doctor, only worse."

"But it's over now," Horst said.

"It's not over," Gudrun said. "You said it yourself. The government isn't going to give up just because it lost this round."

"No, it isn't," Horst said. He looked nervous. "Gudrun... I have something important to tell you."

Gudrun looked up at him. Konrad had sounded similar, very similar, when he'd asked for her promise of marriage. And Horst... did he want to ask her to marry him? Or...?

"I've been keeping a secret from you," Horst confessed, slowly. He slowly released her shoulders. "They sent me to spy on you."

It took Gudrun a moment to put it together. When she did, she slapped his face as hard as she could. Horst recoiled backwards, one hand going to his face; Gudrun flinched herself as she realised what she'd done. She'd slapped an SS officer... she'd just got out of one dingy prison cell and now she'd go straight into another, if he didn't just throw her into the camps and gas her. And yet, if he was an SS officer, why wasn't she dead? Horst knew the names and faces of every one of the Valkyries.

"I suppose I deserved that," Horst said, finally. "But please don't do it again."

He rubbed his face as Gudrun stared at him. She'd left a nasty mark on his right cheek, just indicative of a handprint. He didn't sound particularly hurt... but then, he wouldn't. Kurt had told her far too much about military training, including being taught how to take a blow and recover. Horst had probably been slapped worse in basic training... if he'd *had* basic training. How much of what he'd told them had been a lie?

"You didn't betray us," she said. She wondered, vaguely, if he'd want to slap her back. "I... why not?"

"Konrad was a good man," Horst said. "I read his file. He was on the fast-track for promotion. And yet, the moment he's wounded, they betray him and his family just to conceal the simple fact that the war isn't going as well as they claim. Everything he's done for them, everything his *father* has done for them, no longer matters. They betrayed someone who served them faithfully."

Gudrun eyed him sharply. "And that's why you didn't report us?"

"I believed what I was told," Horst said, after a moment. "It never crossed my mind that a person like Konrad could be betrayed by his own superiors. I... I knew I might be abandoned myself, but I knew the risks when I started. Konrad was *Waffen-SS*. They should have kept faith with him as he kept faith with them."

He could have betrayed us, Gudrun thought. She'd never suspected him, not once; hell, she'd *liked* him. As bad as being stuck in jail for a night had been, it would have been far worse if the police had known who they'd caught. *And if he'd betrayed us, we would all be dead by now.*

"I believed in the ideal of the SS," Horst added. "A body of men, the black knights of the iron cross, who would fight for the *Vaterland* and never surrender. I saw them in their uniforms, back in the east, and knew I wanted to be one of them. And then I discovered that my superiors were prepared to betray their own people, just to preserve their power."

"The SS has done terrible things," Gudrun said.

"Crushing the enemies of Germany isn't a terrible thing," Horst said. "But betraying its own people... yes, that's terrible. And so I decided to help you."

"Rather than report us," Gudrun said. She wondered, idly, just what would happen to Horst if his superiors ever found out. Gudrun and her fellow students might be mere dissidents, but Horst had actively betrayed his oaths. "Why did you tell me now?"

Horst looked down at the steering wheel. "That bungling idiot of a spy..."

Gudrun had to smile. "Which one?"

"Krabbe," Horst said. He sounded as though he wanted to say something worse. "That bungling buffoon approached me when I was with Sven and Leopold and, if that wasn't bad enough, gave an excuse that wouldn't fool a drunken husband. I should have shoved him down the stairs and sworn blind it was a terrible accident."

"So they may know what you are," Gudrun said, slowly. "What do you want to do about it?"

"I'm going to put together a cover story, but I don't know how well it will hold up," Horst said, thoughtfully. "I don't think I could rely on that idiot to count to eleven without taking off his shoes, let alone stick to the script. Still, if someone raises concerns about me, could you deflect them? I think we're going to have a lot of work to do in the next few months."

"I'll do my best," Gudrun said. "The mere fact you didn't betray us should count in your favour."

"I hope so," Horst said. "But undercover groups have torn themselves apart before, just because one member became suspicious of another. That's what they did in the French Resistance."

"I'll do my best," Gudrun repeated. She looked up at him, feeling a strange mixture of emotions. "You're braver than me, Horst."

"I'm trained for this," Horst said. "I wasn't joking when I said I learned to carry and use a gun almost as soon as I could walk. The insurgents made sure of it. I came under fire a long time before I joined the Hitler Youth. The SS only gave me better training. You... you weren't taught how to be anything but a housewife. No one would have thought any less of you if you'd married at sixteen and concentrated on turning out babies. You're far braver than I am."

"Perhaps," Gudrun said. "Would you teach me? To fight?"

Horst blinked. "It wouldn't be easy to teach you how to fire a gun," he said. "The handful of private shooting ranges in the city are closely supervised."

"But you could teach me how to fight hand-to-hand," Gudrun said. "If everyone in the east fights, doesn't that include the women?"

"They fight with guns," Horst said. He gave her a long look. "All other things being equal, Gudrun, a man will always be stronger than a woman."

Gudrun scowled. "But if you taught me how to fight, their strength might not be a problem," she argued. "And I do need to know."

"I can try," Horst said. "But it will hurt. It will hurt a lot."

"Thank you," Gudrun said.

She impulsively leaned forward and kissed him, gently. Horst started in surprise, then kissed her back, his hands reaching out to hold her tightly. Gudrun pulled back for a second, surprised at the sudden rush of feeling. She'd survived another incident that could easily have ended her life, but this was different. Horst had chosen to take a stand, rather than betray them, and she couldn't help feeling a rush of affection. She kissed him again, harder this time. His hands started to slip around to her breasts as his kisses became more passionate; she wrapped her arms around him and felt the strong muscles hidden under his clothes. No wonder he'd always worn loose clothes. The Hitler Youth might insist that boys spent most of their time engaged in healthy outdoors exercise, but Horst was far more muscular than Sven or Leopold...

"We shouldn't go any further," Horst said, pulling back. "Not here."

Gudrun looked around and flushed with embarrassment. There were only a handful of cars in the road, but anyone passing by could see them making out in the car. Maybe they'd even call the police. *That* would be embarrassing.

Horst gave her a final kiss, then let go of her and restarted the engine. They drove back to her house in silence.

"My father might kill me as soon as I walk in the door," Gudrun said, slowly. She knew her father would be furious and, if she'd been missing for a day, he would have had plenty of time to grow angrier. Her mother probably wouldn't be able to calm him down. "But if he doesn't kill me..."

"He won't," Horst said, as he turned the corner and drove towards the house. "I'll see you at university, tomorrow."

"If I'm allowed out of the house," Gudrun said, although she had no intention of letting her father stop her. The butterflies in her stomach might be nasty, but there were worse things to endure than parental disapproval. "I might have to tell him we're courting."

"I would be happy to court you," Horst said. He held up a hand. "But, for the moment, we have to be careful. I'm not the only agent at the university."

Gudrun nodded, then opened the door as soon as the car came to a stop. She fumbled for her keys as she walked towards the door, but it opened before she could find them. Her father was standing there, looking furious. The butterflies in Gudrun's stomach mated and produced babies. Her father hadn't been so angry since Siegfried had mocked Konrad's injuries to Gudrun's face.

"Get inside," he snapped. "Now!"

"Yes, father," Gudrun said.

CHAPTER THIRTY-TWO

Berlin, Germany
13 August 1985

It was hard, so hard, for Herman to remain calm. He knew *precisely* what had happened to his daughter, even before he'd managed to get a glimpse of her file at the station. Even if she hadn't been marked as anyone special, even if she'd only been in the wrong place at the wrong time, she would be processed like any other prisoner. He'd administered the procedure himself, countless times. His fists clenched in helpless rage as recalled forcing prisoners to strip, both to make sure they weren't carrying anything and to ensure they knew they were no longer the masters of their own destiny. Gudrun... how *could* she put herself in such danger?

She stood in front of him, breathing hard. Her clothes looked badly rumpled; her hair hung down in clumps, suggesting she hadn't been allowed to shower while she'd been in the prison cell. She'd probably been left naked too - and, if they'd been feeling malicious, shoved in with a handful of tougher female prisoners. What had she been thinking? Didn't she *know* what could happen to her? She could have vanished into the penal system and never been seen again. Even if she'd been exiled, as a young German lady of pure blood-line, she would still have had a very hard time of it.

He honestly didn't know what to say, let alone do. Boys were easy to raise; it was simply a matter of letting them run free, combined with firm boundaries and strict discipline. But girls? His sisters had been good little housewives, obedient to their parents and then to their husbands. Gudrun... it had been a mistake, he was sure now, to allow her to go to the university. It had given her all the wrong ideas. He wished, now, that he'd forbidden her to sit the exams, let alone remain as a student. It would have been simple enough to find her a suitable man and ensure she married him. Now...

Gudrun looked at him, her face a strange mixture of defiance and fear. He'd seen it before on countless prisoners, mostly males; prisoners who weren't broken, but unsure of themselves enough to remain quiet rather than risk compromising themselves. It was easy to see her grandmother in her face, the mixture of a strong chin and long blonde hair... Herman wished, suddenly, that his mother had remained alive. *She* would have known what to say.

And she never put up with any nonsense either, he thought, feeling a twinge of pain. Why had his mother died while Grandpa Frank, the drunken old bastard, survived? *She would have taken Gudrun under her wing if I'd asked.*

Gudrun broke the silence, finally. "Where's mother?"

"Out," Herman growled.

He glowered at her until she lowered her eyes. His entire world seemed to be shifting around him and he didn't like it. His daughter was arrested and *then* his wife went out onto the streets with a gaggle of other housewives, bringing the entire city to a halt. He'd get an earful from the Captain tomorrow, he was sure, while the other policemen jeered at him for being unable to control his wife. But what was he supposed to do? Handcuff her to the kitchen stove? Beat her like a child? Adelinde would cut his throat the moment he fell asleep or poison his food. She was too proud to forgive him for such a humiliation.

"Tell me," he said, as gently as he could. "What *were* you thinking?"

Gudrun raised her eyes. "I was thinking that I don't want to be scared anymore."

Herman blinked in surprise. "And you thought being arrested would keep you from being scared?"

"I didn't know I would be arrested," Gudrun said.

"Strikes are illegal," Herman pointed out, coldly. *That* had changed, if the radio broadcast was accurate, but Gudrun had still gone to the scene of a crime. "You could be arrested merely for supporting the strikers. Several of your fellow students *died* supporting the strikers."

Gudrun winced. She hadn't known that, Herman realised. The student who'd brought her home - and damn the government for refusing to allow him to collect his daughter - hadn't told her anything. No doubt he'd kept his mouth firmly shut, rather than deal with a torrent of female emotion. Young men tended to be cowards that way.

"You did something very stupid," Herman told her, flatly. "I don't know what they're teaching you at the university, but defying the government can be very dangerous."

Gudrun tilted her head, defiantly. She *did* look like her grandmother. "*Someone* has to take a stand."

"But not you," Herman snapped. "Did it occur to you that your family could have been destroyed? Your older brother's career would come to an end, your younger brothers would be under permanent suspicion, your father would lose his job... do you really imagine that the government would not have hesitated to make an example out of all of us?"

"They'd have to do it to the families of *everyone* who got arrested," Gudrun pointed out, coldly. "Father..."

Herman clenched his fists. "You were lucky," he told her. "Do you know what could have happened to you? You could have been *raped*, Gudrun! You could have been sold to one of the combines as a farming wife..."

Gudrun looked shocked, then angry. "Is that what you do to the girls you arrest?"

"You..."

Herman bit off his words. He'd never taken advantage of his uniform - his wife would have been furious if he'd even *thought* about molesting a prisoner - but he knew what happened in some of the less pleasant prisons in the *Reich*. Young girls, sometimes younger than Gudrun, were raped and abused by the prison guards or their fellow inmates. No one in authority cared, either, not when the victims were criminals. Anyone in jail, as far as the authorities were concerned, had done something to deserve it.

"The prison guards are less concerned with the niceties," he said, finally. "And you could easily have been sold to the farms, Gudrun. You would have been given to some farmer and expected to be his wife."

Gudrun shuddered, then gathered herself. "But it didn't happen."

"It could still happen," Herman insisted. "Gudrun..."

His voice trailed away. He'd never been good with words. He didn't know how to tell his daughter just how scared he'd been, when he'd heard she'd been arrested. His sons were tough young men - he was proud of all three of them - but Gudrun was a girl, the apple of his eye. The thought of her being stuffed into a brutal prison, even one solely for female prisoners, was horrifying. Some of the female prisoners could be far nastier than the men.

"You will not return to the university," he said, finally. "You will remain here, at home, until we find you a suitable husband."

———

Gudrun felt as if she had been punched in the belly. That, or a beating, would have been far preferable to a strict ban on returning to the university. Her father wouldn't give her an opportunity to sneak out, either. She'd be working for her mother from dawn till dusk, if she wasn't being watched by Johan or Grandpa Frank. The thought was maddening. After everything she'd done, after even spending a night in jail, she was *damned* if she was becoming a housewife.

She could see the fear on her father's face. He wasn't scared *of* her, she could tell, but *for* her. She'd heard rumours about what happened to prisoners too, although she'd never dared ask her father before now if there was any truth in them. She hadn't really wanted to know, not when her father might have been involved. And there was something else bothering her father, something to do with her mother. Where *was* she?

"No," she said. Perhaps it was a bad tactic - it might be better to pretend to surrender for the moment and argue later, when her father had calmed down - but she was no longer the young girl she'd been. "I will *not* leave the university."

Her father purpled. "You are my daughter and you will do as I say," he snapped. "I will visit the university tomorrow and inform them that you are no longer a student..."

"You won't," Gudrun said. She met his eyes, knowing he would take it as a challenge. "I worked too hard to pass those exams to just throw them away."

"Yes, you did," her father snapped. "And what will spending the next four years at the university *get* you? A piece of paper that no one will respect?"

"The world may change," Gudrun said. She was sure demand for computers would only grow throughout the *Reich*. If the stories of America were true, every household had a computer, perhaps even more than one. "And computer experts will be much in demand."

Her father snorted. "You're a young woman," he said. "You should be turning out babies, not trying to find a job."

"My boyfriend is a cripple," Gudrun shouted at him, feeling her temper snap. "They didn't even have the decency to *tell* me what happened to him! His father had to find out himself!"

She forced herself to calm down. "Father," she said, "I understand how you feel. But I'm not going to throw this opportunity away because it could turn sour. Being a housewife could also turn sour."

"Not if you treat your husband with respect," her father said. There was a hint of something *ugly* in his tone. "Gudrun..."

"I won't quit," Gudrun said, drawing herself up to her full height. "And you can't make me."

She braced herself, unsure just how her father would react. He might order her to bend over the sofa for a thrashing or send her to her room while he called the university and informed them that she was no longer a student. She was directly challenging his authority, after all, just as she'd challenged the government. His pride in his role as head of the household wouldn't let her get away with it.

But whatever he dishes out, she told herself, *I can take it.*

"I will discuss your future with your mother," her father said, finally. "*And* your punishment for being so stupid as to put your life at risk."

Gudrun bit down a comment about double standards - her father had congratulated her brothers for putting their lives at risk more than once, although she had to admit that they'd only ever risked themselves - and held herself at the ready. She'd been arrested by the police and threatened with a whole series of unpleasant fates. Her father's punishments no longer sounded so fearsome. If Kurt had been a different person after his first deployment into a combat zone, she was a different person too.

"Go to your room," her father ordered, finally. "Have a shower, then wait."

"Yes, father," Gudrun said.

Her father watched her through tormented eyes as she walked past him and up the stairs, but said nothing. There was no sign of her brothers, she noted; Kurt would be at the barracks, of course, but she had no idea where the younger boys were. Perhaps they were with friends, if her father had anticipated a row, or maybe they were just keeping their heads down, knowing their father was in a foul mood. It wouldn't be *safe* to be seen.

She closed the door behind her, then undressed rapidly. Her skin felt unclean, reminding her she hadn't showered for over a day... *and* that she'd been groped by a couple of policemen, one of whom had inspected her private parts. She shuddered at the memory - she no longer felt safe when she was naked - and then forced herself to don a towel rather than hastily dressing herself. It was no longer easy to walk down the corridor to the bathroom, she discovered. The sense of being watched was strong, even though she *knew* she was unobserved. Being in prison, even for a day, had left her with mental scars.

But I didn't break, she told herself, as she stepped into the bathroom and locked the door. *I didn't tell them anything.*

The thought made her smile before the implications caught up with her. As far as the police knew, she was just another student who'd been in the wrong place at the wrong time. They hadn't connected her with Sigrún, the writer of proclamations and dissident... they certainly hadn't connected her to Konrad. There had been no *reason* to do more than strip-search her, no reason to ask more than a bare handful of questions. But if that ever changed...

Her body was shaking as she clambered into the shower and turned on the water. She'd never suspected Horst, not once. Many of the new spies were too obvious to be taken seriously, but Horst? He'd become a friend, even a potential boyfriend, without her having the slightest hint that there was something wrong with him. And if he'd done his duty and reported her from the start... she would have been thrown into prison, along with the rest of the Valkyries.

She shivered, even though the water was warm. Her father was worried for her, she knew; her mother would probably feel the same way. She'd tasted the coercive power of schoolmasters and BDM matrons from a very young age, but she'd been spared a glimpse at the true power dominating the *Reich*, keeping everyone in line. Now... she scrubbed at her body, trying to eradicate the sensation from where she'd been touched. It would be easy just to give up, just to surrender and allow her father to withdraw her from the university. Who knew? Her husband might be a kind man, willing to allow her to be more than just a housewife...

But that would be giving up, she thought, angry at herself. *And I've come too far to give up.*

She'd sneaked into a hospital, she'd started the Valkyries, she'd triggered the process that was bringing more and more people onto the streets, proving that the government was far from invincible. She was *damned* if she was just surrendering now. Konrad deserved better than to be forgotten by his girl-friend. If she couldn't have him back, and she feared his father would simply turn off the life support, she could at least fight in his name.

There was a loud tap on the door. "Gudrun," her mother's voice said. She sounded different, somehow. "Are you in there?"

"Yes, mother," Gudrun said, tiredly. Really, where else would she be, if she wasn't in her room? It wasn't as if she made a habit of sneaking into any of the other bedrooms. "I'm just finishing."

"I'll wait in your room," her mother said.

Gudrun sighed, reminded herself that she could take whatever her parents chose to dish out, then dried herself hastily. Who knew *what* her mother would find if she decided to search Gudrun's bedroom? She was sure there was nothing incriminating in plain view, but she didn't want to take chances. Wrapping the towel around herself, she opened the door and hurried back to her bedroom. Her mother was sitting on Gudrun's bed, resting her hands on her lap. She looked... *different*, in a way Gudrun couldn't quite grasp. And there was no sign of her father.

"We need to talk," she said, firmly.

"Yes, mother," Gudrun said, closing the door and picking up her dressing gown. "I'm all ears."

———

Oh, Gudrun, Kurt thought. *What have you done?*

He hadn't expected the last two days to be anything more than constant physical training, shooting at the range and a host of other tasks to prepare the soldiers for combat operations in South Africa. The horror stories some of the experienced men had told him were enough to make it clear that they needed as much training as possible before they saw the elephant, despite the limitations of any training scenarios. But instead, the Berlin Guard had been ordered to muster and placed on alert. The old sweats insisted they'd never been ordered to prepare for immediate operations since the sixties, when Kurt's *father* had been in the military. Kurt had been convinced there had been some kind of disaster. What *else* could explain the sudden shift in priorities?

But they'd mustered and waited... and waited... and finally been sent back to barracks. There had been so many rumours flying through the base that the CO had had to make an announcement, but it had been utterly incoherent. Strikers in Berlin, women on the streets, schoolchildren throwing mashed potato at their teachers... Kurt had been left wondering if it had been nothing more than an unscheduled drill. The explanation had just sounded impossibly absurd.

And then he'd heard the broadcast, when he'd gone on watch, and put the whole story together. The leaflets - the leaflets his sister had written - had been replaced with something else, a mass - and thoroughly illegal - labour movement. And their strike had brought women and children out onto the streets in support.

We might have been ordered into the city, to fire on strikers and students, he thought, as he checked the bulletin board. They'd been due to go out of the city for mountain training, but apparently the entire training schedule had been cancelled. *And what would have happened when we'd been ordered to open fire?*

The government had backed down, according to the radio, but he knew better than to take that for granted. If the training schedule had been cancelled, when the unit was due to go to South Africa, it could only mean that higher command had a use for the Berlin Guard closer to home. And that meant...?

He shuddered. *What do we do if we are ordered to fire on women and children?*

CHAPTER THIRTY-THREE

Berlin, Germany
15 August 1985

"I'm glad to see you made it back alive," Ambassador Turtledove said. "I was starting to worry."

"It could have been a great deal worse," Andrew assured him. "And we got the pictures out, which is something."

"Definitely," the Ambassador said. He waved a hand at the comfortable chairs. "Please, take a seat. I trust they weren't too unpleasant?"

"Just slammed us into a cell for a couple of days," Andrew said. "No search, no beatings... they must be going soft."

"They certainly backed down when the entire city ground to a halt," the Ambassador agreed, calmly. His secretary appeared with a couple of mugs of coffee. "Washington needs a full report, Andrew. What the hell is going on?"

"The cracks in the *Reich* have finally started to break open," Andrew said. He took a long sip of his coffee before continuing. He'd expected worse when the Germans had swept him and Marshall off the streets, but the *Reich* had had worse problems than a pair of Americans poking their noses into the strikes. "We always knew they would, one day."

The Ambassador nodded. His family was Jewish, although Andrew didn't think he practiced himself. The *Reich* had slaughtered every Jew it could catch, without exception; there was no group in the United States that hated the Nazis as much as the Jews. He was mildly surprised the Nazis hadn't protested Turtledove's appointment - he was human, unlike the shambling monsters German children were taught to fear - but the Ambassador rarely met anyone outside the highest echelons of the *Reich*. It was unlikely the German population even knew his name.

"My contacts were predicting trouble," Andrew added, after a moment. "The real question is just how far the *Reich* will reform."

"It looks as though they have conceded everything," the Ambassador noted. "Do you believe that's true?"

Andrew shook his head. "I don't see the old regime surrendering power so easily," he said, carefully. "They were caught by surprise, I suspect, by the sheer volume of the strikes and street protests. The next time, sir, they will be a great deal better prepared."

He took another sip of his coffee. "Legalising unions and protest groups may seem like a concession," he added, "but it forces the leaders to come out into the open. They'll paint targets on their backsides for the *Waffen-SS* to kick. I would be surprised if they weren't already seeding the protest groups with spies and agent provocateurs, just to provide an excuse for crushing the crowds and arresting the leaders."

"If the soldiers agree to fire," the Ambassador noted.

Andrew shrugged. "The *Waffen-SS* will definitely fire," he said. "Obedience and loyalty to appointed authority has always been one of their strengths. And... they're like the marines, in some ways: a self-selected elite that considers themselves a cut above the rest."

"As a retired marine," Turtledove said stiffly, "I find that comparison highly insulting."

"The principle is the same," Andrew said, unfazed. He'd done his military service in the Rangers, before transferring to OSS. The lure of being like James Bond had drawn him into intelligence work, although supervillains and hot girls seemed to be remarkably thin on the ground. "The *Reich* has worked hard to ensure that the *Waffen-SS* owes loyalty to the *Reich*, to the concept of the SS, rather than to the German population. It doesn't help that most of their eastern recruits see the westerners as..."

Turtledove smirked. "Cappuccino-sipping liberals?"

"More or less," Andrew said. "The real problem, sir, is what happens *after* the protest movements are crushed?"

The Ambassador sighed. "That's what Washington wants to know," he said. "And it's a question I can't answer."

CHRISTOPHER G. NUTTALL

"There are three possibilities," Andrew said. He'd given the matter some thought while waiting in the prison cell. "First, the *Reich* goes back to normal. Second, there is a prolonged period of instability that will weaken the *Reich* over the long run. Third, outright civil war breaks out."

"And the *Reich* has nuclear weapons," the Ambassador said. "Do you think they'd start something with us, just to divert their people from the current crisis?"

Andrew frowned. He hadn't considered *that* possibility.

"They'd need to provoke a bigger crisis than the Falklands War," he said, after a moment's thought. "One they could use to appeal to their own people. A shooting incident between the Brits and Germans? Something they could cool down if necessary. The real danger would be accidentally ending up with a full-scale war."

He scowled, remembering a handful of war games he'd been required to observe during his last stint in Washington. There were too many questions over just how many advanced jet fighters, missiles and nuclear-powered submarines the *Reich* actually possessed, but it was generally agreed that the Germans could give the British a very hard time if they launched a major airborne offensive into British airspace, while using the *Kriegsmarine* to prevent reinforcements from the United States and Canada. And yet, could they do more? There were so many British and American troops in Britain itself that outright invasion might well be impossible.

But then, the same is true for us, he thought. *Invading France would be one hell of a bloodbath.*

The war games had suggested, even with both sides refraining from using nuclear weapons, that the war would be long, perhaps even terminating in a stalemate. Invading France would be costly, advancing through Iran into Germany Arabia marginally less so... it could be years before either side scored a decisive victory. And there were no silver bullets, no way to speed up the process. The United States and Britain would have to gird themselves for a fight that would make the *last* major war look like a minor spat.

"They'd have to be insane to provoke us," the Ambassador noted. "They need shipments of computer tech from the United States."

"They're not exactly sane," Andrew said. He knew too much about the *Reich's* crimes to have any doubt about the nature of the beast. The Jews

262

weren't the only people marched into the concentration camps and gassed to death. Germany was a prison camp above ground and a mass grave below. "They may even feel that they can win a nuclear war."

The ambassador shook his head in disbelief. Andrew understood. A nuclear exchange would devastate both sides, even with the ABM system. He doubted the *Reich* could survive after losing its cities, military bases and transit links to American nukes. God knew the enslaved populations would see a chance for freedom and take it, lashing out at what remained of the *Reich*. But the SS truly believed they were the *Herrenvolk*, the Master Race. They might feel they could survive a nuclear war and rebuild from the ashes.

"Washington would like to know if there's anything we can do," the Ambassador said. "*Is there anything?*"

Andrew frowned. Of all the personnel stationed in the embassy, he had the most contact with ordinary Germans. But even he didn't know *precisely* what was going on in the *Reich*. The Germans themselves didn't know.

"I don't think so," he said, finally. "We don't know *precisely* who's behind the protest movement, so we don't know who to contact. And if we were *caught* speaking to the leadership, the *Reich* would have every right to declare us *Persona Non Grata* and toss us out of the country. They'd play the incident for all it was worth, sir. I think the only thing we can reasonably do is watch from a safe distance."

Turtledove snorted. "*Is there such a thing?*"

"Maybe not, sir," Andrew said. "But better the *Reich* remains concentrated on its own internal problems than looking at us and contemplating war."

"There are some in Washington who'll want to use this opportunity to put the boot in and end the cold war," Turtledove said. He finished his coffee and placed the cup on the table. "Of course, they might just replace the cold war with a hot war."

Andrew nodded. The *Reich's* leadership had to be getting desperate, if they were prepared to make concessions rather than send in the *Waffen-SS* to bust some heads. They'd see the prospect of a war with America as a relief, perhaps. God knew they'd spent the last forty years preparing their population for one final war against the capitalist Jew-ridden pigs in the United States.

"Write a full report and include any suggestions you might have," the Ambassador ordered, as Andrew finished his own coffee. "And make sure they know just how dangerous the situation is becoming. We don't want to stumble into a war because some back-seat driver in Washington thinks he knows better than us."

"Yes, sir," Andrew said. There *might* be a way to help the growing protest movement, but the Germans would turn against it if they believed that outsiders were helping the protesters. Hell, the *Reich* might see fit to portray them as American stooges. "Has the *Reich* said anything formally?"

"Not to us," the Ambassador said. He didn't sound surprised. The German Foreign Ministry talked to the Americans as little as possible. "I suspect they don't want us to know just how bad things are becoming."

Andrew nodded. "They're likely to get worse," he said. "I don't see the regime just surrendering its grip on power. They're not *Americans*. There aren't regular elections with peaceful winners and losers. The *Reich* is a party-dominated dictatorship."

"The federal government endures, no matter which party is in power," the Ambassador said, curtly. "The Nazis may just need a few new figureheads."

———

When, *Reichsführer-SS* Karl Holliston asked himself, had the *Reich* ever actually *surrendered*?

It hadn't, as far as he could recall, certainly not to feckless civilians. The west had truly gone soft, if it was prepared to coddle strikers rather than punish them... and, for that matter, allow married women to march onto the streets as if they were men. Didn't they *know* their duty was to remain at home, having babies and raising them while the men took care of the hard work? How *dare* they have political opinions of their own? How dare *anyone* have political opinions of their own?

Should have set the dogs on them, he thought. There were canine units in the east, deployed against work gangs of *Untermenschen* that rioted against their rightful superiors. *And then have them publicly stripped and flogged to teach them a lesson.*

But the Reich Council had surrendered. The Reich Council had made concessions. The Reich Council... had betrayed the *Reich*.

It wasn't a pleasant thought, but it had to be faced. Karl had thought he could count on Voss, as a matter of course, and several of the other ministers, yet they'd seen the protesters on the streets and turned against their sworn duty. Who *cared* how many students were arrested or killed on the streets when the *Reich* was in danger? The strikers... if they refused to work, they could be shot! And yet, the Reich Council - even the military - had betrayed its own people.

Two days, he thought, savagely. *Two days and the world turns upside down.*

He gritted his teeth in frustration. The reports had flowed in faster than the RSHA could handle them, long lists of new political committees all over the *Reich*. Thankfully, the rot hadn't spread past Old Warsaw - Germany East wouldn't tolerate dissent when the easterners had to fight constantly to defend their settlements - but it was everywhere else. Even a handful of warship crews had been caught holding political meetings, in defiance of naval regulations. The *Kriegsmarine*, which had failed in its duty once before, was now failing again by not stringing the crewmen from the nearest yardarm. And the French were growing bolder in their resistance to authority. It wouldn't be long before strikes started to spread through the occupied territories.

And no matter what they say about the economy, he thought, *the real threat is political.*

Karl had never been to America, but he'd read the reports from German spies and political agents within the United States. America was a tottering country, permanently on the verge of collapse. The act of allowing the races to mingle *alone* had crippled the United States; allowing women the right to vote, to steer the course of global politics, had been worse. It was horrific to contemplate the destruction of all that was good, of all that was German, by a tidal wave of *Untermenschen* under the delusion that the state owed them something. One day, he was sure, the Americans would beg the *Reich* to save them from themselves, but until that day...

I have to make sure the madness doesn't spread into the Reich, he told himself. *And if the Reich Council cannot be relied upon, I have to handle it myself.*

It was a bitter thought. He'd never liked or trusted the civilians, particularly the Finance Minister, but he'd thought he could count on the regular military as a fellow defender of German values. Young German lads might go reluctantly into the army - the *Heer* took conscripts, unlike any of the other services - yet when they left, they were imbued with the fighting spirit of Germany and a willingness to die in defence of the *Reich*. He'd expected better from the Field Marshals, the supreme commanders of the military, but they'd refused to do their duty and stand up to the whining civilians. They'd even allowed the rot to spread through their soldiers! It was worse than 1918-19!

"*Herr Reichsführer*," Marie said. "*Sturmbannfuehrer* Harden is here to see you."

"Good," Karl said. "Send him in, then inform all callers that I am busy."

He rose to his feet as *Sturmbannfuehrer* Viktor Harden entered the room and snapped off a perfect salute. He was a tall man, wearing a black uniform with a single death's head pin on his shoulders. Harden lacked imagination, Kurt recalled, but he made up for it with bloody-minded ferocity that made him perfectly suited to one of the police battalions that supervised concentration camps, rounded up *Untermenschen* for work gangs, hunted down insurgents and policed *Untermenschen* townships in Germany East. There had been a whole string of complaints against the man, Karl reminded himself, mainly from senior military officers with weak stomachs, but Karl didn't care. Harden got the job done and that was all that mattered to the SS.

"*Herr Reichsführer*," Harden said. He sounded vaguely surprised. It was rare, vanishingly rare, for an SS police battalion to be ordered to Berlin. "You wanted to see me?"

"I did," Karl said. He sat back down at his desk and studied Harden for a long moment before continuing. "You've heard the reports from Berlin?"

"Yes, *Herr Reichsführer*," Harden said.

"The civilians" - it was hard not to spit in disgust - "believe that making concessions to the protesters will be enough to prevent another set of strikes," he said. "Those concessions, however, will only whet their appetite for *more* concessions, for more political surrenders, for - eventually - the end of the *Reich* itself. It cannot be allowed."

"Yes, *Herr Reichsführer*," Harden said.

"The Berlin Guard cannot be relied upon," Karl hissed. It was unthinkable, but it had to be tolerated, for the moment. The guard would be purged later or sent to South Africa. "Nor can the police. They will both be there, as a sign of strength, when the next protest begins, but they will do nothing to stop it. Their men have already been contaminated by the protesters, by the fear of injuring their women and children."

He saw a smile of anticipation flicker across Harden's face. The man was a monster, even by the SS's standards, and his subordinates were, if anything, even worse. They had no qualms over slaughtering male prisoners and raping female prisoners before throwing any survivors into the army brothels - or worse. The unit existed purely to spread terror, purely to remind the *Untermenschen* that their lives belonged to the *Reich*. Bringing them to Berlin and turning them loose on Germans was a gamble, but it was one he had to take. There were times when even *good* Germans needed to be reminded that their sole duty was to the state.

"Yes, *Herr Reichsführer*," Harden said. "My men will be happy to crush them for you."

"Billet your men in the garrison," Karl ordered. He'd been careful to ensure that only a handful of SS officers, let alone soldiers or civilians, knew he'd moved Harden's unit to Berlin. "And stand ready to intervene when I call you."

He watched Harden go with a cold smile. The man was thoroughly unpleasant - even a couple of SS officers had filed complaints - but he did good work. It didn't matter to him just who his unit was told to attack; they'd slaughter helpless women and children, even *German* women and children, with the same enthusiasm they'd slaughter Slavic terrorists. The streets of Berlin would run red with blood. And, if something did go wrong, he would take the blame for the whole affair.

It was a shame, Karl thought. There were many good young women in the university, young women who should have been churning out the next generation of Germans. And the older women who'd spearheaded the protests in support of the strikers had good connections. They couldn't be purged as long as their husbands held positions of power and influence. But that would change after Harden's men had cleared the streets. The unmarried girls would be sent east, where they would become farm wives, while the married women were taught a sharp lesson before being returned to their husbands. They'd never dare go onto the streets again.

And the Reich Council will have no choice, but to back me, he thought, as he rose. There were other preparations to make. *I will become the next Fuhrer and save my country from itself.*

CHAPTER THIRTY-FOUR

Albert Speer University, Berlin
16 August 1985

Horst hadn't been sure if Gudrun would be allowed to return to the university or not, even though she'd been released from jail without charge. Her father might have refused to allow her to return to the university, as several other fathers had apparently done in the wake of the strike and protest movements, or she might simply have been expelled for daring to get arrested in the first place. The university might try to be a little freer than the average school, but there were limits. He was relieved - very relieved - when he saw her entering the university two days after she'd been released, only to discover that half of the lectures they were due to attend had been cancelled.

"I'm glad to see you again," he said, as they slipped into a meeting room. He wouldn't have blamed her for taking advantage of the opportunity to drop out of the growing protest movement, but he was pleased to see she hadn't. "What did your parents say?"

Gudrun winced as she sat down on a hard chair. "My mother apparently joined the crowd after she'd heard I was arrested, even defying my father to do it," she said. "They bawled me out, then had a huge argument afterwards. Father wanted me to stay home for the next eternity, but mother insisted that I should return to university."

Horst raised his eyebrows. "Your mother must be a very strong woman," he said. He sat down next to her, close enough to touch... if she wanted to touch. "Did they impose any conditions on you?"

"Just wanted me to make sure I stuck to my classes and kept my head down," Gudrun said, rather ruefully. "Father... was not very happy with me. I know he was worried..."

"He had good reason to worry," Horst pointed out. "Better than he knows."

Gudrun gave him a sharp look, then leaned forward until her lips were practically brushing his ear. "Is it safe to talk in here?"

"Someone has been sweeping the building and removing all the bugs," Horst said. He smiled at her stunned expression. "As far as I can tell, there isn't a bugged room left in the university."

"The SS must love that," Gudrun muttered. She kept her lips close to his ear. "Have you had any other orders?"

"Keep an eye out for troublemakers, but otherwise do nothing," Horst said. "Right now, just about everyone in the university is a troublemaker. There's going to be a big meeting this afternoon in the cafeteria."

"I'll be going," Gudrun said. "I'm already marked as a troublemaker."

"You were arrested for being in the wrong place at the wrong time," Horst reminded her, dryly. "But they'll use that against you if they catch you causing trouble."

"I can't give up now," Gudrun said. "Are you going to stop me?"

Horst wished he could. It would be simple to ring her father and tell him that Gudrun wasn't staying out of trouble. She'd be kept home... and he probably wouldn't see her again, even if she was released after a few weeks of grounding. The thought of her mad at him was almost painful...

Admit it, he told himself, sternly. *You're falling in love with her.*

"No," he said, finally. "But you do realise I'd have to report it? And you'd be at the top of the list because you were already arrested?"

"I understand the risks," Gudrun said, softly. "I've *been* arrested."

"It will be worse next time," Horst hissed. "Gudrun, there are worse things than spending a night in a cell."

"You forget the bit about being stark naked," Gudrun snapped. "Is *that* normal?"

"You'd be amazed at what can be turned into a weapon with a little ingenuity," Horst said, dryly. "Keeping the prisoners naked not only makes them uncomfortable, it ensures they have problems hiding anything from the guards."

"Yeah," Gudrun said. "You promised you'd teach me how to fight."

Horst flushed. "I'm going to have to give that some thought," he said. He knew there were SS tutors who specialised in teaching the handful of female SS operatives, yet he'd never met any of them, let alone watched them in action. He'd been pounded mercilessly by his teacher, but the thought of hammering Gudrun like that was intolerable. "How did you do with your exercises in the BDM?"

"Well enough," Gudrun said. "They never taught us to fight, though."

"I doubt you have time to learn," Horst said, reluctantly. There were sparring chambers they could use, on the lower levels, but they weren't truly private. Taking Gudrun back to the apartment he shared with the other SS operatives would be far too revealing. "Let me sort out where and when we can get together, then we can arrange something."

"Very well," Gudrun said. "And now... what's been happening in my absence?"

"An uneasy peace," Horst said. "I don't expect it to last for long."

———

Gudrun had never really expected to be grateful to her mother, not after she'd realised she didn't want to be a housewife, a nurse, or any of the handful of other socially acceptable female professions, but she had to admit that her mother had stood up for her, even when her father had been in a foul mood. The smouldering ache in her backside, the droll reminder that her parents were displeased with her, was nothing compared to the knowledge of just how close she'd come to being locked away in her room until her father found a suitable man. And yet...

She cursed under her breath as she met up with the others and *listened*. Hilde's mother was arranging more female groups, trying to set up a hierarchy of women demanding the same rights and freedoms as men, while Leopold's father was still working with the growing network of strike committees. Clearly, Konrad's father didn't believe the government had been beaten either, even though it had conceded the first round. New committees were being set up all time, while experienced workers were sorting out what demands to present to the Reich Council.

"Volker Schulze is planning to run for the *Reichstag*," Sven commented. "He's organising thousands of men to support him."

Horst looked unimpressed. "How does one even get *elected* to the *Reichstag*?"

"Good question," Sven said. "I looked it up. One can win a seat through being selected by the local party committee. It's just that most party committees rarely put forward candidates."

"Because the *Reichstag* is nothing more than a glorified rubber stamp," Horst commented, after a moment. "Finding a way to change that will be the next step, I think."

Gudrun shifted, uncomfortably. "Can't the elections be opened to everyone?"

"The voters have to be members of the Nazi Party in good standing," Sven explained. "I don't think they'll let us change that in a hurry."

"But most of the population *are* members of the Nazi Party," Horst pointed out. "The trick would be getting them into the beer halls to vote. Have any of you seen your parents vote?"

Gudrun shook her head. Her father had never voted, as far as she knew; she hadn't even known people could, technically, vote until she'd started the whole movement. But then, Horst was right; the *Reichstag* was nothing more than a rubber stamp. True power came from climbing up the ladder in the civil bureaucracy, the military or the SS. And yet, if that were true, what would happen when Volker Schulze started trying to change things?

She was still mulling over the problem as they went for lunch - another of their classes was cancelled without explanation - and walked down into the cafeteria. Someone had hung a black-edged photograph of Hartwig and a couple of other students, one of them a young woman, from the wall, a chilling reminder that their new freedom of speech had come with a price. Gudrun had never been sure what to make of Hartwig - he'd seemed more interested in chasing girls than actually doing his studies - but he hadn't deserved to die on the streets of Berlin. The handful of testimonials written below the pictures suggested that Hartwig had died on his feet, fighting the police. She had no idea if that were actually true.

"I didn't see him fall," she said, when one of his friends saw her and asked. Everyone knew she'd been arrested by now, thanks to Sven and Horst. It was embarrassing, but perhaps she could use it. "It was a nightmare."

"Tell us what happened," someone shouted.

Gudrun braced herself as all eyes turned to her. She'd never been particularly shy, but being in prison, if only for a night, had left her with scars. She wondered, suddenly, if Horst had watched as she'd stripped naked for the policemen, then decided he probably hadn't been able to go to the police station without an excuse. Gritting her teeth, knowing that she was committing herself, she climbed onto a chair. Thankfully, she *had* been taught how to recite sections of *Mein Kampf* at school.

"The strikers wanted to be paid for their work," she said. Most of the students surrounding her wouldn't have had a proper job. "But the corporations were demanding more work for less money."

She ran through the whole story, somewhat awkwardly, then changed the tone. "My boyfriend went to South Africa," she said. "And then I lost contact with him. It wasn't until his *father* demanded answers that I found out the truth. My boyfriend was badly wounded, so badly wounded that he hangs on the border between life and death. He will probably never recover, but they won't even let him die.

"They lied to us," she added. She wished she'd had a chance to write a proper speech, instead of speaking from the heart. "They told us that the war in South Africa would never be anything more than a police action, that only a handful of soldiers would have to die. But they were lying! What *else* are they lying about?

"I went to prison, but we are *all* in prison, a prison camp called the *Reich*. We went to school, where we were taught our lessons by rote and punished for asking questions, and then to the Hitler Youth, where we were made to march in unison. How many lies were we told in school? How many times were we told never to question our superiors? How much has been buried beneath a wave of lies?"

She was tempted to mention what Grandpa Frank had told her, but she knew it would be wasted effort. Her audience had been taught to hate and fear Jews, even though none of them had ever *seen* a Jew - and, if Grandpa Frank was right, wouldn't even recognise one if they did. Nor would they shed many tears over the hundreds of thousands of *Untermenschen*, worked to death in the labour camps or struggling to build the giant *autobahns*. But they'd understand their own people, students and workers, being punished just for speaking out.

"I'm sick of the fear," she said. "I'm sick of never daring to speak, of never daring to say a word for fear it will be used against me. I'm sick of being told I should be a good little girl and never question the men; I'm sick of hearing my brothers told they should be proud to fight for the *Reich*. I'm sick of being forced to deny it when I see the discrepancy between their lies and objective truth. I'm sick of being trapped in this prison camp!"

She took a moment to steady herself, then went on. "I know; many of you are scared, many of you are nervous about stepping forward and taking a stand. We have all been taught that questioning authority, that failing to parrot back their words brings us nothing but pain. We have all been taught that the *Reich* is invincible, that any who dare to stand against it die horrible deaths. And yet, who *told* us that? Who ordered punishment for those who didn't accept it at once? *The people who wanted us to believe it!*

"They told us a lie. They told us that the *Reich* was invincible. They told us that anyone who dared to question the *Reich* was a naughty child at best, an evil American spy at worst! But look around you. Look at your friends and tell me - are they evil? And when we showed our strength, the *Reich* stumbled rather than trying to fight. Alone, none of us have any power; together, we are strong enough to shake the *Reich*. And as long as we stay together, we will win."

She stepped down from the chair and was instantly surrounded by a mob of students, some cheering her name and others patting her on the back. It had been a risk - her father was likely to explode with rage when he heard about it, while she might get arrested again within the hour - but she'd spoken from the heart. She *was* sick of living in the *Reich*. And there were more cracks in the edifice than she'd dared suppose. If Horst could forsake his duty, how many others in the SS, the bastion of the state, felt the same way?

And if we remain united, she told herself firmly, *we can win.*

———

Horst had been taught to keep his head down, to avoid being noticed. It was dreary tradecraft, all the more so when he was forced to play the role of a loud student at the university, but he'd long since mastered the trick of appearing to be one of them without compromising himself. And yet, Gudrun - in a moment of madness - had stood up and openly declared herself to be a dissident. Her speech had been clumsy, with none of the polish he heard from the *Reich's* broadcasters, but it had transformed the mood of the student body. They now had a leader.

That was careless of her, he thought, savagely. How could she put herself in so much danger? Anyone else, male or female, would have been a better choice. Gudrun simply knew too much to risk attracting attention. A session with the *Reich's* interrogators, men experienced in inflicting unimaginable levels of pain, would probably break her. *She could get us all killed!*

There was nothing he could say, in public, so all he could do was watch as Gudrun worked to rally the students, encouraging them to work together. Perhaps it was better that *she* steer the growing protest movement, rather than someone who hadn't been there at the start, but it was still a security nightmare. Horst would have been surprised if someone in the room - someone *else* - hadn't been an undercover SS agent, watching and waiting to see what happened. He'd have to come up with *something* to tell his handlers or they'd start wondering just what he'd been doing at the university. Gudrun might just have accidentally exposed his duel loyalties to his superiors. By the time she slipped out of the room, back towards the meeting room, he'd had plenty of time to get angry.

"That was stupid," he hissed, as soon as they were alone. The walls were meant to be soundproofed, but he wouldn't have bet money on them. A spy didn't *need* an expensive bug to listen to a conversation, something he felt many in the *Reich* had forgotten. "What were you *thinking?*"

"I was thinking that I had to make sure the entire student body was moving in the same direction," Gudrun said, defiantly. "Don't I have reason to speak *now?*"

Horst was tempted to point out that the BDM *also* made sure the girls moved in the same direction, but bit down on the thought. Gudrun meant well, yet... she could have put him in terrible danger. And if he were to come under intense suspicion, he wouldn't be able to do anything other than make a run for Switzerland and hope he got there ahead of the manhunt.

"Your father didn't thrash you hard enough," he said, instead. "What do I tell my superiors?"

Gudrun reddened. "My father has nothing to do with this!"

"My superiors *do*," Horst snapped. "What do I tell them?"

"Just that you watched me give a speech," Gudrun said. She paused, her face paling. "Or you could claim you weren't there."

"And if there was someone in the crowd I don't know," Horst said, "I would be exposed as a liar. They'd *know* I was lying to them and they'd start to wonder why."

Gudrun looked down at the floor. "I'm sorry," she said. "I... I just got carried away."

"Yes, you did," Horst said. Was it worth a gamble? Was it worth pretending he wasn't there when she made the speech? The risk would be appalling. Or... he took a breath. "Your speech isn't exactly illegal, now."

"No," Gudrun said. She still looked pale. "They were kind enough to concede freedom of speech."

"And you're hardly the only one shooting her mouth off," Horst added. "Maybe you can hide in the crowd."

"There were others talking when I left," Gudrun said. "They can't arrest us all."

Horst was tempted, very tempted, just to shake her. "No, they can't," he agreed. "But they know you already. They won't hesitate to haul you in for the second time."

"Then we have to keep running," Gudrun said. Her voice was low, but grimly determined to carry on. "I might die - you might die - but the ideas we're spreading will live on."

"I hope you're right," Horst said. Gudrun was brave, he had to admit; he'd always thought that insane bravery was a male trait. "Because if you're wrong, we'll be hanging from meat hooks by the end of the day."

CHAPTER THIRTY-FIVE

Berlin, Germany
20 August 1985

"We need to make budget cuts," Hans said, flatly. "Now."

"And there I was under the impression that making concessions would save us from having to make budget cuts," Holliston sneered. "Haven't we already tolerated far too much?"

Hans eyed him dubiously. The *Reichsführer-SS* sounded oddly unfocused, as if he was concentrating on some greater thought. Watching the spread of political activity across the *Reich*, from student debate clubs to industrial unions, hadn't been easy for any of them, but the SS had been surprisingly muted about the whole affair. Hans had wondered if Holliston's position was under threat, yet his sources within the RSHA hadn't heard the slightest *hint* of dissent within the SS. He couldn't help thinking that wasn't a good sign.

"The problem is that the bills are finally coming due," he said, pushing the thought aside for later consideration. The civilians and the military were, for the moment, united. It would take the SS weeks, perhaps months, to break the alliance and reassert their power. "The Americans are not helping. Their newspapers have been covering the protest movements in the *Reich* with great interest."

"It isn't as if they haven't had riots of their own," Voss pointed out. "What does their displeasure mean for us?"

"It means we can no longer buy anything on credit, if we can find anyone in America willing to sell to us," Engelhard Rubarth said. The Foreign Minister looked tired. He'd been talking to his American and British counterparts non-stop over the last week. "Their corporations have to listen to their customers - and the American population. We've been told that several corporations will not be selling anything to us, even if we *do* pay up front."

"They have agreements," Holliston said. Oddly, it sounded more as though he was protesting because he thought he was *supposed* to protest. "Americans *worship* money. They signed contracts!"

"They may be willing to pay the penalties, if - of course - we can get an American court to rule in our favour," Rubarth said. "Politically, *Herr Reichsführer*, their business with us is only a small fraction of their total sales. They cannot afford a boycott from their other customers."

Hans tapped the table. "The Americans are not the only problem," he said. "Thanks to the French, thanks to the protest movements, thanks to the strikes, we're looking at a major cash shortage over the next month. There is no way the cracks can be papered over any longer."

"Seize cash from the major corporations," Holliston suggested. "They have reserves, do they not?"

"That would destroy our economy," Hans said. It didn't help that many corporations kept their money in Swiss banks, rather than the *Reich*. "Their reserves are simply not great enough to cover the holes in our budget. We have to stop the cash outflow."

"The military budget cannot be cut while we have a war on," Voss insisted. "We *need* new equipment and weapons for South Africa."

"And we shouldn't stop paying our fighting men now," Holliston added, darkly. "Who *knows* which way they'll jump?"

Hans silently cursed his predecessors under his breath. The *Reich's* economy had been a hodgepodge of competing factions ever since Adolf Hitler had risen to power, so weak that a single military defeat would probably have started a cascade reaction of failures that brought the entire system down. Even after the war had been won, even after the *Reich* had settled down to stripping Europe bare of everything from manpower to raw materials, the system was a mess. Cutting the budget in one place would have nasty effects in another.

And if we cancel the new aircraft carrier, he thought, *we'll put thousands of trained workers out of work.*

It wasn't the only problem, of course. He had never anticipated - none of them had ever anticipated - dissent within the military, the police and perhaps even the SS itself. The rot had spread far - endless anticorruption campaigns had produced no solid results - but he'd always believed that corruption was manageable. He'd never suspected the police would be reluctant to do their jobs, just because their wives and children were on the streets. In hindsight, it had been a major oversight. And cutting the wages of the men who kept the *Reich* in order would be cutting their throats.

"I don't propose to cut the military budget," he said, "although we are going to have to make some adjustments over the next two years. I have planners working on the best way to make those adjustments without causing an economic crisis. However, right now, we need to cut support payments."

"There will be trouble," Voss predicted.

"Not if we do it carefully," Holliston said. "Cut the payments for families living within Germany Prime, but offer to keep paying for families who are willing to move to Germany East within five years."

Hans blinked in surprise. Had Holliston *ever* supported him? The SS *liked* the idea of paying mothers to have as many children as possible, even though it was a growing drain on the economy. No matter how he looked at it, cutting the payments was going to be painful. God alone knew how many families would no longer be able to afford their children if their state payments were cancelled. Soldiers, in particular, would be hit hard. They were encouraged to get their wives pregnant every time they went home on leave.

It makes sense, he told himself. Holliston and the SS had been trying to urge more Germans to move to Germany East, despite its bad reputation. *They want to use cuts in the payments to encourage immigration.*

"We could simply stop paying for new mothers," Rubarth said, nervously. Economic policy was outside his bailiwick. "The mothers who have been drawing support payments for years *need* them."

"It is something we'll have to do, but it won't help us with the current problem," Hans said, producing a paper from his briefcase. "Assuming we manage to cut support payments by fifty percent over the next two months, we should be able to re-stabilise the economy - if, of course, the Americans don't make any major new deployments. We are already spending far too much money producing new missiles to overwhelm the American ABM system."

"Which we need," Voss said. "If the Americans successfully shield themselves against nuclear missiles, they can simply dictate terms to us at will."

That was true, Hans knew. If the *Reich* had such an advantage, the *Reich* Council would not hesitate to use it to force America to disarm and submit to German rule. The Yankees were cowards, certainly when compared to the *Reich*, but even cowards could pluck up the nerve to fight, if they thought they had an overwhelming advantage. Being able to turn the *Reich* into a pile of radioactive ashes, without fear of major retaliation, would be enough to convince even a coward to strike. It would be unfortunate for Britain, too close to the *Reich* to be shielded properly, but he doubted the American planners would care. The *Reich* wouldn't give a damn if Vichy France were to be turned into rubble, if it gave the *Reich* dominance over the entire world.

"So we make the cuts," he said, out loud. "We do our best to present them to the people as *necessary* cuts, cuts we have to make."

"And offer incentives for people to move east," Holliston added. "There's plenty of unclaimed land for farmers in Germany East."

But most of the people who'll move are not farmers, Hans thought. *They don't want to spend the rest of their lives staring at the back end of a mule.*

He pushed the thought aside. For once, he had the cooperation of the SS. That wouldn't last, but he needed to take advantage of it. No matter how the cuts were spun, it would be impossible to avoid pain. The sooner it was over, the better.

"We can put the question to the *Reichstag*," Holliston added. "Let the protesters try to rationalise their opposition after the *Reichstag* votes in favour."

"That wouldn't be hard," Voss commented. "We haven't held free elections yet."

Hans shrugged. A freely-elected *Reichstag*, dependent on the whim of the population, wouldn't agree to pass any spending cuts, let alone a cut as deep as cutting support payments to German mothers. Holliston had a point, he had to admit; a democratic nation simply couldn't make the hard choices that would secure its future, once and for all. Who knew what would have happened if the Americans had joined the British in war against the *Reich*, back in 1945? The *Reich's* control over Europe had been so tenuous, in places, that it might have come apart at the seams, giving the world to the Americans.

No, he thought. *This isn't a decision we can trust to the people.* He smiled, rather thinly. "Shall we vote?"

———

It was a weakness of civilians, Karl Holliston had often felt, that they thought in terms of money and power, rather than the racial imperatives that had driven the *Reich* from the very first day Adolf Hitler had become the ruler of Germany. A civilian would compromise on issues that an SS officer would know could never be compromised. The world was red in tooth and claw; those who failed to be strong, those who failed to dominate, would be dominated themselves. There was no way the *Reich* could tolerate weakness in its ranks.

And weakness there was, he knew. He'd done nothing to purge the student activists, the female protesters, the unionists... giving them time to stand up and be countered. It didn't seem to have occurred to any of them that going public, no matter what the laws said was legal now, turned them into marked men. Karl's agents had been compiling a long list of men and women, ranging from old unionists to students barely old enough to marry, who would be ruthlessly purged once the old order reasserted itself. And it would, he knew. The civilians might delude themselves that the population would accept cuts in their support payments, but Karl knew better. He had no illusions about the leaders of the protest groups, male or female. They wanted power...

... And, like himself, they would do whatever it took to grab hold and keep it for themselves.

He'd played his cards carefully, as much as it galled him not to oppose the civilians in their madcap schemes. Let them think he would support their cuts, at least in Germany Prime; it was, in many ways, a defensible position. God knew Germany East needed a major population boom and encouraging young families to immigrate was a means to that end. But it would also lure the civilians into a false sense of security. They would assume he had no intention of stepping outside the normal rules of political dispute, within the *Reich*.

But the Reich itself is at risk, he thought, as the vote was taken. Only two junior ministers voted against the cuts, although the military officers looked

CHRISTOPHER G. NUTTALL

dubious. They were probably relieved they'd been spared painful budget cuts of their own. *And I must do whatever it takes to save it.*

Word would spread, long before the official announcement. He'd make sure of it. His agents would even make the cuts seem worse than they actually were, although in truth they were probably painful enough already to cause a major protest in the streets. And then, the SS would be waiting. Blood would flow on the streets of Germany and the *Reich* would be saved.

He glanced at Adolf Bormann, sitting silently at the head of the table. Who knew what *he* was thinking? *Karl* would never have accepted such a title without the power that went with it, even though the *Reich* was determined to prevent another Hitler, another lone man wielding supreme power over Germany. But the civilians and the military would no longer be able to stand in his way, after the protest was brutally crushed. *He* would be *Fuhrer*, in fact as well as name, and he would lead Germany back to greatness...

... And the civilians, who had drained the *Reich* of the vitality it needed to survive, would be ruthlessly wiped from existence.

———

"So tell me," Caius said, as they completed their shift and left the station. "How does it feel to have important relatives?"

Herman clenched his fists in rage - and helplessness. It was bad enough that everyone at the station knew his wife was one of the protesters - he wasn't the only policeman whose wife had gone out onto the streets - but to have his *daughter* leading a student protest movement was unique. He didn't know *what* to do about it. None of his sons had ever caused this much trouble. He'd remonstrated with her, pointing out the dangers of being arrested (again) or simply being expelled, then he'd beaten her and then he'd finally threatened to withdraw her from the university for good. But Adelinde had told him, in no uncertain terms, that if he ever wanted to see her naked again, he had to forget about removing Gudrun from the university. Herman didn't know what to do about her either.

"Just you wait," he said. Caius's sons were in the military, if he recalled correctly; his daughters were still at school, too young to either marry or try to get into the university. "Your wife might be out on the streets too."

282

"My wife has too much sense," Caius said. He pulled a packet of cheap cigarettes from his pocket and offered one to Herman, who took it with practiced ease. "And my daughters are too young to want to do anything more than keep their heads down and avoid the teachers."

He sighed as he struck a match and lit the cigarettes. "But they're already talking about quitting the BDM..."

Herman snorted, privately relieved that Gudrun had left the BDM last year. Kurt and Johan had both loved the Hitler Youth, but Siegfried hadn't found it quite so enjoyable. He had a feeling that his youngest son, like many other teenagers, would start demanding to be allowed to quit soon enough - and if the BDM had been hard on a policeman's daughter, he was sure it would have been worse for many other girls. How many teenagers would demand to be allowed to spend the time elsewhere, instead of being taught how to serve the *Reich*?

He breathed in the smoke as they walked past the front desk, through the armoured door and out onto the streets. Berlin felt *different* now, as if it were hanging on the knife edge between chaos and order, as if the population was no longer inclined to obey orders without asking questions and demanding answers first. It made him feel uneasy; he'd grown up in a world where saying the wrong thing could lead to jail or worse. Even spending most of his life in the military and police hadn't cured him of the corrosive fear that he could say the wrong thing, in front of the wrong pair of ears, and wind up dead. And, even though children learned to be careful of what they said at school, his daughter was still standing up for the right to free speech.

She's brave, he thought. *And yet she's naive.*

It was a bitter thought. Gudrun had endured so much more than the lash of his belt, yet she had no conception of just how bad things could become. *Herman* knew; he'd been a paratrooper before leaving the military and joining the police. He knew the savage horrors of war - and the worse horrors unleashed by the SS, intent on keeping the government in power at all costs. If she was arrested a second time, after opening her mouth in front of hundreds of witnesses, there would be no mercy. She'd be lucky if the rest of her family wasn't scooped up off the streets and marched into the concentration camps.

"I understand how they feel," Caius said. "I had to beat the shit out of one of the matrons, after she hurt my daughter. None of them signed up for the BDM."

And what happens, Herman asked himself again, *to girls who don't have powerful protectors?*

It was easy to push *Gastarbeiters* around. He certainly didn't feel any guilt about it. They were *Untermenschen.* No one in power would care if a handful got their skulls cracked, if they didn't obey orders or merely looked at the policemen the wrong way. But it was different when the people on the streets were wives and children, ordinary Germans who had relatives in the police and the army. Herman would have cheered if an agitator was taken off the streets, until he'd discovered that his own daughter was one of them. He remembered feeling angry when Gudrun had come home sporting bruises, after playing games with the BDM; it would be worse, far worse, if she was beaten bloody by the police. And he *was* the police.

"I don't know," he said, finally. "Just be glad they're not old enough to cause trouble yet."

"Hah," Caius said. He sounded bitter. "One of them is already suggesting a strike at school."

Herman laughed, then sobered. It would take a brave child to stand up to the teachers at school - the teachers had little compunction about inflicting corporal punishment on their charges, if they misbehaved - but his son *was* brave. Poor Siegfried had two older brothers - and now one sister - to emulate. And Siegfried already knew the teachers weren't particularly fair. Some of them lashed students because they enjoyed it, not because their victims deserved punishment.

He shuddered. His perfect family was gone. The world was changing. He no longer felt comfortable in the city he'd patrolled for the last fifteen years...

... And, in all honesty, he had no idea what was going to happen next.

CHAPTER THIRTY-SIX

Berlin, Germany
21 August 1985

"This just popped up on the network," Sven said.

Horst glanced up, interested. He'd taken to spending more time with Sven over the last week, although the orders he'd received - after he'd made a carefully non-committal report to his handlers - had told him to stick close to Gudrun. Gudrun herself had claimed to be unconcerned, but Horst was fairly sure that was nothing more than bravado. She'd set herself up as a student leader, *the* student leader, and she couldn't really allow herself to show fear.

And she keeps nagging me to teach her how to fight, he thought. *But where can we do it without attracting attention?*

He pushed the thought aside. "What is it?"

"It's a note from a friend in the Finance Ministry," Sven said. "Apparently, they're going to cut the *Mutterkreuz* support payments completely."

Horst leaned forward. "Are you sure?"

"The source has proven reliable before," Sven said. "He was the one who provided us with the comparative price data."

Horst frowned. The upside of all the students involved in protest movements, on one level or another, was hundreds of minds studying the government's official statistics and comparing them with reality. It hadn't taken long to realise that the real prices for everything from food to clothing were slowly creeping upwards, forcing families to spend more and more on basic necessities. Horst was no economist - it was a closed field to him - but he'd been taught the basics of budgeting at his stepfather's knee. A person - or a family - simply couldn't spend more than they earned.

Or at least not for very long, Horst thought sardonically. *A bank would be happy to give a loan to a farmer, if the farmers used their farm as collateral.*

It wasn't a pleasant thought - and it would be worse, he knew, in Berlin, where civilians couldn't live off the land. Growing one's own foodstuffs, let alone rearing meat animals, was strictly forbidden within the city. A family of six, with the husband away in the military, would find it very hard to survive if the *Mutterkreuz* payments were halted. Indeed, there was no way the current system was sustainable *without* the payments. The more he thought about it, the more he wondered if it was a trick of some kind. But what sort of person would want the population to believe their throats were about to be cut?

"It says here that the *Reichstag* will be meeting later today to discuss the cuts," Sven said, breaking into his thoughts. He looked up, sharply. "They'll... they'll just approve it, won't they?"

"They will," Horst confirmed. The government might have conceded free elections to the *Reichstag*, but none of those elections had been held - yet. He couldn't decide if someone was playing games or if they genuinely believed the *Reichstag's* blessing would stop the backlash. "All the *Reichstag* does is approve what the government *wants* it to approve."

He looked down at his hands, thinking hard. Word would already be spreading, thanks to the hundreds of computer users - and experts - who were joining the protest movement. He wouldn't be surprised if the unionists weren't already being informed - their families would be threatened by the cuts - and it wouldn't be long before Hilde's mother found out. She might not need any support payments from the state, but she'd hardly underestimate the threat to the rest of the city's women. They'd be out on the streets within an hour...

"I'm going to find Gudrun," he said, rising. "Start spreading the word as far as you can."

"*Jawohl,*" Sven said.

———

Volker Schulze had been expecting the government to do something - anything - about the unions, ever since the government had been forced into a humiliating retreat. He had no illusions. The only way to rise into power - civilian, military or SS - was to have a ruthless drive for power combined with a slavish loyalty to one's branch. And even if the government had been prepared to let bygones be bygones, the corporate managers wouldn't let them. The thought of their workers actually standing up to them, resisting their demands and even shutting down the factories, would be too much.

But he'd never expected the government to threaten to cut support payments.

They had to be out of their minds, he thought. The government had been encouraging Germans to have large families since 1944, since the official end of the war. They'd been helping to fund the families too, awarding payments to women who had more than three children. How many families were completely dependent on those payments? Their husbands didn't bring in enough money to make up the shortfall. They had to be mad...

... *Unless they're deliberately planning to punish the women*, he thought. The state had *rarely* seen women as anything other than mothers, daughters and wives. Indeed, there were only a handful of professions routinely open to women. *They must have been horrified when the women went out onto the streets.*

"We can't let them get away with it," Joachim said. "I have a wife and four appetites to feed."

Volker nodded in agreement. "Start calling everyone," he said. "We're leaving our work and going to the *Reichstag*."

———

Gudrun couldn't help a flicker of fear as she led the tidal wave of students out of the university. There was strength in numbers, strength in the certainty that hundreds - perhaps thousands - of people were behind her, yet there was also a sickening nervousness that made her want to throw up. Horst - and her father - had told her, in great detail, what would happen if the SS decided, *truly* decided, to crush the students. Machine gun bullets, her father had said, would go through flesh like hot knives through butter. Part of Gudrun almost wished she'd let her father beat her into submission, but then she looked at the students and knew she couldn't let them down.

It might have been a mistake to stand up and declare herself their leader, it might have painted a target on her backside, but now she'd done it she was committed.

"The *Reichstag* believes we will accept its judgement," she'd said, when she'd assembled the students. Most of the tutors had made themselves scarce; the SS spies - the known spies, at least - had been isolated. "We have to show them that we will *not* tamely accept their rulings any longer."

She kept walking forward, feeling her heartbeat starting to pound as she led the way towards Victory Square. They'd spread the leaflets there - it felt as through she'd done that years ago - but now, now she was going there openly, with thousands of others at her back. Whatever happened, she promised herself silently, there would be no more hiding. The state would no longer be able to hide its crimes under a facade of respectability.

"No cuts," she shouted. "No cuts!"

The students took up the chant. More and more people - workers, women, even ordinary civilians - were flowing out of their homes and joining the march. Gudrun wished she'd thought of producing a handful of banners, but it hadn't occurred to her before the march had begun. Horst had advised her not to plan a march and she'd listened to him. She caught sight of a handful of policemen, staring in horror, and winced inwardly. Was her father watching her as she marched towards Victory Square?

We need some better organisation, she thought, as the crowd swelled still further. She'd wanted to set up a network of student leaders, and march stewards, but Horst had warned her that the regime would have no trouble targeting them. Better to avoid having many known leaders, he'd said. *We have to put women and children to the front.*

She glanced to the left as Horst appeared beside her. He had to shout to be heard over the din. "What do we do when we reach the *Reichstag*?"

"March in circles," Gudrun shouted back. There were armed SS guards defending the colossal building. They'd shoot, she was sure, if the marchers tried to break into the *Reichstag* itself. "March and shout ourselves hoarse."

Horst didn't look happy, but he held his tongue.

———

"There are thousands of people on the streets," a frantic messenger reported. "They're advancing on the *Reichstag!*"

"Call for police reinforcements," Voss suggested. "And the Berlin Guard!"

Karl smirked inwardly as the Reich Council started to panic, hastily issuing orders and countermanding them seconds later. By his calculations, the marchers would be at the *Reichstag* within twenty minutes at most, although the growing stream of newcomers would slow them down. No one had any real experience with unplanned protests in the *Reich*, not when the only permitted mass movements were parades and ceremonial marches. Some of the students would probably trip, fall and be crushed below the marching feet before they had a chance to escape.

He took one last look at the council, currently issuing more orders to the Berlin Guard, and slipped out of the chamber. *Sturmbannfuehrer* Viktor Harden was on alert - the police unit had been ready to move ever since the first rumours had been allowed to leak - and his men would be on their way within minutes. And then the protesters were in for a nasty surprise.

And the Berlin Guard can keep its hands clean, he thought, nastily. The Guard would be purged when he was *Fuhrer. They can walk straight into the concentration camps after they help us clear up the mess.*

———

"They want us *where?*"

"There's a crowd of marchers heading towards the *Reichstag,* the CO bellowed, as soldiers hastily grabbed weapons and equipment. "The *Reich* Council wants us in place to turn them away from the building, if necessary!"

Kurt shuddered as he checked his rifle while heading down to the vans. They'd anticipated deployment onto the streets, but now the call had come chaos reigned supreme. He couldn't help noticing that many of the soldiers under his command were exchanging nervous glances, clearly unsure of themselves. They'd been preparing to fight barbarian terrorists in South Africa, where it was kill or be killed, not German civilians on the streets of Berlin. They all came from Berlin, Kurt knew; their friends and families might be their targets, not *Untermenschen.*

And Gudrun will be out there somewhere, he thought. He'd taken a great deal of ribbing from his fellow officers about his sister's role in the university protests, although - thankfully - his superiors had either not made the connection between him and Gudrun or chosen to ignore it. They had too many incidents of mutinous chatter to worry about a junior officer with an unfortunate relative. *What do I do if they order us to open fire?*

He sucked in his breath as he looked at the men. The younger ones looked eager - this would be their first taste of action, although it couldn't compare to a battlefield - but the older ones were clearly concerned. Many of them had wives and children... how could they bear the thought of firing into a crowd of protesters? *German* protesters. As God was his witness, Kurt honestly didn't know which way to jump. If the CO ordered him to open fire on the crowds, what should he do?

"Into the vans," he ordered, curtly.

He wasn't the senior officer on the scene, not by a very long way. The CO would take personal command, unless one of the *really* high-ranking officers from the *Reich* Council decided to come out into the streets. Kurt doubted it, even though he was sure the Field Marshals were brave men. They wouldn't want blood on their hands.

The thought chilled him to the bone as he followed his men into the van, then inspected his rifle as the engine roared to life. *Do I want blood on my hands?*

Sturmbannfuehrer Viktor Harden had always seen people as not quite *real*. He had no idea why he'd never been able to make an emotional connection with another person, even the men under his command, but it wasn't something he wanted to change. At nine years old, he'd killed his baby sister, just for distracting his parents from tending to his needs; at thirteen, he'd poisoned a teacher who'd dared to punish him in front of the class; at fifteen, he'd raped and murdered one of his classmates merely to see what it was like to combine sex and murder. He'd never had anything resembling a conscience...

... And, when he'd been arrested after a moment of carelessness with his seventh victim, he'd been given a choice between joining the SS and being unceremoniously executed. It hadn't been a hard decision.

Viktor didn't understand - honestly didn't understand - why so many of his fellow officers had qualms about carrying out anti-terrorism procedures. *He* didn't give a damn how many *Untermenschen* died, let alone *how* they died. Slaughtering entire villages was perfectly acceptable, as far as Viktor was concerned; using their deaths to intimidate thousands of others into submission was a bonus. The men under his command, too, used their impulses in the service of the SS. Others might sneer, others might look away, but Viktor gloried in the nightmares he unleashed. Let the *Untermenschen* hate, as long as they feared; let them stare in horror at what he did to their men, women and children, before bowing the knee to the *Reich*.

He had no qualms about unleashing hell onto the streets of Berlin. He had, after all, no emotional connection to the marchers at all. They were common people, just like his parents; they weren't quite real. Viktor had always snorted at SS officers who said, as if they were paragons of morality, that they would never rape an *Untermensch* woman, that they would never sully themselves by fucking a subhuman animal. To him, it mattered little if his targets were *Untermenschen* - or Germans. All that mattered was that his superiors allowed him to indulge himself, in exchange for unquestioning service.

"Take aim," he ordered, as the marchers slowly came into view. "Prepare to fire."

His lips curved into a cruel smile of anticipation. Some of the girls advancing towards him were young, young enough to be innocent, young enough to be untouched by the world... and yet, old enough to understand what he would do to them. Manipulating them like putty was a pleasure - and, when one was burned out, he slit her throat and moved on to the next girl. There was never any shortage of *Untermenschen* women for his games.

———

Horst hadn't been sure just what to expect as the marchers closed in on the *Reichstag*. The SS guards in front of the building were nowhere to be seen - perhaps they'd retreated inwards and shut the gates - while a line of Berlin Guardsmen were jumping out of vans at the far edge of Victory Square. Judging from their frantic movements, mixed with confusion, they weren't sure *what* they should be doing. Their training hadn't covered peaceful protest marches in Germany itself.

He turned his gaze past the *Reichstag* and froze. Men, black-clad men, were forming a rifle line, pointing weapons towards the marchers. He'd seen it before, in Germany East; men standing ready to repel a charge of *Untermenschen*. Except, in Germany, their targets weren't *Untermenschen*, but Germans...

"Get down," he barked, hurling himself at Gudrun. "Get down..."

She fell under his weight and hit the ground, Horst landing on top of her, just as the riflemen opened fire.

————

Gudrun thought, just for a second, that Horst was attacking her. He'd knocked her down hard enough to hurt, pinning her so soundly that she could barely move. Panic flared in her mind as she tried to struggle, even though it was useless. Horst was just too heavy for her to budge until he wanted to let her go. And then she heard the sounds of shooting...

The crowd recoiled in shock. She twisted her head, just in time to see a young girl fall to the ground, blood leaking from what remained of her head. Others were falling too, some dropping to the ground to avoid the bullets, others wounded - or dead. Horst pushed her down hard, shielding her with his body. She couldn't even move her head any longer.

"The SS are shooting," Horst whispered. He was still holding her down. "Lie still and play dead."

————

Kurt had barely had any time to deploy his men before the CO arrived, just as the marchers came into the square. They looked... harmless; there were girls in the lead who looked no older than Gudrun herself, followed by middle-aged women who could easily have been *his* mother, if things had been different.

He forced himself to relax, despite the chant; the crowd might be loud, but it didn't sound threatening.

And then the SS opened fire.

For a long chilling moment, Karl just stared. Girls were falling to the streets, their blood staining the roads. He'd thought himself used to horror and yet, watching innocent Germans gunned down was more than he could stand. His *sister* could be there, either in the midst of the students or on the ground, slowly bleeding to death.

"Do not fire," the CO bellowed. He sounded shaken, but resolute. "Do not fire!"

Kurt lifted his rifle in one smooth motion and shot the CO in the head. His men - and the other units - just stared as his body dropped to the ground. Grumbling was one thing - soldiers *always* grumbled - but actually shooting the CO...? It didn't happen. Kurt turned his weapon, pointing towards the SS, and opened fire.

Seconds later, his men joined him.

CHAPTER THIRTY-SEVEN

Berlin, Germany
21 August 1985

Viktor opened his mouth in shock as his men started to fall.

He hadn't anticipated armed resistance. This wasn't Russia, where the *Untermenschen* hoarded what weapons they could steal from Germans; this was Germany, where possession of automatic weapons was strictly regulated. The marchers should have been incapable of doing anything other than running for their lives - or dying, when his men shot them down like dogs. And he *certainly* hadn't anticipated the *soldiers* opening fire on his men. The *Heer* might have its doubts over what his unit did, but they understood its value...

"Return fire," he snapped. The army was in revolt. It was the only explanation. Thankfully, the SS existed to keep the army in line. "Kill them all..."

A bullet slammed into his chest. Viktor stumbled and fell, just as another bullet cracked into his skull. He was dead before he hit the ground.

———

Kurt had always wondered just how the Berlin Guard would do against a crack unit of the *Waffen-SS*. The SS certainly boasted of their fighting prowess - Konrad had certainly been happy to insist that they were unrivalled on the battlefield - but the unit that had fired on unarmed civilians had disintegrated under the first salvo. He had expected more of a fight, honestly; men experienced in counter-insurgency warfare should take into account, he thought, the prospect of suddenly coming under fire from an unexpected direction. But the SS had melted away, leaving him with an unexpected problem. He'd just killed the CO and slaughtered an SS detachment. What the hell did he do now?

A man lurched out of the pile of marchers and stumbled towards him, blood trickling down his face. Kurt almost shot the newcomer before he *recognised* him; Volker Schulze, Konrad's father. The man had been a factory foreman, if Kurt recalled correctly; if rumours were to be believed, he was also one of the unionists. And yet, he'd also been an SS officer before retiring to civilian life.

"Kurt," Schulze said. It was suddenly easy to believe the man had been a soldier. "Get your men organised. We need to take the *Reichstag.*"

Kurt stared at him. "The *Reichstag?*"

"Yes," Schulze insisted. "We have to stop the SS before they do something stupid. I'm getting everyone who has military experience lined up, but they don't have any weapons."

I've just started a civil war, Kurt thought, numbly. Had *any* unit mutinied so badly since the dark days of 1918? And he'd taken the lead. *They'll kill me when they catch me.*

Training took over. "*Jawohl,*" he said. Schulze was a good man - and he was right. They could take the *Reichstag* and force the government to surrender before it was too late. "I'll get my men organised now."

———

"The... the troops mutinied?"

"Yes, *Herr Reichsführer,*" the observer said. He had to speak loudly to be heard over the alarm echoing through the building. "The Berlin Guard opened fire on *Sturmbannfuehrer* Harden's men. They have been scattered, while the guardsmen prepare to storm the building."

Karl had to fight to keep his expression under control. He'd expected a quick slaughter, followed by a long period of cleaning the blood from the streets and purging the politicians and activists who'd brought Germany low. But now... all of a sudden, it dawned on him that he might have made a deadly mistake. He was no coward - the thought of dying for the *Reich* held no terrors for him - but everything could be lost along with him. He'd been careful not to anoint a successor, knowing it would cause problems in the future. And yet, that too had been a mistake. If he died, there would be a power struggle within the SS at the worst possible moment.

I can't allow myself to die, he thought. He knew just what the crowd would do to anyone they caught within the *Reichstag*, now the myth of the government's invincibility had been shattered once and for all. *And I cannot let the Reich Council make any more mistakes.*

He rose. "Have my security detail escort me to the helipad," he said. There was always a helicopter ready and waiting, just in case the *Reich* Council needed to leave in a hurry. "And then send out a message on the emergency channels. Condition Wilhelm. I say again, Condition Wilhelm."

"*Jawohl, Herr Reichsführer*," the observer said.

Karl cursed savagely as he hurried out of the office and into the antechamber, where a trio of heavily-armed stormtroopers were waiting for him. Condition Wilhelm was a coup, to all intents and purposes; SS officers and infantry on thousands of military bases would take control and put the bases into lockdown, ensuring the mutiny couldn't spread. And, by the time the dust had settled, the SS would be in complete control of Germany. But there hadn't been time to make *all* the preparations...

And word will be spreading, he thought. He wondered briefly if he had time to lead the way to the council chamber and execute the councillors, starting with the damned Finance Minister, but he knew he didn't dare. *They'll be screaming to the Heer, telling them to join the mutiny and turn on the SS.*

"*Herr Reichsführer*," the lead stormtrooper said. He carried a rifle in one hand, held at the ready. "The building has gone into lockdown; the corridors are clear."

"Excellent," Karl said, checking the pistol at his belt. He wasn't the only one with a security detail, but the SS controlled the building. Everyone else would, hopefully, be running around in confusion while he made his exit. "Take me to the helicopter."

"*Jawohl, Herr Reichsführer*," the stormtrooper said.

———

Gudrun had thought the last protest was bad, but this was a nightmare. She stood as soon as Horst rolled off her, yet she almost wished she hadn't as she glanced around, taking in the horrors surrounding her. Hundreds of dead bodies lay on the ground, while the wounded were screaming for help, help she feared would never come. Even the sight of the soldiers finishing off the remains of the SS was no consolation. She'd led the dead and wounded to meet their doom.

She swallowed hard, wondering if anyone would still listen to her, and cleared her throat. "If you're not wounded, start helping those who are," she shouted. Thankfully, the BDM *had* taught basic first aid, even if it had been more focused on helping children than adults. She silently promised herself she'd thank her tutors if she survived the day. "Bandage their wounds... sort out who can be saved!"

Her eyes caught sight of a boy she knew to be a skilled runner. "Get to the nearest hospital," she ordered, hoping he wasn't too stunned. None of the students had any real experience with uncontrolled violence. "Tell them we need doctors and ambulances out here now!"

Horst grabbed her arm. "Send someone to the nearest computer station," he ordered. "We have to spread the word."

Gudrun stared at him, wildly. "We *have* spread the word," she said. "And look what happened!"

"It's going to get worse," Horst said. "You know what the SS will do, if the bastards have a chance to rally. The military needs to be warned!"

———

Herman hurried onto Victory Square with the remainder of the police reinforcements - and stopped in horror at the sight that greeted him. Dead bodies, wounded students and adults... it was like stepping into a war zone. And they were *Germans*, not *Untermenschen*. He looked at the soldiers, readying themselves for an assault on the *Reichstag*, and the bodies of the SS men lying where they'd fallen, and knew civil war had begun. The soldiers wouldn't have attacked the SS unless they'd stepped well over the line.

"Get in touch with the station," he ordered. The Captain was nowhere to be seen, unsurprisingly. He probably couldn't decide which side to take and was hiding, rather than commit himself. "Tell them to send all the medics they can find."

He caught sight of Gudrun and shivered. His daughter seemed unharmed, but her white shirt was stained with blood and she was organising the students to take care of the wounded. He wanted to drag her away from the scene, yet he knew it was far too late. Gudrun had asserted her independence, no matter what he thought about it. He looked up at the brooding *Reichstag* - a sniper could easily start raining bullets down on the crowd - and then reminded himself it was time to take a side.

"And warn them to arrest any SS officers in eyesight too," he added. He glanced up as a helicopter lifted off from the building's roof and vanished into the distance. Thankfully, either it wasn't armed or the pilot thought the soldiers had antiaircraft missiles on hand. "It's the only hope of preventing a civil war."

———

Hans was in shock.

He'd been tricked, he saw now, and the hell of it was that he'd practically tricked *himself*. He had been so grateful for Holliston's support for the budget cuts that he hadn't really considered *why* Holliston had supported him. He'd seen one reason - Holliston *did* have something to gain from budget cuts - but he hadn't seen the other. Holliston had deliberately provoked a protest march, which he'd then turned into a massacre.

And even he didn't expect to see the Berlin Guard turn on the SS, Hans thought. *The whole world had been turned upside down.*

"He's gone," Voss said. The building was in lockdown, but the military security detachments were trying to open a pathway to safety for the *Reich* Council. "Left his secretary and ran for the helicopter."

Hans closed his eyes in bitter pain as a low rumble ran through the building. There was no point in trying to escape, not now. The secret passageways led directly to the various ministries dotted around Victory Square, but the mob had the streets under control already, even if they hadn't stormed the buildings themselves. They'd counted on using the helicopter to escape Berlin, if the Americans launched a surprise attack, and Holliston had beaten them to it. It was impossible to escape the feeling that the SS *Reichsführer* had *intended* to cause a riot and leave his comrades to die.

"I managed to get a brief message out to the nearest garrison," Voss added. "They'll warn the rest of the *Reich* about the SS."

The building shook, again. Hans sighed and sat down, wondering just what would happen when the mutineers burst into the chamber. It wouldn't be long now.

———

Kurt had no idea what sort of opposition would await his men in the *Reichstag*, but there was no time to do more than the most basic planning before knocking down the gates and swarming the building. Several of his men had vanished in the chaos; a number of policemen had offered to bring up the rear, including - he was surprised to see - his own father. Kurt ordered them to be ready to take prisoners, then led the way into the building. There was almost no opposition, save for a pair of SS troopers who were blasted out with thrown grenades after they made a stand. Kurt couldn't help being glad the murdering bastards he'd killed hadn't been anything like as determined to hold the line.

"Hands on your heads," he bellowed, as they cleared the ground floor and made their way up to the next level. "Get the prisoners down to the halls and leave them there, under guard."

There was no further resistance as they slipped further and further up the building. Kurt couldn't help being astonished by the sheer opulence of the decorations - including hundreds of artworks he'd only seen in books - and just how quickly the low-level bureaucrats surrendered, when they saw the soldiers. The building was solid enough to ensure that a determined defence could hold it for quite some time, particularly when the intruders had no idea which corridor led where. But he was grateful for the lack of resistance, right up until they broke onto the highest level. A hail of fire greeted the soldiers as they climbed up the stairway.

"Surrender," Kurt shouted. A handful of grenades would be more than sufficient to clear the way. "Give up now and you won't be harmed."

There was a long pause, then someone shouted back. "What about the *Reich* Council?"

"They will not be harmed either, provided they surrender," Kurt said. He had no idea if he was authorised to make any such promises - it wasn't as if they had a command authority - but it would encourage them to surrender without further delay. "Tell them to give up and they will remain unharmed."

He muttered orders to his men as he waited for a reply. God alone knew what sort of equipment the *Reich* Council had on hand. They could be calling for help, even now, although the Berlin Guard itself was the closest military unit to the city. Unless, of course, the *Waffen-SS* had another division on hand. He didn't think there were any closer than Warsaw, but he hadn't thought the SS would bring a police unit from Germany East to Berlin either.

"They want to negotiate," the voice shouted, finally.

Kurt shook his head. It sounded like a delaying tactic to him. "They can surrender now or we'll force our way into the chamber," he said. "You have five minutes to decide."

He braced himself, unsure just what to expect. The *Reich* Council didn't seem to have expected trouble, not if they were gathered in the *Reichstag* rather than observing events from a safe distance. Indeed, if the SS hadn't opened fire, there probably wouldn't have been *been* any trouble. Everything he'd seen suggested that the *Reich* Council had been as surprised as the Berlin Guard... although there was the lingering question of just who'd been in that helicopter.

"They would like to surrender, but they insist on talking to the dissident leaders," the voice said, after four minutes. "Is that acceptable?"

"Fine," Kurt said. Volker could talk to them. He'd been in control of the unions, after all; he was probably the most powerful man in the dissident movement. "We're coming up now, so put your weapons on the ground and step away from them."

He forced himself to walk up the stairs, unsure of what he'd see when he reached the top. A handful of soldiers wearing combat battledress - close-protection specialists, he guessed - and a couple of civilians, looking nervous. They were rapidly cuffed as Kurt led the way into the next room, where a dozen men waited for him. The *Fuhrer* and Field Marshal Voss were instantly recognisable - their portraits hung in the barracks - but the others were strangers.

"This is an outrage, soldier," the other Field Marshal said. "Stand down at once and..."

"So is ordering troops to fire on innocent civilians," Kurt snapped. He lifted his rifle and gestured threateningly. "If any of you are carrying any weapons, say so now."

He gave them a moment, then jerked his rifle barrel, indicating they were to rise. "You will be kept separately from the other prisoners until we have decided your final disposition," he said. He had no idea what would be the best thing to do with the former *Reich* Council; that, too, was best left to Volker - and Gudrun. "Do not attempt to speak without permission or you will be shot."

And if they do regain power, he thought morbidly, as his men searched the uppermost level and marked offices as temporary cells, *they'll have problems deciding precisely which of my crimes to put on my execution warrant.*

———

It felt like hours before Gudrun could take a rest. Horst by her side, she had thrown herself into helping the wounded and preparing the dead for honourable burial. It had been a nightmare - the streets were slippery with blood - but there had been no choice. *Someone* had to take charge and deal with the chaos. By the time Kurt - wearing his combat uniform - came to find her, she was tired and cranky.

"Gudrun," Kurt said. He looked around, then back at her. "If I'd known this would happen when I helped you sneak into a hospital..."

"She did the right thing," Horst said. He somehow managed to sound fresh. "The government had to be beaten."

Kurt gave him a sharp look. "And how much of the country do we control?"

"Good question," Gudrun said. She rose and peered at her brother. "Who's in charge right now?"

"Konrad's father," Kurt said. "He wants to see you."

"I'm coming," Gudrun said. "Horst?"

"I'll come with you," Horst said. "If you'll still have me."

Gudrun slipped her hand into his. "I wouldn't miss it for the world."

She sobered as she followed her brother through the remains of the gates and into the building. She'd never been inside and part of her was quietly fascinated, a feeling that faded as she realised just how much of the country's wealth had been lavished on the building while large parts of the population barely had enough to eat. Hundreds of prisoners, their hands cuffed, sat in the hallway, looking at the floor despondently. It was easy to tell that they expected to be shot out of hand.

"They stole the artwork from all over the *Reich*," Horst commented quietly, as they walked up the stairs. "Herman Goring used to collect pieces of irreplaceable art. When he died, his family passed it to the *Reich* Council."

Gudrun nodded. She wasn't surprised.

"Gudrun," Volker Schulze said. He was standing alone in a large war room, covered with maps of Germany and the *Reich*. "Did you know what you'd start?"

"No," Gudrun said. How much did he know? Kurt could have told him she'd known about Konrad long before anyone else - no, he merely thought she'd pushed him into using his contacts to check up on his son. "I didn't."

"But you started this," Volker Schulze said. He waved a hand at one of the maps. "You can now help me clean up the mess."

CHAPTER THIRTY-EIGHT

SS Deployment Base/Reichstag, Germany
21/22 August 1985

It had not been a comfortable flight.

Karl Holliston had hoped to fly directly to the *Reich* Command Bunker in East Germany, or perhaps loop round Berlin and head to Wewelsburg Castle, but the endless series of confused reports on the radio made it sound dangerous. There were outbreaks of fighting at military and SS bases, mutinies on the high seas and even clashes between jet fighters... if, of course, the radio could be believed. Karl was sure that most of the reports were badly exaggerated - he'd been taught there was always a period of confusion when something happened without warning - but it was hard to know for sure. The *Heer* might be divided, yet he had no doubt that the *Kriegsmarine* and the *Luftwaffe* would side with the rebels. They'd been infected with rebel propaganda right from the start.

He gritted his teeth as the helicopter, running on fumes, dropped towards the SS Deployment Base. *SS Skorzeny* had been preparing for its deployment to South Africa and - he cursed in frustration - most of its equipment had been boxed for transport. The unit, the only wholly reliable unit west of Poland, would need time, more time than he had, to prepare for a full-scale attack on Berlin. He grunted as the helicopter hit the pad, then staggered to his feet and hurried to the hatch. The ground crew were already moving in to secure the helicopter and refuel the craft. Behind them, a uniformed officer waited.

"*Herr Reichsführer,*" SS-*Obergruppenfuehrer* Felix Kortig said, as Karl clambered out of the helicopter. In the distance, the sun was setting over the mountains and darkness was falling over the land. "We have a briefing for you in the situation room."

"Good," Karl said. Perhaps, just perhaps, the situation wasn't as bad as it seemed. "Have some coffee brought to the room too. We're going to need it."

He allowed Kortig to lead him into the base, barely noticing the stormtroopers standing guard at the doors. The entire garrison had gone into lockdown, although - as far as they were from civilian towns or military bases - it was unlikely there was any immediate danger. But that would change, he reminded himself, as they passed through a pair of armoured doors and into the situation room. The deployment base was hardly a *secret*.

"I have two companies on readiness," Kortig informed him, "and a third picketing all the approaches. However, most of our equipment is already *en route* to South Africa..."

"I know," Karl said, cutting him off. He wasn't in the mood for excuses. "I need a situation briefing, right now."

He took a seat as an orderly entered, carrying a tray of coffee. Behind him, a young analyst stepped into the room, looking pale. He seemed too young to wear SS black, Karl noted; the young troopers seemed to get younger every year. Karl felt a sudden flicker of wistfulness for his younger days, when all that mattered was getting the job done, which he pushed aside savagely. He might have made mistakes - bad rolls of the dice were inevitable - but the contest for supremacy in the *Reich* was far from over.

"*Herr Reichsführer*," the analyst said. "Most of our communications network has been badly damaged. What reports we have are often imprecise or wildly exaggerated. However, we do have a picture of just what's been happening over the last few hours."

Karl nodded impatiently, sipping his coffee.

"The police and military bases in Berlin itself seem to have gone over to the rebels," the analyst continued. "I was able to speak briefly to an officer in the RSHA, *Herr Reichsführer*: he confirmed that the building was surrounded and on the verge of being stormed. None of the other SS installations within Berlin responded to our calls. They may simply be isolated or they may have been overwhelmed."

He paused, waiting for Karl's response. "Outside Berlin, the situation is confused. A number of military bases turned into war zones as our forces attempted to take control of the troops, provoking the soldiers to mutiny. At last report, *Herr*

Reichsführer, most of the military bases in Germany Prime are probably in rebel hands. However, as it is clear the rebels didn't *plan* for an uprising, they may be as uncertain of what's actually going on as ourselves. It will take them at least a week, I suspect, to re-establish a chain of command and decide what to do next.

"Germany East remains solidly in our hands. The *Heer* units within Germany East are seemingly unaware of anything happening to the west, *Herr Reichsführer*. Germany North, Germany Arabia and Germany South are, so far, quiet, but Germany South may declare for the rebels when they finally work out what's going on. We are not particularly popular there."

Karl sipped his coffee, thoughtfully. "And the forces in South Africa?"

"No word," the analyst said. "I don't know which way they'll jump."

"Keep monitoring the situation and inform me if there are any major changes," Karl ordered, looking at the map. The deployment base was looking alarmingly exposed. How long would it take the rebels to deduce where he'd fled? Not long, he suspected, if some of the *Reich* Council joined the rebellion. "How many men can you send to Berlin?"

Kortig frowned. "Right now, twenty-five at most," he said. "We only have four assault helicopters fuelled up and ready to fly. The transport aircraft we were planning to use for Operation Headshot are already in Germany East. If we had a few days to make preparations..."

"We don't have a few days," Karl said. Right now, the rebels controlled Berlin and Berlin alone. Given time, that would change rapidly. "We need to launch a strike as quickly as possible and kill the rebel leadership."

"That would be tricky," Kortig observed. "Berlin is not exactly undefended."

"Right now, the defences are confused," Karl argued. "We can slip four helicopters back into Berlin and attack the *Reichstag*."

"There isn't time to mount the operation under cover of darkness," Kortig said. "By the time the helicopters reached Berlin, the sun would be rising. We'll have to launch the attack tomorrow night."

He was right, Karl knew, even though it was bitterly frustrating. Twenty-five men, even *Skorzeny* commandos, would be hellishly exposed if they tried to launch an attack in broad daylight. The rebels would probably have already moved mobile antiaircraft missile launchers into Berlin, if they were expecting an immediate counterattack. It was what *he* would have done. Sending the troops in daylight was asking for disaster.

And yet, he asked himself, *just how badly can they damage the Reich in a day?*

"Start making the preparations," he ordered. If the assault failed, if the rebel leadership survived, they'd have to prepare a far more elaborate response. "And make contact with our forces in Germany East. We have to prepare for war."

"*Jawohl, Herr Reichsführer*," Kortig said.

———

Under other circumstances, Hans would have savoured the thought of being locked up in one of his own offices. The rebels had searched it, removed anything that could be used as a weapon and then told him not to try to leave the chamber on pain of death. Hans hadn't tried to argue. Instead, he'd sat down as the door was closed and tried to get some sleep. There was no point in doing anything else. If he tried to escape, and succeeded, where would he go?

He was half-asleep when someone opened the door, but the sound jerked him awake instantly. A pair of soldiers stood there, looking down at him. Hans braced himself, wondering if he was simply going to be taken outside and shot, then rose to his feet, ready to meet his death with dignity. The soldiers searched him - again - and then escorted him through the network of corridors into a small office. Volker Schulze - instantly recognisable from the files on union activists - was sitting behind a table, looking tired. A large mug of coffee was perched in front of him.

"*Herr* Schulze," Hans said. It was hard to keep the bitterness out of his voice - it had been hard enough trying to save the economy without the unions driving up costs and limiting production - but he had tried. "What can I do for you?"

Schulze looked up at him. "Answer me a question," he said. "Where do your loyalties lie?"

"With the *Reich*," Hans said, flatly. He had no objection to enriching himself at the same time as building the *Reich's* economy, but there were limits. It was a constant headache - it had *been* a constant headache - that others didn't seem to recognise those limits. "Where do yours lie?"

"With the *Reich*," Schulze said. "Your subordinates speak highly of you, *Herr* Krueger."

"Thank you," Hans said. He'd played the political game long enough to have a very good idea of where the conversation was leading. "You want me to run the economy for you."

Schulze didn't bother to pretend to be surprised. "Most of the ministries haven't had *time* to slip into disarray," he said, instead. "Bureaucrats weren't murdered, save for a handful who were killed to pay off old grudges; files weren't destroyed, even in the RSHA. We need those ministries in working order just to take control of the *Reich*."

Hans nodded. "And how much *do* you control right now?"

"Not as much as we'd like," Schulze admitted. He smiled, rather darkly. "I should tell you that the *Reichsführer* sentenced you to death. The police unit that fired on the protesters had orders to sweep the *Reichstag* afterwards, capturing or killing the *Reich* Council. You would simply have been killed out of hand."

"I wish I could say I was surprised," Hans said. Holliston, damn the man, had clearly had his own plans for taking advantage of the chaos. Hans had thought Holliston respected the balance of power - the SS might not have come out ahead if the balance had shattered - but the protests had already crippled the *Reich*. "He always was a ruthless bastard."

Schulze nodded in agreement. "You have two choices, *Herr* Krueger," he said. "You can join us and help us to build a new government. Or you can refuse, whereupon you will be moved to a detention facility until you can be tried, afterwards, for your role on the *Reich* Council."

"I thought I was doing the right thing," Hans protested, without heat. "Legally..."

"Legal is what the people in power say it is," Schulze snapped. "You taught the entire *Reich* that lesson, *Herr* Krueger."

He paused. "I might add that the *Reichsführer* and the SS are unlikely to roll over and play dead for us," he warned. "You may be taken from *our* detention centre and thrown into an SS detention centre, if we lose the war."

"I have no illusions about what they'll do to me," Hans said. Holliston had a whole string of grudges to pay off. "Or you, if you lose."

It wasn't a hard choice. The prospect of being put on trial chilled him to the bone. He understood the value of scapegoats - the *Reich* Council had turned quite a few people into scapegoats merely for being in the wrong place at the wrong time - and the rebels, if they used him as a scapegoat for the

Reich's ills, could draw some political advantage out of his death. He'd done the best he could, he knew, but the population wouldn't see it that way. The unionists alone had good reasons to want him dead.

And Holliston wants me deader, he thought, wryly. The rebels would probably shoot him out of hand, but the SS would torture him first, then slaughter his entire family. *Joining the rebels is the only hope for any kind of survival.*

"I'll join you," he said, simply.

"Glad to hear it," Schulze said. "You can have some sleep, then you can start work tomorrow morning. By then, hopefully, we should have a clear idea of just what's going on."

Hans shuddered. It was possible, he supposed, that most of the military would join the rebels, just like the Berlin Guard. But it was equally possible that Holliston would take control of the entire *Reich*, save for Berlin itself. If that happened, the city would come under siege... and no one, not even newborn children, would be spared the consequences when it finally fell. He might just have joined the losing side.

But it doesn't matter, he told himself, as the guards reappeared. *I'm dead anyway.*

He frowned. "If I may ask," he said, "what happened to the *Fuhrer?*"

"He's going to make a nice speech handing over power to the provisional government," Schulze said, "and then he's going to go into exile. There's nothing to be gained by killing him."

"I suppose not," Hans agreed. He had no particular dislike of the *Fuhrer*. Besides, killing him would give the SS a martyr they could use for their propaganda. "He was always a harmless fool."

"Gudrun," Herman said, as he entered the office. It had taken him nearly an hour to work up the nerve. "Can I have a word?"

His daughter looked tired, too tired. She didn't have any experience in administration - hardly anyone did, outside the bureaucracy - but she was doing her best. Herman couldn't help wondering just how long she'd keep the post, even though she'd been a student leader; there were others who were far more experienced. And yet...

"Yes, father," Gudrun said. She sounded tired too. She'd changed her shirt, at some point, but she looked as though she needed a shower and several hours of sleep. "What can I do for you?"

"I just wanted to say I'm proud of you," Herman said, closing the door behind him. "And of your brother."

"It could have gone very badly without him, father," Gudrun said. She waved him to a chair in front of her desk, pushing her paperwork to one side. "And you."

Herman nodded. He'd believed in the new order, he'd believed in the state... but, in the end, the state had tried to gun down his daughter and thousands of innocent Germans. And his entire family had turned against the state. How could he argue with his wife, his daughter and all three of his sons?

"I do wish you hadn't done it," Herman said. The thought of his daughter in jail, or hanging naked from meat hooks under the RSHA, or being raped to death was terrifying. Even now, even after the regime had been crippled, he still shivered at the thought. "I..."

He shook his head, unable to find the words. His father had told him that there would come a time when he'd look at his daughter and see a different person, but he hadn't believed the old man until now. Gudrun was no longer a girl, or a young woman; she was an adult who'd taken her destiny into her own hands. He still wanted to protect her, but he could no longer try to control her life.

"It had to be done," Gudrun said, stiffly. "I wrote those leaflets."

"Yes, it did," Herman said. "And I'm proud of you for doing it, but I wish it hadn't been you..."

He blinked in surprise as he registered what she'd said. "*You* wrote those leaflets?"

"I did," Gudrun said. She met his eyes with a defiant stare that reminded Herman, once again, of his own mother. Gudrun's grandmother had never taken any backtalk from her son when he'd been a child. "I lied to you, father, but I'm not sorry."

Herman shook his head. A month ago, he would have exploded with rage. He hadn't raised his children to lie to him, even if they did have to be less than honest with their teachers and the BDM matrons. Now... now he understood. Gudrun's boyfriend had been crippled and the state had lied about it... and she'd taken a terrible revenge. The rebellion might still be crushed - Herman rather doubted they'd rounded up *all* the SS personnel in Berlin - but the state would never be the same again.

"I understand," he said, finally. "Please don't lie to me again."

"I'll try not to," Gudrun assured him. She changed the subject hastily. "Did you get mother and the others here?"

"I did," Herman said. He would have preferred to keep the rest of his family well away from the *Reichstag*, but Gudrun was a known rebel and Kurt might well have been marked too. If there *were* roving SS officers on the streets, Gudrun's family might be targeted. There just weren't enough police officers to ensure their safety anywhere else. "They're all in rooms in the *Reichstag*, even Frank."

Gudrun's face flickered. Herman frowned, inwardly. Gudrun had *never* liked the disgusting old man, even though her mother insisted that Gudrun clean his room every day. Frank had *never* been a particularly decent man. Hell, he'd been slipping into the bottle long before Herman had met and married Frank's daughter. The wretched drunkard had been a plague on the family ever since he'd moved in with his daughter. And yet, there was something on Gudrun's face...

He dismissed it. There were too many other things to worry about.

"Get some sleep," he advised. "You'll need it, I think."

Gudrun yawned. "There's too much to do," she said, softly. Another yawn put the lie to her words. "I have to work..."

"You'll be making mistakes if you're tired," Herman told her, firmly. "You have a bedroom here, do you not? Get a shower, get into bed, get a good night's sleep. Things will look better in the morning."

"Yes, father," Gudrun said. "And you get some sleep too."

CHAPTER THIRTY-NINE

Reichstag, Germany
22 August 1985

"Using *Herr* Krueger is a gamble," Gudrun said.

Beside her, Horst nodded in agreement. He'd appointed himself Gudrun's bodyguard as soon as she'd been given an ill-defined role within the *very* provisional government, rather than trying to obtain a high office for himself. Given his role, which was probably included in one of the files taken from the RSHA, he'd felt it would be better if he avoided attracting attention. Gudrun didn't seem concerned about his former masters, but not everyone would take the matter so lightly.

"Yes, it is," Volker Schulze agreed. He turned to stare out of the window at the afternoon sky, then looked back at them. "Using *any* of the *Reich* Council is a gamble. But we don't have many other experienced people."

Horst had to admit he had a point. The provisional government was slowly making contact with military bases and police stations outside Berlin, trying to build up a picture of just what was happening, and it was becoming alarmingly clear that a great many senior officers were dead or sitting on the sidelines. Thankfully, the SS hadn't quite realised just how much the *Heer* had focused on training its soldiers to use their initiative. SS troopers had killed senior officers, only to be killed themselves by junior officers, NCOs and ordinary soldiers. But it had created a horrible mess that wouldn't be solved in a hurry.

"We can't trust him," Gudrun said, slowly. "Can we?"

"He hasn't enriched himself excessively," Schulze said. "I believe he has the best interests of the *Reich* at heart - and, right now, those include a peaceful transfer of power."

"I hope you're right," Gudrun said. "Has there been anything from Germany East?"

"Nothing," Schulze said. He smiled, rather tightly. "But apparently there *have* been a few mutinies in South Africa. The SS dropped the ball rather badly."

Horst wasn't so pleased. The troops in South Africa were unlikely to side with the SS, but they'd be reluctant to fight the *Waffen-SS*. They'd been fighting beside them for the last two years, after all. But it probably didn't matter. Getting the troops back to the *Reich* would take far longer than they had, he suspected. The impending civil war would be fought with what weapons and manpower both sides had on hand. Thankfully, Schulze's union included hundreds of men with military experience and there were thousands more in Berlin - and hundreds of thousands in Germany Prime.

"I may need you to speak to the French," Schulze added. "*And* the Italians. God alone knows which way they'll jump."

"Offer them their political freedom," Gudrun said. "Trade that for them staying quiet for the next few months."

Schulze looked uncomfortable. "They'll want parts of Germany Prime too."

Horst nodded, sourly. Occupied France had been annexed, to all intents and purposes; native Frenchmen had been driven out and replaced with German settlers. If the provisional government tried to return the territory to France, there would be another outbreak of civil war. But the French would never forgive the Germans for keeping their land.

"We can sort that out after the war," Gudrun said. "Can't we?"

"Perhaps," Schulze said. "But they'd have to be fools *not* to take advantage of our weakness to demand concessions. Their government is so unstable that it might go under any day now."

He dismissed Gudrun. Horst followed her back to her office, then smiled as she closed and locked the door. But Gudrun seemed to have something else on her mind.

She met his eyes. "Does he *have* to worry about the French?"

"The government in Berlin, no matter who runs it, has to worry about the French," Horst said, thoughtfully. "They're not going to go away."

"No," Gudrun agreed, after a moment. "But we're not going to go away either."

Horst settled back in his chair as she returned to her desk and went to work. It was astonishing just how much paperwork was involved in forming a new government, particularly when very few of the people involved had any experience at all. Schulze, at least, had founded and run a union for a few weeks before becoming the leader of the provisional government. Gudrun had nothing more than theory and his advice to guide her.

"You might want to watch Voss," Horst advised, when she read through his file. "He was always ambitious."

"That's the problem," Gudrun agreed. She yawned suddenly. "Everyone who climbed to the top in the old government was ambitious."

"Time for you to get some rest," Horst said. He rose and held out a hand. "You can sleep in the bed. I'll sleep on the floor."

"You take this bodyguard job too seriously," Gudrun said, rising. A faint blush coloured her cheeks as she checked her watch. "I could stay up for longer..."

"It's nearly midnight," Horst said, firmly. "It's time for you to go to bed."

He concealed his amusement with an effort as they headed up to the residence level and walked down towards Gudrun's suite. Her entire family was currently living in the *Reichstag*, along with the families of several other rebel leaders. Horst was surprised she'd managed to wrangle herself a separate suite, but he had to admit it was a relief. He knew her father would have made a fuss if he *knew* he was sharing a room with her, even if they weren't sharing a bed.

"You know," Gudrun said, as they entered her suite and closed the door, "you need a shower."

Horst blinked. "I do?"

"Yes, you do," Gudrun said. She pointed to the door leading into the bathroom. "Get in there."

Horst did as he was told. Moments later, she joined him - and, when he turned to face her, wrapped him in a hug and kissed him as hard as she could.

———

Hauptsturmfuehrer Arul Falkenhayn braced himself as the helicopters swept over Berlin, heading directly towards the *Reichstag*. Night had fallen - half the city was in darkness - but he doubted they could maintain the advantage of surprise for very long. There was no such thing, despite American propaganda, as a truly silent helicopter. The rebels would have to be deaf as well as dumb not to hear them coming.

He glanced at his men, suited up and ready to go, and braced himself. He'd have felt better if the entire battalion had been prepping itself to jump into hell, but he only had twenty-one commandos and three helicopters under his command. The fourth helicopter had developed a fault that had proven maddeningly impossible to trace, let alone fix, before the mission had to be launched. There was no way to know if it was just another example of the Demon Murphy striking at the worst possible time or deliberate sabotage. Arul knew himself and his men to be loyal to the *Reich* - they'd planned to jump into Pretoria, after all - but the ground crews might not feel the same way. One of them might just have been cunning enough to do something to a helicopter and get away with it.

"Ten seconds," the *Strumscharfuehrer* shouted. "Get ready!"

Arul stood, grabbed hold of the rappelling line, and prepared to dive out to meet his destiny.

———

Gudrun lay in her bed, staring up at the ceiling.

She honestly wasn't sure why she'd given herself to Horst. He was everything she wanted in a man - strong, capable and understanding - and yet, she hadn't been taught to be so forward as to invite a man into her bed. She had wanted him, and she was sure he wanted her, and yet part of her knew their relationship had just changed for good. Konrad had wanted to go further than they had, she knew, and yet she'd been reluctant to commit herself to him completely. Now...

But the world has changed, she thought. *Konrad and I thought we would have a whole life together. Now... Horst and I may not survive the month.*

It scared her, scared her more than the sharp pain and blood when he'd gone inside her for the first time or the dull awareness that he could easily have gotten her pregnant. They'd overthrown a government! The *Reich*, a government that had endured since Adolf Hitler had taken supreme power, had been broken. There was no going back. And there was no future if they lost, either. Perhaps that was why she'd finally given in to temptation. What was the point in waiting for marriage, or at least parental approval, when they might be dead within a month?

She twisted her head to look at Horst, sleeping on the bed. There was no SS tattoo marring his skin, unsurprisingly; he'd have some trouble explaining one if he'd ever managed to get naked with a student. He was strong... but then, Konrad had been strong too. No wonder he'd always worn loose clothes, she thought. Students were not expected to exercise regularly, unlike boys in the Hitler Youth, but Horst was still more muscular than the average university student. Someone might have been suspicious if they'd seen him shirtless...

Horst jerked awake as the alarms began to ring, one hand grabbing for the pistol he'd left on her bedside table. Gudrun rolled over and out of bed, cursing her own nakedness as she searched for the light switch. She didn't want to run out of the room without even a pair of panties... she clicked on the switch, then grabbed for her dressing gown. It was better than nothing.

"Turn off the light," Horst snapped, jumping to his feet and running around the bed. His gaze snapped upwards as shots rang out over their heads. "We have to get to the lower levels."

He caught her hand, holding his pistol in the other, and dragged her towards the door. She wanted to tell him to put some clothes on, but she was suddenly very - very- afraid. The SS had managed to mount a counterattack, even though the military officers had believed it to be impossible. Berlin was heavily defended, after all...

"They're not trying to retake the building," Horst muttered, as he opened the door. His thoughts must have been running along the same lines. "They couldn't have put together a large force or it would have been a great deal louder. They're just trying to kill as many of us as possible."

"Just," Gudrun repeated. The building shook, violently. Dust drifted down from the ceiling. "What do we do?"

"Get out of the firing line," Horst said. He didn't seem troubled by his nakedness, even though doors were opening all the way down the corridor. "Move it!"

———

Arul knew there was no point in playing games, not when the element of surprise was rapidly slipping away. The helicopters swept their machine guns across the rooftop, wiping out the guards before they could put up a fight, as the commandos dropped down to the roof. He silently saluted the designers - the layer of armour under the stone had resisted the bullets effortlessly - as a missile slammed into the hatch, opening a pathway into the *Reichstag*. A second later, another missile lanced towards one of the helicopters, which exploded with staggering force. Thankfully, its complement of commandos were already on the roof and heading into the building.

No hope of escape now, Arul thought, as he heard the chatter-chatter-chatter of machine guns, deeper and heavier than the weapons mounted on the helicopters. The forces on the streets had responded with remarkable speed, despite the confusion. *But then, this was always a suicide mission.*

He cursed under his breath as he threw a grenade ahead of him, hastily recalling the building plans he'd seen. There hadn't been any time to plan a proper operation, let alone gain the intelligence they needed; they'd been forced to decide, eventually, that all they could do was storm the building and kill everyone they met. There was no way they could escape, not once the enemy was alerted. All they could do was kill as many people as they could before they were wiped out themselves.

And at least we're coming in through the roof, he thought, tossing another grenade into a doorway as they ran past. *Most of their forces are down on the ground.*

A pair of soldiers appeared at the far end of the corridor, weapons at the ready. Arul fired a long burst from his rifle, then hurled a grenade as more soldiers appeared. Clearly, the enemy had anticipated a helicopter attack... although, if they had, why hadn't they cleared the *Reichstag* instead of turning it into their headquarters? Who gave a damn about the symbolic value of the building Hitler and Speer had designed if the rebel government was wiped out?

"Franz is hit," the *Strumscharfuehrer* snapped. "Albus is dead."

Arul nodded, then hurried onwards. There was no point in worrying about the wounded - they'd all be dead, soon enough. He heard someone screaming over the racket and glanced through a door. A woman was lying on the bed, staring at the body of her husband and screaming; a young boy sat next to her, his face in shock. Arul shot them both and moved on, leaving the room behind. They were rebels or related to rebels. Either way, they had been sentenced to death.

"Get further down the stairs," he ordered. The rebels would be confused, but if they'd done any planning at all they'd either be sealing themselves in the panic rooms or trying to get out of the building. "Try and cut them off."

———

Frank Reinecke had been having a nightmare when the alarms went off. He jerked awake, so dazed and confused that it took him several moments to remember that he was in the *Reichstag*, after Gudrun had succeeded beyond his wildest dreams. There was no way he could ever wash the blood from his hands - he would have killed himself, if he hadn't feared the fires of hell - but at least the government had been toppled. And yet, it seemed the government wasn't dead after all. Frank had never really been a combat soldier - the *Einsatzgruppen* had rarely been called upon to do more than slaughter defenceless victims - yet he had no trouble recognising the sound of a firefight. It was hard to be sure - he'd been going deaf over the last three decades - but it sounded very much as though the enemy were heading down from the roof.

Grabbing his cane in one hand and his service revolver in the other - he'd kept it ever since he'd left the *Einsatzgruppen*, despite his daughter's objections - he staggered towards the door and out into chaos.

———

Gudrun was never quite sure what hit her. One moment, she'd been running down the corridor with Horst; the next, she'd been picked up by... *something*... and hurled into the wall. She banged her head hard enough to stun her, leaving her dazed and confused as she fell to the ground. Somehow, she managed to twist around, just in time to see a pair of black-clad figures running towards her. They'd seen her move. It was too late to play dead...

She closed her eyes and waited.

———

Arul didn't feel any guilt as he saw the half-naked girl on the floor, even though she was young enough to be his daughter. Like everyone else in the *Reichstag*, she was either a rebel or related to a rebel; he had no compunctions about gunning her down as casually as he'd killed his other targets. He walked towards her, intending to crush her neck and save the bullet he would have wasted on her, then looked up as he saw a man staggering out into the hallway. Just for a second, Arul stared in disbelief. The man was old, leaning heavily on a cane...

... And carrying a pistol in one hand.

The moment of hesitation proved fatal. Arul heard the *Strumscharfuehrer* grunt in pain as the old man opened fire, bending over as the first bullet slammed into his chest and the second smashed his goggles, slamming right through them and into his brain. The *Strumscharfuehrer* was dead before he hit the ground. Arul shouted in rage, pointing his rifle at the old man and pulling the trigger. He could have sworn he saw a smile on the man's face before three bullets struck his body, sending him falling to the ground. What did *he* have to smile about?

He turned back to the girl and - too late - found out.

———

Horst had been knocked ass over teakettle by the blast - a grenade, he thought - but he'd managed to keep hold of his pistol as the commandos ran up behind him. They'd been looking at Gudrun - she'd been too dazed by the impact to play dead - and he'd been bracing himself to intervene when Frank Reinecke, of all people, had appeared and opened fire, killing one of the SS commandos. Horst sat upright, despite the aches and pains, and took aim at the other commando. The man had no time to react before Horst fired, putting a bullet through his mask and into his brain.

He staggered to his hands and knees and crawled over to Gudrun. She was almost certainly in shock - there was a nasty bruise on the side of her head - and staring at the remains of her grandfather, mumbling to herself. Horst wasn't sure if she liked him or not, but he'd given his life to save hers. That, at least, deserved recognition.

"It's all right," he said, wrapping an arm around her. The sound of shooting was slowly dying away, although he knew that jumpy soldiers would be firing at shadows for the next few hours. "They can't hurt you any longer."

But, in all honesty, he wasn't sure if that were true.

CHAPTER FORTY

Berlin, Germany
25 August 1985

"There's no hope for recovery," Volker Schulze said. There was a bitter tone in his voice as he looked down at Konrad's body. "The life support can be turned off."

Gudrun felt sick as she took one last look at her former boyfriend. The medical report had been clear, all too clear. Konrad had been dead, to all intents and purposes, from the moment he'd been wounded. His comrades had done a fantastic job keeping his body alive, but the brain was dead and the soul was gone. She'd started the whole affair for Konrad, yet he would never live to see the new world.

"Goodbye," she said, very quietly.

"He loved you, I believe," Volker Schulze said. "But he would also have wanted you to live your life, not waste it in mourning."

"Too many people are dead," Gudrun said. Hundreds dead in the march, dozens killed when the SS had attacked the *Reichstag*. It galled her that she knew only a handful of their names, although she'd promised herself that they would be immortalised afterwards. "But I will try to live for his sake."

She sighed as she turned and walked towards the door, not wanting to watch as the doctors finally cut off life support. Konrad was dead - and so was Grandpa Frank. The old man she'd spent half of her life loathing had given his life to save hers, despite his own fear of death. She had no idea what was awaiting him in the afterlife - and she knew far too much about his crimes - but she hoped he would not be judged too harshly. He *had* tried to make up for his crimes, after all.

Horst met her outside, looking uncertain. "Are you all right?"

Gudrun gave him a tight hug, fighting down the urge to cry. "They're taking him off life support now," she said, bitterly. "He'll be buried tomorrow with the others."

"It's not over," Horst said. "You and I might still end up dead too."

"I know," Gudrun said. "The SS isn't going to let us win without a fight."

She contemplated it as they walked through the doors and out into the car park, where her official car was waiting. The provisional government had control over most of Germany Prime - although Wewelsburg Castle was still holding out - but the SS, the rump government, was in firm control of Germany East. And they controlled tanks, aircraft, missile launchers and thousands of trained soldiers. There would be war. Germany East couldn't survive without the rest of the *Reich*.

At least we have control of most of the nukes, she thought. *And it will take them some time to rewire the warheads they do have under their control. We did keep them from getting the launch codes.*

It wasn't a reassuring thought. Gudrun knew little about nuclear weapons, but one of the government officials who'd briefed her had admitted that a skilled engineer would probably be able to bypass the security codes and prepare the nuke for detonation. The SS hadn't been trusted with sole control of nuclear warheads since they'd been used to crush a rebellion in 1950, yet they had hundreds of engineers in Germany East. Triggering the tactical nukes probably wouldn't be that hard.

But they'd have to be mad to use them, she thought. *We have hundreds of nukes too.*

Horst opened the door for her, waited until she was seated and then climbed into the driver's seat. "Where do you want to go, *Frau* Gudrun?"

Gudrun almost suggested they find a quiet place to spend some time together, but she knew it wasn't a possibility. There was just too much for her to do at the *Reichstag*. Besides, they would be noticed. There were far fewer cars on the streets now, as the provisional government fought to conserve fuel as much as possible. If the SS managed to convince the Turks to cut the oil pipelines that ran from Germany Arabia to Germany Prime, they might have fuel shortages to add to their other woes. Hell, even *food* would be in short supply if the SS started cutting shipments from Germany East.

"Back to the *Reichstag*," she said, finally. They'd have time to relax together once the day came to an end. "I have work to do."

Berlin seemed stunned, she saw, as they drove through the streets. The schools were closed - a number of BDM matrons had vanished, according to the reports - and most workplaces had followed suit. It had only been two days since the *Fuhrer* had formally announced the formation of a provisional government, complete with a whole string of freedoms, and no one seemed quite sure how to handle them. The population had spent their whole lives guarding their mouths, after all; she suspected that some of them feared the SS was still watching them from the shadows. And they might well be right. There were hundreds of SS personnel still unaccounted for in Berlin alone.

And so we have to make the new government work before it's too late, she thought, as the car rolled into Victory Square. *And if we fail, the SS will tear the Reich apart.*

———

"The real question," Ambassador Turtledove said, "is just what we do."

"Nothing," Andrew advised. He'd spent the last four days struggling to keep abreast of the changes running through the *Reich*. "Both sides in this brewing civil war have nukes. The loser might just decide to pop their missiles at the United States and call it a draw."

"Assuming the ABM network doesn't protect us," General William Knox pointed out. "This is an opportunity to actually put an end to the *Reich*, once and for all."

"It's also a chance to commit suicide," Andrew said, tartly. "Are you willing to bet thousands of American lives that the ABM system will do a perfect job?"

He tapped the table firmly. "There's also the minor problem that the *Reich's* population is reflexively anti-American," he said. "If we send in the Marines to help stabilise and secure Germany Prime, the bad guys will gain one hell of a propaganda advantage."

"We'd be coming to help," Knox objected.

"They wouldn't see it that way," Andrew warned. "They are an intensely patriotic people, General. How pleased would our population be if they saw

German troops coming up Main Street and parking their tanks in Central Park?"

He looked at the ambassador. "There are ways, sir, to support the provisional government," he added. "We can make offers of economic assistance, loans and suchlike... we can even offer covert military support, if they need it. But overt support is likely to blow up in our face. We might accidentally kill the people we want to help."

"Not everyone in Washington will agree," the Ambassador said. "The chance to get rid of the *Reich*, once and for all..."

He cleared his throat. "For the moment, we will continue to monitor the situation, attempt to develop ties with the provisional government and report to Washington. I'm sure the Pentagon has contingency plans for the Germans causing trouble in hopes of diverting their own people from their woes."

Andrew shrugged. Germany Prime and Germany East had been drawing apart for decades, although the Nazi Party had been desperately papering over the cracks. It was quite possible that the *Reich* would split into two entities, although that would raise the issue of just what would happen to Germany Arabia and Germany South. The latter might not last long, not once South Africa went under, but the former was relatively secure after the native population had been largely exterminated and the handful of survivors enslaved.

"I don't think they'd try now," he said, finally. "The crisis facing the *Reich* has gone far beyond anything a manufactured confrontation with us can settle."

"Let us hope you're right," Turtledove said. "And let us hope that the Germans are actually *sane*."

———

"If the last report is to be believed, the SS has secured every military base in Germany East," Voss said. "We don't know what happened to the personnel, but I suspect most of them have either agreed to fight for the SS or gone straight into the camps."

Volker nodded, curtly. The SS was *popular* in Germany East, after all; soldiers and airmen stationed there for a few years would certainly come to respect the SS, even if they didn't *like* the men in black. And it wouldn't make any difference if they refused, he suspected; they'd simply be arrested and put to one side while the SS prepared an offensive into Germany Prime.

"We have the beginnings of a defence forming down the Gdansk-Warsaw-Lubin line," Voss added, "but it isn't very solid and won't be until we get more armoured units and aircraft into the region. Thankfully, they won't be prepared for war either. They'll be doing their best to change that as quickly as possible."

"They'll want to launch an offensive before the winter," Volker agreed. Campaigning in winter was difficult, to say the least. But then, the SS had plenty of experience fighting in the harsh Russian winters. The horror stories of frozen weapons, useless clothing and frostbite he'd heard as a young trooper were in the past. "They certainly won't want to give us time to reboot the economy."

"Probably not," Voss agreed. "I have a number of contingency plans for your attention."

Volker sighed, inwardly. Voss was a hard-charging man, a loyal soldier... and Volker wasn't entirely sure he *trusted* the man. He smiled too much, too brightly. But he was popular with the troops, genuinely respected even by men who didn't like him. Removing him would certainly cause the troops to lose faith in the provisional government... if, of course, they'd had any in the first place. They'd known where they stood with the *Reich* Council. The provisional government was a whole different kettle of fish.

I can keep an eye on Voss, he told himself, as he turned his attention to the plans. *And hope he wants nothing more than to command our forces in war.*

———

"I saw Kurt at dinner," Horst said, as he stepped into Gudrun's office. "He was sitting with Hilde, chatting."

Gudrun smiled at him. "Kurt and Hilde?"

"They're an odd couple," Horst agreed. Hilde was aristocracy, insofar as the term had any meaning in the *Reich*; her father, like so many others, had agreed to continue to work for the provisional government. "But maybe they'll be good for one another."

He smiled. It would be the young, he was sure, who would take the greatest steps in overthrowing the old rules. Kurt and Hilde would never have been allowed to marry in the old world, even if he managed to get her pregnant. Her formidable mother would have *destroyed* Kurt, while the child would have been given away to an orphanage... if, of course, Hilde wasn't given a thoroughly illegal abortion. But now, Kurt's sister was a high-ranking government minister, his mother was involved in organising the women and the SS had been driven out of Germany Prime. Who *cared* what Kurt and Hilde did together?

"Maybe," Gudrun said. She rose, putting her paperwork aside. "I believe you made me a promise."

Horst gave her a long look. "You want me to teach you how to fight?"

"Yes," Gudrun said. "There's a shooting range in the basement, I notice."

"Yes. Yes, there is," Horst said. It was clear she wasn't going to give up on the thought, even if they were sleeping together now. And how could he blame her? She was in grave danger at every moment. "Come on, then. We'll draw some weapons from the armoury and shoot a few rounds at the targets."

Gudrun gave him a tight hug. "Thank you," she said. "For everything."

"It isn't over," Horst said. It was hard to think with her breasts pressed against his chest. "I don't expect this peace to last for long."

"No," Gudrun agreed. "They'll come for us. But we'll be ready."

EPILOGUE

𝕲ermanica (𝕸oscow), 𝕲ermany 𝕰ast
25 𝕬ugust 1985

The operation had failed.

Karl Holliston, *Reichsführer-SS* and *Fuhrer* of the Greater German *Reich* - he'd claimed the title in his broadcast to Germany East - cursed under his breath as he read through the final set of reports. The commandos, thrown into action with minimal preparation, had killed dozens of people, but failed to decapitate the provisional government. It had been a desperate throw of the die and it had failed.

And so there will be war, he thought. There was no other alternative, not now his plans had misfired so badly. *But perhaps that's what we need.*

The *Reich* had been forged in fire. The humiliations inflicted on Germany after the Jews and Americans had stabbed the Germans in the back, the suffering of its people, the sneers of the French and British... they'd fuelled a desire for revenge that had created and shaped the Nazi Party. And then the war of conquest had carved the Greater German *Reich* out of decadent and corrupt Europe, while the Jews and countless other undesirables had been purged from the land. And the endless war against insurgents in the east had turned Germany East into a fortress of true Aryan values, even as Germany Prime slowly collapsed into decadence.

We had a war, he told himself. *But it was too far away to be noticed.*

No one had cared, he was sure, about the death toll of Hitler's war. They'd *known* the *Fuhrer* was fighting for their future, that the bodies of young German men were all that stood between the *Reich* and hordes of murdering *Untermenschen*. Children were prepared, in school, to fight for the *Reich* or support those who fought for the *Reich*, while young women were taught to bear children, many children, and older women encouraged to keep the younger ones in line. But they hadn't been able to *see* the South African War. No bombers had flown over Berlin...

... And so they had forgotten the truth of human nature. The world was a dark place, red in tooth and claw. Let the Americans prattle, if they wished, about right, wrong and morality; let the British talk endlessly of the white man's burden. The *Reich* rejected all such concepts as unspeakably wrong. There was no morality in the world, but what one made of it; there was no reason to assist the *Untermenschen*, if only because the *Untermenschen* would take what they were given and use it to slit the giver's throat. The world was divided into the dominators and the dominated. Those who did not choose to dominate became, in time, the dominated. It was a law as old as humanity itself.

"The war will remind our people of the truth," he said, out loud. Germany Prime had been a safe place to live. It wouldn't be safe for much longer. "And they will be purged of their weakness in fire."

End Of Book One

The Story Will Continue In
Chosen of the Valkyries
Coming Soon!

APPENDIX: THE WORLD OF STORM FRONT

In our world, Adolf Hitler declared war on the United States after Japan attacked Pearl Harbour. But in another world, an American counterattack, which sank a Japanese carrier before it could make its escape, made him think better of it. The racism that was so much a part of his mentality came to the fore and, instead of supporting Japan, Hitler declared war on her.

President Roosevelt had no illusions that Germany's declaration of war on Japan was anything other than a paper gesture. Roosevelt believed that Nazi Germany was the greatest threat the United States had faced since the Civil War. However, Roosevelt was unable to manipulate Hitler into starting a war or take the United States to war himself. Therefore, as Nazi Germany completed the conquest of Russia, North Africa and large parts of the Middle East, America waged a titanic war against Japan. By the time the Japanese Home Islands were physically occupied (the invasion was launched in 1944), the war in Europe had largely ground into stalemate. Once Churchill's successor took office, Britain agreed to a surprisingly decent truce with Germany. The Second World War (the European War) was over.

It is now 1985.

———

Nazi Germany is politically divided into five component sections; Germany Prime, Germany North, Germany East, Germany Arabia and Germany South.

Germany Prime is the core of the Greater German Reich, stretching from the coasts of France (the 1940 occupation zone) to Poland. States such as Belgium, the Netherlands and Poland have completely disappeared from the map. Populations deemed insufficiently Germanic have been forcibly relocated, enslaved or exterminated. In their place, German settlers have taken their lands and established their own settlements. Germany Prime is considered the best place to live in the Reich, but that isn't saying much.

Life within Germany Prime is quite regimented. Children go to state schools from age 5 and join the Hitler Youth from 12. The Hitler Youth isn't precisely compulsory, but membership can open doors - and refusing to join can mark someone as a potential enemy of the state. Exams are held at sixteen for anyone wishing to apply to the universities; anyone who doesn't apply is liable for conscription (see below) or being streamlined into a job.

Education is segregated and intensely focused on one's role within the state. Young men are taught that they might have to sacrifice themselves for the *Reich*, while young women are prepared for a life as homemakers. Once old enough to marry (17), men and women are encouraged to marry and have children as soon as possible. (See below.) Young women rarely enter the workforce; older women, who have had two or three children, make up a female professional class.

Freethinkers are barely tolerated; many of them are either sent to the universities or reported as potential troublemakers. The secret police keeps an eye open for sedition and a single report is often enough to ruin a person's life.

Hardly anyone in Germany knows that Jews are human. Indeed, Jews (and anyone non-white) are portrayed as barely-humanoid monsters. (If they met a Jew, they wouldn't recognise him.) Very few truly understand the level of the crimes perpetrated by the Nazis - or, indeed, recognise them as crimes.

Despite the best efforts of the secret police, there exists a criminal underground within Germany Prime.

Germany North consists of Denmark and Norway. Both states have been declared 'Germanic' (with the exception of the usual undesirables, who were marched off to concentration camps and killed) and German rule is very light, provided neither state causes trouble. The *Reich* maintains a considerable number of naval and air bases within both states, but otherwise relies on collaborators to keep the countries under control. Germanic propaganda has been wearing away at the resistance ever since the British bowed out of the war; it isn't uncommon for Norwegians to join the SS or be invited to settle in Germany East and marry into German families.

Germany South consists of the former Belgium Congo and South West Africa (Namibia). It has a fair claim to being one of the most horrific places on Earth; the Germans, having taken both colonies after the European War ended, rapidly reminded the natives why they were glad to see the back of the Germans in 1918. Oddly, it is also one of the most liberal places in the Reich; German settlers are rather less concerned about blood (as long as the newcomer looks white) than they are about having another pair of hands to work the fields, mind the slaves and keep the natives under control. (The SS has periodic witch-hunts for Jews in Germany South, although these searches are deeply resented by the local Germans). As of 1985, the endless bloodletting of the South African War has spread into Germany South.

Germany Arabia consists of everything between the Suez Canal and Iran. Hitler's original promises to the Arabs were forgotten once the Germans won the war; the Arabs, having helped slaughter the remaining Jews in Palestine, found themselves under the yoke of a master far worse than the British Empire. This lead to a brutal uprising in 1950 which, after giving the Germans some very nasty moments, was eventually crushed. As of 1985, the original population has been sharply reduced and German settlers have established new homes near the seas.

Germany East has a well-deserved reputation as the worst place in the *Reich*, which puts it up against some pretty stiff competition. Formally, Germany claims all the territory from Poland to Kamchatka; practically, Germany controls much of the terrain as far north as the Urals. Much of the original towns and cities of Russia have been destroyed; in their place, the Germans have established massive plantations and slave labour camps. The Slavic population, declared subhuman, is brutally mistreated; unsurprisingly, most of the German settlements are actually fortresses. (Notably, Germany East is the only place in the *Reich* where the SS is genuinely popular).

———

The death of Adolf Hitler in 1950 (after a long struggle with Parkinson's Disease) left the *Reich* with something of a quandary. Hitler had presided over a divided state, allowing him to serve as the final arbiter; he had never named a successor (at least not one who was unchallenged by everyone else.) The different factions within the government nearly started a civil war over just who should succeed Hitler; indeed, it is quite likely that the uprising in the Middle East saved the *Reich* from internal collapse. Even so, the post-Hitler government was extremely unstable.

Formally, the *Fuhrer* is the Head of State, with the Deputy *Fuhrer* as his designated successor. However, neither of them possess any real power; the latter, in particular, is seen as a place to dump awkward sods who are too prominent to place on the *Reichstag* or simply shove out of power altogether.

Practically, *real* power is vested in the *Reich* Council, which is dominated by the *Reichsführer-SS*, the Finance Minister and the Head of OKW (effectively, the uniformed head of the German military.) Each of them rules a shifting bastion of smaller factions; the Finance Minister, in particular, must balance an array of competing elements to hold his place within the troika. Confusingly, several factions that appear to have a natural bent towards one of the councillors have a habit of going in other directions; army commandoes, for example, trend towards the SS while the navy is generally more supportive of the Finance Minister's 'government' faction.

Government is generally by consensus. The SS can be said to be the hardliners of just about any decision, while the civilian (insofar as the term can be used in Nazi Germany) departments favour a more balanced approach. Personality clashes between the two are constant, with the military taking sides or not as it wills. Partly in order to keep the clashes from turning into open war, it is generally agreed that the SS has near-complete control over Germany East while the remaining parts of the Reich are ruled by the civilians.

The *Reichstag* is, in theory, a parliament. In practice, it exists to rubber-stamp decisions and nothing else. Technically, German citizens can vote for members, but this hardly ever happens.

———

Every full-blooded German is, technically, at the disposal of the state. In practice, one-third of the male population in Germany Prime is conscripted into the military when they turn seventeen, although the precise number is often altered to reflect the number of volunteers who sign up. Students who do particularly well in their exams - and win a place at one of the growing number of universities - are not conscripted. (They can, of course, volunteer.)

Volunteers are given first pick of the assignments; conscripts are generally allocated where tests say they should go and complaints are given short shrift. The SS and rocket forces do not take conscripts, while both the navy and air force prefer to avoid them.

Legally, females can also be conscripted, but the Nazi Party's stance on the importance of motherhood (and raising the next generation of Germans) tends to ensure that relatively few women are conscripted into the military. When they are, they're normally assigned to either clerical or medical work. (A handful of SS commando units make use of women, but this is extremely uncommon.)

Males are given basic military training at school, as part of their education. Females are not given military training outside Germany East, where everyone may have to pick up a gun and fight if necessary.

———

Complicating any attempt to understand the *Reich* is the simple fact that the different arms of its military are rarely united to a single purpose. For example, the *Luftwaffe* claims control over all aircraft, but all three of the other major services operate their own aircraft. Furthermore, each service has its own equipment and standardisation is largely non-existent.

The *Wehrmacht* (army) is charged with the defence of the *Reich*. In this role, it competes with the *Waffen-SS*, which deploys its own powerful forces and commandos. It remains, however, the largest single military force on the face of the planet.

The SS is an oddity. Parts of it are effectively a second army, other parts are effectively cults, with ceremonies that claim to worship the old gods, or a giant combination of repressive state mixed with social services. It is rarely clear just how seriously some members of the SS take their own claims.

Originally, the SS also controlled Germany's nuclear arsenal, but after nukes were used to smash the Arab revolts the other services insisted on dividing up the nuclear arsenal between them.

The *Kriegsmarine* (navy) claims to be the most powerful naval force on Earth, although this is flatly inaccurate. It deploys five nuclear-powered carriers, seven battleships and 137 smaller surface ships, but is significantly outgunned by the USN and barely superior to the Royal Navy. Its real power lies in its force of ninety-seven nuclear submarines, which it intends to use - in the event of war - to cut Britain off from America.

In recent years, the Kriegsmarine has been humiliated by the failure to assist Argentina during the Falklands War - see below - and has consequently become the most liberal of the military services.

The SS handles much, although not all, of Germany's foreign intelligence gathering. Internally, the *Gestapo* is responsible for security (its independence hangs by a thread) while the *Abwehr* handles military intelligence collection. A semi-independent service - the Economic Intelligence Service - has become a *de facto* civilian spy agency.

———

The Nazi Party is obsessed with breeding the next generation of full-blood Germans. Accordingly, females are encouraged to marry young and give birth to as many children as soon as possible. A German woman who has more than three children is eligible for the Mother's Cross and, more practically, benefits from the state in exchange for having more children.

Bastardry does not carry a stigma in Germany Prime, provided the father was a full-blooded German. Mothers who do not wish to keep their children tend to hand them over to SS-run orphanages, where they are either parcelled out to women who do want them or raised by the state. In certain circumstances (the father being killed on active service before the wedding) the mother will be treated as his legal wife, with all the benefits that accrue to the widow of a dead soldier.

The SS takes it a step further. Polygamy is technically legal in Germany East, with one man being married to two or more women. Typically, the second wives would have been married already, then lost their husbands to an insurgent attack.

Contraception is banned to women with less than three children - there's a thriving underground trade in condoms and American-made Pills - and abortion is rarely permitted. Women who are *not* full-blooded Germans can expect a contraceptive injection after having their second child.

Notably, a fake paternity claim can get a woman thrown into a concentration camp. The party takes bloodlines *seriously*.

———

Of all the nations in Europe, the only one that holds any form of true independence is Switzerland. The Swiss, by dint of mountains, an armed population and a willingness to deploy every weapon at their disposal to protect themselves (it is generally believed that the Swiss have nukes) maintain a careful distance from the *Reich*. Sweden and Finland claim to be independent, but their economies are dependent on Germany.

Vichy France controls the remains of France and French North Africa, a giant territory in Africa. The government has sought to secure *some* form of status within the *Reich*, but as Hitler's dislike of France pervaded German foreign policy, it is clear that Vichy France holds very little freedom of movement. Over the years since the end of the war, vast numbers of Frenchmen have immigrated to North Africa, where they have tried to build new lives away from the looming power of Nazi Germany. Vichy has not hesitated to exterminate vast numbers of Arabs and Africans to provide living space for the colonists.

The French are not permitted more than a small army in mainland France, nor are they permitted nukes, modern aircraft or warships. It is generally acknowledged that the French habit of conscripting males for two years, giving them basic military training and then releasing them makes the French more powerful than they seem on paper, but the French lack the tanks and air support to stand up to the Germans.

The Free French control French Polynesia, but are otherwise utterly powerless after the end of the war.

Italy started the war with high hopes, which were rapidly quashed by Britain in 1940, forcing the Germans to step in to help. Once the war was finished, Hitler allowed Italy to keep Libya, Ethiopia, Egypt (apart from the Suez Canal), Greece and large parts of the Balkans, but not much else. The latter two, in particular, are constantly restive; Italy would like to simply abandon them, but the fascist government is afraid of the German reaction. Italy has a strong infantry force; it is generally agreed that its navy and air force wouldn't last long if pitched into battle against the NAA (see below) or the Germans.

Spain, Turkey and Portugal did very little heavy lifting during the latter half of the war, Portugal (a former British ally) in particular did absolutely nothing beyond a *pro forma* declaration of war on Britain in 1944. Hitler was incensed when Franco failed to take Gibraltar and assumed, perhaps correctly, that the Spanish were trying to play both sides against the middle. Accordingly, while Turkey was rewarded with tracts of sand in the Middle East, none of the three powers received much else for their puny efforts. (It is probably lucky for Spain that Hitler died before remembering he had to settle accounts with Franco.)

In 1985, the Turks have a powerful army and air force; Spain and Portugal have strong armies, but little else. Both states account for a considerable degree of immigration to South and Latin America.

———

Opposing Germany is the North Atlantic Alliance; an association of America, Britain, Canada, Australia, New Zealand, India, Iran, Iceland and Brazil. All of these states, with the exception of Iran, are democracies and most of them have powerful navies. Britain and Iran serve as the forward bases for alliance striking power; both states play host to sizable American air bases as well as their own not inconsiderable forces. There are occasionally degrees of friction amongst the alliance partners, but the threat of the Third Reich keeps them unified.

The NAA faced its greatest test in 1980, when German-backed Argentina invaded the Falkland Islands. (It is generally believed that the Reich authorised the invasion to test the alliance's resolve.) While British forces reoccupied the islands, American and Canadian warships stood ready to intervene if the Germans pushed matters. The German Navy was reluctantly forced to admit that it couldn't hope to save the Argentineans and the war was concluded in 1981 with a British victory.

———

The British Empire was replaced by the British Commonwealth in 1951, when India was formally granted independence from the British Crown. The remaining states of the empire (India, Australia, Canada, New Zealand and South Africa) agreed to merge their resources into an alliance, mainly to prevent the United States from completely dominating the NAA.

South Africa, however, formally withdrew from the Commonwealth in 1965, after friction arose between the more liberal-minded states and the apartheid regime. Oddly, despite allying with Nazi Germany the year later, South Africa is still remarkably liberal compared to the Nazis - it's population of Jews, for example, remains untouched despite being marked for extermination by the *Reich*. Even so, with a growing war underway, it remains unclear just how long South Africa can survive.

———

Iran was formally occupied by Britain and Russia in 1941, after the Iranian Government was caught attempting to set up links with the Germans. Maintaining the occupation, however, proved increasingly difficult and, after the US entered the war against Japan, it was agreed that a US force could relieve the Anglo-Soviet occupation force. In partial compensation, Iran was added to the lend-lease program and received billions of dollars worth of war material and economic assistance.

As of 1985, Iran is still a monarchy, but otherwise remains fairly liberal and a strong ally of the United States. Relationships with Britain are cool and strictly formal.

———

Japan was invaded in 1944 by the Americans, after the Japanese Government refused to surrender. (Nukes were not available yet.) The combination of fanatical resistance (the US was still shooting diehards in 1955), mass starvation and the near-complete collapse of government power led to the death of roughly 60% of the Japanese population, even though - as American forces tightened their control over the islands - the Japanese began to seem more human to their occupiers. Although officially banned, relationships between American servicemen and Japanese women started almost at once. Many of these relationships were between black soldiers and Japanese girls.

The near-complete destruction of large parts of Japan effectively extinguished the native culture. In its place, a strange combination of Japanese and American influences took form, particularly when Japan was opened to settlement by Americans. Black Americans, in particular, were encouraged to move (a consequence of Civil Rights, embraced by Truman) and eventually created a very mixed culture. Japan is about the only place in the alliance where racism can be said to be completely non-existent and, indeed, claiming multiracial ancestry is regarded as a badge of honour. (Claiming to be one-eighteenth Cherokee would be seen as rather puny.)

Japan is formally a US Territory. There is a strong statehood movement in both Japan and mainland America, but so far Congress has refused to admit Japan.

———

President Truman, once he succeeded Roosevelt in 1943, started breaking down racial barriers within US society almost at once. This met with heavy resistance from some sections of the American population, although the combination of the threat from Germany (particularly once Germany led the way into space) and the existence of Japan as a sinkhole for 'radicals' kept the opposition largely muted. An economic boom, powered by the war (and the need to keep a strong defence against Germany) has largely transformed American society.

As of 1985, American-led efforts to colonise the moon and mine the asteroids have started to bear fruit. Combined with a powerful ABM system - and a navy that is second to none - a number of Americans have seriously proposed leaving the Reich to collapse under its own weight. However, the President and most of Congress remains committed to holding the line until the Iron Curtain (a term popularised by Winston Churchill) falls for good.

The Chinese barely noticed when the European War ended; Chinese Nationalists, Chinese Communists and various warlord factions were engaged in a bloody civil war from 1944 (after Japan was invaded), once the Japanese armies in China were either exterminated, repatriated back to Japan or absorbed into various Chinese militias. China remained torn apart by war until 1951, when the Chinese Nationalists - with a great deal of American assistance - defeated most of the warlords. The remaining Chinese Communists retreated into Manchuria and held out until the Nationalists finally agreed to a ceasefire. North China is now the only genuinely communist state on Earth.

China saw substantial economic growth after the end of the war, but an increasing bent towards authoritarianism saw China slowly slip into the German orbit. However, the combination of distance and wariness of German racial theories ensured that the Chinese were never full-blooded allies and, with the Chinese economy growing rapidly, the threat of a clash between the Chinese and Germans has become a viable possibility. Thankfully, the vast tracts of wasteland between China and Germany East ensure that war is unlikely to result.

Korea is a relatively stable democracy and an American ally. With the US unchallenged in Asian waters, most of the other states in Asia have followed suit.

Although the *Reich* appears stable, a number of problems bubble below the surface.

The first, and most prominent, is the South African War. What began as a genuine effort to assist South Africa against its black population has snowballed into a major war against an elusive and deadly enemy. Thousands of German troops have been killed and thousands more have been badly injured, with only a relative handful of the wounded formally acknowledged as such. The war has become a death match, sucking up German resources at the end of a very long supply chain while thousands of South Africans seek to flee their country as it is consumed by civil war.

The second is the constant arms race with the United States. Although Germany achieved a number of successes in the early stages of the Cold War, the defection of Von Braun in 1950 and the introduction of Nazi Ideology into German schools crippled German science and, despite their best efforts, Germany has fallen behind in the arms race. The deployment of the American ABM system has forced the Germans to invest billions of *Reichmarks* in building a new force of ICBMs, SLBMs and other weapons. Trying to match American deployment of smart weapons, stealth aircraft and other advanced systems may prove beyond the *Reich's* capabilities.

The third, connected to the second, is a growing economic crisis. The *Reich* is simply not very efficient; in a sense, it has all the weaknesses of a command economy without any of the strengths, a problem caused by the division of German economic facilities among the various branches of the state. In particular, intelligent young men are fleeing Germany for America where they won't have to work in an inefficient system. Furthermore, social security payments (particularly to mothers with more than three children) are slowly draining the system dry.

In trying to tackle these problems, the *Reich* may have sown the seeds of its own disintegration...

APPENDIX: GERMAN WORDS

Abwehr - German Military Intelligence

Bund Deutscher Mädel (BDM) - League of German Girls/ Band of German Maidens, female wing of the Hitler Youth.

Einsatzgruppen - SS extermination squads

Gastarbeiter - Guest Worker

Germanica - Moscow, renamed after the war

Hauptsturmfuehrer - SS rank, roughly equal to Captain.

Heer - The German Army

Herrenvolk - Master Race

Kriegsmarine - The German Navy

Luftwaffe - The German Air Force

Mutterkreuz - Mother's Cross

Oberfeldwebel - *Heer* rank, roughly equal to Master Sergeant

Oberkommando der Wehrmacht (OKW, 'Supreme Command of the Armed Forces') - The German General Staff.

Obergruppenfuehrer - SS rank, roughly equal to Lieutenant General.

Ordnungspolizei - Order Police (regular police force)

Reichsführer-SS - Commander of the SS

Reichssicherheitshauptamt (RSHA) - Reich Main Security Office

Sigrunen - SS insignia (lightning bolts)

Standartenfuehrer - SS rank, roughly equal to Colonel.

Sturmbannfuehrer - SS rank, roughly equal to Major.

Strumscharfuehrer - SS rank, roughly equal to Master Sergeant.
Untermensch - Subhuman.
Untermenschen - Subhumans, plural of *Untermensch*.

Unterscharfuehrer - SS rank, roughly equal to Second Lieutenant.
Vaterland - Fatherland
Volk - The German Population.
Wehrmacht - The German Military (often taken to represent just the army (*Heer*)).

CPSIA information can be obtained
at www.ICGtesting.com
Printed in the USA
BVOW09s0318201217
503303BV00018B/2648/P